OREGON!

is the fourth unforgettable saga
in the WAGONS WEST series—

INDEPENDENCE!

In 1837 a dauntless band of pioneering men and
women set out for parts West, led by Claudia
Humphries, the fiery young widow, and Sam
Brentwood, the bold wagon master. Traveling
under secret orders from President Andrew Jackson, Brentwood must win a desperate race against
England and Russia, to bring the great Pacific
Northwest under the American flag.

NEBRASKA!

The legendary caravan drives onward in a story
of hard-won ideals, betrayal from within, and
sabotage from British and Russian agents. Above
all, it is the story of Whip Holt, the ruggedly
quiet leader of this leg of the migration; and of
Cathy van Ayl, who leaves her family behind to
continue on with Whip's train—perhaps to win
his heart.

WYOMING!

Attacked by savage Indians, stalked by a lone,
war-crazed Blackfoot, America's first wagon train
pushes through the Rockies. Survival depends on
Whip Holt, who is torn between the passions of
Cathy van Ayl and the Indian maiden La-ena.
Each wants him, and either has the power to
become his fatal weakness.

✳✳✳✳✳✳✳✳✳✳✳✳✳✳✳✳✳✳✳

WAGONS WEST

OREGON!

THE CONTINUING SAGA OF THE BRAVE MEN AND WOMEN BLAZING THE FIRST WAGON TRAIL ACROSS THE BREADTH OF AMERICA

CATHY VAN AYL,
the new bride, who may never
forget her first love.

LEE BLAKE,
Lieutenant Colonel in the U.S. Army,
he courageously dares the British
to fire the first shot in
a war to win Oregon.

WHIP HOLT,
the taciturn mountain man whose frontier
skills are no help in handling a wife.

EULALIA WOODLING,
a former South Carolina belle,
who must fight to overcome her handicap
and gain her husband's love.

★★★★★★★★★★★★★★★★★★★★★

IGOR DOZNEVKOV,
a member of the *Cheka*, the Czar's
secret police, a dangerous man sent to
Oregon to investigate the loyalties
of a band of Russian settlers.

COLONEL PHILLIPS MORRISON,
the tough, aggressive Royal Army commandant.
His orders: "Take any measures you deem
necessary" to keep Oregon in British hands.

MAJOR ROLAND PITTS,
young, straight as an arrow, he plans to
claim the territory for Great Britain—peacefully.

LISOLETTE ARBO,
only nineteen, a lovely half-French,
half-Russian girl who wants to be an American,
but is forced to spy for the Czar.

NANCY WADE,
a fiery, flirtatious hellion. Scornful of
convention, she is turning the town upside down.

RICHARD RAMSEY,
a former mountain man. Whip dislikes
him and distrusts him; rumors say
Russian gold can buy him.

Bantam Books by Dana Fuller Ross
Ask your bookseller for the books you have missed

WAGONS WEST ★ VOLUME 4

OREGON!

DANA FULLER ROSS

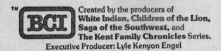

™ **BCI** Created by the producers of
**White Indian, Children of the Lion,
Saga of the Southwest,** and
The Kent Family Chronicles Series.
Executive Producer: Lyle Kenyon Engel

BANTAM BOOKS
TORONTO · NEW YORK · LONDON · SYDNEY

OREGON!

A Bantam Book / published by arrangement with
Book Creations, Inc.

Bantam edition / April 1980

2nd printing ..... April 1980	9th printing ..... May 1981
3rd printing ..... April 1980	10th printing . September 1981
4th printing ..... April 1980	11th printing . December 1981
5th printing ..... April 1980	12th printing ..... May 1982
6th printing ...... May 1980	13th printing . December 1982
7th printing .... August 1980	14th printing . September 1983
8th printing .. December 1980	15th printing . December 1984

Produced by Book Creations, Inc.
Chairman of the Board: Lyle Kenyon Engel

ISBN: 0-553-24088-9

Published simultaneously in the United States and Canada

PRINTED IN THE UNITED STATES OF AMERICA

H   24 23 22 21 20 19 18

OREGON!

THE SWEEPING TALE
OF THE MEN AND WOMEN
OF WAGONS WEST
AS THEY FORGE THEIR WAY
TO THE PACIFIC SHORE.

I

Martin Van Buren, eighth President of the United States, stared gloomily out of his office window. The glorious spring weather of Washington City was perversely responsible for his sour mood. Daffodils were blooming in the garden, the grass was a fresh, green carpet, and the White House itself was dazzling in the bright sunlight. A fresh coat of paint hid the last of the scars made a quarter of a century earlier when—during the War of 1812—British invaders had tried to burn down the building.

"Every morning as I look out there," he said, waving a pudgy hand, "I can't help wondering how soon spring will come to the Rocky Mountains, how soon our wagon train can resume its journey to Oregon."

Major General Winfield Scott, the army's dashing Deputy Chief of Staff, was beginning to acquire presidential aspirations of his own, but nevertheless he felt sorry for his superior. Walking in the footsteps of the enormously popular Andrew Jackson, Van Buren had been suffering the burden of an unexpected, severe financial depression. In addition, the expedition to Oregon was a constant source of concern to him. "The last letter we had from our representative, Colonel Blake, said the severe winter weather was beginning to moderate," Scott responded. "So I'd guess the wagon train is either on the move again or soon will be."

"It can't be soon enough," Van Buren grumbled. "It's essential to our national future that we establish a firm claim to the Oregon country without delay. A second train is already heading toward Independence, Missouri, from the eastern states, and a third is being organized."

"I'll grant you it will be a catastrophe if the first train doesn't reach the Pacific and if our settlers fail to set up their farms and a town, Mr. President," the General replied. "But there's no cause for despair. Lieutenant Colonel Blake is highly competent, and so is the train's guide, Whip Holt. The man they elected as their president, Ernst von Thalman, is also an able executive. They've survived Indian attacks, floods, sabotage, and God knows what. So, I'm confident they'll reach Oregon."

"There are developments since I last saw you, Scott, that make me apprehensive."

"Sir?"

"Our legation in London reports on excellent authority that Great Britain is in the process of strengthening her garrison at Fort Vancouver, her port near the mouth of the Columbia River. Please keep in mind that the British claim to Oregon may be as valid as our own. The nation that takes the greater amount of land—and holds it, developing it rapidly and successfully—will make that claim real."

"Are you asking me for a recommendation, Mr. President?"

"I am," Van Buren said.

"My colleagues at the War and Navy Departments and I have anticipated this problem, sir. We'll make our recommendations official by putting them through the departmental secretaries. But the generals and commodores are already of one mind. We want to send a sea expedition of our own to Oregon. One or more warships, carrying as many army troops as they can comfortably hold. We'll set up a fort of our own, with Blake in command. He already knows what we have in mind, and he's eager to accept the responsibility."

The President frowned. "When two nations set up garrisons in close proximity to each other in disputed territory, the chance that sparks will be struck rises rather dramatically. We're still feeling the effects of the Panic of '37, even though it's been two years since that disaster first struck us. We simply can't afford another war with the British. What's more, I don't believe the public would support such a war. Most people know very little about the rich Oregon country and aren't aware of its potential."

"According to the most careful analysis the War and Navy Departments have been capable of making, sir, the British don't want another war with us, either. We've beaten them twice, and we'd beat them again for the simple reason that they can't maintain supply lines that far from home. Remember that London is six thousand miles from Oregon. Oh, they may bluff us, if they can, but two can play at that game."

Martin Van Buren sighed. "I'm inclined to accept your recommendation, Scott, because I can see no practical alternative to it. But I'll discuss it first with the Cabinet and with the leaders of the Senate and House of Representatives before I give my final approval."

"We have little choice, Mr. President. The United States has an obligation to the members of the first wagon train that we must fulfill. They have the right to expect the government to give them full support and all the help that can be mustered."

The officer had touched a raw nerve, and the sensitive Van Buren reacted strongly. "I need no lectures on my responsibilities, General," he said, his voice stiff.

Winfield Scott flushed and ran a hand through his prematurely gray hair. "I meant no personal criticism, sir. I was merely speaking in terms of the overall situation."

Well aware that his subordinate was by far the most brilliant of his generals, the President allowed himself to be mollified. "The British constitute only one phase of our problem. I'm worried also about Imperial Russia, Scott."

"Oh, the Russians have sabotaged our wagon train and have renewed their claim to Oregon after abandoning the country, but the Czar's claim is theoretical."

"There's nothing theoretical about his government's most recent actions," Van Buren declared. "Our legation in St. Petersburg has sent positive information to the effect that Russia has also sent a colony of volunteer settlers to Oregon."

"Good Lord! How are they traveling all that distance?"

"They've gone overland through Siberia, and our St. Petersburg legation says they're currently sailing by the short northern route to their North American colony, Alaska. There, I presume, they'll be transferred to another ship."

"The poor devils! How many of these so-called volunteers are there, Mr. President?"

"The original party consisted of about two hundred and fifty settlers, Scott."

"The Russians will be lucky if as many as one hundred survive a journey of that length, sir."

"I know." Van Buren nodded gravely. "And even if they reach Oregon, it will be a terrible strain for the Russians to send them supplies and reinforcements. We have the natural advantage. Not that I'm decrying the hardships our trains must undergo, but at least they're making the entire journey by land across territory that we've either incorporated within our borders or claim."

"Then you don't see the Russian expedition as a threat to our own activities and plans?"

4

love with him, and she had become convinced he had eyes only for Cathy, in spite of her marriage.

Only a few weeks earlier a disease called the mountain fever had swept through the company, killing many, and Eulalia had been one of the survivors; however, the ailment had left her crippled. Whip had astonished her by proposing to her, and in a moment of weakness, because of her love for him, she had accepted.

That had been the worst mistake of her life, she reflected as she changed her position on the buckboard in the hope that her crippled leg would stop aching. Whip had married her only because he had felt sorry for her. She realized that now.

Oh, his tender, considerate lovemaking on their wedding night had astonished and delighted her, and he had been just as passionate the next night. But the following morning, when they had left their winter camp and resumed the journey, everything had been changed. Whip dutifully joined her at the communal meals, and at night he slept beside her in her wagon, now their wagon. But he had retreated into his shell, and once again had become remote and uncommunicative with everyone including his bride.

Certainly it was no accident, Eulalia thought, that he had carefully refrained from making love to her ever since they had been on the trail. It was possible he was devoting himself to the well-being and safety of his charges, but that wouldn't prevent him from reaching for the woman who slept beside him. It seemed likely to Eulalia that he had changed his mind and regretted the charitable impulse that had led him to marry her.

She could try to break the impasse herself by reaching out to him when he joined her beneath the blankets, but something in her nature prevented her from making the gesture. The pride of someone who had been reared as a lady was partly responsible, but her reasons for holding back were far more complex.

Had she been healthy, her beauty would have caused many men to want her, as she knew from experience. But in her crippled state she was capable of inspiring only pity, so she couldn't and wouldn't use the remains of her sex appeal as a means of holding Whip. Either he wanted her or he didn't, and if he was rejecting her, which seemed likely, she couldn't blame him.

What made Eulalia's dilemma such hell was the forty-eight-hour honeymoon she had shared with Whip. She had been his woman, he had been her man, and all had been right with her world. But his desire had ebbed so quickly she felt positive he had found it impossible to pretend he wanted a girl who was lame.

She guessed she would have to live with her hurt, for she had married for better or worse. But it was bewildering that her happiness had been so short-lived.

Lee Blake rode at a slow canter to the head of the column, joined Whip, and accompanied him for a time. The professional soldier who was a graduate of the Military Academy at West Point and the mountain man who had been a hunter, trapper, and guide since his youth were men of far different backgrounds and approaches to life, but their months on the trail together had given each a respect for the other's talents, so they had become friends.

There was no need for conversation. The wagon train created its own music as it moved, and both men were aware of it. The wheels of the wagons creaked on the hard ground, harnesses flapped, and plodding work animals strained. The uneven rhythm of the blending sounds was soothing, and if a wooden yoke or an axle broke, one of the monitors soon would know it.

This was a special day, but at the same time it was

like so many others, and both men enjoyed it. Neither was aware of the thoughts of his wife. They relished the pine-scented smell of the clean, cool breeze, the heat of the sun, the grandeur of the snow-capped peaks, and the sense of peace that enveloped them.

"I hope it's this quiet when we get to Oregon," Whip said at last.

"That will depend on the welcome the British at Fort Vancouver give us. And whether the Russians make a fuss," Lee replied.

"I reckon that, between us, you and I can handle most things that come up," Whip said, grinning slightly.

"Most," Lee said. "Now that you're a married man I suppose you'll be staying on in Oregon yourself."

"I reckon I will. That's one of the reasons I decided to settle down. If you live long enough in the mountains, you'll either get killed or start to drink too much because the life is so lonely."

"Well, you qualify as a settler, so you'll be able to choose your property and get a grant of six hundred acres."

"I'm not cut out for the life of a farmer," Whip said. "I'm thinking, maybe, of getting a loan so I can buy the claim of somebody who doesn't want one. That way, I'd have eighteen hundred acres, including Eulalia's land, and I could set up a ranch."

"You plan to raise cattle?"

"Horses. I know where there are wild horses a-plenty and I'll start my breed with them. Wagon trains by the dozen will be following in our tracks, and when all those settlers reach Oregon, the demand for horses will be tremendous."

"You're onto something," Lee said, then became thoughtful. At last he said, "As I'm on the government payroll, I'm not entitled to a land claim, and I'd have no use for one because the army has other plans for me. But Cathy has a legitimate claim because she wasn't married to me all along. I'll speak to her, Whip, and I'll let you know whether she's willing to release her claim to you."

"That's decent of you, Lee, but I wouldn't want either one of you to feel obliged—"

"We wouldn't. I can see no reason we shouldn't work out something reasonable because Cathy will have no use for property, either. An officer never knows where he'll be sent next, so he doesn't think about land until he's ready to retire."

Whip nodded, and they rode in companionable silence for a time. Then the guide said quietly, "We've moved into the South Pass. It'll take about an hour for the whole train to clear it."

"I'll give the good word." Lee immediately moved to the rear, pleased because his wife would be the first to hear the news.

By the time he had spoken to her, then to Eulalia, and had moved on to the third wagon, several of the monitors realized something out of the ordinary was happening and rode forward to join Lee.

None reacted with greater pleasure than Tilman Wade, a prosperous widower in his thirties who had sold his profitable farm and had joined the company in order to start life anew. Always dependable and even-tempered, he long had been a member of the elected council of representatives that was responsible for establishing and enforcing the rules that the company observed.

Grinning broadly, Tilman cantered toward the rear, then approached each wagon in turn in his assigned sector of the line. Most of the future settlers responded with shouts of joy, and soon women and children in wagon after wagon were beating with wooden spoons on skillets and cooking pots. The eruption shattered the quiet.

Tilman unconsciously tilted his hat at a more rakish angle as he rode toward his own wagon, which was being driven by Ginny Dobbs. A young seamstress from New Jersey, she had come to the camp early in the winter after crossing the mountains from Spanish California. Tilman had learned from others, although not from the girl herself, that Ginny had gone to the town of Yerba Buena to become the mail-order bride of a wealthy Spanish rancher, but the arrangement had been canceled, leaving her to her own devices.

Perhaps her disappointment was responsible for her shrewish behavior. She was a vixen, all right, no two ways about it, and she had as sharp a tongue as any woman Tilman had ever encountered. All the same, he had been drawn to her, and in recent weeks, after he had shaken and spanked her in exasperation, she had become more civil toward him. Feeling sorry for her—no, it wasn't really pity, but he wasn't quite certain what he felt—he had asked her to drive his wagon so he could work as a monitor, and she had seemed grateful for the opportunity.

Now, however, her attractive face was bland, almost expressionless, as he rode up to her.

"We've reached the South Pass," he told her. "We're moving through it right now."

"I don't see any difference," Ginny replied, her tone indifferent. "We're in a valley like all the others, with mountains all around us. I'm so sick of mountains I could scream."

"You'll see plenty of them before we reach Oregon, that's sure." He fell in beside her for a few moments.

"Apparently you forget that I've already crossed the Sierra Nevada going east. And here I am, traveling west again. Not that I'm unhappy about joining these people. Oregon is as good a place as any to settle, I suppose. But having already crossed the Continental Divide in nasty weather—and almost freezing to death while I was at it—I'm not exactly thrilled right now. Thanks all the same."

As Tilman moved on to the next wagon he told himself that, in all justice to Ginny, he couldn't blame her for her lack of enthusiasm. If he had undergone all that she suffered on the trail, he would be less than ecstatic himself.

When Tilman saw the occupant of the next wagon, he was puzzled. Dave Evans's wagon wasn't assigned to his sector, but the man apparently had changed places with someone else. Evans was a well-to-do, self-assured man in his forties, the former owner of several sawmills, who made no secret of the fact that he had found no more challenges in his native Ohio and was going to Oregon because he intended to repeat his past success there.

Tilman didn't like the man, but had to admit he was prejudiced. Ever since the journey had been resumed, Evans had taken notice of Ginny and had been spending a great deal of his free time with her, and she appeared to be interested in him, too. At least she was polite enough to him, smiling instead of going into one of her tantrums, Tilman thought. Well, that was their privilege.

But it was annoying that the man had moved to a new position in the line without first notifying the monitor in charge of the sector. Ernie von Thalman had made such notification a hard rule, but Evans seemed to think he could break it with impunity.

No, that wasn't really the problem. What really bothered Tilman was the fact that he was only ten years older than Ginny, yet she wasn't being as nice to him as she was to a man like Evans—who was old enough to be her father.

As he drew near to the other man's wagon, Tilman was laconic. "We're crossing the divide, Dave."

"Is that a fact?" Evans showed no excitement.

Before he could stop himself, Tilman blurted, "I wish you had told me you were moving to a new place in the line."

"I plumb forgot." In no way was Evans apologetic. "But there's no harm done."

"Is this a permanent move?"

A gleam appeared in the older man's eyes. "You just bet it is!"

"All right, I'll mark it on Whip's chart." The annoyed Tilman moved on to the next wagon. He guessed he had been thinking more about Ginny than was good for him, but if she really liked a boor like Evans, he'd be wise to put her out of his mind.

Ultimately the entire caravan moved through the pass, and the day's march continued for another hour. Whip finally called a halt on a section of tableland bisected by a swift-moving stream, its waters swollen by the spring thaws. The wagons were drawn up in a circle, teams of horses and oxen were turned loose in the enclosed area, and the cooking detail immediately began to prepare supper under the direction of Cathy Blake. Having made camp so near the bank of the river, the water-gathering detail had no work to do.

Eulalia Holt felt bitter as she limped forward and began to unhitch her team. Other husbands helped their wives in such chores, but Whip, as always, was too busy answering the questions of the many people who invariably surrounded him at the end of a day.

Then someone came up beside her and took over the task. "Let me give you a hand," Lee Blake said. "I've already attended to our own team, and you look as though you wouldn't mind some help."

"I'm grateful for it." Eulalia smiled at him and told herself Cathy was fortunate to have married a gentleman. Why couldn't she have been so sensible? A mountain man didn't have the common courtesy to remove his hat when he went indoors or to stand when a lady approached him. Not that such gestures were all-important to her any more, she reflected.

Damn Whip! She wouldn't mind if he never removed his hat provided he remembered he had a wife who might be crippled but was very much alive! Eulalia wanted to approach him, take his arm, and draw him away from the people who were pestering him with their minor problems. But her pride was too great. As far back as she could remember, males had made a fuss over her, and she refused to give some of these cowlike women the satisfaction of thinking she was jealous of her husband.

Because of her leg she had been assigned to no work detail, and she felt at loose ends. Perhaps if she went to the cooking unit, where she had formerly worked, Cathy and Cindy would give her something to do. Eulalia started toward the fire, then halted when she saw her brother come up to Cindy and lift a huge iron kettle onto a tripod over the fire for her.

Never had she seen the expression that appeared in Claiborne's eyes when he looked at Cindy. If Whip ever looked at her like that—just once—she would melt. The way Cindy was melting at this moment. The animation in her face made her look even prettier than usual, and Eulalia forgot her own problems long enough to rejoice for her brother and her friend. It was obvious to her that Cindy and Claiborne were in love, although she knew Cindy had yet to admit it. It would be wonderful to have her as a sister-in-law.

Eulalia couldn't help thinking how much she had changed since leaving South Carolina. Had anyone told her, as recently as a year and a half ago, that she would welcome a former whore into the family, she would have laughed. The experience of being forced into prostitution by her Indian captors had made her a better, far more tolerant person. She didn't recommend the experience, to be sure, but she and Cindy would be sisters in more ways than one. Like Eulalia, Cindy knew a real man when she encountered one, and Claiborne also would be fortunate.

Someone was lurking in the shadows of a nearby wagon, and Eulalia called a greeting to him. "Good afternoon, Ted."

Ted Woods, the giant blacksmith from Indiana, spoke without turning his head. "Howdy, ma'am."

Eulalia saw that his gaze was riveted on Cindy, and

she felt desperately sorry for the man. Cindy had confided to her that Ted had murdered his wife and brother when he had caught them together. He had paid the penalty for his crime by spending years in prison. Then he had started a new life by joining the wagon train, and he had become one of the most needed and useful members of the expedition.

His deep interest in Cindy had been obvious for a long time, but as she had told Eulalia privately, "Sooner or later he'll meet the woman who can tame him, I hope, but I'm not that woman. His jealous rages are so violent he scares me half to death. If I were married to him, I'd be afraid to as much as speak to another man. I honestly think he'd choke or beat me. Ted needs somebody he can trust, and I'm not that person."

Looking at Ted now, watching him devour Cindy and then stare with unreasoning hatred at Claiborne, Eulalia knew what her friend meant. Ted could be a dangerous enemy because he was so moody and his temper so ungovernable.

Shivering slightly, Eulalia rubbed her arms. Claiborne knew what Ted thought of him, of course, and was capable of looking after himself. She wasn't really concerned about Claiborne or, for that matter, about Cindy. Her heart went out to Ted because she could understand the feeling of bleak despair that enveloped him. She was feeling more and more the same way herself.

It was Danny, the former bound boy, who was the first to observe what everyone else in the company should have noted immediately. His changing voice rising from a deep baritone to a squeak, then sliding down two octaves again, he shouted, "Look at the river! That water is flowing toward the west!"

There was a moment of stunned silence. Danny was right! On the eastern side of the Continental Divide, the major rivers flowed toward the Atlantic Ocean. Now that the divide had been passed, the rivers moved toward the Pacific! Here, after the seemingly endless months of hard travel, was positive proof that their goal at last was within reach.

A frenzied spirit swept through the throng. The dignified Ernie von Thalman began to dance a waltz with his sedate wife, Emily, who was clutching a ladle in one hand, and they were cheered by her young sons, the Harris boys. Lee Blake went to Cathy, who turned away from the cooking fire and, after standing rigidly for a moment, returned his kiss.

A score of men and women formed a line and began to play an impromptu game of follow-the-leader. Others, including a number of children, joined in the procession, and so did Ginny Dobbs. Tilman Wade was only a step behind her, beating Dave Evans to the place.

Claiborne Woodling exuberantly lifted Cindy into the air and held her there. "Now will you marry me?" he demanded in a voice loud enough for his sister to hear above the hubbub.

"Put me down!" Cindy demanded.

It was plain to Eulalia, if not to her brother, that the protest was mild.

"Not until you give me an answer," Claiborne said. "The right answer!"

"If you're going to be that way about it, all right, I will!" Cindy replied.

Claiborne slowly lowered her to the ground, her arms slid around his neck, and they embraced.

The only person other than Eulalia who was aware of the couple was Ted Woods. The color drained from his swarthy face, and for an instant Eulalia thought he would find release in a violent explosion. Instead, he averted his face and slowly walked away from the scene, his huge fists clenched.

Eulalia caught a glimpse of his eyes as he turned away, and his pain was so intense she lowered her own gaze to the ground.

She was unaware of Whip's approach until he stood

beside her. "I never expected all this whoop and holler," he said. "If I'd thought of it, I would have called folks' attention to the river myself." He shook his head and smiled wryly. "The trouble is, I've gone back and forth across the divide so many times that I just didn't think about the way the rivers flow."

"Well, I think it's wonderful," Eulalia said firmly. "I'm as excited as all the others."

Whip's expression indicated that he didn't believe her, but he refrained from challenging her. Instead, he shoved his hat onto the back of his head, hooked his thumbs into his belt, and studied her for a long moment before he said, "On the trail today, I got to thinking about you."

A trace of her old spirit impelled her to respond, "Should I be flattered or abashed?"

"Neither." His mood was serious. "It seems to me I remember that before you took sick you were a fair enough horseback rider."

"I was far better than that," she said with dignity, wondering whether he was deliberately trying to hurt her by reminding her of past pleasures she had enjoyed. "My brother and I both learned to ride before we could walk. There isn't a woman in this train— including Tonie Martin—who is a better rider than I am. Than I was. For all the good it does me now."

"It's odd you should mention Tonie. She's been so busy helping her husband tend to the sick that she almost never rides that mare of hers anymore. It seems to me we could get young Chet Harris or one of the other lads to drive your wagon, and you could ride Tonie's mare every day. I'm sure she'd be pleased. That animal needs a rider."

"I'm afraid I don't care for your sense of humor, Mr. Holt," she said, hoping she sounded dignified.

Whip blinked in surprise, and Eulalia pointed to her crippled leg. "You seem to forget that my illness left me with a handicap."

"I don't forget it, Mrs. Holt, not for a minute. That's

why I want you to ride. So you can work out the kinks."

She was astonished. "Surely you don't actually believe that spending the day in the saddle—every day—will improve my leg and heal it, Whip."

"The way I see it, the exercise can't do you any harm. We'll ask Doc Martin about it right now. Come along." He stalked off in the direction of the so-called hospital wagon, refusing to walk at a slow pace because of her condition. Eulalia had to struggle to keep up with him and was annoyed by his lack of consideration for her.

Bob and Tonie Martin were seeing a patient out of the wagon and were about to join in the increasingly hilarious celebration when the guide and his recent bride blocked their path.

Whip never minced words. "Doc, would it do Eulalia's leg any good if she rode horseback every day and stopped favoring her hurt?"

The question was unexpected, and the physician considered it for some moments. "Very little is known about the fever that Eulalia and so many others suffered," he said. "Most authorities at our best medical schools, places like Harvard and Pennsylvania, admit they understand almost nothing about the causes of the disease and nothing at all about the cures. But I do recall something in a textbook written by a professor of medicine at Edinburgh. He advocated exercise—and lots of it—as a cure."

Eulalia remained silent.

"Aha!" Whip grinned.

Dr. Martin addressed himself exclusively to the young woman. "I advise you not to get your hopes up too high, Eulalia. Exercise as a cure for your condition is effective in only one case out of three, and so far no one has been able to predict when it will help a patient and when it does nothing."

"I have no hopes," she said in a flat voice.

"One chance in three is better than no chance at all," Whip said. "Like the winter I nearly froze when I was caught above a pass in the Colorado country after a snowslide. I had about one chance in ten of working my way through that pass and staying alive. I took the chance, and here I am."

"Certainly I see nothing to be lost by trying," the physician said.

Whip turned to the doctor's wife. "Tonie, that mare of yours is getting rusty, trotting along behind your wagon every day. Would you be willing to let Eulalia ride her?"

"Willing? I'd be delighted!" Tonie turned to the girl. "She's a temperamental, high-spirited beast, but I've seen you ride, and I'm sure you can handle her."

"You saw me," Eulalia said in a low tone, "before my illness. I'm not sure I could even keep my foot in the stirrup now."

"It's settled," Whip said, a rare note of impatience creeping into his voice. "We'll get hold of Chet after he stops prancing around out there with all the other crazy people, and tomorrow morning you'll start riding. I'm much obliged to you, Tonie." He paused, then added, "And so is my wife."

Eulalia's tentative smile indicated she regarded the brash experiment as dubious at best. Then she resolutely put her own problems out of her mind. "Claiborne proposed to Cindy just now, and she accepted. I want to wish them well."

Whip thought about the couple, then nodded in approval. "I'll come with you," he said, taking her elbow to guide her through the throng of celebrants.

The touch of his hand on her arm thrilled Eulalia, and she wished it didn't.

News of the betrothal was spreading, and Cindy and Claiborne were surrounded by well-wishers. Whip gently but firmly cleared people out of his wife's path.

Eulalia kissed Cindy and hugged her, then beamed at her brother. "You don't deserve her," she said, "but I wish you every happiness."

Whip wrung his brother-in-law's hand. When he turned to Cindy, he became shy, as he so often did in the presence of women. "Welcome to the family," he told her stiffly.

Cindy was aware of the effort he was making and kissed him on the cheek, which made him even more uncomfortable.

Cathy Blake, who had already offered her good wishes to the betrothed couple, interrupted at an opportune moment. "Supper will be spoiled if we don't get back to work, Cindy."

Cindy laughingly disengaged herself from Claiborne's grip. "Spoken like a true army officer's wife, Cathy. Duty, duty, duty."

"Let me help, too," Eulalia said. The other young women exchanged quick glances.

"Let her help," Whip said. "It will be good for her."

Eulalia held her head high as she limped toward the fire.

The festive air in no way diminished throughout supper, even though the main dish was standard fare, venison and antelope meat, stewed with cornmeal and fresh dandelion greens. A quarter-moon rose in a cloudless sky filled with stars, and the night gradually became chilly. Small children were led to bed, more tired than usual after all the excitement, and a few of the elderly retired, too. But the majority of the adults continued to sit around the fire.

Most of the talk tonight centered on Oregon. Farmers assured each other that the soil was far more fertile than any they had known anywhere, and Whip confirmed for them, as he did frequently, that there were at least two growing seasons in the Oregon country, perhaps three, depending on the crops they planted. Some of the women talked longingly about planting orchards, and recipes were exchanged for preserving apples and pears. In the minds of these future settlers, they were already arriving in Oregon, and they happily ignored the hard facts that hundreds of miles of hard travel still awaited them, that they would have yet another mountain range to cross after they put the Rockies behind them.

The sharp crack of a sentry's rifle brought them back to the harsh reality of the present. Then a second rifle sounded.

Lee Blake, Ernie von Thalman, and Whip were on their feet immediately, directing the men to defense positions between the wagons and urging the women to move into the shadows beyond the light still cast by the cooking fire.

Within a moment everyone was on the move. The men carried their rifles, ammunition, and powder with them at all times and were able to take their places in the line without delay. Some of the teen-age boys ran to the supply wagon for spare rifles, which they would load for the sharpshooters who formed the core of the company's defense. This informal group, consisting of fewer than a score of men and one woman, Tonie Martin, refrained from moving up to the wagons. They banded together without being told, but they were waiting to see where the spearhead of the assault would develop before committing themselves to the battle. Meanwhile, mothers hurried off to take their places beside their children, and other women took the responsibility for keeping the horses and oxen calm.

There was no panic in the camp, no hysteria. The wagon train had been subjected to so many sudden attacks that everyone knew what was expected of him or her, and even the little children did not cry. Self-discipline was the key to the company defense, and these veterans responded instinctively to the crisis.

A shrill Indian war cry sounded outside the circle, confirming what people already knew. A raid on the train was under way.

The warriors were not mounted, and as soon as the sharpshooters realized that the brunt of the assault was in the vicinity of four or five small wagons, they hurried to that sector. Lee Blake dropped to one knee and methodically began to fire at the invaders, taking a loaded weapon from Danny as soon as he emptied the chamber of the one he held.

Whip was firing from a prone position a few feet away, with Chet Harris beside him to provide him with loaded rifles. Whip peered hard at the foe, trying to make out the colors of their war paint.

It was Stalking Horse, the Cherokee scout and Whip's close friend, who first identified the enemy. "Paiute!" he said, and there was no mistaking the urgency in his voice as he spoke.

Random arrows were falling inside the circle, and Emily von Thalman calmly directed the women to withdraw the work animals from that area.

"It looks to me like there are a couple of hundred of them," Whip said.

Further conversation was impossible because at that moment the Paiute made a concerted rush toward the wagons they apparently regarded as the weakest sector.

"Hold steady!" Lee Blake shouted to the sharpshooters. "Make every bullet count!"

A steady crackle of deadly rifle fire greeted the invaders.

"I got one," Claiborne Woodling muttered grimly.

"Me, too," Tilman Wade told him, but he, too, felt no satisfaction.

Tonie Martin was as calm as the men, taking careful aim, squeezing the trigger, and reaching for another rifle. She had grown up on the ranch of her uncle, Arnold Mell, near Independence, Missouri, in the days when that region had been the frontier, and her training showed.

Arnold, now one of the scouts in spite of his advanced age, was equally tranquil. "Raise your sights a little, Tonie," he called. "You're hitting them in the legs."

The girl nodded and adjusted her fire. Although she was married to a physician dedicated to the saving of lives, a goal she shared, she well knew that in battle it was essential to kill rather than inflict injury on an enemy.

Two farmers were wounded by Paiute arrows, but neither was seriously hurt, and both managed to make their way to the hospital wagon without assistance.

The unrelenting fire of the sharpshooters took a heavy toll, and the attackers withdrew to regroup out of range of the defenders' weapons.

Lee rested the butt of his rifle on the ground and, still watching the open area outside the circle, spoke to Whip. "Any special reason for this raid?"

The guide did not take his eyes from the open area, either. "I reckon it's spring fever. The Paiute have been cooped up in their canyon villages all winter, and they thought they saw a chance to grab free food and booty without taking much of a risk. Ordinarily they aren't troublemakers like their cousins, the Paiute to the south."

"You mean they're stupid."

"Not really, Lee. They've never faced heavy rifle fire, and they're just now finding out what it can do to them. If we teach them enough of a lesson, you can bank on it that they won't come near us again."

"I see." The army officer was silent for a moment. "We'd better be ready to move the sharpshooters elsewhere for the next assault."

Stalking Horse surprised him by laughing.

Whip shook his head. "Some tribes, maybe, but not the Northern Paiute. They're proud warriors, and

25

they'll want to prove to themselves they can break through our line in the same place. I'll give odds of ten to one they'll attack again right here."

His prophecy proved to be accurate. Instead of spreading out around the circumference of the circle, the warriors concentrated their renewed assault on the same sector, sending all their men against the one place.

Lee promptly sent for reinforcements, and other members of the company, using the wagons as cover, made their way completely around the circle to their new positions. "Hold your fire until I give the signal," Lee told them. "We'll wait until they make a rush before we respond."

An arrow severely wounded one of the oxen, and a short time later the animal had to be put out of its agony.

Grace Drummond, a robust hearty woman who was helping keep the work animals calm, was astonished when she felt a savage thrust in her shoulder and saw an arrow protruding from it. She had been wounded once before, in winter camp, when a crazed member of the wagon train had taken a shot at her. That experience had nearly unhinged her, but it had taught her a valuable lesson in endurance. Now, refusing assistance, she walked stolidly to the hospital wagon to have the arrow removed.

Chet Harris brought the news of her injury to her husband Nat, a diminutive but aggressive farmer, who was a member of the band of sharpshooters.

"How bad is she hurt?" he asked.

"She wouldn't let anybody help her when she went to see Doc Martin," Chet told him.

Nat chuckled. "It would take a half-dozen arrows to knock Grace off her feet," he said. "My place is right here."

An arrow sang past Cindy, missing her face by inches, but she did not flinch. Never had she expected to find happiness with any man, but now that she had given her heart to Claiborne, she believed she was, somehow, impervious to enemy weapons.

The Paiute charged in a solid mass toward the wagons, sending streams of arrows through the openings between the vehicles as they ran.

Lee remained silent, carefully gauging the approach of the enemy. A number of the defenders, particularly the newcomers to the position, became apprehensive. Left to their own devices, they would have opened fire without further delay. But Lee Blake was a veteran of four Indian wars, and he coolly waited until the warriors leading the advance were no more than ten or fifteen feet from the wagons. Then at last he gave the order, "Fire at will!"

Thirty-two rifles spoke simultaneously, then were exchanged for another set of weapons that spoke again. The blistering fire cut down the braves like a giant scythe, and those in the vanguard either dropped to the ground or fell back. Within moments, however, their places were taken by others.

The defenders kept up a steady fire, which so disconcerted the Paiute that they were unable to return it. The hail of arrows coming from the Indians ceased abruptly.

"Keep it up!" Lee shouted above the din. "Don't ease your pressure on them!"

The rifles continued to roar until the warriors finally broke their ranks, and although they managed to take their wounded with them as they fled, their dead littered the ground.

Members of the wagon train company were too weary to celebrate their victory. They were relieved that their own casualties had been light, with a total of five wounded, including Grace Drummond. Dr. Martin assured the leaders that none of the injuries were serious.

As a precaution the vigil inside the circle was maintained. Whip went out into the open, accompanied by the scouts, and ultimately they assured themselves that the Paiute had retreated from the area and would not strike again.

Eulalia was already in bed by the time Whip finally returned, and she pretended to be asleep as he undressed and crawled in beside her. Tired after his exertions, he fell asleep almost immediately, and Eulalia listened to the sound of his deep, even breathing.

The celebration that had followed the crossing of the Continental Divide had been premature, she told herself. Tonight's attack had demonstrated that many perils still awaited the company on the long road to Oregon.

As for her own situation, she thought it was hopeless. The others rightly thought of Whip as dependable, a rock of strength in an emergency, dependable when danger threatened. He was all of those things, but he was not a loving husband. His only contribution to her peace of mind and welfare was to order her to ride a horse each day, which would only make everyone else more conscious of her physical handicap.

But Eulalia would not allow herself to weep. Somehow, after this nightmare journey ended, she would find a solution for her problems.

II

The crippled Russian sailing ship moved slowly into Sitka Sound at the southern tip of the Russian colony of Alaska, then limped toward Baranof Island. The harbor, filled with small islands, was dominated by an extinct volcano on one of them and was surrounded by forests that ascended to the timberline. Above these thickly wooded areas on all sides were majestic, snow-capped peaks.

The scene inspired awe in some of the one hundred and sixteen weary travelers who had begun their long journey many months earlier in St. Petersburg. To most, however, the view was bleak, and they were not impressed by their first glimpse of the town of Sitka, sometimes called New Archangel, the capital of Alaska, which lay directly ahead and where, if their ship didn't fall apart, they would land in another hour. Only two buildings of consequence loomed above several dozen drab, one-story structures of wood where the residents lived and worked. One, obviously, was the bulb-domed Russian Orthodox Church, and the other, as the newcomers would learn, was the palace of the Imperial Governor, the Czar's personal representative in the New World. As the travelers could see, even from a distance, Sitka was dominated by the warehouses and offices of the Russian-American Trading Company that lined the waterfront. Here were gathered the furs and lumber that were dutifully sent back to Russia, along with quantities of fish, the only products that made the vast colony worth the efforts of administering it.

A man and a woman stood near each other on the deck of the ship, each wrapped in private thoughts. Anton Wizneuski, a young physician who had received his medical degree at Edinburgh, couldn't help wondering, as he looked at the grim view, why he had elected of his own free will to join the expedition to Oregon. His family was well connected in St. Petersburg, he was handsome and personable, and his future in Russia had been assured. Why, in the name of all that was holy, had he volunteered for this expedition? He knew the answer, of course. Russia, ruled by a handful of aristocrats in the name of the Czar, was stifling, and anyone who dared to complain would soon find himself imprisoned or sent to exile in Siberia by the secret agents who were everywhere. Anton had learned the meaning of real personal freedom during his years in Edinburgh. Foolishly, perhaps, he had hoped to find—or create—a similar atmosphere in Oregon, where he would have a voice in the colony's establishment.

Well, it was too soon to give in to despair. The young physician's knowledge of New World geography was hazy, but he realized that Oregon lay far to the south of Alaska, so at least the weather would be warmer there. Sitka reminded him of the convict villages he had seen when the party had crossed Siberia, and he shuddered.

Olga Runkova was so miserable she was unaware of the doctor's unhappiness. At the age of thirty she was the widow of a kulak, a farmer, who had been well-to-do, but died with debts unpaid. Her finely chiseled features, and her slender figure made her look like an aristocrat. Vanity was responsible for her presence in this company, so she had no one to blame but herself.

She had wanted to better her state, refusing to contemplate marriage to one of the poor serfs in her village not far from Moscow. But she couldn't imagine why she had thought any man of consequence would be making this journey. There was Dr. Wizneuski, to be sure, but he was several years her junior, so she ruled him out.

In a sense, Olga reflected, she had lost little. To be sure, she had no money. The profits from the sale of her farm had all gone to pay off back taxes and her husband's debts. But at least she was free and owed nothing to anyone. And she was lucky, in a way, to be leaving Russia. No member of the higher classes in Russia would have even contemplated marriage to a kulak's widow, although she was acquainted with several who had offered her other propositions, which she obviously would have nothing to do with.

At least she was still alive and healthy. She had lost count of the number who had died on the journey, but many of the survivors were ill. Well, if she stayed healthy she would claim a large plot of land in Oregon, and if there were no potential husbands in the St. Petersburg company, perhaps she would meet an eligible Englishman or American in Oregon. Always one to look ahead, she had been learning English from the doctor, and she addressed him now in that language.

"I didn't see you in the main saloon just now when Igor Doznevkov gathered us there to hear his announcements."

Anton shook his head. "I was looking after a patient below."

"That Doznevkov makes me so angry!" Olga removed the shawl from her head, and her hair, resembling fine-spun gold, tumbled down her back. "For one thing, he says we're going to continue to live on board this miserable, leaking tub until another ship is ready to sail us to Oregon. Imagine! He insists there are no facilities in Sitka for so many of us."

"That doesn't surprise me." Anton smiled sardonically and waved a hand in the direction of the drab town toward which the vessel was crawling under reduced sail. "Judging by the look of the place, I don't believe we'll be missing much. Sitka reminds me of Siberia."

"It isn't the place that bothers me. It's the food. Doznevkov made quite a point of telling us we'll have to eat the rest of the food on board before we'll be given any fresh Alaskan supplies."

Anton stared at her, his face hardening. "Doznevkov actually said that?"

The young woman nodded, disturbed by the anger she had aroused in the physician.

"We'll see about that!" He turned and started off down the deck.

Olga hurried after him and caught his arm. "Let me come with you Anton."

"It's better for you if you don't. What I intend to say won't be very pleasant, and I hardly need remind you that, as the official leader of the party, Doznevkov undoubtedly has access to the government's secret agents. For all we know he may be one of them."

"I'm so furious I don't care." She was exaggerating deliberately, and her reason for wanting to accompany him was simple. She had seen evidence of his blazing temper, and if he became embroiled in an argument with Doznevkov, she felt she could be a moderating influence.

The young doctor shook his head. "I'm protected by my profession. I'll allow you to come with me only if you promise to say nothing."

"Very well." She looked resigned.

They found Doznevkov in his private cabin, where he had just changed into formal court attire, a gorgeous long-tailed coat of embroidered yellow silk, a green satin waistcoat, white satin breeches, black silk stockings, and shoes with gold buckles.

Olga stared at him. Not once on the journey had anyone worn such clothes.

Igor Doznevkov, a burly man in his mid-thirties, looked as though he were glowering even when his face was in repose. "I'm calling on the Governor as soon as we tie up at the dock," he said.

"I hope," Anton said slowly, emphasizing each word, "that you'll also have time to order fresh food supplies that will be delivered before the end of the day."

Doznevkov was irritated. "I've already made it plain that the food on board will have to be eaten first."

"The biscuits are filled with weevils, the preserved meat is spoiling, and the pickled fish has become so sour it's no longer edible." Anton Wizneuski accented his points by thumping his fist into the open palm of his other hand.

"The members of this company," Doznevkov replied, "are receiving their meals free of charge through the kindness of His Imperial Majesty. Are you criticizing the Czar?"

"I'm quite certain," Anton retorted, "that His Imperial Majesty doesn't want immigrants to a new colony fed the slop given to prisoners in Siberia. There must be cows in Sitka. Our people, especially the mothers and children, need milk, butter, and cheese. There must be chickens in Sitka. Everyone in this party needs eggs. The weather may be chilly, but I believe vegetables are grown here. Our people need fresh greens!"

"You have grand ideas, Wizneuski."

Olga couldn't help interrupting. "Anton is right. People get sick on what we've been forced to eat. It's a disgrace."

"It's worse than that," Anton declared. "The food supplies on board this stinking ship are a hazard to the health of the entire party."

"You go too far, Wizneuski," the leader of the group said in an icy tone.

"I refuse to debate with you, Doznevkov! Unless

33

our people are given proper, nourishing food, still more of them will die. And I shall pay a visit to the Governor myself. It's my duty as a medical practitioner to submit a full report in writing, with copies to be sent to all of the appropriate ministries in St. Petersburg, protesting this intolerable situation. Either provide us with decent food or my report will be on the Governor's desk by nightfall!"

Igor Doznevkov silently cursed the interfering physician. He was assured of a tidy sum if he could force the stupid immigrants to consume what was left of their supplies before he bought more for them, and Wizneuski was taking gold out of his pocket.

"Before we left St. Petersburg we were assured of every convenience on this journey," Anton said. "Our quarters as we crossed Siberia were a cruel hoax. This ship is loathsome. And most of those who are sick have been made ill by the food. I shall spell out the full details in my report, and I shall emphasize your flat refusal to cooperate in this matter." All at once he was glad Olga had come with him. "It is fortunate I have a witness. I shall read my report to Madame Runkova, and she can put her mark on it to testify that I speak the truth."

"I can read and write, thank you," Olga said with great dignity. "And I shall be delighted to sign your report as a witness."

Igor Doznevkov knew he had to back down. "The authorities in St. Petersburg have better things to occupy them than to wade through the reports of dissidents. However, as the Czar himself is interested in the success of this mission, which depends on the harmony of its members, I shall—just this once—give in to your outrageous demands. Supplies of fresh food will come on board."

"Ample supplies," Anton said as he turned away. "Today."

The cabin door closed behind the pair.

Doznevkov stood still, his eyes narrowed. These

34

two were real troublemakers, that was certain. Well, he had the authority to take care of them in his own way. As a senior secret agent, he had the legal right to dispose of Wizneuski and Runkova as he saw fit. He would do nothing rash, of course—nothing to attract attention—but on the high seas or in the wilds of Oregon, an "accident" could easily be arranged. Yes indeed, Dr. Wizneuski and Olga Runkova had better mend their ways, or else their days would be numbered.

The palisades that surrounded Fort Vancouver were constructed of individual logs, each twelve feet high, each with a pointed top. The barracks inside the compound were made of logs, too, as were the officers' quarters and storehouses. Only the personal dwelling of the garrison commander, Colonel Phillips Morrison, was made of stone.

The architecture in the so-called lower town that stood beneath the fort, overlooking the Columbia River estuary, was more varied. Here houses and shops were made of clapboard fashioned in the sawmill owned and operated by the Hudson's Bay Company. The company's warehouses near the water's edge, filled with furs and timber, grain and dried fruit awaiting export to England, were constructed of solid stone. But rocks were no longer readily available, so the new warehouses being built to take care of the company's growing needs were of wood.

As Dr. John McLoughlin, the factor—or supervising manager—of the Hudson's Bay outpost often said, he was partial to clapboard. The large general store operated by his subordinates—an establishment that was a magnet for hunters, trappers, and friendly Indians—was shingled, as was his own house. In it his combined office-library had a window that boasted the largest single sheet of glass on the entire Pacific coast, but that window had not been designed to impress anyone. Dr. McLoughlin could tell at a glance what ships were arriving at Fort Vancouver, what ships still lay at anchor, and what ships had sailed to ports in Europe or the United States.

The window also afforded the craggy-faced Scotsman a luxury he thoroughly enjoyed. From his desk he had a magnificent view of the area where the river widened, and on the south bank he could see the huge trees of the lush forest. And by standing at the window and craning slightly, he could look off to the east and catch a glimpse of the superb, perpetually snow-covered peak that later generations would know as Mount Hood.

John McLoughlin loved Oregon with all his heart, and his enthusiasm was the principal reason Fort Vancouver was flourishing, even though London was sending no colonists to the area to support the garrison and trading post. The reason, which he accepted as valid, was that Canada, already a British possession, was sparsely populated and therefore colonists were being sent there. It didn't seem to matter to the government that the land here was incredibly fertile, that the hunting and fishing were marvelous, and that the area could support a large population.

That was not to say John McLoughlin was ignored in London. The Hudson's Bay Company was privately owned and theoretically had no direct connection with the government. But one of its seventeenth-century founders had been Prince Rupert, a cousin of King Charles the Second. So everyone knew that young Queen Victoria and other members of the royal family were major stockholders. Dr. McLoughlin was the most important man in Oregon, and everyone there knew it, with the single exception of Colonel Morrison.

Certainly the British Foreign Minister, Lord Palmerston, was well aware of the relative positions of the pair because he addressed his letters to them jointly.

Today, Dr. McLoughlin paid no attention to the

view from his office as he listened to the communication being read aloud by Major Roland Pitts, who had brought it from London and was to assume the post of second-in-command of the garrison.

Colonel Morrison listened, too, his boots propped on one of John McLoughlin's hardwood tables, his head lolling, and his eyes closed. Contrary to appearances, however, Phillips Morrison was not asleep; that was how he concentrated best. "Be good enough to read the second and third paragraphs again, Pitts."

"Yes, sir." The Major read obediently. "'As you know, gentlemen, Her Majesty's Government are laying claim to the whole of the Oregon country, regardless of the counterclaims being made by the United States. So it becomes obvious that the wagon train now traveling across America to Oregon, the first of many, constitutes a direct threat to our position. Oregon must remain British. Therefore, I urge you to take any measures you may deem necessary to insure that this is done.'"

"Ah." The Colonel exhaled slowly, sat upright, and rubbed his hands together. "That does it! I shall direct any Royal Navy warship that may be in port here at the time the Yankees arrive to fire on them. And if that doesn't send them flying, my redcoats will chase them back into the mountains with their bayonets!"

John McLoughlin was so agitated that his Scottish burr was even more pronounced than usual. "Surely you're not serious, Morrison!"

Major Pitts was horrified, too. "You'd be committing acts of war, Colonel! The United States will be certain to declare war the very day the news reaches Washington City."

Phillips Morrison shrugged, and a tight smile appeared on his puffy face, creasing it. "I've worn this uniform for a quarter of a century, and I know how to obey orders."

Major Pitts became even more upset. "But Lord

Palmerston gave no orders, sir. He *urged* you and Dr. McLoughlin to take certain steps. He didn't *order* you to take them."

"Quite so," McLoughlin said. "I've dealt with Palmerston for years, and he's a canny one. The lad is right. What's more, I'm quite certain the Foreign Minister was referring to peaceful means, not acts of war."

"No one in London wants a new war with America!" Major Pitts exclaimed.

Colonel Morrison was smug. "In my opinion Lord Palmerston's instructions are quite clear. His letter speaks for itself."

"Even if it did," McLoughlin said evenly, mastering his sense of outrage, "Palmerston is mistaken. What does matter is that civilized men occupy Oregon and take advantage of God's bounty here. There's no land like it anywhere on earth."

Morrison was incredulous. "Do you advocate American occupation of Oregon, Dr. McLoughlin? That's treason!"

The factor was amused. "Hardly. As I've written to my company's directors—and to the Queen herself—it may be true we were the first to set up a trading post here, then the first to establish a military garrison. But we haven't taken proper advantage of our situation. Great Britain has sent no farmers to till this fine soil, no fishermen to take the salmon that leap out of the river. The American claim is honest, you know. Their explorers were the first to find this area. And I say that if they send colonists here before we do, let them have the territory. Any nation that shows that initiative deserves it!"

The Colonel's cheeks ballooned. "My duty is clear!"

Roland Pitts looked first at one, then at the other. The clean-cut young officer's own view was less liberal by far than that of the generous McLoughlin, to whom Oregon meant more than the claims of rival nations. But he also realized that Morrison's attitude represented the greater danger. "Colonel, you can't open fire on Americans!"

Phillips Morrison glared at his new deputy. "Are you presuming to give me orders, Major Pitts?"

"No, sir. I'm just urging you to be sensible."

"It makes very good sense to me to drive the Yankees out of Oregon. That will settle the problems of sovereignty here once and for all."

"On the contrary," Dr. McLoughlin declared. "No nation could refuse to accept that kind of challenge. Not only will the United States send troops in large numbers across the continent to take and hold this territory, but they'll invade Canada and capture Quebec. They'll engage us on the high seas. They'll take Oregon, and they'll also claim large parts of Canada by right of conquest."

"We can't win a war with them," Pitts said. "Our divisions must travel three thousand miles before they enter combat, and we can't maintain supply lines that long."

"I regard Lord Palmerston's letter as sufficient authority for what I see fit to do," the Colonel replied.

John McLoughlin rarely lost his temper, but his eyes blazed, and, although he didn't raise his voice, he spoke with greater resonance. "If you set North America aflame, Morrison, I won't rest until I see you court-martialed and dismissed from the Royal Army in disgrace!"

The commander of the Fort Vancouver garrison drew himself to his feet and tugged at his gold-encrusted scarlet tunic. "I shall gladly take that risk, McLoughlin. I am determined to keep the Union Jack flying in Oregon!"

The U.S.S. *Washington*, a fifty-two-gun frigate, sliced cleanly through the waters of the Atlantic on the long voyage that would take her around South America into the Pacific, then north. There were few clouds in the early evening sky, promising fair weather for the next day, and the members of her crew, most of them experienced sailors, were in high spirits.

So were the two hundred and twenty United States Army infantrymen who were being transported to the Oregon country. They had acquired their sea legs since sailing from Baltimore, and now, having eaten their supper, they strolled on the main deck, enjoying the salty spring air. All were volunteers, and all were filled with a spirit of adventure. They had agreed to spend three years in Oregon, and they were buoyed by the knowledge that they were taking part in a historic undertaking. They laughed and joked, and, when out of sight of the duty officers on the quarterdeck, some of them broke the navy's rule forbidding smoking at sea.

The atmosphere in the spacious cabin of the *Washington's* commander, Captain Robert Ingalls, was more subdued. His dinner guest was Major Eli Moser, the acting commander of the army troops, and the two officers spoke in sober, restrained tones.

"We'll put into seven or eight ports for supplies during the course of the voyage," Captain Ingalls said. "In the Caribbean, South America, and Mexico, with our last stop at Yerba Buena. The Mexicans won't welcome us with open arms there, but they won't deny us the facilities of the port, either."

"What you're saying, sir, is that the British in Oregon may learn of our coming before we arrive," Major Moser said.

The navy officer shrugged. "Anything is possible, especially when we move north through the Pacific. The Oregon trade is fairly lively, and any number of merchant ships who sight us might well guess our destination and take the word to Fort Vancouver before we ourselves arrive there."

Moser's smile was tight. "I welcome that possibility, Captain. And, between us, I hope we reach Oregon before our wagon train gets there and I relinquish the command to Colonel Blake. There's nothing I'd enjoy more than a tangle with the redcoats!"

Ingalls, who was at least ten years older than the army officer, spoke softly. "This voyage is being timed so we reach Oregon on the heels of the wagon train, not ahead of them. The administration considers it important that they arrive first and establish their claims to the land."

"Well, if they suffer any delays of consequence, we'll beat them."

"Surely you've been ordered to avoid hostilities with the British, Moser!"

"Oh, yes," the Major replied easily. "General Scott made it very plain that, if I still hold the command, I'm to fight only in defense."

"I'm sure that means you're not to pick a quarrel with the British garrison."

"Right, sir," was the cheerful reply. "But they may pick a quarrel with me, and if they do, they've chosen the wrong man. I was too young to fight them the last time, but I know of no better way to win a double promotion than to beat them in a battle."

Captain Ingalls ate the last of his meal, then waited until his orderly cleared away the dishes and brought them mugs of coffee before he spoke again. "I'm afraid of the Royal Navy," he said slowly. "They still have more ships, but we proved to them in the War of 1812 that our gunnery was superior. It still is. If anything, we've improved. If necessary, I could give a good account of myself against a ship-of-the-line—or two frigates. But I don't relish the idea of a new war with Britain. Especially a war over Oregon. I believe our dispute with them can be solved peacefully, and I think Lee Blake agrees with me."

"You know Colonel Blake, sir?"

"We were members of the same class in a joint command course a couple of years ago. He's level-headed, and his trigger finger doesn't itch."

"But mine does, sir?" Major Moser laughed.

"I sincerely hope not."

"I'm not one to start a ruckus," Moser said. "On the other hand, I'd prefer an overnight promotion to the rank of full colonel to waiting another ten years. I intend to be civil to the commander of the British garrison at Fort Vancouver—"

"I'm glad to hear it."

"—but if he tries to create problems for me, he'll soon learn his mistake. The United States has become big enough and strong enough not to swallow the insults of any other country on the face of this earth."

Captain Ingalls could only hope, fervently, that the wagon train would reach Oregon before he dropped anchor at Fort Vancouver. The presence of Lieutenant Colonel Lee Blake in Oregon was urgently needed to cool the ambitions of this hotheaded young officer.

Every morning that Eulalia Holt spent riding the mare was an agony almost too great to endure, but she endured it all the same. grimly spending each day in the saddle. Sometimes the pain in her leg was so intense she wanted to cry, but she refused to give Whip that satisfaction. Whenever she faltered or sought an excuse to ride in her wagon, he firmly refused to permit the indulgence.

"Ride," he told her repeatedly, "if you ever want your leg to get better."

Well, there was no real improvement in her leg. She had to admit it was growing stronger, that when she first arose in the morning she could put her weight on it without feeling discomfort. But she could see no change in her basic condition, and she saw no reason to bother the busy Dr. Martin by asking him to examine her again.

Eulalia spent most of her time riding with the monitors of the line because, as she quickly discovered, she was less conscious of her acute discomfort when she forgot herself by conversing with others. Tilman

Wade soon became her favorite riding companion because he was so solicitous, never mentioning her pain but exerting himself to keep her distracted. Tilman, she learned, was kind to everyone.

At the end of the day's ride he frequently held long talks with the almost eighteen-year-old Sally MacNeill, whose parents had died earlier on the journey. As Tilman confided to Eulalia, Sally was in love—or imagined she was in love, which was more or less the same thing—with Paul Thoman, a Harvard College man who had joined the expedition after spending a year as a mountain man for the sake of adventure. Only three years older than Sally, Paul came from a far different world. He was a member of a prominent Boston shipbuilding family, he immersed himself in classical literature, which he quoted frequently, and although he was attracted to Sally, he had little in common with her.

"I've been trying to tell Sally that she and Paul wouldn't have looked at each other twice if they'd met back East. In fact, they wouldn't have known each other in the first place. People from Boston's Beacon Hill don't become acquainted with farm girls. But Sally won't listen to me, and every time Paul's attention wanders when they're together, she's miserable."

Sally MacNeill, Eulalia told herself privately, wasn't the only woman in the company who had made a bad mistake. She had met Whip only because he had been hired to guide this train. But why she had fallen in love with him—and why she continued to love him—was beyond her understanding. If only he would allow her to relax and would stop forcing her to ride that confounded mare!

One bright spring day, in mid-morning, the train reached the Snake River. Whip announced they would follow it for about three hundred miles, which would take approximately one month. When possible, they would move along the bank of the river, but when it cut through gorges and ravines, they would be forced to travel along the heights above it. Soon the Rockies would be behind them, and only the Cascade Range would stand between them and Oregon.

That same afternoon, when the lead wagons were already moving into place at the campsite the scouts had selected for the night, Eulalia was riding with Tilman at the rear of the column. She knew that if she spurred forward she would be able to dismount at last, but something perverse in her nature forced her to wait. Whip was not going to accuse her of being a quitter!

The wagons still in line slowed to a temporary halt while those in the front were maneuvered into their night positions in the circle, so Eulalia and Tilman rested their mounts.

Eulalia was about to speak, but she saw that Tilman's attention had been diverted. Following his gaze, she noticed that Dave Evans had left his wagon and had gone forward to exchange a few words with Ginny Dobbs.

Tilman's expression was stormy, and Eulalia quickly understood the reason: Ginny, who was normally phlegmatic, was smiling and speaking with animation as she flirted with Dave. Well, Eulalia didn't think too highly of Evans, although she wasn't certain why she shied away from him.

It was far more significant that Tilman was interested in Ginny. Eulalia had actively avoided the girl for a long time, as had Cathy Blake and Cindy, and it was her private opinion that Tilman was too good for her. A man of his sensitivity deserved better.

Tilman forced himself to stop looking at the couple. "It's taking longer than usual to get organized for the night," he said. "Maybe the campsite is cramped. At least, that's how it looks from here—" He broke off suddenly, an expression of stunned surprise on his face.

Then, as he slumped forward in his saddle, Eulalia saw an arrow protruding from his back. She screamed.

Paul Thoman was the first of the monitors to respond, arriving at a gallop. Taking in the situation at a glance, he immediately headed for a nearby boulder and dismounted, his rifle in his hand.

Others quickly arrived, too, and Whip made remarkably good time from his place more than half a mile away. Before he joined Paul he looked quickly at Eulalia to make certain she had not been hurt. That glance hinted to her that, perhaps he wasn't as indifferent to her as he appeared.

But this was no time to think of herself. While the men searched for the attacker, she had to look after the unconscious Tilman. She dismounted long enough to strap him to his saddle so he wouldn't tumble to the ground, then she mounted the mare again and rode forward as rapidly as she dared.

Whip and Paul were studying the ground behind the boulder. "It looks to me like there was just one man here," Whip said.

"A Rogue warrior who had nothing better to do than create mischief," Paul agreed. "I'll take a couple of men and go after him."

Whip shook his head. "He had a head start, and he can make better time in those woods on foot than you can on horseback."

"But I'm damned if we can let him get away with this!" Paul declared vehemently. "Have you ever read Sir Walter Scott's *Lay of the Last Minstrel?* 'Vengeance, deep brooding o'er the slain—'"

"Save the fancy talk," Whip interrupted. "We'll double the sentry detail tonight, and tomorrow you can take charge of a strong rear guard, Paul. You'll know what to do. If you see a lone warrior anywhere, put a bullet through him fast!"

The order was sensible, and Paul reluctantly abandoned the idea of giving chase.

Word of what had happened spread swiftly, and Dr. Martin was waiting for his patient when Eulalia reached the hospital wagon. He undid the strap holding Tilman in the saddle, then gently carried him inside.

A crowd had collected around the hospital wagon, and people were talking in low tones.

Tonie Martin came to the entrance. "Please," she said, "go about your business. I'll let you know if Bob needs any help."

The normal evening routines were followed. Firewood was gathered, preparations were made for the evening meal, and the water detail dipped their buckets into the swiftly flowing Snake River. But Tilman's injury had cast a pall over the company, and as time went on with no word from the hospital tent, even the children became subdued. Night came, and most people were finishing their supper when Dr. Martin appeared.

He moved to a place near the fire and said, "It wasn't easy to remove the arrow, but Tilman Wade will be all right. I had to give him a couple of doses of laudanum during surgery, so he's sleeping now and won't wake up until tomorrow. But I'm going to need help. He'll spend at least a week in the hospital wagon, and I'll need someone with him whenever we're in motion to make certain his bandages don't slip."

Sally MacNeill immediately turned to Dolores, the tiny half-breed girl who shared her wagon. "You take care of the wagon," she murmured, and jumped to her feet. "I volunteer, Dr. Martin!" she called.

Bob Martin thanked her and immediately returned to the wagon.

An irate Ginny Dobbs materialized in front of Sally. "I was going to volunteer," she said, "but you beat me to it. What gives you the right to nurse Tilman?"

"The right?" Sally was puzzled. "He's a friend. He's been kind to me, and I want to return the favor. But

I'm sure there's enough for both of us to do. I'll gladly share the time with you."

"Never mind." Ginny tossed her head. "You asked for the job, so you can do it." She stalked off, muttering to herself.

Dolores had spent several years as a medicine woman with her father's tribe and apparently saw visions that enabled her to foretell the future. Sally was skeptical of that talent but nevertheless knew her friend was wise, so she turned to her in confusion.

"Why was she so nasty?"

"Sometimes," Dolores said, "when a woman cannot decide whether she wants a man, she is still jealous. Until she makes up her own mind, she wants no other woman to have him."

"But that's ridiculous! You heard what the doctor said. Tilman will need someone to keep an eye on his bandages, that's all."

Dolores's only reply was an enigmatic shrug.

It was late morning when Tilman awakened. Conscious of a throbbing pain in his back, he felt the motion of the wagon, then realized when he saw its hard sides and top that he was in the hospital wagon rather than a covered wagon. Then Sally came into his line of vision. "What's all this?" he asked hoarsely.

"You were wounded by an Indian's arrow yesterday," the girl told him. "Dr. Martin cut it out and patched you up. You'll be fine in a few days."

He digested the information. "But what are you doing here?"

Sally waved self-deprecatingly. "Oh, he needed somebody to make sure your bandages stay in place, so I offered to help. It's nothing."

"It sounds like a great deal to me."

She changed the subject. "Would you like a drink of water?"

"That's a thought. Now that you mention it, I feel as

though I've spent months in the desert." The wagon bounced over a rock, and he winced.

"Are you in pain, Tilman?"

"Well—"

"Dr. Martin said to mix this medicine with a glass of water if you're hurting."

"Let me smell the medicine, please."

She held the vial under his nose.

"Ugh. That's laudanum. No, thanks. It'll put me back to sleep."

"You have nothing better to do," she said, smiling.

"But I do. I can talk with you."

"We'll have a good many days for that before you're allowed out of bed."

"Tell me what wonderful deeds Paul has performed lately," Tilman said.

Sally needed no urging. "He wanted to give chase to the Indian who shot you, but Whip wouldn't allow him to go off into the woods. Instead, he's been put in charge of a strong rear guard. I think it's wonderful that he's given so many responsibilities at his age."

"Very impressive," he said, the pain in his back so intense he wanted to shout.

"Oh, I think so, too. I—Tilman Wade, you're hurting bad!"

"I'll admit there have been times when I've felt better than I do at this moment."

Sally poured the opiate into a glass, which she filled with water. "Drink this down. Every last drop!"

"You remind me of a drill sergeant I knew in our militia back home."

"Is that good or bad?"

"In your case it's quite good. What's more, it must be very pleasant to give orders to someone almost twice your age." Tilman made a valiant attempt to smile.

"But you're no such thing. You're only fourteen and a half years older than I am." Sally was indignant.

"How do you know?"

"Because you told me yourself." She held his head while he drank the concoction. The taste was so bitter that Tilman almost gagged, but he forced himself to drain the glass.

"I'm going to tell Dr. Martin you're a wonderful patient."

"Sally," he said, trying in vain to smile, "when you marry and have children, you're going to be a perfect mother."

"Tell that to Paul."

He suspected she would have a number of other beaus before she settled down, but he refrained from expressing the thought, knowing he lacked the strength to argue with her. He felt as though a huge knife were digging into his back, and the pain was excruciating, but he had to bear it for another ten minutes or more until the opiate took effect.

"Sally," he asked, clenching a fist, "have you ever seen a grown man cry?" She shook her head. "It isn't a pretty sight."

Her father had wept when he had died, but this was not the moment to mention such things. "You go ahead and cry, if you want," she told him.

"I'd rather not."

Impulsively she reached out and put her hand over his tightly clenched fist. Tilman caught hold of her hand and held it in a grip that hurt. "That's better," he said.

Sally smiled at him, tolerating the discomfort. In a few minutes, as the wagon train drew to a halt for the brief rest period called the nooning, he fell asleep, still clutching her hand.

A few moments later the rear door opened. Ginny Dobbs stood in the frame. Sally raised the forefinger of her free hand to her lips.

But Ginny's temper flared, and she paid no attention to the signal. "Excuse me for interrupting," she said and flounced away.

When Bob Martin came in to check on his patient, he found Sally, her hand still imprisoned by Tilman's, smiling broadly to herself. All Sally knew was that Ginny was vexed, and the knowledge pleased her. Tilman was far too good for that shrew.

Tilman had to remain in bed for eight days, and when he was allowed to return slowly to normal living, Sally insisted he ride with her and Dolores until he regained his strength. The girl's chatter amused him, so he accepted the invitation. He would have preferred to ride with Ginny, but she didn't ask him.

On Saturday, when camp was made, Tilman walked beside Sally toward the bank of the Snake River. Dolores and Hosea, a diminutive former slave whose exploits in battle and clever work with a miniature forge had made him one of the company's favorites, walked close behind them.

The entire company was gathering for an unexpected ceremony. Cindy and Claiborne had agreed to wait until they reached Oregon before they were married, but that very morning at breakfast he had demanded, "What's to stop us from being married today?"

Cindy had been startled. "Well—nothing, I guess."

"Tomorrow is Sunday, so we'll stay in camp for the whole day. I mean—"

"I know what you mean," Cindy said, smiling.

"I see nothing to be gained by waiting until we get to Oregon," Claiborne said.

She drew a deep breath, then said tremulously, "You might change your mind."

"I can think of no reason I would."

"We haven't talked about this lately, but are you sure you want to marry a woman with my past?"

"I want to marry *you*," he said firmly. "I know what you are, so I don't give a hang about what you were. It's *now* that counts. And our lives together in Oregon."

"Well," Cindy said, weakening, "if you're really positive—"

"I'll speak to Reverend Cavendish right now, before we hit the trail," Claiborne said, leaping to his feet.

There was no time to prepare for a proper wedding, but Cindy didn't care. The clothes she had brought with her from Louisville were too blatantly bold for a bride to wear, so she borrowed a gown of pale lilac lace from Cathy Blake. Hosea set up his tiny forge outside of Ted Woods's wagon, and he promised he would have a wedding ring made long before the day ended.

Mack Dougall, one of the scouts, shot an elk for the occasion, and several of the men helped him butcher it and haul it to the campsite. There the quarters were roasted over a huge fire, and the children, under Dolores's direction, gathered sweet mountain berries for the feast.

Reverend Oscar Cavendish put aside his buckskins and wore his one black suit as he stood beside the river bank. A high cliff formed the backdrop, and the rushing waters provided the music, augmented by a breeze that caused the pines in the forest to sigh.

Out of deference to Eulalia, the matron of honor, who was so painfully conscious of her limp, the bride walked only a short distance toward the clergyman. Claiborne's poise had deserted him, and he looked pale. Of all the wedding party, only Whip, standing beside the bridegroom, looked composed.

No one spoke, and no one moved as Reverend Cavendish read the familiar words that began the ceremony. "'Dearly beloved, we are gathered together here in the sight of God and in the face of this company, to join together this man and this woman in holy matrimony. . . .'"

No one thought it strange that this ceremony, whose roots were as old as the civilization of Western man, was being conducted in a primitive wilderness

51

more than a thousand miles from the nearest American outpost. A few scattered Indian tribes lived in these forests and mountains, and occasionally a white hunter or trapper made his way through the passes. The only other inhabitants were wild animals and birds.

It was more than the background, though, that made the ceremony so impressive. Every adult in the train knew Cindy's past, but she had been so firm in her loyalties and had worked so hard that even those women who had avoided her for a time now wished her well. Claiborne had been unpopular for a long time after he had joined the train, too, but his courage, resourcefulness, and willingness to share hardships had won him many friends. Perhaps only the Austrian-born baron, Ernst von Thalman, realized that in this land where all men were said to be equal, the travails of wagon train living brought out the best or the worst in people. Certainly Cindy and Claiborne had been changed for the better.

Whip looked past the bridal couple at his wife, but she was lost in her own thoughts.

A little more than a month had passed since Eulalia had been married, and a tear trickled unheeded down her face. She realized that anyone who might glance at her would think she was just being sentimental, but she knew she was crying because she felt sorry for herself. It was her right to break down, just a little, on this very special occasion.

Ted Woods stood alone at the back of the crowd, staring first at the bride, then at the groom. A feeling of great emptiness filled him, and he thought he might drown in that void. No, he was damned if he would! Bitter experience had taught him that he could survive alone, and much as he might want a woman, he was self-sufficient. When these people reached Oregon and began to farm there, they would need a blacksmith even more than they needed him on the trail. Well, he wouldn't fail them—or himself.

Whip reached into a pocket of the only suit he had ever owned as an adult, the suit he had bought when he had been summoned by President Andrew Jackson and offered the job of guiding this train. He fumbled for a moment, then handed the ring to Claiborne, the ring Hosea had made from one of Eulalia's thin gold bracelets.

The ceremony ended, and the bride and groom kissed. Their embrace was so protracted that Nat Drummond whistled, earning a glare from Grace.

Eulalia kissed her new sister-in-law and brother, then stood aside as people thronged toward the bridal couple. Suddenly a firm arm encircled her shoulders and held her in a tight grip.

She recognized Whip's touch instantly, even before she looked at him. His gesture of affection was so unexpected that she didn't quite know what to make of it. Surely he, of all men, wasn't becoming sentimental.

His jaw worked for a moment before he spoke. "Seeing tomorrow is a rest day," he said, "there's no need for you to go riding. You've been looking a mite peaked. You could stand a whole day of not doing anything much."

"Yes, I'd like that." She looked at him more intently.

Whip averted his eyes, but his grip on her shoulders did not slacken.

He was shy, as Eulalia had realized for a long time, but there was something other than shyness in his attitude. Her instinct told her he would make love to her tonight, and she knew she would respond to him with her whole heart, mind, and body. Lovemaking would not even begin to resolve the issues that drove them apart, but at least she knew he wanted her and wasn't repulsed by her crippled leg. She would cling to that realization.

Ted Woods was one of the last to approach the bridal pair. Seeing him, Claiborne stiffened, and Cindy's smile froze on her face. But Ted, for the first time in years, kept his emotions completely under control. "Good luck," he told Cindy, brushing her cheek with his lips. Then he gripped the bridegroom's hand. "You have a wonderful wife," he said. "Appreciate her."

Before Claiborne could reply, he moved away.

There was a wedding feast of roasted elk meat and cornmeal cakes. Since no fresh vegetables were available this early in the spring, especially in the mountains, everyone appreciated the berries the children had gathered. Cathy Blake and Emily von Thalman had used a quantity of precious flour to bake a wedding cake, and there was enough for every member of the company to be given a tiny square.

Cindy threw her bridal bouquet of wildflowers that some of the smaller children had picked for her, and the unmarried women reached for it. There was a peal of laughter when they realized that Sally MacNeill had caught it. Sally's face turned as red as her hair, and she didn't dare glance in Paul Thoman's direction.

It was just as well, Tilman thought, because Paul, deep in conversation with several of the men, had no idea she had captured the bouquet.

The bride and groom ate very little, and when the parents of the younger children began to remove them from the scene, Cindy and Claiborne exchanged a quick glance. With one accord they rose. Then, sauntering with seeming unconcern, they paused to speak to various people. But after they moved beyond the light cast by the fire, they walked more rapidly as they made their way to Cindy's wagon.

Both were convulsed with laughter, and Claiborne's hand shook so violently he found it difficult to light the candle just inside the entrance. They sat side by side on the bed, laughing until they were on the verge of weeping. The hazing of bridal couples was strictly forbidden because the wagon train had enough real troubles, but Cindy and Claiborne were pleased because they had given everyone the slip, or so they thought. Not until later would they realize that most people had carefully pretended not to see them when they had stolen away.

Gradually their laughter subsided. They embraced and kissed, and all at once the interior of the wagon crackled with the tension caused by passion. They stood, and Cindy moved toward the candle, intending to blow it out.

"Let it burn," Claiborne said. "I want to be able to see you."

She hesitated for no more than an instant before she turned away from the candle. She couldn't and wouldn't tell him that undressing in front of a customer had been one of the time-honored rituals in the Louisville brothel in which she had worked.

Looking at each other, they undressed slowly, deliberately, and Cindy knew this experience in no way resembled what she had ever done in the brothel. This man was her husband, who loved her. That made all the difference in the world.

When they were nude, he picked her up and, kissing her, carried her the few steps to the bed. He deposited her gently, then joined her there.

Cindy quickly realized that Claiborne was experienced in the art of lovemaking, and she was relieved. She had dreaded the thought of being forced to become his teacher, and for the first time she began to relax.

She was fully prepared to simulate, to pretend she was gradually becoming aroused while actually feeling nothing, as she had done on countless occasions with men in the past. To her astonishment, however, her response to him was genuine, and her desire, combined with a real sense of erotic pleasure, grew within her. Never had she known such joy, and she abandoned herself to it, no longer thinking, allowing her urges to express themselves as they would.

They were united, then moved steadily, swiftly toward a mutual climax. Suddenly, when Cindy could no longer tolerate the anticipatory suspense, she found release. Only then did it occur to her that the same thing was happening at the same moment to Claiborne.

They remained locked in an embrace as their passion subsided, and Cindy knew that the shackles that had held her in bondage to her sordid past had been removed. This man—her husband—not only wanted her for herself, but made certain that her gratification was as great as his.

Her eyes shining, she looked at him. The candle had burned itself out, and neither of them even noticed that the interior of the wagon was dark.

III

Sir Harold Wilkins, the British Minister to the United States, had spent his entire adult life in the diplomatic service of his country. Tall, lean, and cosmopolitan, he was looking forward to his retirement in another year, meanwhile enduring his present life in the raw, unfinished town the Americans called Washington City.

But there were compensations, and as he descended from his carriage at the White House entrance, Sir Harold, elegantly attired as always, was looking forward to his meeting with the President of the United States. He was pleased that the crude, aggressive Andrew Jackson no longer held the office. Martin Van Buren, who had served as the American Minister in London, thought of himself as civilized and thoroughly enjoyed a good meal, a glass of rare port, and a conversation with an attractive lady. It was the considered opinion of the British Minister, frequently expressed in his dispatches to Lord Palmerston, the Foreign Secretary, that Van Buren was weak and could be maneuvered into corners from which there was no escape.

The President greeted the envoy cordially, amenities were exchanged, and Sir Harold accepted a Virginia cigar, which he pronounced excellent, although he preferred West Indian tobacco.

"Mr. President," he said at last, "I've been instructed by Her Majesty's Government to seek a solution to the Oregon question that has been disturbing our amicable relations."

"I'm delighted to hear it," Van Buren replied, still smiling. "We've been at war with each other too often in the past, and certainly the two principal English-speaking nations of the world should be able to settle their problems peacefully."

"Precisely our sentiments."

The President folded his hands over his paunch and leaned back in his chair. "Have you been authorized to make any specific proposals?"

"To be sure." Sir Harold reached into an inner pocket and produced a map of the Oregon country, which he unfolded and spread on the desk.

There was no need for Martin Van Buren to look at the map. He was already thoroughly familiar with the geography of the Pacific Northwest.

"Her Majesty's Government are prepared to offer the United States a compromise. All territory below the forty-fifth parallel will be American. All territory north of that parallel will be incorporated into Canada."

Without bothering to look at the map, the President knew the proposal meant that the great Columbia River, its rich basin, and the fertile land that lay to the north of it for hundreds of miles would become British. The offer was so absurd that, had the situation not been so serious, he would have laughed aloud. "We have already made an offer to settle the boundary at the forty-ninth parallel, you know."

"Quite so, Mr. President. But we regard that line as arbitrary rather than natural."

"The forty-fifth would be even more arbitrary. You've simply chosen to take a ruler and draw a line across a map at a spot that suits you."

Now, the British envoy thought, he would begin to

apply pressure. "That's the best we can offer," he said flatly.

Van Buren leaned forward, resting an elbow on the desk. "The United States," he said quietly, "prefers to establish the boundary at a line at fifty-four degrees, forty minutes."

Sir Harold studied the map briefly, then stared across the desk in astonishment. "Surely you can't be serious, Mr. President! That would extend the boundary of the United States to the southern tip of Russian Alaska."

"So it would." Van Buren was unflustered. "I've consulted a great many people on this matter, Sir Harold, and I tell you plainly that not only is my Cabinet of one mind, but I have the full support of both houses of the Congress. In the interests of fairness, we've offered you the forty-ninth parallel. If you come back to us with an offer that's ridiculous, and you know it as well as we do, then we shall insist on fifty-four, forty. What's more, we're prepared to back up that claim by any means necessary."

The President wasn't reacting as the British Minister had anticipated. "Are you saying you're prepared to go to war over this matter?"

"We seek no war, and we prefer to remain at peace with all nations. But we're fully determined to do what we must in order to protect our basic national interests."

The British envoy was forced to revise his estimate of the President's character. Although much quieter and far less bellicose than Andrew Jackson, he was just as firm. The realization created a different situation and required a more delicate approach. "As you know, Mr. President," he said, "the Hudson's Bay Company established a trading post on the Columbia River opposite where the Willamette River drains into it. That post has grown into a town of some hundreds of persons. So Her Majesty's Government felt obliged

to set up a fort there in order to protect British subjects."

Van Buren nodded. "Of course, Sir Harold. So, in
the light of your experience, you can understand our
position. The United States feels the urgent need to
support our citizens migrating to Oregon in wagon
trains. I refer not only to our initial train, with which
you're familiar, but with future trains being organized. In the years immediately ahead, we anticipate
that there will be thousands of Americans settling in
the Oregon country. I'd be derelict in my duty if I
failed to shield them with our army and navy."

In spite of his lifelong diplomatic training, Sir Harold could not conceal his surprise. "You're intending
to send troops and warships to the Pacific, sir?"

The President preferred not to reveal that the frigate *Washington*, carrying an army contingent was
already on the high seas. The move would be far more
effective if London learned of the action after the
arrival of the troops and warship became an accomplished fact. So, rather than answer the question, he
said only, "You may inform your government, Sir Harold, that—like it or not—this country is actively settling the Oregon country. Our people are moving in,
and there they shall stay."

The British Minister soon took his leave. On the
short ride back to his legation, he was lost in
thought.

When he returned to his office, Sir Harold called in
his deputy, the chargé d'affaires, before writing his
disturbing report to Lord Palmerston. Sir Harold explained the situation to him. Listening to his superi-
or's account of the interview with Martin Van Buren,
the younger man shook his head. "It appears," he said
at last, "that the President couldn't be bluffed."

"Correct. And I don't believe he was bluffing, either."

"Then you think there's going to be a direct confrontation between our people and the Americans in Oregon, Sir Harold?"

"Anything is possible, and nothing will surprise me. All I know for certain is that an explosive situation between England and the United States is being created in the Pacific Northwest, and one way or another, there's going to be hell to pay."

For a long time, Yerba Buena, the principal Mexican port in her colony of California, had been a sleepy little town. A small garrison was stationed at the fort known as the presidio, but the half-battalion there had remained inactive. The duties of the assistant governor in charge of the area had been light, and only the missions, established to convert the Indians of the region to Christianity, had been active.

But Yerba Buena was changing, particularly in the neighborhood of the waterfront. Twenty ships flying the flags of a half-dozen nations were either tied up at the docks or rode at anchor in the magnificent natural harbor. Increased trade with the British in Oregon and the Russians in Alaska was partly responsible, and so was the opening of trade with China. For the first time in history, tea and silk and cotton were being exported from China in return for goods from the West.

Most of the newcomers to Yerba Buena were Americans, the majority of them New Englanders. They owned the warehouses and stores being built so rapidly in the port area, and they were the proprietors, too, of the proliferating saloons, brothels, and eating places that served the various needs of the transient seafaring population.

It was no accident, either, that most of the ships were American-owned and their crews made up in the main of Yankees. Even before the departure of the first wagon train for Oregon, Americans had been discovering Yerba Buena, and so many of them were coming to the town that the assistant governor was mildly perturbed. "English," he declared in a report to Mexico City, "is being spoken here as commonly as is Spanish."

One Yankee who felt completely at home in Yerba Buena, as he did at a number of ports, was the bearded Harry Canning of Connecticut, owner and master of the *Wendy Anne*. His schooner had a somewhat shabby, disreputable air but was completely seaworthy, and the ship was a reflection of Harry Canning himself. Self-educated, since he had run off to sea as a cabin boy at the age of eleven, he had crowded a vast number of experiences into his thirty-two years. At ease with the gentlemen in a merchants' club or with the residents of a bordello, his affable mien concealed a sharp mind and a burning ambition. His schooner represented a major step up the ladder of worldly success.

Indistinguishable in appearance from an ordinary sailor in his wool shirt and pea jacket, worn, shapeless trousers, and run-down seaman's boots, he stood on the deck of his vessel, directing the loading of rakes, hoes, scythes, and sacks of grain seed into his hold. His voice, which he rarely raised, was authoritative, and his manner was crisp, indicating that he knew precisely what he wanted.

Dock workers labored harder for Harry Canning than they did for other captains. They knew he paid handsome bonuses when they accomplished their tasks in less than the contracted time but that he would pay nothing if they loitered. They had learned, too, that one did not argue with Harry Canning, who was not only a terror with his fists, but did not hesitate to draw a knife or pistol, which he was prepared to use if he thought someone was cheating him.

The day's work progressed so smoothly that the longshoremen were finished by mid-afternoon. Canning paid each of them in silver, which he fished out of a patched canvas bag, obtaining a promise from each man that he would return at dawn the next day, no matter what the weather. Then, his own chores completed, he turned to his fellow American, Ed Bellows, the owner of the warehouse from whom he had bought the supplies. "If you're as thirsty as I am," he said, "you'll come to my cabin."

The grinning, gray-haired Bellows happily followed him.

The master's cabin was startling to anyone who had not seen it. The bed, desk, and chests of drawers were made of handsomely carved mahogany. An exquisite rug purchased in Constantinople covered most of the floor, and hanging on two of the bulkheads were Flemish tapestries that the wealthiest of Americans would have been delighted to own.

Harry opened a chest and removed a jug of superior, potent rum. Carefully measuring quantities into two clean glasses, he added generous splashes of water to weaken the drinks, then handed one to his guest. Seating himself on one chest and propping his feet on another as he leaned against the bulkhead, he raised his glass in a silent toast, then took a small sip. He was relaxing for the first time that day.

Ed Bellows knew valuable property when he saw it. "Your furnishings are worth a fortune."

Harry shrugged. "Wait until you see the home I build in about ten more years, when I've made enough money to go into your end of the business the way I want to go into it." He removed his battered hat, sailed it across the cabin, then ran a hand through his thick hair. "Not that I'd consider living in Yerba Buena under the Mexicans. I want a voice in making the laws I'm obliged to obey."

"The only reason I'm here is because it's profitable," Bellows said defensively.

"Hell, my friend, I'm not being critical." Harry's quick smile lighted his face. "I have a long-range plan, that's all. And so far I'm a couple of years ahead of schedule." He sipped again, then placed his glass on the chest beside him, after fastidiously wiping the bottom with his sleeve to make certain it left no mark on the wood. "I suppose you're wondering why I've been buying so much farm equipment from you."

"I never question my customers," Bellows said. "I've assumed you're planning to sell it to Russians at Sitka or Mexicans at San Diego."

"Guess again. Who is going to have the greatest need for tools and grain? Americans! Those who are moving toward Oregon at this very hour in our first wagon train and all those who are going to follow them in more and more trains. They'll be hungry for what I have to sell, and I plan to make only a small profit on any one sale. I'll make up for it in volume. Eventually I hope to run a shuttle service between Yerba Buena and Oregon."

"You're clever, Captain Canning. I approve of your scheme, and I admire your motives. But you may just be a mite too clever for your own good."

Harry was unperturbed. "How so?"

"You forget the Hudson's Bay Company has a monopoly on goods and other merchandise purchased in the Oregon country."

"According to the British, yes. But I'm not subject to their laws."

"They have some persuasive arguments in their favor," the merchant replied dryly. "Fort Vancouver, with some hundreds of troops stationed there. Plus the firepower of whatever Royal Navy ships may be in nearby waters."

Harry laughed. "Let me tell you a couple of secrets. First, I have the roughest, meanest crew of sailors you've ever seen. We've thumbed our noses at the rulers of the Barbary Coast states in the Mediterranean. We've faced the warships of the Ottoman Empire and never flinched. Right now, my lads are spending every last penny of their pay in the waterfront dives here, and by the time I'm ready to sail up the mouth of the Columbia River, they'll be hungry again, spoiling for a fight and ready to take on anybody who stands in their way—including the redcoats of Fort Vancouver and the crews of the whole blame Royal Navy!"

"Surely you don't mean that!"

Draining his glass, Harry stood and beckoned. "Come with me," he said, leading his guest to the main deck.

On the deck were four large mounds, two fore and two aft, all covered with tarpaulins of heavy canvas. Bellows had noticed them in passing and had assumed they were piles of merchandise that had not yet been removed to the hold for storage.

Harry loosened the lines on one of the mounds and raised a portion of the canvas cover. Bellows was astonished when he saw the muzzle of a large cannon.

"I carry four of these guns, all of them nine-pounders," Harry said proudly. "What's more, they aren't for show. Not only do I carry plenty of ammunition and powder, but my lads are expert gunners. They practice on every voyage so they don't get rusty. I'll put my bets on them in a contest with any gunners on the high seas, including those of our own navy."

Bellows realized he wasn't boasting, but was confident of his own abilities and the skill of his crew. "I reckon you could put up a stiff fight, Captain Canning," he said. "But this schooner would be no match for a Royal Navy warship that carries ten or twenty times as many cannon."

"Numbers don't mean much in this kind of combat," Harry replied evenly. "There's no warship in the British navy that can match our seamanship and gunnery—as I'm willing to prove if they try to stop us from unloading our merchandise for sale to American citizens in Oregon. In fact, we'd welcome the opportunity to prove how good we are. I don't carry a chip on my shoulder, but nobody can ever accuse Harry Canning of running away from a fight."

"But if you damage a British warship or shell Fort Vancouver, you'll be committing an act of war!"

"They'll be starting the war if they lift one finger to prevent me from engaging in honest trade with fellow Americans, especially in a place where our claim to the territory is as good as theirs. Our wagon train people need what I have to offer them, and I won't tolerate anybody coming between them and me!"

Sitka was as drab and inhospitable as its weather was raw and damp. But Lisolette Arbo nevertheless stayed ashore as long as she could in order to avoid going back to the cramped ship that had brought her to the New World from Siberia. The few shops in the town offered little merchandise of interest for sale, and the two inns that a lady could visit without annoyance or embarrassment were exorbitantly expensive; so she wandered aimlessly through the dirt streets, telling herself as she skirted piles of snow that at least she was obtaining much-needed exercise.

Passers-by, Russians and Indians alike, stared at her, but Lisolette, now twenty, had been ogled by men since her mid-teens and paid no attention. One thought was uppermost in her mind: she had made the worst mistake of her life when she had joined the expedition to Oregon.

She was willing to admit the idea had seemed promising. The daughter of a French mother and Russian father who had spent her entire life in Paris and London until two years ago, she had gone to St. Petersburg after the sudden death of her parents in an accident to claim her inheritance from her father's estate. That had been her first error.

In spite of her legitimate Russian citizenship, she had been treated as a foreigner, in part because her

Russian was so heavily accented, and she had quickly discovered that Russians of all classes hated foreigners. Two cousins of whose existence she had been unaware had contested her claim, and she had spent an entire year fighting them in court, only to lose out because the judge regarded her as a foreigner, too.

Then, to her astonishment, she hadn't been allowed to return to France or England, where friends would have given her temporary shelter and helped her find work, even though there were few positions open to an exceptionally attractive young woman who had been reared as a lady and had received no training for any vocation. At first she had laughed when the Russian authorities had forbidden her to leave because of her dual citizenship, but they had been serious when they claimed she might be a French spy, and they had closed the border to her.

With her funds running low, she had seized the chance to join the settlers leaving for Oregon. She knew little about America and hadn't even heard of Oregon, but that hadn't mattered. She had volunteered without hesitation to join the company because here was the opportunity to escape from an impossible situation, from a world that stifled and frightened her.

Most of her companions on the long journey were goodhearted enough, but they were ignorant provincial dolts who blindly obeyed orders and never complained about their living conditions, food, or the callousness of Russian authorities. Only the friendship of Dr. Anton Wizneuski and the sympathy of Olga Runkova, neither of whom wanted anything in return, had enabled her to retain her sanity.

"Life will improve after we reach Oregon," they had told her again and again. "Just wait, and your feelings will change."

Lisolette realized she had drawn an idealized portrait of the New World in her mind, and she knew, too, that Alaska wasn't Oregon. But Sitka, with its

ugly, squat wooden buildings and cold climate, reminded her of the many horrid towns she had seen in
Siberia on the interminable journey. She knew she
was giving in to a mood, but life seemed to hold so
little in store for her. She wasn't afraid of work, but
she knew nothing about farming, and having lived
only in great cities, she didn't know how she would be
able to accustom herself to a wilderness. Well, she
had no choice.

Thoroughly chilled after her long walk, Lisolette
forced herself to return to the crumbling ship for
supper. At least the quality of the food being served
the settlers had improved sharply after Anton and
Olga had complained. She didn't quite know how
they had accomplished the miracle, but she was grateful for the results. Meals had become edible, even
though the fare was still plain.

Most of all, Lisolette reflected as she made her way
up the rickety gangplank, she hated this miserable
ship and its stench. Certainly the new vessel that
would carry her and the others from Sitka to Oregon
couldn't be any worse.

Someone loomed up out of the twilight shadows on
the deck, and she immediately recognized the tall,
bulky figure of Igor Doznevkov. The leader of the
party made her feel uncomfortable, and Lisolette,
who had never had cause to fear anyone, had to admit
to herself that she was afraid of him. He represented
the unreasonable, unreasoning power of the autocra-
cy, and, although he had been unfailingly polite to
her, he nevertheless reminded her of the officials in St.
Petersburg who had made her so miserable.

Igor Doznevkov beckoned and, not bothering to
make certain she was following, made his way across
the rotting deck to the prow, beyond mounds of supplies piled high in a haphazard fashion. The young
woman had no way of knowing he despised her because she reminded him of the wives and daughters of
the aristocrats for whom he worked and in whose

presence he had to behave humbly. Like them, Doznevkov thought, she was slender and haughty, carrying herself with an independent air, as though she owned the world. Like them she had never worked a day in her life, and she looked through those she regarded as her inferiors, not even seeing them. Well, he had waited a long time for a day like this.

"I trust you enjoyed your excursion on shore," he said.

"I bought a few bits of ribbon. There was nothing else I could afford." Lisolette wondered why he had summoned her to this isolated spot. If he intended to make advances to her, she would teach him manners fast enough. Under cover of her long, voluminous cloak, she removed a tiny, double-edged knife from its case. Her mother had given it to her on her fifteenth birthday, and on this journey she had carried it day and night. Its blade was no longer than her thumb, and she could conceal it easily in the palm of her hand, but it was capable of inflicting severe wounds, as more than one man had learned to his sorrow in the past.

"If I had known your funds were low, I'd gladly have advanced you some rubles," he said. "In fact, I'm offering you the opportunity to earn a steady income."

If he wanted her to become his mistress, Lisolette thought, she would give him cause to change his mind in a hurry.

Doznevkov was encouraged by her silence. "I've noted over the weeks," he said, "that you're on friendly terms with the troublemakers."

The unexpected turn in the conversation puzzled Lisolette. "Troublemakers?"

"Dr. Wizneuski and the Runkova woman."

Anton and Olga were her friends, but the two years she had spent under the authority of the Czar made her cautious, so she did not reply.

"I have cause to believe they are dissidents plotting against the crown."

The charge was so absurd she had to bite her lip to prevent herself from laughing.

"What I mean," Doznevkov amended, "is that they're trying to sabotage this expedition. Since it has been sanctioned by the Czar himself, anyone who opposes it makes himself an enemy of the throne."

"I know of no plots," she said firmly.

"It is your duty to unearth them," he told her.

Lisolette could only stare at him.

"Young woman, your own position in our society is highly questionable. Your mother was a citizen of France, and you yourself spent more than ten years in England."

He sounded so much like the officials who had interrogated her for days at a time in St. Petersburg that she became irritated. "If you know so much about me, then you also know my father was the London and Paris representative of several Russian exporting companies. He lived in those cities—with the blessings of the Ministry of Trade—because he sent gold francs and silver pounds to St. Petersburg."

Doznevkov ignored the interruption. "Even your Russian, grammatically correct though it may be, is spoken with a foreign accent."

The officials in St. Petersburg had made the same absurd accusations. "Since you know so much about me, you also know I tried and tried to return either to Paris or London, but I was refused an exit permit. Why am I being persecuted again?"

"You and I are having an informal conversation. I am not persecuting you, I am offering you a chance to dispel all doubts about you. I am giving you the opportunity to prove your loyalty to the regime. Demonstrate your fidelity to the Czar, and you will never be questioned again. Quite the contrary, as I've already indicated, you shall be rewarded."

"Exactly who are you, Doznevkov?"

He drew himself up to his full height and folded his arms across his chest. "I happen to be in a position that enables me to speak with the full authority of the Ministry of the Interior and Public Safety."

No wonder he spoke with such self-assurance, and no wonder she disliked him so much. It was his colleagues who had made her existence in St. Petersburg so miserable. "I'm afraid you've come to the wrong person," she said. "I know nothing of any plots or conspiracies of any kind, and I have no interest in such matters. I ask only to be left alone. I'm making this journey to Oregon because it was the only way I could leave Russia, where I couldn't call my life my own."

"I have come to the right person, I assure you." A gleam of malicious humor appeared in Doznevkov's eyes. "You are far more vulnerable than you realize, my dear young woman. Your refusal to cooperate with me will be regarded by my superiors as a sure sign that their suspicions about you were well founded and that you are disaffected."

"That's ridiculous!" Lisolette knew it was wrong to lose her temper, but he sounded like his colleagues in St. Petersburg, and she had no patience with the breed. "Next you'll be telling me I look dangerous."

"You well may be," he replied gravely.

"I celebrated my twentieth birthday just last month, if you can call anything on this horrid ship a celebration. I weigh one hundred and fifteen pounds. I wouldn't know one end of a rifle from the other. My friends in London and Paris were people like myself, and I had no opportunity to become friendly with anyone in Russia. How could anyone in his right mind call me dangerous?"

"You have a physical appeal, and I have no doubt many men find you attractive. If you are in the employ of a foreign government, you could compromise imperial officials and force them through threats of blackmail to reveal government secrets. I give you only one of many possible examples." Doznevkov became more strident. "Your opinions in this matter are of no concern to us. Our experience has taught us that our judgment of individuals is accurate. Either you will agree to work with us or you will suffer the consequences."

"Be more specific." Her resolve was faltering, but she did not show it.

"If I say the word," he declared, "you will be returned to St. Petersburg or perhaps only as far as Siberia—in chains, if necessary—regardless of whether you are placed under arrest here in Sitka or later, after we reach Oregon. The arm of the Czar's justice is very long, and it has a sure, strong grip."

When she had been interrogated in Russia, Lisolette thought, her tormentors had been more subtle. But here, in this bleak town on the edge of a raw, forbidding wilderness, there was no need for the subtleties of a more civilized place.

Her dual French-Russian citizenship made her vulnerable to the manipulations of the secret agents. Her funds were virtually exhausted. Had she made a great fuss in St. Petersburg, where her lawsuit had made her known, it might have been inconvenient to apply too much pressure on her. So she had been allowed to accompany the Oregon settlers, and now she found herself backed into a corner. If she were placed under arrest and disappeared, only a handful of people would notice, and the few who cared would have no one to whom they could complain.

Lisolette suddenly realized that her personal freedom meant more to her than anything else on earth. She had agreed to make the journey to the New World because she had yearned for liberty, and now she would be deprived of it if she failed to do the bidding of this horrible man. She was tempted to plunge her tiny knife into his chest, but she was afraid she lacked the physical strength to kill him. And there was no way she would be able to conceal what she had done.

Beneath her cloak she dropped the knife into its pouch again, and without the comforting feeling of the steel resting against her palm, she was swept by a sensation of helplessness. "What do you want me to do?" she asked, lowering her head.

Doznevkov knew better than to gloat, but his voice was smug. "Become even friendlier with Dr. Wizneuski and the Runkova woman. Encourage them to talk about themselves and their aspirations. Sooner or later they'll reveal their true natures, and when they speak treason, report at once to me. In private."

Lisolette nodded, too unhappy now to speak.

"Keep your ears open at all times. Others in the company will speak more freely by far in your presence than they will in mine. I want to know what all of them are thinking. It is far easier to control a group when one knows what is passing through the minds of its members. You will be my eyes and my ears. Do you understand?"

Again she could only nod.

"But you will come to me only in private. Outwardly you and I will continue to have little or nothing to do with each other. No one must know who I really am or that you are working for me."

"Your instructions are very clear," she murmured.

Doznevkov reached into a pocket of his greatcoat and removed a small purse filled with silver coins, which he handed to her.

Lisolette wanted to throw the purse into his face, but instead, to her shame, she meekly placed it inside her cloak.

"There," Doznevkov said. "You begin to taste the rewards of cooperation. Buy yourself something pretty in Sitka tomorrow, and think of me whenever you look at it or use it. But I warn you, I expect concrete results."

She fought back a rush of tears.

"And remember, when I give an order, I want it

73

obeyed instantly!" Not waiting for her reply, he went off down the deck, after first picking his way around the small mountain of supplies.

Lisolette continued to stand at the prow, staring with unseeing eyes at the windows of Sitka lighted with oil lamps and candles. It served no useful purpose to curse herself for cowardice, to berate herself because henceforth she would be obliged to spy on her friends and betray their confidences. She had been caught in a trap and had become the lowest of the low, a paid informer. There was no escape, regardless of whether she was in Russia, here in Alaska, or in the supposed land of plenty, Oregon. She wished she were dead, but she knew she lacked the courage to kill herself.

The very thought of going to Oregon filled her with dread and self-loathing.

The journey along the bank of the Snake River came to an end after more than a month of grueling travel, and soon the wagon train found itself entering a pleasant, broad valley, with heights on either side. To the north stood a range of mountains, but unlike those they had been seeing for months, these peaks were pine-covered.

That night at supper Whip made a casual announcement. "Those are the Blue Mountains yonder," he said, "and we've arrived in the Grande Ronde Valley. That means we're nearing the beginning of what I consider the true Oregon country. The Columbia isn't more than a couple of weeks away."

The excitement was so great that members of the company staged another impromptu celebration.

Eulalia and Cindy were working together at the cooking fire when Whip made his announcement, but within moments they were interrupted by Claiborne, who lifted his bride off her feet as he hugged and kissed her.

Eulalia smiled, inwardly crying. Cindy and Claiborne were behaving as newlyweds should, she reflected, but she and Whip had been married only a month longer, and no one would know it. Even Lee Blake, who was usually sedate, had made it his business to join Cathy at the fire, while elsewhere whole families were dancing or laughing and chatting animatedly. Dolores and Hosea retired to a far portion of the circle to discuss their own plans for the future, and the Reverend Cavendish wandered from group to group, enthusiastically shaking hands with everyone he encountered.

But Whip was too busy to pay any attention to his wife. He was surrounded by several people asking about the next stage of the journey, and he answered their questions patiently.

Eulalia tried in vain to curb her resentment. She knew he had duties to perform, but they always seemed to be at her expense, and she had a right to expect at least token consideration from him. Nevertheless, she managed to conceal her feelings, and when the excitement began to die down, she carried on the task of feeding people who formed in line for their supper. Ultimately she would fill two plates for Whip and herself and then would pry him away from those who never tired of bombarding him with requests for information.

Cathy and Lee also made it their practice to eat after most of the company had received their food. Tonight Lee Blake seemed troubled, and at his suggestion the two of them took their plates to their wagon, then sat on the back stoop to eat.

"It's so wonderful to realize that we've actually reached Oregon," Cathy said. "Why are you upset?"

"I'm afraid people are expecting too much," Lee told her. "Some of them have traveled almost three thousand miles, as you have, and they've been sustaining themselves with the thought that they're going to inhabit a Biblical land of milk and honey, but it won't be that easy."

"After all this time I'm sure they're realists," she replied. "They know they'll have to work hard to build their houses and establish working farms here. They know the land is generous, but not without toil."

"That's the least of what awaits them," Lee said. "It's the political situation that has me worried. According to the letter from the War Department that Sam Brentwood sent on to me from Independence by courier, the British may not give us a very cordial reception. Between us, I expect fireworks."

"You don't mean that literally."

He shrugged. "I can't predict what may happen. All I know is that if they use force of arms to prevent us from settling on the land, there will be hell to pay."

"You'll lead the company in active resistance?" Cathy began to share his concern.

"I hope that won't be necessary. The army is sending me an initial contingent of troops to establish an American garrison, and more troops will follow. So I certainly don't rule out a showdown between the British and us. I also expect another complication. The Russians are sending their own party of settlers to Oregon by way of Alaska. I know no details, but if their company is made up of armed men prepared to resist our establishment of a colony, I'll have to rid them of their misconceptions. The War Department has authorized me to take any steps I regard as necessary to protect our interests."

"Don't say anything tonight, Lee, not when people are so happy. Besides, perhaps your fears won't be realized."

"Maybe not," the officer said, "but I've got to be ready for anything unpleasant that may develop. And I'd like to put people on their guard."

"Wait for a few more days before you say anything," she urged. "They've gone through so much in order to come this far. They're entitled to their joy.

Just look at those faces! I don't think there's an unhappy person in the whole company."

"They're living on false hope. Our problems will be starting, not ending, when this trip comes to an end."

His attitude irritated her. "I realize that what you're saying is right. All I ask is that you give them a little breathing spell. I gather we'll be spending two weeks on the trail, so you'll have plenty of time to warn them there's trouble ahead."

Her tone annoyed him, and he stiffened. "I've got to do my duty as I see it," he said.

"I'm not suggesting that you neglect your duty. That's the last thought in my mind. But what harm will it do to wait?"

"The letdown will be that much more severe! They have the right to know what may lie ahead." Lee finished his meal, stood, and hitching up his belt, walked quickly to the fire, where he clapped his hands together to gain the attention of the company.

Cathy couldn't help putting her hands over her ears. Lee was just being stubborn by refusing her advice, and he was being unnecessarily cruel. She could see no reason he couldn't have waited a few days to pass along his unpleasant news.

Watching the reactions of the people, even though she couldn't hear what Lee was saying, she could see the joy drain from the gaunt faces of the men and women who had suffered so many hardships on the long trek. Duty, indeed!

Ordinarily Cathy wouldn't have interfered in military matters, but the people who now stood glowering and scowling were her friends, and it was her husband who had cut short their fleeting pleasure. It would be difficult for her to forgive him.

Whip and an exceptionally quiet Eulalia sat together on a flat rock beyond the light cast by the fire, eating their half-cold meal in silence. They listened attentively to Lee's announcement, and Whip didn't seem in the least surprised.

"You already knew about the British and Russians," Eulalia said.

He nodded. "Lee showed me the War Department letter right after he got it a couple of weeks ago."

"But you didn't mention a word to me!"

Her unexpected stridency made him blink. "It didn't cross my mind to tell you," he said, making matters worse.

She sniffed audibly. "Sometimes I wonder whether you married me for any reason other than to have someone who'll wash your shirts and hand you your meals."

"Hold on now." Her fury startled him.

"You pay no attention to me except to keep hounding me about riding that confounded mare. It doesn't matter that every hour I spend in the saddle is an agony or that I see no improvement in my leg. For some insane reason I've got to do it. Beyond that you ignore me!"

She was exaggerating wildly, and Whip felt compelled to protest. "I still have a job to do, you know. My time won't be my own until we reach the end of the trail and pick a site for our ranch."

"Other men know their wives are alive, which is more than I can say for you, Michael Holt!" All of Eulalia's resentment was bubbling to the surface, and she was becoming even more frenzied. "As long as I'm docile, don't make a fuss when you forget I exist, and obey you when you force me to ride the mare, you reward me. Once a week you actually condescend to make love to me."

Her charge was absurd. He was awake before dawn every morning and was the last to retire, making the rounds of the sentry posts to assure himself that all was in order before he went to bed. Not only was she asleep most nights he joined her, but he was too tired to think of lovemaking. His dignity prevented him from making a direct reply, however, and he could only say, "All that will change, too, after we settle down."

"I'll believe that when it actually happens!" Eulalia said. "And I'll tell you one thing right now. I'm not riding the mare tomorrow, no matter how much fuss you make. I'm spending the day in the wagon, giving my leg a rest. I see no reason to be subjected to torment just to satisfy your whim!"

Whip looked at her reproachfully. Granted that he had never understood women, but Eulalia was making no sense to him. "I know riding isn't easy for you," he said. "But there's a chance the exercise will get rid of the crimp in your leg muscles, so you've got to ride. Every day, even though it hurts."

"Not tomorrow, not if the whole future of our marriage depends on it!" She spoke in a low, intense voice.

He saw she was so furious she was shaking, and he reached out a hand to mollify her.

"Don't you touch me! Just remember what I said! I—will—not—ride—the—mare—tomorrow. No matter what the consequences!" She jumped to her feet and limped off toward their wagon.

He watched her as she vanished into the night. Then, pushing his hat onto the back of his head, he sighed aloud. He had married the woman and was prepared to support her for the rest of her life, so he was damned if he knew what else she wanted from him. Certainly she had known for a long time that he was not glib, that he was not demonstrative.

Hurt and disturbed, Whip left the circle of wagons and made an early tour of the sentry outposts. The activity, as he well knew, was nothing more than a way of calming himself a bit. He was expecting no trouble from Indians in this part of Oregon, so his gesture was nothing more than routine.

By the time he returned to the wagons, most of the company had retired. But Whip had no desire to join

Eulalia. She might still be awake, and he was afraid
that if she launched into another blistering tirade he
might respond in the same spirit. He had learned
during his years as a hunter and trapper in the Rocky
Mountains to choose his words with care before he
spoke. He had seen too many men lose their lives
because they hadn't been able to control their
tongues.

He wandered toward the fire, which was dying
down, and stood for a long time staring at the glowing
embers. With any luck Eulalia would feel better now
that she had unburdened herself. In any event, he had
no intention of returning to the subject in the morning
or any other time. And if she wanted to take a day off
and ride in the wagon, he guessed he couldn't blame
her. Maybe it was too much to ask a woman in her
condition to subject herself to grueling punishment on
horseback day after day. Had he been suffering from
her ailment, he would have ridden, no matter how
great the pain, but he wasn't Eulalia, and he couldn't
object too strenuously if she rested for a day. If she
elected to continue riding in the wagon, however, it
would be his duty to intervene, no matter how loudly
she might protest.

As Whip turned away from the fire, he came face to
face with Cathy Blake, and he halted abruptly. Cathy,
who had been lost in her own thoughts, saw Whip at
the same moment, and she, too, stopped short.

Everyone on the train had expected these two to
marry each other, but instead they had turned elsewhere for their mates. They had consciously avoided
each other since the day Cathy had accepted Lee's
proposal, and Cathy was flustered by the unexpected
encounter.

"Well, hello," she said.

Whip was jarred, too, but a lifetime of training
enabled him to hide his feelings. "Evening, ma'am,"
he said and touched the brim of his hat.

80

"I wasn't sleepy," she said, hoping she didn't sound too inane, "so I was just wandering around."

"Same here." He wished he could think of something significant to say, like telling her he was glad their paths finally had crossed. "The fire is still giving off heat," he said. "It's warmer there."

With one accord they moved closer to the coals. "What a long time it has been since you and Sam Brentwood came to our house on Long Island and we began this long march."

The memory of her late, first husband, Otto van Ayl, intruded on them, and Whip felt even more uncomfortable.

Cathy knew what he was thinking, as she had so often in the past, and deliberately laid the ghost to rest. "Poor Otto. Going to Oregon was his idea, you know, but he had no idea he was letting himself in for so many hardships. He'd have been far happier if he'd stayed on Long Island, counting his gold coins." Gently she changed the subject. "I cooked supper for you and Sam that night, but that was so many hundreds and hundreds of meals ago I couldn't possibly tell you what I served you."

"I remember," Whip said promptly. "You roasted a big chunk of beef, and you made some potato dumplings. Best I ever ate."

She had to be honest. "That was my sister's recipe."

Whip chuckled. "Then I'll bet Claudia is making potato dumplings for Sam a couple of times a week back in Independence. He loved them, too."

"After all of us get settled, Lee and I will have you and Eulalia over for supper, and I'll make some dumplings." She felt him stiffen at the mention of their respective mates, and she was sorry she had spoken without thinking.

"That'll be right nice of you, ma'am." He was almost excessively polite.

"Lee says you're interested in my land claim. I told him I'd speak to you about it." There was no time like the present.

"I surely am. With eighteen hundred acres I'd have enough land for the kind of ranch I have in mind, provided your price isn't too dear and you don't mind waiting until Colonel Astor back in New York sends me the rest of my pay for guiding this train."

"I'll gladly give you the claim, Whip," she said. "It isn't costing me anything, and with the government providing us with housing, I have no use for it."

"I couldn't accept it for free," he said.

Cathy shook her head. "Lee knows how I feel, and he agrees with me. Consider it a way of thanking you—from everybody on the train—for taking us safely from the Atlantic to the Pacific."

Whip was embarrassed. "You might want to settle in Oregon yourselves."

"I can't look ahead twenty-five years to Lee's retirement. Long before then, if he's made a general—as I'm sure he will be—he's certain to be transferred to Washington City for a tour of duty. After that, we'll be too old to come all the way out to Oregon again. It'll be difficult enough to visit Claudia and Sam in Independence."

"By that time," Whip said, a huskiness in his voice betraying his deep feelings, "there will be roads stretching back and forth across the continent."

Cathy started to laugh but changed her mind. She had a hunch his prediction might well prove accurate. "If it works out that way, a lot of the credit will belong to you."

He fidgeted, shifting his weight from one foot to the other. "I'm not looking for any medals, any more than I am a free land claim that I don't deserve."

"If you refuse it, then I'll simply have to give it to Eulalia as a wedding present. After all, you shot a buffalo for us as a gift, and we accepted it. So what's fair is fair."

He bowed his head, admitting defeat with as good grace as he could muster. As long as he had known Cathy, she had displayed a remarkable talent for getting her own way. "I reckon that'll please Eulalia," he said.

Something in his tone told her that something was amiss in his relationship with his wife. "I do admire her for exercising regularly," she said quickly. "She deserves to have her leg become strong again."

"I wish you'd tell her. Seeing you're her friend, maybe she'll listen to you." His voice became bleak.

"I hope you're going to have happy lives together," Cathy said impulsively.

The spell of the past was broken. "The same for you and Lee," Whip said and stalked off in the direction of the wagon he and Eulalia had been given.

Eulalia was asleep, as he had hoped, and he stretched out silently beside her, trying not to awaken her. All at once, conscious of her proximity, he felt a wave of guilt. Damnation! Cathy van Ayl Blake was the girl he should have married, and now it was too late. He remained awake for a long time, hating himself, despising his lack of loyalty to Eulalia.

Cathy continued to stand in front of the embers for another quarter of an hour after Whip's abrupt departure. But the fire was casting no warmth now, and she made her way back to her own wagon.

An oil lamp was lighted, and Lee, still fully dressed, was writing in his journal, a meticulous record of the journey that he intended to send to the War Department for the benefit of later settlers. He looked up at her and knew at a glance that she was no longer annoyed with him for having refused to heed her advice.

"I saw Whip just now," she said. "He wouldn't accept my land claim, so I'll have to give it to Eulalia."

Lee nodded, smiled, and continued to write in his journal.

Cathy watched him surreptitiously as she changed into her nightgown. He was such a fine, upright person and so considerate of her that she hated to hurt him. So there was no way she could tell him that her chance encounter with Whip had shaken her badly.

She had been shortsighted when she had discovered that the Indian girl who had appeared at the winter camp had lived with him. Well, the poor creature was dead now, after deliberately vanishing into the wilderness, burdened by the knowledge that she could never make him happy.

Cathy had known he had wanted her, yet she had turned to Lee. Was it possible she should have been more patient, that she should have forgotten her pride? Now she would never really know whether she should have married Whip.

Lee completed his journal entry, undressed, and extinguished the lamp. He crawled into bed and reached for his wife.

"I'm sleepy," Cathy murmured.

He desisted immediately and turned over.

That was a lie, the wide-awake Cathy told herself, and frightened by the implications of what she had done, she did not sleep for a long time.

IV

The sun sparkled on the clear waters of New York harbor off the lower tip of Manhattan Island as a brass band blared the tune of "Columbia, the Gem of the Ocean." A huge crowd was on hand to watch the festivities. Four covered wagons stood in a line in Battery Park, and their occupants, self-conscious because of the stares of the multitude, said their farewells to friends and relatives. Only the former mountain man who had been hired as a guide showed any signs of impatience, but he knew the spectacle was being staged for a purpose, so he curbed his desire to give a premature signal to start.

Two men stood apart and observed the proceedings. One was heavyset, resplendent in an immaculately tailored suit, and beaver hat. He carried a gold-handled walking stick, and occasionally the fingers of his free hand slid across the heavy chain of gold links that spanned his waistcoat.

No one in the crowd recognized him, which suited his purposes, and only his companion and employee, Homer Jennings, knew he was Colonel John Jacob Astor, one of the wealthiest men in the United States, who had made his initial fortune in the Pacific Northwest fur trade.

Astor chuckled indulgently. "Look at the envy on those faces, Jennings. When we announce the next wagon train, half the places will be taken by New Yorkers. The lure of Oregon and the romance of the wagons is irresistible."

"There's little doubt of that, sir," Jennings replied. "With the second train already on its way to Independence and this one starting out, the Oregon country won't be able to absorb the immigrants in the fourth train fast enough."

"Ah, but they will be absorbed at just the right pace, because we won't announce the next train for several months. And I don't intend to send it on its way until early next spring. We've got to give our settlers time to acclimate, or they'll stumble over each other and create chaotic conditions."

The subordinate nodded. No one ever disputed the word of John Jacob Astor, particularly on matters relating to the Oregon country. It was he, along with a group of associates, who had first proposed the settlement of the Pacific to President Andrew Jackson, and he was matching the federal government's contributions dollar for dollar.

Not that he was engaging in philanthropy. He owned the supply depot managed by Sam Brentwood at Independence, his ships would soon engage in Pacific trade, and he already controlled the lion's share of the region's furs and lumber. It was in his very best interests that Oregon be annexed by the United States.

Satisfied that he had seen enough, Astor turned and walked at a rapid clip toward his nearby office. "I had no time to read Sam Brentwood's letter before we left this morning," he announced. "What did he say?"

"The smoked hams and flour he ordered from St. Louis have arrived, and he finally received the shipment of rifles and ammunition we had sent from Connecticut. So he's ready for the second train. I want to make certain all the orders for the third have been confirmed before I notify him that the train is starting out, or Brentwood will blister my hide."

"I'm grateful to Andy Jackson for recommending him and Whip Holt to us, I must say. They're good men."

"I'm afraid we're going to lose Holt, Colonel," Jennings said. "Brentwood writes that he's married one of the women on the first train, and apparently he's going to settle in Oregon himself."

"We'll miss him, but our loss is Oregon's gain." Astor rarely wasted time on regrets. "Anything else of interest from Brentwood?"

"Yes, sir. He seems convinced the second train will reach Oregon six months after it leaves Independence, and he actually suggests that later trains will make the journey in as little as four months." Jennings was incredulous.

"That makes sense to me." Astor's walking stick tapped the cobbled street with authority. "Holt has blazed the way, and later trains will follow the trail he's created. Oh, some of them will have troubles caused by the weather or fights with Indians bent on creating mischief, but they know the way now. Remind me to tell Brentwood he'll be wise to double his storage capacity—and his staff—before the end of this coming winter."

"Yes, sir." Jennings hesitated for a moment. "It appears to me, Colonel, that we've pulled the cork out of the jug and are pouring people into Oregon."

"So we are," Astor replied smiling with satisfaction.

"I can't help wondering if that's wise."

Astor's thick eyebrows seemed to blend into one line as he frowned. "Why shouldn't it be?"

"I just read in this morning's newspapers that Great Britain is protesting rather strongly."

"Let 'em protest!"

"They also point out that Great Britain has been augmenting her garrison at Fort Vancouver."

"It's their fort—for the present. So they're privileged to station as many men there as they please. But John McLoughlin, the Hudson's Bay man there, is an old friend of mine. Very sensible. I'm sure he sees the handwriting on the wall, so he'll do whatever he can to keep the troops in line."

"We hope, sir."

No one was within earshot, but Astor lowered his voice. "I've been notified—very privately—by President Van Buren that we're also establishing a garrison there. So let the British make of that what they will."

Jennings whistled under his breath. "If they open fire on each other, it'll create a ticklish situation."

"Ticklish? I dare say. But mark my words, Jennings. Come what may, our flag will fly over Oregon. It's our destiny, and no other power on earth can prevent the American people from spreading out coast to coast!"

Andrew Jackson Brentwood awakened from a light nap and announced in no uncertain terms that he was hungry.

Claudia Brentwood, Cathy van Ayl Blake's older sister, was preparing her husband's dinner in the kitchen of their ranch house just outside Independence. She heard the baby's wail, instantly identified it, and went to his room to nurse him. Then she changed his diaper, a process in which he took no interest. After gurgling happily as he smiled up at his mother, he obligingly dropped off to sleep again.

Glancing at the clock on the dining room mantel as she returned to the kitchen, Claudia realized Sam was late. He had gone into town to attend to several quick errands and should have returned long before now. Not that she was in the least worried about him. In spite of his arthritis, Sam Brentwood could take care of himself in any situation, and in a fight he was the equal of at least four other men. Everyone in Independence knew it, including the gamblers, brothel owners, and petty criminals who came to the booming town because it was the jumping-off place for Oregon. They gave Sam a wide berth, just as they avoided Claudia when she went into town.

Oh, well. The potato dumplings needed to simmer a little longer, although the boiled brisket of beef was ready whenever he appeared. Claudia poured herself a cup of strong coffee from the pot she kept on the stove, then seated herself at the kitchen table and resumed her frequently interrupted work on the supply depot books. Sam lacked the patience for such labors, so she had been in charge of the books ever since they had established the place in partnership with John Jacob Astor. Now, however, so many goods were being sent to Independence in such large quantities that Claudia was constantly in danger of falling behind.

Well, that situation would change when the new bookkeeper from Chicago arrived. Then Claudia would supervise the accounts but would do little of the actual work. What amazed her was that she wouldn't miss it in the least. In fact, it surprised her that she, once the most fiercely independent of women, now gloried in her domesticity. Next year, she hoped, she and Sam would have another baby, and this time she wanted a girl. A son and a daughter would be just right, and it was comforting to know they could give their children the luxury of a good education in the East. It hadn't occurred to her, any more than it had to Sam, that they would become so prosperous in so short a time.

At the sound of hoofbeats, Claudia finished adding a column of figures and then got up from her work. When she went to the kitchen window, she saw two people emerging from the horse barn. One was Sam, who was scowling, and the other was Nancy Wade. That girl! Claudia felt a quick premonition of more trouble.

Nancy's problem was that she was too flamboyantly pretty for her own good. No, pretty wasn't the word. With her ripe, young body and her long, pale blond hair and laughing eyes, she exuded sex appeal, and unfortunately she knew it. She was spoiled, incorrigible, and flirted with every man she saw; even now, walking to the house beside a stiff-legged Sam, whose old wound aggravated by arthritis was bothering him, she couldn't help flirting.

Claudia sighed aloud. Nancy was driving them to distraction, but they would have to put up with her antics as best they could until the second wagon train reached Independence and she accompanied it to Oregon. She was Tilman Wade's cousin, and because she and Sam were so fond of Tilman, they felt obliged to look after her for the present. But Tilman was welcome to her!

Nancy burst into the house, unable to control a fit of giggling. "Sam says I've been naughty again," she announced, then fled in the direction of her own room.

"Dinner will be ready in ten minutes!" Claudia called after her, then turned for her husband's kiss.

Sam—preoccupied with the willful Nancy—didn't notice his wife's gesture. Instead, he stomped to a cupboard and poured himself a small drink of corn whiskey, which he drank neat. "Nancy is the reason I'm late, of course," he said, his voice even deeper than usual. "I should have been home an hour ago."

"What was it this time?"

"Maybe you'd like a drink, too."

"Why, Sam Brentwood! How dare you forget I'm still nursing Andy?"

He raised a hand in apology as he sank down opposite her at the kitchen table. "You know that big brothel down at the river front?"

Claudia laughed. "Well, I know it when I see it."

"Nancy was walking past it this morning. I never

did find out what in thunderation she was doing in that part of town. Some man—a mean devil, as it turns out—stopped her in front of the place, thinking she was one of the girls who works there."

Claudia moaned. "Oh, dear. Don't tell me she encouraged him!"

"You're right the first time, honey. She led him on and on. Enjoying herself thoroughly at the man's expense, of course. Naturally, he wanted to take her inside. Nancy hadn't bargained for that—"

"She should have known!" Claudia interrupted.

"Sure, but she never thinks ahead. Fun for its own sake right now, that's her motto. Anyway, when the fellow grabbed her and tried to haul her into the brothel, she took her purse from her belt. It was filled with coins she had taken with her to go shopping, so it was pretty heavy, and she whacked him proper on the head. Raised a lump the size of a goose egg."

Claudia laughed without humor.

"The fellow raised an awful fuss. He yelled and carried on until a constable came—one of the new members of the force who got in from Cincinnati only a few days ago. She tried to identify herself, but the constable hadn't heard of the Brentwoods and hauled her off to the police station."

"It served her right!"

"They finally found me over at the arsenal, where the army is keeping the new consignment of rifles safe for me. So over to the police station I went. By that time she had Lieutenant Healey reduced to putty. For my sake he lectured her before he released her into my custody, but he was grinning at her the whole time, and she kept flirting with him."

"So she learned nothing from the experience."

"Nancy never learns," Sam said.

Claudia rose. As she went to the stove, she bent down to kiss him. "What's going to become of her, Sam?"

91

"I'll wager she'll turn our settlement in Oregon up-side down and inside out. People like Whip, Ernie von Thalman, and Colonel Blake will be tempted to turn her out of the colony."

"Would they really do that?" she asked as she picked up a ladle and began to spoon out potato dumplings.

"I reckon not," he conceded. "But poor Tilman will be even more strongly tempted to send her back to Pennsylvania."

"He can't do that, Sam. She has no one there. Unfortunately, Tilman is her only living relative."

"Then the only hope for our settlers in Oregon," Sam said, "is that she falls in love with some man who manages to tame her."

"He'll need to be quite a man," Claudia said.

The last of the new cargo would be loaded within another five days, but the *Wendy Anne* wasn't prepared to sail. Harry Canning wasn't in the least surprised when he discovered that five members of his crew were leaving his ship. Two of them had been knifed in a saloon fight, and their wounds would not be healed for many weeks; two others had found employment on a merchantman ready to make a voyage to South America; the fifth had simply disappeared.

Undeterred by the setback, he passed the word ashore that he would hire replacements, and the following day a crowd appeared on the dock. He interviewed them one by one on the main deck, and long experience with seamen enabled him to weed out the shifty, the unreliable, and the perennial drunks. By the end of the day, he had hired three fellow Americans who had been stranded in San Francisco when their ships had sailed without them.

By the next morning the crowd had thinned considerably, but he raised an eyebrow when the first to board the schooner was a short, wiry Mexican who said his name was Murillo.

"What's your experience?" Harry demanded.

"I spend fourteen years at sea. For the last three years I was bo's'n's mate on ship out of Valparaiso."

"Why did you leave her?"

"She old tub. She sink."

"Let me see your papers." To Harry's astonishment the man produced a sheaf of authentic-looking documents that appeared to be in order. One major question was as yet unanswered. "Why have you come to me instead of going to a Mexican ship?" There were at least three riding at anchor in San Francisco Bay.

Murillo grinned. "Yanquis the best sailors. And I hear you pay better."

The reply was honest. "I demand loyalty," Harry said, "and it won't be easy to give. We may be in for some rough times on this voyage."

The Mexican nodded complacently. "I recognize guns under canvas. And I know you don't pay big wages for nothing. You need a man who knows how to fight, you hire Murillo."

As always, Harry relied on his instinct. "You're hired," he said. "I need a bo's'n, so you have the job. If you can't handle it, you'll be demoted."

"I handle," Murillo said.

Only riffraff applied for the one remaining opening, and after three more days Harry began to feel pressed. He used the smallest crew possible, working his men hard and compensating them accordingly, and he was reluctant to put to sea short-handed. So he continued to interview the few applicants who appeared.

A Royal Navy sloop of war lay at anchor, putting in for sea stores after paying a visit to Fort Vancouver. Murillo, who seemed to know everything that was happening in the port, told Harry the warship was sailing for England by way of China and India. The master of the *Wendy Anne* had no interest in the sloop of war and dismissed her from his mind. His own problem preoccupied him.

The British warship sailed at dawn one morning, and soon after she vanished at sea, Harry was summoned from his cabin by a grinning Murillo. "New sailor waiting for you on deck," he said. "I think maybe we find right man."

When Harry made his way down the deck, he saw a balding giant with reddish-blond hair lounging against the rail. His nose apparently had been broken years earlier and seemed to spread across his square face. A long scar on his left cheek made him appear even more disreputable. Although the weather was cool, with a stiff wind blowing, he was attired only in a shirt, pants, and boots.

To Harry's astonishment he suddenly stood at rigid attention. "Who are you?"

"Billy Sullivan is me name." The man spoke with a thick brogue. "I've heard you need a seaman to round out your crew, and I'm the very lad you're seeking."

Harry went through his usual routine. "What's your experience?"

"I've sailed on so many ships it would take me all day to list them, sir."

Harry studied him briefly, then grinned. "You lie. You're a deserter from that British sloop."

Sullivan's returning grin was hearty. "So I am," he said cheerfully, "and I'd be the last to deny it. Eleven years I spent before the mast under the Union Jack, with a spar or a cat-o'-nine-tails across me backside every time I told the bloody English what I thought of them."

"Why did you enlist?"

"Enlist, say you?" Sullivan snorted derisively. "Eleven years ago, when I was but a broth of a lad, I left County Cork to seek me fortune in England. The very day I landed, a press gang caught me. From that day to this, I've ne'er saluted their bloody flag or drunk a toast to Queen Victoria."

The man's potential was interesting, but Harry remained cautious. "Can you hold your liquor?"

"That I cannot, sir," Sullivan said. "Rum was near the death of me, and for six years I've touched nary a drop, nor will I as long as I live!"

Perhaps, as Murillo had said, this was the very crewman the *Wendy Anne* needed. One matter remained to be settled. "We're making a very short voyage," Harry said. "No farther than Fort Vancouver."

"I've just come from the place. There's not much there."

"Soon there will be hundreds of Americans in the area. My hold is loaded with goods I intend to sell them. And if I'm successful, as I intend to be, we'll sail back and forth between Oregon and Yerba Buena, coming here for fresh supplies. You'd not only need to avoid the British authorities ashore, but there may be trouble with them. I'm prepared to resist if they try to send me packing."

A hard gleam appeared in Sullivan's eyes. "If that be right, sir, I'll gladly work for a berth and food. Never mind the pay. For the joy of evening the score with the English, I'll join you free of charge."

It was plain he meant what he said, and Harry laughed as he shook his head. The belligerent Sullivan was a rare find. "You'll be paid regularly, the same as all the others. But I won't tolerate brawls at Fort Vancouver. I don't want to give the British any excuse to throw me out."

Sullivan was disdainful. "I couldn't crack the heads of more than three or four of them in a brawl," he said. "I've learned patience these eleven years. So I'll gladly wait until you unlimber the cannon you're hiding under that canvas—and blow down the walls of the bloody English fort. Just waiting for that day will be joy and comfort to me, sir."

"You're hired," Harry said, extending his hand.

The Irish seaman grasped it in an iron grip. "This is a lucky day for both of us!"

Harry could only hope his instinct was right.

Two more of the Russian settlers died on board the ancient ship that continued to remain tied to the Sitka dock, and the survivors were in despair. The quality of the food they were given was deteriorating again, and although they were promised a transfer to the vessel that would carry them to Oregon, they remained on board the old ship, where the stench grew worse every day.

The heartsick, weary travelers, afraid they would never reach Oregon, grumbled to each other about the inefficiency of the bureaucracy, but only Dr. Anton Wizneuski had the courage to raise his voice in protest. His patience exhausted, he waited at the rail on the main deck until Igor Doznevkov came on board after spending the entire day ashore. Making no attempt to hide his anger, he spoke firmly. "When are we being transferred from this pestilential tub to a decent ship? When will we sail for Oregon?"

"Soon," Doznevkov replied soothingly. "I spent several hours with our officials here today, and, although they are occupied with many important matters, they will attend to our needs as quickly as they can. These arrangements always take time."

"For days you've been telling us there will be action soon," Anton replied heatedly. "How soon is soon, Doznevkov? On behalf of more than one hundred people whose lives are in greater danger every day they spend on board this disgraceful ship, I demand a specific answer!"

"You demand?" Doznevkov raised an eyebrow.

"I do, as a physician, as an escort and as a loyal subject of His Imperial Majesty. I hold you personally responsible for our situation!"

Doznevkov became sarcastic. "Do you speak for yourself or as the spokesman for the company?"

"I've taken no poll, although I'm sure all the others agree with me. Just look at them! They droop more and more each day. In another fortnight there won't be enough of them still alive and healthy enough to establish a colony in Oregon. Think of what St. Petersburg will say to that news! Think of what Prince Orlev will say!"

Doznevkov had already devoted a great deal of thought to the excuses he would make to Prince Orlev, the Czar's counselor and friend who had inspired this expedition as a way of establishing Russia's claim to the Oregon country. Like any official familiar with the intrigues of the court in St. Petersburg, Doznevkov felt it would be easy enough to find scapegoats onto whom he could shift the blame. Everyone in the service of the government was skilled in such maneuvers.

"I warn you," Anton said, "if there is no action taken in the next twenty-four hours, I will write to Prince Orlev myself!" He stormed off down the deck and went below.

Here was a nasty turn of events, Doznevkov thought. Most of the kulaks and peasants in the company could neither read nor write, so there was nothing to fear from them. But Wizneuski was different. Not only was he a respected young physician, obviously literate, but his family was prominent in St. Petersburg, and one of his uncles held a fairly high post at the Czar's court. Prince Orlev would not only read what he wrote, but would pay attention to his complaints.

Doznevkov well realized his personal role would not bear close scrutiny. By cutting corners on the journey, buying inferior food, and renting this aged ship, he had already saved enough money to enable him to retire in comfort after he spent an obligatory token year or two in Oregon. If the threat was genuine, he would have to find some way to neutralize Wizneuski effectively. First, however, he would need to know whether the doctor would actually write a letter to Prince Orlev and, if he did, what he would say in it.

There was one way to find out. Waiting until members of the company began to assemble for their meager supper, he indicated to Lisolette Arbo that he wanted to speak to her in private.

As soon as she ate her meal, the girl dutifully but reluctantly made her way to the prow of the ship.

There Doznevkov awaited her. "Now," he told her, "you will begin to earn your pay. Wizneuski, your friend, informs me he intends to send a letter to a nobleman in St. Petersburg, Prince Orlev."

The girl nodded dully. "The aide to the Czar who sponsored this company."

His new agent wasn't stupid, and Doznevkov was pleased. He wouldn't have believed that any member of the expedition other than Wizneuski had ever heard of the Prince. "Find out if such a letter is really sent. If it is, I want to know the full contents."

Lisolette caught her breath. "You ask the impossible! How can I find out what is said in a letter?"

"I hold you responsible for the information I want. How you get it is your business. A woman has a natural advantage in these matters when she is dealing with a man." Doznevkov smirked, then chuckled quietly as he went off.

Returning to the cramped cabin she shared with several others, Lisolette felt ill. She was being required to commit a specific act that would betray a friend who had been kind to her. Anton had encouraged her when she had felt despondent, and twice when she had been ill on the long journey, he had treated her for her ailments, showing great solicitude. It was obvious to her that any letter sent to a high government official in St. Petersburg would be critical of Doznevkov, but she couldn't reveal to Anton that the man was a government agent without placing herself in even greater jeopardy. She was trapped, and there was no way she could extricate herself from her predicament.

Lisolette lay awake for the better part of the night, and the following morning she wanted so badly to avoid her companions that she appeared very late for the usual breakfast of bread and cabbage soup.

Someone hailed her as she entered the main saloon. "Lisolette! The very person I want to see!"

The girl cringed, promptly losing what little appetite she had mustered. She would have preferred to avoid Anton more than anyone else.

"Join me after you've eaten," he called from the corner of the cabin, where he sat near a window as he wrote furiously on a pad of paper.

She went through the motions of consuming a small portion of the miserable meal. The bread was stale, and the odor of the cabbage soup, which had been cooked the previous day, made her want to retch. Anton, she saw, kept glancing in her direction. If only she could find some way to tell him she was being forced to work for the man who was their common enemy.

When she stood, Anton beckoned impatiently. Her feet felt like heavy lead weights as she went to him. They were alone in the saloon, and she wondered how she could summon the nerve to seek the information that Doznevkov had demanded. Never had she felt so cheap, so degraded, but she knew if she failed she would be thrown into prison. The mere fact that her mother had been French was enough, in Russia, to condemn her to years in a jail or a Siberian convict camp.

Anton moved to the end of the plain wooden bench so there would be a place for her beside him. He addressed her in a low tone. "I challenged Igor Doznevkov yesterday," he said. "I told him that unless our

situation is improved by this evening I'll send a letter
to Prince Orlev, and so I will. I've been composing it
for hours. Here, read this and tell me what you think
of it." He thrust a sheaf of papers at her.

That took care of the problem of learning what the
letter contained, and the knowledge made Lisolette
feel even worse. She read slowly, and the contents
stunned her. Anton was brutally candid, withholding
no facts about living conditions on the journey and
making it clear that the fault was Igor Doznevkov's.
Now the agent was certain to retaliate against the
man who was attacking him, and as months would
pass before Prince Orlev received the letter and
could act, Doznevkov held all the advantages in the
duel.

"What do you think of it?" Anton demanded.

"It's very strong," Lisolette replied, her voice trembling.

"Naturally." Anton was still seething. "I see no reason to mince words. I've even hinted that our Igor
may be pocketing funds that should have been spent
on the people. I'm sure that's what he's been doing,
although I can't actually prove it. But Prince Orlev
will pick up the hint, and I dare say he'll know how to
start an investigation."

"I—wonder if you should go so far," the girl murmured.

"I'm not afraid of Doznevkov," Anton said contemptuously. "His neglect has already cost us dearly.
What can he do that he hasn't already done?"

Lisolette took a deep breath, but fear gripped her,
and she backed down. "I—I wish I knew."

"May he rot in the forests of Siberia," Anton said. "I
refuse to do anything behind the man's back, so I'm
making a copy of this letter and will present it to him.
Let him get in touch with St. Petersburg and defend
himself as best he can. The facts speak for themselves,
very loudly and very plainly."

For an instant Lisolette felt relieved. She found it

almost incredible that Anton would give the man a copy of the blunt letter, but there was no need now for her to betray her friend. Anton unwittingly was saving her from committing a reprehensible act.

At the same time, however, she realized he was placing himself in grave danger, and her relief gave way to fear for him. It would be far better if she reported to Doznevkov; she could soften the impact by saying he had complained about living conditions but had not made charges about any individual. It would be another half year, perhaps much longer, before Doznevkov learned the real truth.

"Must you give Doznevkov a copy of the letter?"

"Of course," the young physician said. "If nothing else forces him to obtain a better ship, put decent food on board it, and sail us to Oregon in the immediate future, that will do it. He'll feel the urgent need to improve his record. Are you ill, Lisolette? You look so pale."

"It's nothing. I—I wish you wouldn't give him the copy, Anton."

"But I must, for the reason I just explained to you."

"Suppose—he—isn't what he seems?" She fumbled for words, trying to tell him what he needed to know without revealing her own compromised position. "What I mean is—suppose, for instance, that he's a government secret agent?"

Anton looked at her in puzzlement for a moment, then shrugged. "That possibility hadn't occurred to me, but in our society anything is possible. Not that it matters. I've told the truth, and Prince Orlev is in a position to confirm it."

"You're declaring war on Doznevkov." She had gone as far as she could, but Anton wasn't really listening.

"So I am. I won't stand aside when his carelessness is costing human lives!"

Lisolette's dread overwhelmed her. She felt certain

Anton would pay a terrible price for his temerity, but there was nothing more she could do to help him. Out of her fear grew another, equally strong emotion, a surge of black hatred toward Doznevkov.

Reared as a lady, she had never in her life committed an act of violence. But now she prayed for the strength and courage to murder Doznevkov.

Late on a Saturday afternoon the wagon train reached the Columbia River, its waters surging and tumbling. They would follow the mighty river through a valley to its navigable mouth, about fifty miles inland, at the place where it was joined by the Willamette River, opposite Fort Vancouver. Within weeks the monumental journey would come to an end.

Sunday was even less of a day of rest than usual. A number of the men and older boys went out at dawn to catch salmon and returned with strings of the large, silvery fish. Whip showed them how to pack the salmon in clay and bake them in the coals of a fire. Meanwhile, Dolores took some of the younger women and girls into the forest and demonstrated a method of removing the bark from birch trees. Boiled and seasoned with wild herbs, the bark made a delicious dish long favored by the Indian tribes of the Pacific.

No one was busier than Ernie von Thalman. Acting in his capacity as president of the company, he sat at a table placed inside the circle of wagons, and there he filled out and signed the federal forms granting land to those who had endured so much for this privilege. Lee Blake, the only government employee in the train, sat beside him and countersigned each document.

The head of every household and the unmarried, regardless of whether they were men or women, each received grants of six hundred acres. Men who had been married prior to embarking on the journey were given an additional one hundred and twenty acres for their wives, and every child in a family brought the father or widowed mother another forty acres.

Only the United States recognized these claims, to be sure, but those who received the precious parchment sheets were indifferent to the probability that Great Britain and Russia would dispute their rights. Some had come as far as three thousand miles, crossing the Great Plains and two chains of mountains and leaving the populated portion of the continent behind them. The grants were positive proof that they had won their great battle. All they had to do, after they reached the junction of the Columbia and the Willamette would be to select the land they wanted, build their homes, and clear the forest. These were formidable tasks, but after what these men and women had suffered, it would be child's play.

Cathy Blake finally approached the table.

"After all you've done," Ernie told her as he signed his name with a flourish, "I wish I could give you a double grant." He handed the parchment to Lee for his signature. "I hope you two will build a house out here so you'll have a retirement home when your career is ended."

"We can't look that far into the future," Lee said.

"Besides," Cathy added, "there are others who can put that land to better use immediately." She turned away and went in search of Eulalia, finding her standing nearby with Whip.

Since Cathy had waited until all the others had received their grants, Lee had no more certificates to sign, so he wandered over to join them.

Whip looked at his own grant, then at Eulalia's, and handed both to her. "You'd best hang on to these for us," he said. "I've had so little to do with papers I'm afraid I might lose them."

Cathy said, smiling, "Here's another to add to your collection. Consider it our wedding present to you."

Eulalia was overwhelmed. "I can't take it from you, Cathy. You're being too generous."

"We want you to have it," Lee said. "Your horses will need plenty of room to roam and graze."

Cathy's smile was radiant as she nodded and looked at Whip.

The thought passed through Eulalia's mind that the smile was unusual. Intimate, perhaps. Of course, Cathy and Whip had been interested in each other for a long time, so she supposed it was only natural that they should still feel close. Or was it natural?

Surely Whip's undemonstrative attitude didn't mean he still cared for Cathy! Or did it? Eulalia tried to dismiss the unpleasant thought from her mind, hating herself for being suspicious.

Lee saw his wife's smile, too, and felt uneasy. She had done nothing to cause him to distrust her, to be sure, and he knew Whip was an honorable man. They wouldn't forget or ignore their marriage vows, either of them. But it was possible, Lee had to admit, that there was still something between them, perhaps a feeling that neither consciously recognized. He told himself not to be foolish. The wise thing to do would be to stop imagining things, but he knew he wouldn't.

The scouts and Dolores had insisted on supervising the preparation of a special dinner to celebrate the issuing of the grants, and their shouts indicated that the meal was ready.

People formed in line for generous portions of steaming salmon, bowls of tender bark, and quantities of wild onions. Only a very few had been privileged previously to taste Columbia River salmon, and everyone agreed with Ernie von Thalman's solemn pronouncement. "I spent most of my life in Vienna, which supposedly has the world's finest food. There are those who argue in favor of France, and I've eaten many meals there, too. But I've never had anything that can compare with this salmon. We've heard many good things about Oregon, but nobody ever told us we were coming to heaven on earth!"

The catch had been so plentiful that most of the

company availed themselves of the opportunity to have second portions. Paul Thoman, whose slim frame seemed at odds with his always-ravenous appetite, heaped his plate high, then returned to his place beside Sally MacNeill.

He plunged his fork into the steaming, pink meat, ate with relish, and then said something incomprehensible in what sounded like a foreign language. Sally looked at him blankly.

"I was quoting Homer in the original Greek," he told her. " 'Men have but a short time to live,' he wrote in the *Odyssey*, and he was right, of course. But it doesn't matter how short life may be, provided we can eat this ambrosia."

She had never heard of Homer, but didn't want to reveal her ignorance.

Paul knew from experience that she had no idea what he was talking about. "The *Odyssey*," he said, "is a story about a journey even longer and more difficult than the one the people on this train have just made."

"That's not possible," Sally said and put the ridiculous statement out of her head. She had other, far more practical matters to discuss. "Dolores says there are dozens of ways to cook salmon. You can poach it or fry it like steak or even eat it cold."

"I have a new ambition in life," Paul declared as he continued to eat. "I intend to try every salmon recipe ever invented."

"I'll cook it for you," Sally said promptly.

"Why, that'll be very kind of you."

She sat back, her hands locked over one knee, and looked up at the benign Oregon sky. Summer had arrived, and the sun was hot, but a breeze blowing down from the snow-covered Cascade Mountains kept the air pleasantly cool. "I can't wait until everything is settled and houses are built. I can see us now, can't you? I'll be working in the kitchen when you come in from the farm—"

There was a faint note of alarm in his voice as he interrupted her. "I don't intend to become a farmer, Sally," he said. "It isn't in our family tradition, of course, and I know nothing whatever about raising crops. It was Vergil, the great Latin poet, who wrote that the present time is the great golden age. He was writing about any age, naturally, and his words certainly have meaning today. The people in this company are just the beginning of a tidal wave of settlers, you know. There will be unlimited opportunities for the ambitious, and I intend to take full advantage of them."

She found it incomprehensible that he didn't plan to farm his own land. "What in the world do you aim to do?"

"I'm not sure yet," Paul said. "I want to look around and take my time. I plan to weigh various prospects before I act. My grant will be as valid two or three months from now as it is this minute, so I'm in no rush."

Sally swallowed hard. "But how will we—I mean, how will you live during those months?"

His laugh was self-confident. "I managed for an entire year in the Rocky Mountains, you know. For one thing, I'll fish. If and when I grow tired of salmon, which I find unlikely, these forests are full of game." He patted his rifle, which lay on the ground beside him. "I don't much care where I sleep, and as long as the weather stays like this, I'll enjoy living in the open. When I've decided how I intend to make my living—and I'll admit I have some thoughts I'm not prepared as yet to discuss aloud—it will be time enough to build myself a little cabin. Until then I'm just going to sniff out the prospects, which is what my great-great-grandfather did before he decided to build the shipyard that's given our family its backbone."

She sat erect and averted his gaze.

Paul noted with surprise that her back was rigid

and her fists were clenched. "What's wrong, Sally?" She made no reply. "Have I said something to offend you?" His bewilderment was genuine.

Sally spoke stiffly so he wouldn't hear the tremor in her voice. "I guess I've been assuming something that isn't so, that's all. But I do thank you, Mr. Thoman, for warning me before I make an even bigger fool of myself."

He had no idea what she was talking about, but decided to find out before he went back to the fire for a third helping of salmon. "If I've hurt you in some way, it was unintended, I give you my word."

"Please don't give it another thought." Her voice was unnaturally high and thin. "Let's just say that I, for one, always keep my word, spoken or unspoken. I'll build my house, and somehow I'll get my land cleared. I'm going to have an enormous kitchen with two stoves, one for wood and the other for charcoal. And any time you want to drop in for supper, I'll be very happy to cook salmon for you."

"I appreciate that," he said. "And perhaps I can give you a hand with your house and land-clearing. Now, if you'll excuse me for a moment, I don't want any of that fish to go to waste."

Not until he had walked part of the way to the fire did the significance of their conversation dawn on him. All at once beads of sweat appeared on his forehead, and he wiped them away with the back of his hand. Lord, Sally was actually serious about getting married in the immediate future, and he had almost committed himself without realizing what he was doing.

That had been a close call, far too close for comfort. Paul had no intention of marrying anyone for a long time. Besides, even though he enjoyed Sally's company, and for a while had been attracted to her, he had come to the realization that she really wasn't his type. Not that he was a snob, far from it, but he knew that when he fell in love it would be with a girl who would be completely at home entertaining members of the Thoman family from Boston and, hopefully, financiers from New York. Sally was sweet, pretty, and thoughtful, but he couldn't imagine her at ease in his parents' Beacon Hill home, either.

His plate refilled, he returned to the place where they had been sitting, only to discover she had gone. Too bad, he thought, and as he ate his salmon he hoped she wasn't too disappointed. At least he had done nothing to encourage her mistaken belief that he wanted to marry her, so his conscience was clear.

What he didn't know was that Sally had fled to her wagon so she wouldn't make a spectacle of herself by weeping in public.

Elsewhere in the circle Tilman Wade—now fully recovered from his arrow wound—his stomach comfortably filled, leaned on one elbow as he chatted with Ginny Dobbs. She might be an unpredictable firebrand, but she sure was pretty, and he wondered why it had taken him so long to realize it. At least Dave Evans was eating elsewhere, so he was grateful for the opportunity to spend some time alone with Ginny.

The young woman plucked a blade of grass from the ground and bit off the white inner tip of the root. "I did this all the time when I was little," she said. "Do you ever eat grass?"

Tilman smiled and shook his head. "I've kept too many cows for too many years," he said. "I'm hoping I can buy some cows out here. A six-hundred-acre plot is plenty big for a dairy farm. And the way I see it, there's going to be a big demand for milk, cheese, and butter when folks settle down."

Ginny was impressed by his foresight and became thoughtful. "When I was in California, I saw cows. You might have to send to Yerba Buena, but I'm sure the Mexicans will sell you at least the start of a herd."

"That's good to know, and I thank you for the information. What are your plans?"

"I haven't really made any. I'm as good a seamstress as you'll find. I did little else at the orphanage after they taught me reading and writing. But I have a hankering to do something other than sew."

"Why is that?"

She shrugged. "Maybe I need new challenges. Maybe I'm too restless for my own good."

Tilman had never heard her speak with such candor about herself, and he thought it was possible their relationship might be entering a new phase. But no further confidences would be exchanged that day.

Ginny suddenly tensed when Dave Evans approached the couple, smoking one of his ever-present cigars. He carried a seemingly unlimited supply of them in his wagon.

Tilman silently cursed the man for butting in.

But Ginny, in spite of her greater tension, greeted the newcomer cordially and appeared to be pleased that he was joining them. "We've just been talking about our plans for the future," she said.

Dave lowered himself to the grass, and it couldn't have been accidental that he placed himself between them. "I've been doing some snooping of my own," he said. "First, I've had a chat or two with Whip Holt, and today I've just been talking to the scouts who also know Oregon. Now I'm all set."

Tilman didn't care how the man intended to earn a living and said nothing. But Ginny encouraged Dave with a bright, expectant smile.

Drawing on his cigar, Dave became expansive. "Back home," he said, "I ran a sawmill that made me a pile of money. When I sold the place, I had duplicates made of my best saws, and I've brought them all the way with me. The demand for finished lumber will be enormous. Most of our people, along with those who'll come here in later wagon trains, will want to build themselves real houses and barns, not log cabins. So I'm going to build myself a sawmill, either on the Willamette or on the Columbia, whichever I like better. On both rivers the water power will be free."

"Haven't we heard that the British already have a sawmill at Fort Vancouver?" Tilman asked.

Dave's offhand wave indicated his lack of concern. "I looked into that, and it's true the Hudson's Bay Company already has a sawmill in operation. But a little competition will be healthy for them. Will Americans buy from me or from foreigners, especially when my product is every bit as good and as cheap as Hudson's Bay can produce? I guess you know the answer to that one!"

It was obvious that he entertained no doubts about the success he would enjoy, and Ginny looked at him admiringly. "I'm sure you'll make out fine, Dave."

"So will you," he replied, totally ignoring Tilman. "I've got plans for you, Ginny."

"You do?" Her surprise was genuine, and it was clear to Tilman that the subject hadn't been discussed previously.

"There ain't many women who can read and write and do calculations," Dave said. "I'm going to need somebody to take care of the office work for me while I run the sawmill. And you're a natural for the job. I'll fix up an arrangement with you for good pay, even before I get the mill into operation. How does that sound?"

The young woman was flattered. "Thank you for thinking of me. This is all so new to me that I want to roll it around in my mind for a spell, if you don't mind."

"Sure, take your time. I know you don't want to go back to sewing, so this here is a way of solving your problems as well as my own."

"It sounds tempting," Ginny said, "and I'm grateful to you, Dave."

Tilman found it difficult to conceal his indignation. Now he knew why Evans had been paying so much attention to Ginny in recent weeks. She was the only available member of the company who was capable of performing the duties he had in mind for her, and no matter what he paid her, she would be well worth whatever she earned. Perhaps his interest in her was personal, too, although that was difficult to judge at the moment. What irritated Tilman was the realization that Dave was taking advantage of Ginny for the sake of his own vocational needs.

Dave hauled himself to his feet and, ignoring the other man, patted Ginny on the shoulder. "This is an offer tailor-made for you," he said, then wandered off.

Tilman had to curb his desire to tell Ginny what he thought of the matter. Her decision was strictly her own business, and he could only hope she wouldn't associate herself with Evans. The offer was legitimate enough, at least on the surface, but he didn't trust the man, and he wished that Ginny wouldn't become involved with him.

V

A grass-covered plain extended for a mile or more on both sides of the Columbia River at the place where the Willamette River flowed into it. To the west and south lay vast expanses of forest, to the east were the hills that rose higher and higher until they blended with the mountains of the Cascade Range, and directly across the Columbia, to the north, Fort Vancouver had been carved out of another expanse of deep woods. The Union Jack fluttered in the breeze above the fort, and another was displayed at the yardarm of a small merchant ship that lay at anchor near the place where the Columbia widened dramatically in its rush to the sea.

It was on this invitingly green plain, at the junction of the two rivers, that the first wagon train ever to cross North America came to a final halt. Plains, plateaus, and mountains had been conquered, attacks by hostile Indians had been warded off, and the attempts of Great Britain and Russia to halt the advance had failed. The first great victory had been won.

But the end of the long journey was anticlimactic, and in a way nothing was changed. Many weeks would pass before the sites for homes, farms, and offices would be selected, the land cleared, and buildings erected. So, for the present, the company would remain united, and people would continue to work for the good of all, as they had during their travels.

The wagons were drawn into the familiar circle for the last time, firewood was gathered, and the water detail brought filled buckets into the compound. In the morning teams of hunters and fishermen would go out in search of food, which was plentiful. Dolores and Stalking Horse would lead groups into the forest for berries and edible roots.

The soil was black and rich, and many of the farmers agreed with Tilman Wade, who said, "It looks so good I could blame near eat it!"

The knowledge that the exhausting journey was behind them caused a few of the women to weep with relief, but most members of the company remained calm. The problems of establishing their homesteads awaited them, and by common consent they postponed the celebration of what they had achieved. When they moved out of their wagons into their new houses, they would have real cause to celebrate.

Sentry outposts were established as a matter of routine, although no Indian attacks were anticipated, and the women of the cooking detail went about their usual business.

Suddenly a sentry's shout alerted the company. "Look across the Columbia!"

Scarlet-uniformed British troops armed with rifles were climbing into longboats, obviously intending to cross the river to the wagon train. Chet Harris and Danny made a quick count and announced that the detail consisted of one hundred men, led by three officers.

The buckskin-clad Lee Blake quickly went to change into his own blue dress uniform, while Ernie von Thalman and Whip Holt, their rifles cradled in their arms, strolled quietly toward the river bank to await the arrival of the soldiers. Virtually the entire company followed them, with the men carrying their firearms, partly out of habit and in part because they knew better than to take unnecessary risks.

The leaders of the train had intended to pay a courtesy visit to Fort Vancouver the following morning, but the British, for their own as yet unexplained reasons, were taking the initiative. There was no need for them to send troops. The settlers wanted no quarrel with anyone, and Ernie von Thalman was concerned. "No matter what's said," he called over his shoulder, "don't lose your heads, my friends!"

He and Whip halted about fifty yards from the Columbia and waited as the troops landed, hauled their longboats onto the shore, and then formed into two platoons, each led by a young officer. Major Roland Pitts took his place in front of the formation and gave several orders in rapid succession. The redcoats jumped to attention, presented arms, and then stood at ease. Apparently they were not going to open fire, at least for the present.

Major Pitts advanced alone toward the Americans, and Ernie and Whip strolled toward him.

The British officer halted, then spoke in a voice loud enough for all to hear. "On behalf of Her Britannic Majesty, welcome to Oregon and Fort Vancouver."

"We're glad to be here," Ernie said.

Pitts's smile was warm and quick. "Your achievement is rather extraordinary, gentlemen," he replied simply. "You have every reason to be proud."

His manner was so friendly that Whip immediately spoke in the same spirit. "There were times along the way we weren't so sure you'd ever have us as neighbors."

The Major smiled again, then sobered and stiffened as he reached into a pocket of his scarlet and gold tunic. Raising his voice again, he said, "Permit me to read you a proclamation prepared by Colonel Phillips

Morrison, commandant of Her Majesty's garrison of Fort Vancouver."

Lee Blake, now wearing his resplendent blue and gold full-dress uniform, with his sword hanging at his side, began to move forward unobtrusively from the rear of the crowd.

The Major began to read. "'In the Queen's name, greetings. You have arrived in the Royal Crown Colony of Oregon, and you now stand on British soil. You are free to settle here and lead your lives as you see fit within the limitations of British law. I require only that, immediately and without delay, you renounce all other citizenships and swear allegiance to Victoria, our Queen.' The letter is signed, Phillips Morrison, Commandant, Fort Vancouver, British Oregon."

There was a shocked silence, and then the crowd began to stir. Lee continued to advance until, standing beside Ernie and Whip, he faced the British officer.

Although surprised to see an American officer superior to him in rank, Pitts was equal to the occasion. Drawing his own sword and saluting, he said crisply, "Roland Pitts, sir, Third Grenadier Guards, Deputy Commandant of Fort Vancouver."

Lee returned the salute with his own sword. Then his voice rang out. "Lieutenant Colonel Leland Blake, United States Army, commanding officer of the First Regiment of Oregon Territorials."

None of the settlers except Cathy had ever heard of such a regiment, and they stared at Lee in astonishment.

"On behalf of President Van Buren, the Congress, and the people of the United States, I categorically deny the allegation that Oregon is a British possession." Lee turned and beckoned.

An eager Danny raced forward, carrying an American flag attached to a pole, its base sharpened to a point. Lee took the pole and, using his full strength, drove it into the ground. The flag stood at eye level. "I hereby lay claim to the entire Oregon country on behalf of the government and people of the United States of America," he declared.

Pitts's expression made it obvious that he felt personal admiration for the American officer who, standing alone and without troops to back up his claim, nevertheless took a defiant position.

"I trust I have given an unequivocal reply to your commandant's demand, Major," Lee said.

"Indeed you have, Colonel."

Every adult present knew a serious crisis had arisen.

"I will make an immediate report of your acts and words to Colonel Morrison, sir," Major Pitts said.

"The members of this wagon train are tired after making a very long journey," Lee said informally. "So I'm sure you can appreciate my eagerness to resolve this issue as soon as possible. If you don't mind, Major, I'll come with you right now and see your commandant."

"I'd be delighted, sir!" Pitts said and meant it.

Cathy was concerned for her husband's personal safety, but he turned for a moment, found her in the crowd, and reassured her with a quick glance.

Lee was in his element now. He knew precisely what he was doing, and he had the full support of the government. Therefore, he was not as isolated as he appeared to be.

Strolling toward the river with Pitts beside him, he said, "I presume you can have someone bring me back across the river after I've met Colonel Morrison."

"Certainly, sir!" Major Pitts ordered his troops to salute the American officer, and they presented arms. Then, after ordering them to their boats, he said in a low tone, "I have great respect for your position, Colonel."

"Well, I have no quarrel with you, either," Lee

replied. "It seems sensible to me that we live side by side as peaceful neighbors while Washington City and London reach some accommodation."

"Quite right, sir. I shudder to think of the complications if blood is spilled here."

As they climbed into a boat and sat together, Lee remarked quietly, "I gather your commandant isn't in full agreement with your opinions in this matter."

"No, Colonel," Pitts said in a dry voice. "Colonel Morrison has his own views, as he does in all things."

The soldiers manning the oars worked together in unison, and the boats crossed the great river in a short time. Lee looked with interest at the houses and shops of the town that Hudson's Bay had established. The civilians who saw him stared at him curiously.

"I think," Pitts said delicately, "that you'll want to meet the company factor, Dr. McLoughlin."

"I look forward to it," Lee replied. "Everyone interested in Oregon knows how much he's accomplished here."

The Major coughed behind his hand. "You and he will find you have a great deal in common, Colonel."

Lee was grateful for the strong hint, and the British situation here became clearer to him. The commandant was setting up obstacles but was opposed by the factor and the deputy commander, who had no authority in his own right, but at least sympathized with the Americans and wanted, as did Lee himself, to avoid a war.

The sentries at the entrance to Fort Vancouver stood at rigid attention and presented arms as the two officers entered the compound. It was only a short walk to the commandant's quarters, and Pitts told an orderly to inform the commandant he had arrived, accompanied by Colonel Blake.

Phillips Morrison was so startled he came to the door of his study. He gaped when he saw Lee's uniform, then returned the American's salute and asked him to come in.

Morrison waved him to a chair, and Pitts took another. "I've never heard of a regiment of Oregon territorials," the commandant said.

"It's still in the process of formation, sir," Lee replied quietly. "But it no longer exists just on paper. I'm expecting my first contingent of troops at any time. They're being transported here," he added deliberately, "by our navy." He was careful not to mention how many ships might be involved.

Colonel Morrison couldn't ask about the size of Lee's troop dispositions, any more than he himself would answer questions about the strength of his own garrison.

Lee saw no reason to evade the heart of the issue. "Colonel," he said, "I replied to your proclamation by raising our flag and claiming the entire Oregon country for the United States."

The amazed Morrison could only stare at him.

"It's my understanding that Britain also claims the whole of Oregon at present, so now we're on even terms," Lee continued cheerfully. "Ultimately our governments will work out a compromise, and each of us will settle for a part of the pie. Until then, as I've said to Major Pitts, I trust we can live near each other as friendly neighbors. I also suggest we set up no artificial borders and that American citizens and British subjects be free to travel anywhere they please in Oregon."

"Surely you're joking, Colonel Blake!" Morrison spoke in his parade-ground voice.

"I'm in earnest, sir. I'm speaking of an informal agreement that will enable Americans and Englishmen to live in peace near each other if not together."

"I cannot be a party to any agreement that will harm the claim of Great Britain to the entire territory!" Morrison trumpeted.

"Of course not," Lee said reasonably. "Any more than I'll allow the claim of the United States to be diluted. All I'm saying is that since you and I aren't empowered to bargain together and reach a settlement, we live as friends until our governments work out the terms of a treaty."

"I am instructed," Morrison declared, "to maintain the full claims of Her Majesty's Government. This I will do. Any persons desiring to live in Oregon are required to swear an oath of allegiance to Queen Victoria!"

"Our people fully intend to make their homes here," Lee told him. "They—and all those who are following them—haven't endured countless trials and privations in order to settle in some lesser place. What's more, I can assure you they won't give up their American citizenship."

"You make it necessary for me to use force, Colonel Blake!" Morrison thundered.

Lee rose slowly to his feet but continued to speak quietly, even though his voice hardened. "Are you threatening to fire on us, Colonel Morrison?"

"I am, if you give me no alternative!"

"In that case, sir," Lee said in clipped tones, "you'll be firing the first shots in the third war between our countries. You may want to inform your superiors that my government is well aware of the repeated attempts to sabotage our wagon by one or more British agents. We're willing to let that matter drop, however, if our mutual problem can be solved in a civilized manner. If you use force, we'll use it in return. You'll fire on us at your peril!"

Turning on his heel, Lee walked out. Major Pitts soon followed and escorted him back to the river.

"Our settlers have faced a number of enemies," Lee said. "They've never fought regular army troops, but I'm quite sure they'll give a good account of themselves."

"I continue to hope we won't become enemies, Colonel."

"So do I." They reached a dock where a boat was waiting, and Lee extended a hand, which Major Pitts grasped firmly. "I give you my word we won't fire first," Lee said, "but we'll sure as hell keep our powder dry!"

As soon as the boat started toward the south shore of the Columbia, Roland Pitts hurried to the house of John McLoughlin and quickly brought the factor up to date on the explosive situation that his superior had created. Dr. McLoughlin, who had been looking forward to selling various products to hundreds of potential customers, was dismayed and went at once to see the commandant of Fort Vancouver.

"I'll tell you what I think, Morrison, and I'll not spare your feelings," the Scotsman declared scornfully. "You're behaving like a brainless jackass."

"I resent—"

"Be damned to your resentment!"

"But the Americans have openly defied me, which means they've defied the Queen. I cannot tolerate—"

"Be damned to your intolerance, too! I've been in the New World since you were a subaltern, Morrison, so I know America and Americans well. Do you think it an accident they won the War of Independence? Do you suppose it was bad luck that let Andrew Jackson beat our regulars at New Orleans, regulars who had defeated Napoleon Bonaparte? Attack them on this continent, Morrison, and they'll declare war on us the very day the news reaches their capital. This time they'll not only take Oregon, but they'll annex all of Canada, too. You'll go down in history as the man who lost North America!"

His withering contempt cooled Phillips Morrison's ardor. "What would you have me do, then?"

"Absolutely nothing! Let them spend their money in the Hudson's Bay shops. Let them settle where they please—because you lack the strength to stop them. Give the diplomats time to make a treaty that will be fair to all. And for God's sake, don't start a war you cannot win!"

Morrison had to back down. "Your opposition cripples me, as I'm sure you know," he said, his manner becoming surly. "However, my instructions are clear, and one way or another I will rid this territory of Yankees!"

As the threat of an open battle receded, the members of the wagon train company began to explore the countryside, and most of them claimed rich land along the banks of the Willamette River. The claims were approximate; an exact measure of the six hundred acres allotted to each settler would have to await a formal survey. The settlers were heartened by the firm stand Lee Blake had taken, and they enthusiastically began the laborious process of building their new homes and clearing their land. Most returned every night to the circle of wagons; long accustomed to helping each other, they continued to observe that same pattern.

Tilman Wade found the land he wanted, and Sally MacNeill followed his lead by claiming the adjoining acreage. Whip, insisting that Eulalia accompany him on horseback for the exercise, roamed through the rolling hills east and south of the junction of the rivers until he came to a place that suited him. It was too remote from the homesteads of most of the others for Eulalia's taste, but she felt somewhat better when Claiborne and Cindy decided to build nearby.

Dave Evans started work single-handed on his new sawmill, Ted Woods elected to build his blacksmith's shop a short distance away, and their two embryonic places of business formed the nucleus of what would become an American village opposite Fort Vancouver. A few who had funds tried to hire Indians who came to the fort to sell furs, but the natives were unaccustomed to such labor and proved unreliable, so the settlers had to do the work themselves. Consequently, progress was slow.

Late one afternoon in October, those who were already back at their wagons saw a warship moving up the Columbia under reduced sail. Someone remarked that she was a frigate, and the settlers were electrified when they saw the Stars and Stripes flying from her yardarm. The U.S.S. *Washington* at last had arrived. Lee, who had anxiously been awaiting this day, changed into his uniform.

Captain Ingalls sent his complement of Marines ashore first, and then Major Eli Moser led his troops, two hundred strong, into the boats that carried them ashore.

"Sir," he said as he saluted Lee, "I am ordered to give the regiment into your command."

Moser also handed him a personal letter. By command of the President, Lee was promoted to the rank of full Colonel and now was the equal of Colonel Morrison. A package that Moser handed him contained the silver eagles that were his new insignia of rank and the full silver epaulets he would wear with his dress uniform.

That night Lee and Cathy dined on board the *Washington* with Captain Ingalls and Major Moser. Both of the newcomers listened intently as Lee told them of his confrontation with Colonel Morrison. "Major Pitts, the deputy, seems like a sensible man," he concluded, "and I'm sure Dr. McLoughlin has been a moderating influence, too."

"I'll stay for a while, Lee," Ingalls said. "In fact, count on me as long as you need me."

"Thanks, Bob, I need your support. And the brawn of your men, particularly your carpenters."

"Don't thank me," Ingalls said, chuckling. "I'm under a personal directive from President Van Buren to help you in every way possible."

123

Major Moser was thoughtful. "How big is the British garrison, sir?"

"I'm not really sure," Lee said. "I've only paid one visit to the fort, and I had no real chance to look around. But Whip Holt, our guide, who knew the place when he was a trapper, has snooped around several times for me, and he thinks the garrison has an overall strength of four to five hundred men."

Moser rubbed his hands together. "We have two hundred, and the *Washington* carried a complement of four hundred and fifty sailors and Marines, not to mention guns that can reduce Fort Vancouver to kindling in an afternoon. We can order the British to clear out!"

Lee looked at him in astonishment.

Ingalls laughed wryly. "Moser has a thirst for British blood, as you'll soon discover, Lee."

Not wanting to reprimand his new subordinate too severely in Cathy's presence, Lee merely smiled. "You'll outgrow the taste, Moser," he said. "More than twenty years ago we and the British tentatively agreed to occupy Oregon jointly. Now both nations are pressing full claims to the territory, and I hope we and they will be intelligent enough to compromise. With so much at stake a war could develop. However," he added firmly, "I won't start it, and neither will anyone under my command."

Eli Moser now knew precisely where he stood.

The following morning the American troops went to work clearing ground for a fort, which would include barracks, offices, a mess hall, officers' quarters, and a parade ground, as well as several storehouses and recreational buildings. They would also construct a house for the commandant, and the compound would be surrounded by a palisade. Captain Ingalls offered the services of his marines and most of his sailors, too, keeping only a skeleton crew on board the *Washington*. Trees were felled so quickly that it seemed as though a giant scythe had been utilized, and before the morning ended, tree stumps and rocks were being removed from the area.

The first of the settlers to approach the site was Dave Evans. "Colonel," he said, "I want to make you an offer. Clapboard is better than logs, but you'll pay a pretty penny at Hudson's Bay for it. Give me enough men to put up my sawmill in a hurry, and I'll return the favor by giving you—and the *Washington*—all the lumber you want. At no charge."

The man was shrewd, Lee realized; the wood itself was free for the taking. But planks were superior to logs, especially for barracks and houses, so he found the offer irresistible. "You have a deal, Evans," he said.

One hundred and fifty soldiers and sailors went to work constructing the sawmill. A scant forty-eight hours later the happy Evans was in operation, his saws cutting lumber furiously.

One week later the commandant's house was ready for occupancy, and several of the carpenters from the *Washington*'s crew began to make furniture in accordance with Cathy's wishes, although the house and any furniture they made automatically would become government property.

The barter deal with Dave Evans had been so successful that many of the other settlers began to clamor for help. So Lee and Captain Ingalls made a bargain with them. The soldiers and sailors would clear land and build houses and in return would be supplied with meat and fish in sufficient quantities so that food not required for immediate consumption could be smoked, pickled, and otherwise preserved. This arrangement served the ends of civilians and the military alike, and the settlers happily accepted. Parties of hunters energetically went into the heavily wooded hills, and fishermen caught vast numbers of salmon.

Thanks to these cooperative efforts, a task that might have dragged on until spring was completed by the early autumn. Farmers were already able to till enough of their land to produce crops they would be able to harvest in a few months. They were just beginning to learn the true "miracle of Oregon," that the growing season lasted for all but one hundred days each year and the ground failed to produce only during the worst of the winter. Wheat, barley, and oats were planted, as were varieties of vegetables, and the forests were searched for wild, fruit-bearing trees. It would not take long before the orchards of the territory would be unrivaled anywhere in the United States.

The most significant symbol of the establishment of a secure community was the disappearance of the wagons from their circle. The fort, soon to be named Fort Oregon, provided the people with the protection they needed, and as they moved into their new homes, they took their wagons with them, freeing their horses and oxen for farm work. By mid-autumn they were ready for the next influx of new arrivals, but the second wagon train hadn't yet appeared, so it was assumed it had been forced to halt for the winter somewhere in the mountains.

Lee and Captain Ingalls saw to it that a church, open to people of all faiths, was built in the village, and a modest parsonage was constructed adjacent to it for the Reverend Cavendish. The *Washington* carried four spare cannon in her hold, and Ingalls gave them to Lee, along with ample quantities of ammunition.

Lee immediately ordered his regimental sergeant major, Hector Mullins, to have mounts built for the guns and to emplace them.

Mullins, a grizzled veteran who had spent more than two decades in the army, stood at his commanding officer's desk. When he grinned he revealed a gap in his mouth, two teeth having been knocked out in a fist fight many years earlier. "Colonel, which way do you want them cannon to point?"

Lee leaned back in his chair and smiled. "I have no

desire to provoke the British at Fort Vancouver, Mullins. You realize that, of course."

"Hell, yes! I mean, yessir!" A deep laugh rumbled up within Mullins. "There ain't many Indians hereabouts, and the ones that come moseying around are housebroke. So it would be a terrible waste to point the cannon at the Willamette River. Or at a patch of woods."

"True enough." They understood each other perfectly, and Lee was pleased.

"Seems to me," Mullins said, scratching his chin, "that we might put up a higher palisade in front of the cannon so they can't be seen from the other side of the river. That way I can keep them aimed straight at Fort Vancouver, and what the redcoats don't know won't hurt them none."

"I'll leave the details to you," Lee said. "I know I can rely on your judgment."

"You damn well bet you can, sir." Mullins swaggered slightly as he left his superior's new office, his rolling gait akin to that of a sailor.

The civilians were as busy as the military, and Whip faced an unexpected crisis one morning when he and Eulalia were eating breakfast in the kitchen of their new ranch house. "I'm going off into the hills for two or three days," he told her. "There's a canyon there with extra sweet grass at its base, and wild horses love it. I plan to catch a few, if I can, and bring them back so I can start my herd. Can you make out all right without me for that time?"

"Of course," she said. "And if I should need anything or encounter any problems, Cindy and Claiborne are only a few minutes' ride from here."

"That's what I want most to talk to you about. Riding. See to it you spend plenty of time on horseback while I'm away."

Eulalia's temper flared. "Sometimes, Michael Holt, you make me so angry I want to scream! I know I've got to ride and ride and ride! You make that very clear to me with your incessant nagging!"

There was a strained silence, and Whip stared into space as he ate his grilled fish. It appeared that he had married the most high-strung mare on earth.

At that unpropitious moment Stalking Horse came into the house, as usual not bothering to knock on the door. Unaware of the domestic tensions, he addressed his friend in the tongue of the Cherokee. "I am here to say farewell to my brother."

Whip was so startled he replied in English. "What the devil does that mean?"

"The work that brought your brother with you to this place is finished. No more is there a need for a scout. No more is there a need for a warrior who will fight bad braves. In these forests there is so much game there is no need for a hunter. So Stalking Horse is leaving."

"Where are you going?"

"I go to the land of the Cherokee in Tennessee," Stalking Horse said.

For the sake of a curious Eulalia, Whip continued to address the Indian in English. "But I need and want you here, my brother. I was planning to find you this morning so you would come with me to round up my first wild horses. I'll need you to help me break them in and look after them. I want you to stay on with me as my foreman. This property is plenty big, so we'll build you a house of your own, and when you find the woman you want and marry her, you can live there with her."

The Cherokee's face was almost devoid of expression.

All the same, Eulalia could see in his eyes that he believed a job was just being created for him out of kindness. Like a woman who was crippled, he was an outsider, someone who felt different and totally alien.

"Until you marry, if you ever do, Stalking Horse,"

she said, speaking slowly, "I hope you'll take all your meals with us. And if you don't want to live in a house by yourself, I hope you'll stay right here. You've been my husband's good friend for so many years that this is your home. He wants you here. And I—I want you here, too."

For a moment Stalking Horse remained impassive. Then a broad smile lighted his face and, without directly acknowledging what Eulalia had just said to him, he turned to Whip. "I stay," he said. "When we go to round up wild horses?"

"Right now." Whip left the kitchen to fetch his rifle, and a few moments later he and his friend had gone off on their mission.

Eulalia was pleased because she knew she was responsible for the reversal of Stalking Horse's decision. At the same time, however, she couldn't help resenting Whip's failure to recognize the effort she had just made. He was taking her for granted, just as he had been doing ever since they had married. No matter how hard she tried, no matter what she did, she seemed to make no impression on him. He had been totally self-sufficient for so long, living alone in the mountains and being responsible to no one but himself, that she was afraid he didn't really want or need a wife.

Well, it did her no good to mope. She had so much to do in order to put the house in working condition that she scarcely knew where to begin. She limped out to the well that Whip had dug for her, brought up a pail of water so she could wash the breakfast dishes, and then began the chores that seemed to have no end.

Sergeant Major Hector Mullins entered the tiny cubicle that served as an office at one end of the new sawmill, then stopped short. Sitting behind the table of raw pine that served as a desk was the most attractive woman he had ever seen. Perhaps she wasn't all that young—he guessed she might be in her late twenties. Quickly, almost instinctively, he looked at her left hand and was surprised when he saw she wore no wedding ring on the fourth finger. Perhaps she was one of the wagon train's widows.

Ginny Dobbs realized that someone had come into the room, but she was adding a long column of figures and didn't want to interrupt herself. So she finished the task before she looked up and found Hector Mullins gaping at her. She touched her topknot to make sure her hair was in place, then assured herself that her dress of linsey-woolsey was properly buttoned.

"What's the matter, soldier?" she asked with asperity. "Has my nose fallen off?"

Hector, who could inspire terror in a squad of recruits on a drill field and who had won citations for honorable participation in eleven battles, responded meekly. "No, ma'am."

"I also have two eyes and two ears, just like everybody else," she snapped.

"Yes, ma'am." He grinned at her, displaying the gap where he had lost teeth. "And it seems like you got a mouth, too, bigger and sharper than most."

Ginny was startled and couldn't help smiling. Obviously the man could not be cowed easily, and she liked a man who showed real spunk.

"That's better," Hector said and, continuing to gaze at her, hooked his thumbs in his broad uniform belt.

His steady scrutiny made her uncomfortable. "You've come to buy some lumber, I assume."

"You assume wrong," he said. "If you work for this Dave Evans—"

"I do."

"—then you know he made a deal with the army. We get our lumber from him for free. And we got us a special job we want done. My men are going to bring in some tree trunks. A heap of them. We want them all eighteen feet long, with one end shaved nice and sharp, like a spike."

Ginny scribbled some notes and tried to speak impersonally. "We'll attend to the order as soon as we can get to it. As I'm sure you can imagine, Mr. Evans is terribly busy these days. Just about everyone hereabouts wants lumber from him."

"Ma'am," Hector said flatly, "my men are on their way here right now with the tree trunks. They'll give Evans a hand if he wants some help. But I tell you plain, the order will be done today."

She glared at him.

"Nobody keeps the U.S. Army waiting," he said. "We need a special palisade for a special purpose, and we need it fast. So your other orders will have to wait."

Ginny was about to retort but thought better of it. The man was an overpowering brute, but, to her surprise, she found she didn't resent him in the least. When a man wanted to be respected he should speak his mind, as she herself often did, and she could hardly blame him for it. "Never fear," she said at last, "the job will be done today."

"That's what I like to hear." He rocked back and forth on his heels. "Tell me something, ma'am. You got a husband? Or be you betrothed to anyone that came out here in the wagon train?"

"I'm neither married nor engaged," she snapped. "If that's any of your business."

"I aim to make it my business," Hector Mullins replied calmly.

Ginny felt herself reddening.

"I'll be back late this afternoon to inspect the job and have my men take the wood away," he said. "And seeing the sun don't go down until late, there will be plenty of time for you and me to take us a stroll along the river."

She became haughty. "What makes you think I'd go walking with you, Sergeant?"

"It's the best way I know for us to get acquainted. I don't even know your name yet, and I don't aim to keep calling you, 'Ma'am,' ma'am."

In spite of herself Ginny laughed.

"That's better," he said approvingly. "You look so pretty when you laugh that you ought to be happy all the time. You can look for me this afternoon. I'll be on time, never fear." He raised his hand in an informal semblance of a salute, then casually left the room.

Ginny was annoyed when she discovered her heart was pounding. The man was rude, insufferably conceited, and far too blunt. All the same, she knew she was attracted to him. Tilman Wade was too much of a gentleman for her taste, and Dave Evans thought only about making money. The Sergeant, for all the faults she had already seen in him, was the sort of man she admired. He knew what he wanted and made no bones about it. In this instance it was plain he wanted her.

Well, she didn't too much mind becoming acquainted with him, as he had suggested. She would put him in his place fast enough if he developed any wrong ideas about her; as he would soon learn, she wasn't afraid of any man. And he did intrigue her.

There was snow on the heights above the timberline, but the sun was warm, and the cliffs on either side of the deep canyon cut off most of the wind, so Whip was comfortable in his buckskin shirt. He and Stalking Horse rode side by side, neither of them speaking. The Cherokee had complete confidence in his old friend's ability to find the wild horses they were seeking, and Whip himself was completely at ease.

This was the world he knew best. He became tongue-tied and confused when Eulalia ripped into him for slights and insults he hadn't intended, but here he was in control of himself and his environment, ready to deal with any situation that might arise. The wilderness was his true home.

Stalking Horse half rose in his saddle for a moment,

then pointed. Whip saw what he meant and nodded. They were in luck. Ahead, grazing on the sweet grass, were a gray stallion, two chestnut mares, and a little foal. So far they hadn't become aware of the proximity of men and other horses.

The pair continued to advance at the same even pace. Then, still not speaking, they separated, with Whip moving a short distance to the left and Stalking Horse edging toward the right.

The stallion raised his head and pawed the ground.

Whip uncoiled the long whip he habitually kept wound around his middle and held it ready for use. This operation wouldn't be too easy, but he had faced worse.

His own stallion snorted. The wild stallion raised his head, and his loud neigh was an invitation to battle. Eager to accept the challenge, Whip's mount started forward, but his master gave him no opportunity to fight. Holding him on a short, tight rein, Whip commanded, "Steady, boy. Stay! Don't move a muscle, or I'll have your hide for it."

The mount halted, his nostrils quivering, ready to spring forward the instant he was given his release.

The wild stallion reared, calling again, and gathered himself for a plunge. Suddenly a whip cracked over his head, missing him by inches. Then it sounded again, directly in front of his face. The sharp, explosive noise startled him and was so alien to anything he had ever heard that he backed away.

Ah, Whip thought. We're off to a good start. The canyon narrowed at its far end, and with cliffs surrounding it on three sides, there would be no escape except by making a break past the two mounted men. Whip left the two mares to Stalking Horse, who would know how to deal with them. The foal, cavorting and prancing beside its mother, would create no problems.

Still keeping his mount under firm control, Whip

advanced a few paces, and the length of rawhide in his hand became a living thing as it leaped and crackled, each snap sounding like a rifle shot near the head of the wild stallion. The beast continued to back toward the end of the canyon. For the moment he was merely confused and a little frightened and wasn't yet thinking of trying to escape.

Stalking Horse fitted an arrow into his bow, took careful aim, and let fly. The shaft landed in the ground no more than a foot in front of one of the chestnut mares, and she halted uncertainly. The arrow trembled in the ground, and she sought safety by racing toward the dead end of the narrow ravine.

The other mare received the same treatment, and she reacted even more quickly, galloping away as fast as she could. Her foal, finding itself deserted, hurried after her on spindly legs.

The cracking whip continued to drive the wild stallion toward the spot where he would be cornered, and Whip's mount appeared to understand the nature of the game and its meaning. No longer straining to prove himself against an enemy, he responded to the pressures of his master's knees, obediently advancing a few paces and halting, then moving forward a short distance again.

Too late the wild stallion realized he and the mares had been trapped. Now he had no choice and, baring his teeth, gathered himself for a gallop past his tormentor.

Whip had been timing his advance with extraordinary care and knew the stallion's intentions even before the beast realized what he had to do. The whip sang out again, coiled around the stallion's neck as effectively as a lasso, and held firmly. The great animal began to buck and plunge in an attempt to rid himself of the length of rawhide that held him captive.

Whip advanced one last time. "Here we stay, boy!"

he told his mount. "Brace yourself and hang on while we try to land him!"

Every time the wild stallion pulled away from the whip, it tightened around his neck. He reared and plunged repeatedly, and then, as he gradually exhausted himself, his convulsive efforts began to lose force. Ultimately he was forced to halt, his gray coat lathered with sweat. The mares and the foal now cowered behind him, using him as a shield between them and the man.

Whip's arm felt as though it had been torn from its socket, but his task was not yet done. On the contrary, he had to strike quickly and accurately before his fortunes were reversed. Holding his whip taut with one hand, he took a coiled lasso from the side of his saddle with the other. Swinging it overhead in an ever-widening arc, he took careful aim and dropped it over the wild stallion's head, swiftly tightening the noose.

Stalking Horse dismounted and took the free end of the lasso from his friend, then tied it securely around the trunk of a large oak tree. Only now did Whip free his rawhide.

Stalking Horse mounted his gelding again, and the two men rode a safe distance from the wild horses. Now, if one of the mares tried to break for freedom, Whip could use his rawhide to drive her back again.

The great gray stallion recovered his breath and courage and desperately tried to free himself. But the lasso held, and whenever it threatened to choke him, he had to pause again.

The mares saw what was happening to him without understanding why he was thrashing. All they knew was that his efforts were being made in vain, so they stood still and waited. The foal, feeling secure again, began to cavort nearby.

Ultimately, after the stallion wore himself out, the mares would be roped, too. Their capture was certain, and Whip had no intention of moving closer until the infinitely more dangerous stallion was no longer a threat.

"My brother," he said in the tongue of the Cherokee, breaking the long silence, "we have won."

"It is so," Stalking Horse replied calmly. In his mind, at least, the outcome of the delicate operation had never been in doubt.

Whip continued to watch the wild stallion wear out his strength. "I reckon it will take about two days to teach the big fellow and his lady friends enough manners so we can take them back to the ranch on tethers," he said.

The Cherokee answered with a nod and a grin.

Whip sighed happily, picked up another lasso, and began the task of snaring one of the mares. He had good cause to feel pleased with his efforts. He would have been satisfied had he returned home with only one wild horse, but he had caught four, and his new business was off to an exceptionally solid start.

During the next two days, Whip and Stalking Horse worked hard with the horses, teaching them to obey rudimentary commands. Their performance was outstanding, and this encouraged Whip. He planned to return to this canyon several more times before the coming of winter, to pick out more horses. There was every reason to hope that he could build a substantial herd, and by this time next year he would be able to start selling horses to the settlers who would be coming to Oregon in ever-increasing numbers.

On the last morning in the canyon, Whip roped the captured horses together so that he could lead them back to the ranch. This task quickly accomplished, he put his forefinger and thumb into his mouth and emitted a curious, two-tone whistle. His own stallion picked up his ears and obediently trotted to his master.

Smiling, Whip reached into his pocket, removed a carrot, and placed it in the palm of his hand. After taking it gently from Whip's hand, the great beast promptly ate it.

Well, now, that was training! For more than three and a half years, ever since Whip had broken in the stallion and taught him the trick, the horse had never failed to respond to the up-and-down whistle that meant he would be fed a treat. In time, perhaps, these wild horses would be tame enough to learn to respond in the same way.

But Whip guessed he would have to learn to live with the basic fact of life that—no matter how great his patience—there was a wild streak in his wife, a streak he would never tame.

Eulalia awakened early, as she always did, and stoked the banked fire in the kitchen hearth, then heated an iron caldron of water for her bath. She was in no hurry to face the long day, and after she dressed she lingered over a breakfast of bread she had baked the previous day, sweetened with wild honey, and several cups of bitter but potable acorn coffee. Within the next year, perhaps, such staples as real tea that she had once taken for granted would be available in this benign wilderness. She looked forward to any little luxuries that would make life more bearable.

She had to build shelves in the parlor, which was still bare, and needed some planks from the new sawmill for the purpose. Well, the ride into the village would be good for her, at least according to Whip, and she sighed aloud as she started toward her bedroom for her riding crop and gloves, vestiges of her life as a lady to which she still clung.

Suddenly she halted and looked down at her lame leg in astonishment. All at once it occurred to her that she had felt no pain as she had been walking around the house and that her limp had been almost imperceptible.

Holding in her breath, she made the experiment of moving her stiff ankle, which had been unyielding ever since she had been stricken with the debilitating fever. To her astonishment she could move her foot independently of her ankle. She had not achieved complete mobility, to be sure, but the improvement was miraculous. Tears came into her eyes, and she brushed them away in a spirit of mounting excitement.

Conscious of her walk, Eulalia went on to the bedroom. Sure enough, her limp was so slight that a stranger might not know she had ever been lame. All right, she wasn't yet totally cured, but she was well on her way. Apparently Whip had been right: the daily physical exercise he had forced her to take was producing remarkable results.

Sitting down on the bedroom's only chair, which Whip had made the previous weekend, Eulalia stared breathlessly at her ankle. Unconscious of the passage of time, she spent more than a quarter of an hour flexing the ankle, then wiggling and twisting her foot.

Now she needed no nagging, and wanting to share her joy, she hurried out to the stable, saddled her borrowed mare, and quickly rode to her brother's adjoining property. No one answered her loud knock at the front door, and then she remembered that Claiborne and Cindy had planned to go into the village to have two of their workhorses shod.

Eulalia was so eager to share her news with them that she decided she couldn't wait until they returned. Instead she would follow them to the village, and while she was there she would obtain the planks she needed for the parlor shelves. The trail that she and Whip, Cindy and Claiborne had made was easy to follow, and in her exuberance she cantered the better part of the way into the village.

Hosea was at work at a small forge in the rear of the blacksmith's shop when she entered the place, and she exchanged waves with him, but he was so engrossed in what he was doing that he couldn't leave his work. Then Ted Woods appeared and lumbered forward to greet her. "Morning, Miz Holt," he said, but did not smile. Since Cindy's marriage no one had seen him smile.

"Have you seen my sister-in-law and brother this morning, Ted?" she asked.

He shook his head. "Not yet I ain't."

Eulalia became aware of an army officer in uniform standing nearby, and she knew she had met him, even though she couldn't recall his name at the moment, so she smiled at him.

Eli Moser had never seen such a radiant smile and was dazzled by it.

"Ted," Eulalia said, "I have an errand to do, so when Cindy and Claiborne come in, tell them not to leave town until they've seen me."

Ted Woods nodded and turned away silently, thinking it inappropriate to comment that he avoided Cindy and her husband whenever he could.

Hosea came forward, carrying a silver spur. "Is fixed," he announced.

Moser examined the spur and shook his head. "Incredible. No one would ever know the tip had broken off."

Eulalia's spirits were so high she couldn't refrain from joining in the conversation. "Hosea is the most clever metalworker I've ever known. He produces wonders on his miniature forge."

Hosea calmly agreed. False modesty was not one of his attributes.

Eulalia left the blacksmith shop, still rejoicing in her ability to walk with only a faint limp. Eli fell in beside her, raising his hand to the visor of his uniform hat. "Major Eli Moser, Mrs. Holt."

"Of course, Major." Compensating for the guilt she felt because she hadn't remembered his name, she was far more emphatic than she otherwise would have been. "How could I have forgotten you?"

He hadn't realized he had made any impression whatever on her, but he was flattered. She was the most beautiful woman by far in the wagon train company, and from the moment he had first seen her, he had envied Whip Holt. In fact, he had wondered how the crude mountain man, regardless of the esteem in which he seemed to be held by those who had crossed the continent with him, could have won the hand of such a lovely lady. He didn't want to build up his own vanity, but she seemed genuinely pleased to see him. He fell in beside her, openly admiring her beauty. "I wasn't sure you knew me just now."

"Indeed I did." It had been a long time since any man had stared at Eulalia with such obvious interest, and her feeling of joy was doubled. Now that her leg was healing, she was becoming attractive again! Unconsciously, with no idea of what she was doing, she began to flirt subtly with the Major, just as she had flirted with scores of swains in South Carolina before her father had lost their plantation.

"What brings you into town this early in the day?" he wanted to know.

She had no intention of mentioning the wonderful healing of her leg. She didn't know him that well, and besides, he didn't appear to have recalled that she had walked with a decided limp on the occasion of their previous meeting. "I've come to pick up some planks that are being made to my specifications at the sawmill," she said.

He was surprised that a woman would assume such a task, and his expression revealed his feelings.

"My husband is off in the mountains for a few days, hoping to catch and bring home some wild horses," she explained.

If he had a wife that attractive, Eli thought, not even the lure of wild horses could drag him from her side. "Perhaps you'll let me walk with you."

"I'll be delighted." They came to a rut in the village's new road, caused by heavy rains that had fallen two nights earlier, and Eulalia took his arm.

Her touch inflamed Eli Moser. He didn't want to

read too much significance into what might be no more than an innocent gesture. At the same time, however, he hadn't had a woman since setting out for Oregon from Baltimore months earlier, and never had he met anyone who turned his head as Eulalia Holt did. He grinned at her, his eyes searching her face for some sign that would indicate whether the intimacy was deliberate.

Eulalia was lost in her own euphoria. Even on this dirt road, its mud caked hard in ridges, she felt no pain in her ankle as she walked. Before she left for home she wanted to stop in at the new combined office and hospital that had just been constructed for Dr. Martin and ask him to examine her. She supposed she wanted confirmation of her new, flaring hope that the change for the better in her ankle would become total.

Eli saw only her bright, steady smile and concluded that she truly liked him. He had no desire to become embroiled in a dispute with Whip Holt, whom he suspected might be a mean and dangerous opponent, but Eulalia's relations with her husband were her own business. Certainly he had every intention of exploring this budding friendship.

Ginny Dobbs was sitting in the sawmill office, smiling to herself as she recalled every word of her conversation the previous evening with Hector Mullins. Abruptly she returned to the present, her eyes narrowing when she saw the attentive Major Moser at Eulalia's side.

The young women greeted each other, and Eulalia explained her errand. Ginny consulted a list hanging from a nail on the wall. "Your planks are ready," she said. "Eighteen of them."

"Eighteen?"

Again Ginny studied the list. "Whip ordered some of them," she said. "They're shorter and broader than the ones you wanted for your parlor."

"They must be for the kitchen." It was typical of

141

Whip to have forgotten to tell her he had ordered them, and Eulalia laughed helplessly. "There's no way I can load eighteen planks onto my mare and ride her at the same time. Whip is away, Ginny, so I'm afraid I'll have to wait until he comes home and picks them up himself."

"Maybe I can help," Eli said. "I'll have a couple of my men tie your planks into bundles and load them on a pack horse. I'll lead him out to your house myself this noon, if you like. Provided you'll give me a cup of coffee."

"It'll have to be acorn coffee," Eulalia said, smiling broadly. "That's all I have."

"There's nothing I'd like better." Eli continued to grin.

They left together after Eulalia paid for the planks and Eli arranged to have them picked up.

Ginny decided she would have to ask Hector about the character of the deputy commander. The way he and Eulalia were looking at each other spelled trouble—lots of trouble if a man who handled firearms as Whip did became jealous.

VI

A sign was posted on the palisade near the gate of Fort Vancouver: *By order of Colonel Morrison, only authorized personnel are permitted inside the military compound.*

Colonel Lee Blake refused to retaliate in kind. "Every day, especially on weekends, more and more of our people cross the Columbia to visit the Hudson's Bay stores, and every day more of the British come over here. That's a healthy sign. People who visit back and forth aren't going to war with each other."

"I hope you're right," Cathy said.

"I'd like to step up the pace of those visits. Suppose we invite their leaders over here for Sunday dinner day after tomorrow. Nothing fancy, and we don't have to put on airs. The weather is still warm enough to eat outdoors, where we can set up a few simple tables. Since this will be an official function, I'll get the regimental cook and his assistant to help out in the kitchen, so you won't have too much of a chore."

"If that's what you want, dear," Cathy said, aware of her obligations as the American commandant's wife. "I have just two questions. First, I don't know what to wear."

143

"You look good in all your clothes," he replied vaguely.

She sighed, realizing she shouldn't have asked for that kind of assistance from him. "Far more important is what we'll eat. I don't have enough food in the larder for a party."

"That problem is solved," Lee said, smiling. "Mullins, my sergeant major, had the day off today and went hunting. He brought down a buck elk, and he's now presented me with the whole carcass, except for the antlers. I'll have the cooks roast half the animal."

Cathy laughed. "Even a quarter would be too much, but it does solve the meat problem. Some Indians who live up the Willamette have started bringing their produce to Cindy, so I'll have her get us some wild melons, squash, and beans. We shall have our party, Lee, right after church."

Lee sent invitations to the senior officers of the British garrison and Dr. McLoughlin. Colonel Morrison promptly sent a stiff note of regret. Just as promptly, however, Major Roland Pitts and three other officers accepted, as did Dr. John McLoughlin, with all of them indicating they would arrive in time to attend church services prior to the meal. Only a few of the American civilians were invited, with Cathy holding down the list to Dr. Martin, Whip Holt, Ernie von Thalman, and their wives. Lee told her in confidence that Ernie had received a letter from the State Department via a courier who had arrived from Washington City earlier in the week. In the spring, Ernie had been told, President Van Buren intended to appoint him as the first United States agent in the Oregon country. Thus he would become the ranking civilian federal official, relieving Lee of many responsibilities. Presumably, as the population of Oregon increased and territoriality was made official, he would be appointed Governor of the Territory. And between now and spring, the army was directed to construct an office building in the village that would serve as the first seat of the Oregon government.

On Saturday afternoon Whip and Stalking Horse returned in triumph to the ranch leading the partly tamed wild horses.

"These horses will form the nucleus of my herd," he told Eulalia. "Now, if I can just rope a few more before winter, we're off to a great start. By this time next year we'll be selling horses as fast as we can breed them."

She was pleased that their financial future looked so promising, but privately she felt hurt. Whip was so full of his own accomplishments that he had failed to notice the dramatic improvement in her leg. She wanted—and intended—to thank him for insisting that she exercise daily, even when she had become discouraged, and she planned, too, to assure him there would be no need for him to nag her again. Perversely, however, she made up her mind not to mention the subject until he realized on his own that she now walked with only a slight limp.

The atmosphere at the ranch was strained that evening. Whip was tired after his expedition into the mountains and retired early. Eulalia remained awake and spent more than an hour going through the wardrobe she had brought with her from South Carolina. The following day she would wear one of her prettiest dresses to the party at the Blake house. Not only did she have few opportunities to wear attractive clothes, but she hoped to outshine Cathy Blake. Uncertain of the extent and depth of Whip's continuing interest in Cathy, she wanted to force him to recognize the fact that his own wife was even lovelier and more feminine than the woman he had long admired.

Sunday morning the sun rose in a cloudless sky that sparkled on the snow-crested mountains that lay to the east. The weather was balmy, comparable to a day in late spring on the Eastern Seaboard, and a relieved Cathy knew the party could be held outdoors.

A section in the front pew of the church was reserved for the community's leaders and their British guests from the far side of the Columbia River. Tilman Wade was one of the early arrivals, bringing his new neighbor, Sally MacNeill, with him. Sally wanted to loiter outside for a time, explaining that she was enjoying the warmth of the sun. Tilman knew her real reason was a desire to see Paul Thoman, but he did not object. On the contrary, he hoped to intercept Ginny Dobbs—perhaps she would sit with them.

When Paul arrived he was surrounded by the parents of some of the children he taught in the temporary one-room schoolhouse that had been built for him in the village. He chatted with them for a few minutes, and the moment he extricated himself, Sally stood in his path.

His greeting was friendly, but Sally was blunt and minced no words. "I'm still waiting for you to come to my house for a salmon supper," she told him. "Every morning before Hosea goes to work in the blacksmith shop he spends an hour or two fishing. So Dolores and I—she's living with me, you know—always have salmon in the house."

"I've been thinking about visiting you," he said honestly, "but if I may paraphrase the Roman writer, Seneca, there are too few hours in the day."

Sally was puzzled, and her reply was candid. "You just teach at the schoolhouse in the mornings." She made a great effort not to sound hurt.

Paul grinned at her and spoke in a low voice. "I'll tell you something in confidence," he said. "You, too," he added to Tilman, who stood beside Sally as he searched the crowd for Ginny Dobbs. "I've started to work on my own private project."

"I didn't even know you had one," Sally replied.

Paul nodded. "I've used half of my land grant to claim three hundred acres on a little cove I found on the Columbia. It's a perfect place for a shipyard. I'm using my wages as a teacher to buy lumber from Dave Evans, and I'm building the yard myself. It will take me a long time, but I'm in no rush. And once I'm actually in production, I'm going to offer my father a deal. I hope to go into business with him, so that my yard will become associated with the family business back home in Boston." His confident smile indicated that he had found himself and knew what he wanted to do in life.

"I'm glad for you," Sally said. But she realized he was slipping away from her, and she felt forlorn.

Tilman grew tense when he caught a glimpse of Ginny. He was on the verge of excusing himself when Sergeant Major Hector Mullins, his hair slicked, almost unrecognizable in the dress uniform he was wearing for the first time since coming to Oregon, made his way quickly to Ginny's side.

He handed her something, and Tilman saw he was giving her a pair of polished elk's antlers. How Ginny might use the antlers was impossible to guess, but that didn't much matter. Her smile of thanks was so glowing that Tilman averted his gaze. Her interest in Mullins was a crushing blow, and Tilman realized there was little he could do to further his own cause.

An honor guard approached, escorting the visiting British officers and Dr. McLoughlin. Lee Blake, with Cathy at his side, came forward to greet the guests. They were followed by Ernie and Emily von Thalman and Whip and Eulalia Holt. Lee made the necessary introductions.

As the settlers started toward the church, Ginny Dobbs muttered something under her breath and shook her head. Hector Mullins bent down to hear what she was saying. "What's that?"

"Look at Eulalia Holt," she said in a low tone. "The very pretty girl in the fancy silk dress. She has Major Moser on one side of her, and now one of the redcoats is competing with him for her attention."

"That's Major Pitts, the deputy commander of Fort Vancouver," Hector told her. "He's all right, even if he is an Englishman."

"Well, Whip doesn't seem to realize what's going on. Just look at the way Eulalia is flirting with those two!"

"I guess she's one of those women who knows she's beautiful." Hector refrained from saying that he preferred the company of the young woman beside him. He didn't yet know her that well, and his instinct told him not to push Ginny too hard or too fast. After spending years as a bachelor, he knew he wanted her as his wife, and he did not intend to do anything that would interfere with his aim.

"You don't know Whip the way those of us who were with him in the wagon train know him," Ginny said. "He's a fair, honest man, and he's quiet, very quiet. But his insides are made of steel, and may the Lord have mercy on anybody who crosses him. How I'd hate to have him as my enemy."

Hector watched Eulalia walking into the church, turning first to Eli Moser and then to Roland Pitts. She seemed to be enjoying herself thoroughly and obviously relished their attention. "Well," Hector said, "I've heard about mountain men. So I just hope, for his wife's sake, that she doesn't cheat on him."

The only music in the church was provided by Pierre le Rouge, a French-Canadian who had become one of the wagon train's scouts. Formerly interested in Eulalia, he had settled down into bachelorhood and, to the surprise of the community, had gone into partnership with Mack Dougall in establishing a fruit orchard. Now, playing a small mouth organ, he set the pitch for the opening hymn.

The congregation, aware of the visitors' presence, sang with even more gusto than usual. A number of people noted that no one sang with greater fervor than Dr. John McLoughlin.

The Reverend Cavendish delivered his sermon on

148

the subject of the brotherhood of man, which was perfect for the occasion. Frequently, as he stressed the urgent needs of men of all nations to live side by side in peace, the American and British officers in the congregation were seen nodding in unison.

After the services were concluded, the community's leaders and their guests paused to exchange a few words with the clergyman, and then Lee and Cathy Blake led the way to Fort Oregon. The sentries at the gate stood at attention and saluted, but there were no formal military ceremonies, Lee having decided that it would not be an appropriate way to mark the historic occasion.

Tables and chairs had been placed on the new lawn behind the commandant's house, and the weather was so pleasant that everyone remained outside.

John McLoughlin became engaged in a deep conversation with Ernie, and most of the others, with the exception of Eulalia and her two officers, listened attentively, too. "When I first came to the Oregon country," the Hudson's Bay factor said, "there was nothing here but a wilderness. I knew I'd found paradise, of course. The Indian tribes in the area are small, and with the exception of the Rogue, whose villages are near the border of Mexican California, they're peaceful. This whole area has been demanding development and trade for many years, and now you Americans are finally doing what's needed."

"True enough, but it's the Yanks, not the British, who are capitalizing on that potential," McLoughlin declared. "You know, Mr. von Thalman, I can see the handwriting on the wall for Great Britain here. Eventually—and the sooner the better—London will be forced to accept a compromise agreement that will set the border far north of the Columbia River. You people, just by being here, have taken the initiative away from us, and the longer we wait, the more of Oregon you'll have settled."

"Not everyone feels as you do," Ernie said diplomatically.

There was no need to mention the absent Colonel Morrison by name, but McLoughlin's smile was pained. "Every nation has its share of the shortsighted. I don't mind telling you I've already written to my directors, urging them to sell our entire commercial complex here to John Jacob Astor or any other American willing to buy it."

The Americans were stunned, and Whip asked, "Do you think they'll follow your suggestion?"

"Not immediately," the factor said. "My operation still brings them a handsome profit every year, and as your numbers increase, we'll make still more. I think it may take a few more years for London to realize that we're playing a losing game here. I've recommended that we establish a new trading post and fort at some such place as Vancouver Island to the north of here. The idea will begin to make sense when it dawns on them that we're isolated, surrounded on all sides by more and more Yankees."

"I hope your directors will see the situation your way," Lee said thoughtfully. "It's an ideal solution."

Major Roland Pitts interrupted his conversation with Eulalia. "The British Isles are so cramped that we don't think in terms of unlimited space. But it seems to me the Pacific Northwest is so vast that there's more than enough room for you and for us."

"I feel the same way," Lee said. "As I've already written to the War Department, there's enough space in the overall area to accommodate a population of millions."

Cathy, who had gone off to the kitchen, reappeared to announce that dinner was ready. Stressing the informality of the occasion, she suggested that the guests sit anywhere they pleased.

Major Moser and Major Pitts promptly escorted Eulalia to one of the tables, and Whip for the first time was very consciously aware of his wife's flirtatiousness. His eyes narrowed as he watched her. It had never occurred to him to mistrust her, but, now that he thought of it, he had known her only on the wagon train and was unfamiliar with her conduct in a permanent settlement that included people other than her fellow travelers. It was absurd to doubt her now, of course, and he tried to push the offending thought out of his mind. After all, she was an exceptionally attractive girl, and her limp had made her feel inferior to other people, so she was enjoying the attention of the two officers.

Suddenly he realized—her limp was virtually gone!

He remembered that she had been strangely expectant when he had returned from his expedition to the mountains. He realized now that she had been waiting for him to notice the improvement in her condition. He could blame only himself for his failure. Walking to one of the tables, he passed the chair in which Eulalia had just seated herself, and he gripped her shoulder in mute apology.

She looked up at him, startled. Unable to read what was passing through his mind, she jumped to the conclusion that her flirtatiousness with Eli Moser and Roland Pitts was paying dividends. So much the better! She would continue to flirt with them. At least Whip knew she was alive!

The main course consisted of elk chops, which everyone regarded as a delicacy. Dr. McLoughlin and Whip alternated in telling stories about wilderness incidents in which elk meat had saved the lives of starving hunters and trappers. The atmosphere became relaxed, and soon the officers of both garrisons were chatting freely.

Lee Blake was pleased. Thanks to Cathy's talents as a hostess, the party was accomplishing its purpose and was a success.

They were finishing their dessert of fresh berries when the lieutenant who was the duty officer approached Lee in obvious agitation. "Excuse the interruption, sir," he said, "but a dilapidated old ship has just anchored off the village, and a lot of people are coming ashore. About one hundred of them, maybe. The ship is flying the Russian flag, and the first man to come ashore also carried a flag. He planted it, as if he were claiming the Oregon territory in the name of the Czar."

The British officers and Dr. McLoughlin joined in the Americans' hearty laugh, but the news brought the dinner party to an abrupt end, and the participants hurried to the waterfront. The thought crossed Lee's mind that it was too bad the U.S.S. *Washington* was at sea for a few days, trying out her new sails prior to leaving on her long voyage home. Her presence would have put a damper on any claims that representatives of Russia might make.

He could handle the situation, however, and with Major Pitts striding beside him, it appeared that under these circumstances, at least, the American and British military would present a firm, united front.

Whip fell in beside Eulalia, and Major Moser, taking the hint, moved ahead to join his commander.

"Your leg is better," Whip said simply.

He sounded pleased as well as humble, and Eulalia's feeling of resentment dissipated somewhat. "I've been wondering when you'd notice," she said.

"I should have realized when I came home last night," he told her. "I'm sorry."

She knew he never lied, so his contrite air was genuine, and she squeezed his arm. "I have you to thank," she said.

"Rubbish. You've done it yourself."

"I couldn't have managed without you to goad me and prod me," Eulalia said, matching his candor. "But you won't need to do it again. I intend to ride every single day until all the lameness is gone."

They soon reached the waterfront, where a platoon of American infantry arrived at a trot in response to the order Lee had given before leaving the garrison. It was apparent that Colonel Morrison also was aware of what was happening because a full company of armed redcoats lined the far shore of the Columbia.

It quickly became clear, however, that military precautions were unnecessary. The last of the Russians, their numbers reduced to slightly fewer than one hundred, were stumbling ashore, and most were in a pitiful state. Clutching their few belongings, they were emaciated, and many seemed dazed.

One member of the group seemed well-fed, however, and he straightened when he saw the American and British officers approaching. "I have the honor to represent the government of Imperial Russia," Igor Doznevkov declared in heavily accented English, "and in the name of our great Czar, I lay claim to the territory known as Oregon."

Dr. Martin had already arrived on the scene, as had many other settlers, and he spoke at once to Lee and Major Pitts, who were facing the Russian together. "From the looks of them, most of these people soon will be dead if they aren't given nourishment." He turned to the man in charge. "How long has it been since they've been fed a decent meal?"

Doznevkov made no reply.

Anton Wizneuski, himself pale and thin, came forward and introduced himself as a physician. Speaking British-accented English, he said distinctly, "It has been so long since we have been given a proper meal that no one can remember the last time it happened."

"Are any of your people suffering from communicable diseases, Dr. Wizneuski?" Bob Martin asked.

"Not to the best of my knowledge," Anton replied painfully. "I've done what little I could for them. Our living conditions were not good when we reached Alaska. We were supposed to change ships there, but no new vessel was available, so we came down the coast in our old, leaking tub. To make matters worse, most of the supplies taken on board at Sitka were spoiled and rotting. We've had no food at all for the past five days, and we've been restricted to a few cups of stale water every day."

"Moser," Lee Blake ordered, "have the platoon escort these people to the garrison. Give them temporary quarters in the new barracks that haven't yet been occupied, and see that they're given a meal from our stores as soon as possible."

"Yes, sir." Eli Moser began to organize the removal of the Russians to Fort Oregon.

He was given unexpected help by two of the Russian women, even though they, like the others, were weak and exhausted. Lisolette Arbo, it quickly developed, spoke good English, and Olga Runkova could also speak the language a little, her lessons with Anton Wizneuski during the long voyage having made her reasonably proficient. The two women were able to translate Major Moser's directives into Russian.

"After they've eaten," Lee said, trying to create some measure of order out of chaos, "we'll take their names and make certain that families are kept together."

"I can't let you Yankees accept the entire burden for these poor people," John McLoughlin said. "I'm going back to Fort Vancouver, and I'll send over a boatload of wheat, beans, bacon, and smoked venison immediately, with more to follow tomorrow. Their claims to Oregon are absurd, but we share the responsibility for not allowing these—these scarecrows to starve."

The British deputy commander and his junior officers took their leave, too, and after thanking their host and hostess, Major Pitts drew Lee aside. "Colonel," he said, "I hope we can make a substantial contribution from our Fort Vancouver stores. If my recommendation carries any weight, rest assured we shall. However," he added in embarrassment ,"as you know, I don't have a final word."

"I appreciate your offer," Lee replied as they shook hands and exchanged salutes. "But even if you can't help, we'll manage."

Ernie had already gone ahead with Whip and the women to see what could be done for the wretched new arrivals, and Lee was the last to start toward Fort Oregon.

Igor Doznevkov was waiting for him and started to walk beside him. "Colonel," he said, "I must protest the manner in which you have taken charge of the people who are in my care."

Lee, who had disliked him at first sight, stared at him for a moment. "Do you have alternatives to offer?"

"They should sleep on board our ship, as they have done for months. And those who are healthy will find food in the forest and rivers."

"From the looks of them," Lee said, "none of them could survive long enough to hunt and fish. As for your ship, the stench is unbearable, even from a distance. I urge you to sink it, but if you refuse, please oblige us by having it moved elsewhere on the river."

Doznevkov bristled. "I warn you, sir," he said, "I will make a full report to St. Petersburg on your assumption of authority."

"Report and be damned to you," Lee said. "You're on American soil now, and neither we nor the British across the river intend to let people die of starvation. As to your claims to Oregon, you're too late. We're already here, and so are the British, and our governments are trying to work out a compromise that's fair to both. Tell that to St. Petersburg."

"Colonel," Doznevkov declared, "on behalf of the Russian government, I cannot accept either your claim or that of the British."

"Accept or reject, it's all the same to me," Lee said. "If you're smart, you'll take my word for it that we're in Oregon to stay."

"And if I refuse to accept your word, Colonel?" Doznevkov demanded haughtily.

Lee gestured in the direction of the Fort Oregon palisades. "My troops and my guns," he said, "are capable of speaking for themselves."

News of the arrival of the Russian immigrants electrified people on both sides of the Columbia River. Scores of the American settlers volunteered their help, and Eulalia, Cindy, and Emily von Thalman spent almost all of their time with the bewildered refugees. Dr. McLoughlin lived up to his promise of generosity, and even Colonel Phillips Morrison unbent sufficiently to send supplies of food, blankets, and other necessities.

On the day after the Russians' arrival, the *Washington* returned from her trial run and prepared to take on food and water before sailing for Baltimore. Her presence gave teeth to Lee Blake's demand that the decrepit Russian ship be moved, but before that could be accomplished, she began to sink. Apparently she was even more exhausted than the people she had transported such a long distance.

Afraid she would be a hazard to both American and British shipping, Captain Ingalls sent his men out in longboats to tow the Russian ship toward the mouth of the Columbia. The sailors rowed for several miles, aided by a strong tide, and then, following their captain's orders, they set fire to the hapless ship, which burned to the waterline.

"I'm afraid the poor devils have really had their bridges burned behind them," Lee said.

Dr. Anton Wizneuski refused to rest, in spite of his own debilitated condition, and spent all of his time ministering to the Russians. Bob Martin accompanied him on his rounds and was deeply impressed by his medical skill and sincerity.

On the third day of the Russians' stay at Fort Oregon, the American physician drew his colleague into an empty room and leaned against the window. "What are your personal plans, Dr. Wizneuski?" he asked.

Anton shrugged. "I have had no time to think of them," he said.

"Well I've had plenty of time to think. Assuming that the Russians accept the offer to join our community, there will be six hundred of us here. Still more are due to arrive in the next wagon train, and I've learned there are no doctors of medicine in that party. So I gladly make you the offer to join me in my practice. You won't grow rich, but I can promise you'll be kept plenty busy. In the spring I plan to expand the hospital that's been built for me. At least you won't go hungry, because most people pay for medical services with food."

"After the near-starvation I've known," Anton replied, grinning, "I need no other incentive. I accept, Dr. Martin, on condition you tell me why you're being so generous to me."

"I not only like the way you work," Bob said bluntly, "but with all the work to be done, I already need an associate, and that demand is going to become much greater. I can tell you from experience, there's more than enough work here for two of us."

Ample food, clean living conditions, and plentiful rest enabled the Russians to regain their health and strength, and thanks to the dedicated care of the two physicians, there were no more deaths. The younger members of the party were the first to recover, and Olga Runkova, aided by a strong constitution, soon was pitching in and helping the American women care for the others.

Lisolette Arbo became much stronger, too, but

spent much of her time alone in one corner of the dormitory facilities in which the Russian women and children were quartered. None of the party seemed comfortable in the presence of Igor Doznevkov, but Lisolette went out of her way to avoid the man, quickly ducking out of the dormitory whenever he appeared.

The settlers' council held a meeting, and a policy quickly was forged. The Russians would be invited to join the American community provided they renounced their loyalty to the Czar and swore to obey the laws of the United States and Oregon. Those who accepted would be housed temporarily in the homes of American settlers, many of whom had already volunteered their hospitality. Those who refused the conditions would be asked to leave.

Doznevkov was summoned to the commandant's office to hear the decision from Lee and Ernie, the former remarking, "He's going to have fits. I don't know who he thinks he is or what authority he believes he wields, but we'll have to straighten him out."

The Russian entered the office, clicked his heels, and stood at attention. Lee waved him to a seat.

Ernie von Thalman carefully and slowly explained the position the council had taken. "We're struggling to establish our own colony in Oregon," he said, "so we're going to the limit of our hospitality. Any of your people who don't want to accept our offer are free to go elsewhere and settle on their own."

"But it's only fair to tell you," Lee added, "that my garrison soon will grow larger, and so will our entire community. We've claimed all of Oregon, and Washington City intends to assert that claim in no uncertain terms. So, wherever you may settle, you'll still be under American authority."

Doznevkov was bitter. "You give us little choice," he said. "With winter coming we have no opportunity to make our homes elsewhere, and you have destroyed our ship."

"It destroyed itself," Lee said, curbing his impatience. "It would have become a wreck in a few hours and would have been a menace to shipping. You can't create an international incident out of that unfortunate occurrence."

"My charges and I will obey your commands because we must," Doznevkov replied.

"Not so fast," Ernie said. "We're holding no guns to your heads."

"Although I am forced to renounce my sovereign," Doznevkov declared, ignoring the comment, "I still have a duty to perform for Russia. I will write letters, some to St. Petersburg, which I hope another Russian ship will pick up, and some to the Russian legation in Washington City, which I plan to hire a courier to carry for me."

"That won't be necessary," Lee said. "We'll gladly give any letters you may write to one of our military couriers. The very next one who comes here."

Doznevkov's expression made it clear he placed no trust in the Americans and preferred to handle the matter himself.

"We're making no secret of our policy, I assure you," Ernie said. "You may be certain the State Department will explain it in detail to the Russian Minister."

"My own explanation," Doznevkov declared, "will make it plain that my charges and I have been coerced. As for myself, I shall refuse your hospitality. Two other members of our party will assist me in building a house in the forest and I will live there for as long as necessary."

Not waiting for a reply, he stood abruptly, turned, and stalked out.

"I won't put too much faith in any oath of allegiance he swears," Ernie said dryly.

Lee walked to the window. "He's mean, all right, and a troublemaker. Between us, we'll have to keep watch on him. I have my own suspicions about him, but I'd rather not talk about them until I have something substantial in the way of evidence against him." Suddenly he started to laugh and pointed toward the window.

Ernie joined him and stared, too. "Good Lord," he said.

The sturdy Olga Runkova was walking across the compound, with a huge iron caldron swinging from each hand, and she seemed unconscious of bearing any physical burden.

"Now there's a woman," Ernie said as they watched her disappear through the gate of the fort, "who can do the work of a man!"

Olga trudged toward the village, never slowing her pace, and soon reached her destination. A search of only a minute or two was all she needed to find the blacksmith shop. As she came in, Ted Woods recognized her as one of the Russian refugees, and he said politely, "Good morning, ma'am. What can I do for you?"

Olga placed the caldrons on the ground in front of him. "These were salvaged before our disgusting ship sank. Soon we are moving into the homes of the Americans, and we will need property of our own. So I bring you these to be repaired, but I warn you—I have no money to pay for the work."

"I don't want any money," Ted said. "Everybody here is helping out." He picked up one caldron, examined it in silence, and then inspected the other. "Sorry, ma'am, these are beyond repair."

Olga knew only how to deal with artisans in her own Russian village. "Aha! So you do want money!"

Ted's dark complexion grew darker. "I've already told you, I don't want a penny!"

"Perhaps you are too lazy to make the repairs, then?" Olga asked sarcastically.

He glared at her for a moment but managed to keep his violent temper under control. Then he picked up a steel spike and, using only his bare hands, drove several holes in the bottoms of the caldrons.

In spite of herself, although she wasn't afraid of him or any other man, Olga was impressed by his overpowering physical strength.

Ted looked contemptuously at his handiwork. "Just like I told you," he said, "these pots weren't worth saving. They must be a hundred years old."

Olga was indignant. "At least they would have lasted us a little longer. Now you've made them useless."

Ted turned and called to someone in the back of the shop. The young woman's eyes widened when Hosea came forward to join his partner. He was not only tiny, the top of his head not even reaching the giant blacksmith's shoulder, but he was the first black man she had ever seen. The pair conferred in low tones for a few moments, and Hosea's gestures were expansive. Then, scarcely glancing at the customer, he returned to his miniature forge at the rear of the shop.

"My partner and me," Ted said, "will salvage the iron in these pots and make one new one for you. A good one." He grinned broadly and suddenly. "And I'll give you my personal guarantee it will last for another hundred years."

She couldn't help returning his smile. "I don't believe I'll need it that long," she said. "How much money will I owe you?"

"I already told you," Ted bellowed. "There's no charge!"

"I cannot accept a free gift," Olga said with dignity. "It is true that my funds are almost exhausted, but there must be some way I can pay you for the work."

Ted knew what poverty meant and couldn't help sympathizing with this woman, far from home and almost penniless, who was being forced to make her way in an alien wilderness settlement. "Do you know how to sew?" he asked tentatively.

Olga regarded the question as absurd. "Naturally," she snapped, her ire rising again.

He guessed she was the only woman he had ever encountered whose hair-trigger temper matched his own, and he backed down hastily. "Well," he said, "I was thinking maybe we could make an exchange. I'll fix this pot for you, and maybe you could mend some shirts of mine that are getting rips in them."

"Gladly," she said. Nodding toward Hosea working at the forge, she asked, "Does he have shirts that also need to be repaired?"

Ted shook his head. "Dolores takes care of things like that for him. They're going to be married one of these days. I'll be right back." He disappeared through a door at the rear of the shop.

As Olga waited for him, the thought occurred to her that the blacksmith appeared to have no wife. It was odd, she reflected, that such a handsome giant should be unmarried. She would have assumed that any single woman in the community would have been delighted to have such a strong man as a husband.

Ted returned, carrying several shirts of heavy, faded wool. "They're clean," he said. "I washed them myself."

That statement confirmed his single status. "When shall I return?" she asked.

"We have some other work to do first," he said. "So it'll be the day after tomorrow before your new pot is ready for you. But there's no rush. Wait until you finish mending the shirts."

"They will be done long before the day after tomorrow," Olga said.

Her words made a sharp impression on him. His late wife had put off such chores, frequently forcing him to wait for many days before she attended to them. This woman was prompt, a virtue he prized, and he looked at her with new respect. "I'll be grateful to you, ma'am. I don't have a decent shirt to my name. Crossing most of North America in the wagon train was hard on most of what I own."

Olga knew what he meant. Her own wardrobe had become dilapidated on the long and tiring journey from St. Petersburg to Oregon. "If you have some material or can obtain some," she heard herself say, "I'll gladly make some new shirts for you."

Ted was stunned. "I'm like you are," he said. "I won't take free gifts. I'd be much obliged to you for the shirts, but I'd have to do something for you in return."

She thought for a moment. "The handle of my frying pan broke off during a storm at sea and has become useless. And my only jewelry, a silver necklace that was a gift from my late husband, is twisted out of shape, and I can't repair it."

Ah! She was a widow! "You just made yourself a deal, ma'am," he said solemnly. "I'll take care of your frying pan so you'll think it's new, and Hosea will help me fix your necklace so you won't even know anything ever happened to it."

Olga extended her hand. "We have made a bargain."

Her clasp, he discovered, was firm and strong, that of a woman long accustomed to working with her hands. He grinned at her as she gathered the shirts and left the shop. Not until she had gone did he realize that he didn't know her name and hadn't told her his. But no harm had been done. He would be seeing her again on at least a couple of occasions, so there would be an opportunity then to become better acquainted.

Hosea grinned broadly when his partner and friend returned to his own forge, but he made no comment.

Ted felt color rising to his face and couldn't understand why he was flushing.

Eulalia spent an hour riding in the morning and repeated the exercise at the end of the day. She no longer needed Whip's urging, and, although the day-by-day improvement in her leg was virtually imperceptible, she fervently believed now that soon her recovery would be complete.

She completed most of her immediate chores at the ranch house after dark, but most of the tasks that had to be done in the unfinished dwelling were put aside for the moment as she continued to spend most of her days with Emily and Cathy, looking after the Russian refugees. Eulalia spent most of her time in the company of the withdrawn Lisolette Arbo.

Little by little Eulalia learned the basic story of the half-French, half-Russian girl who had spent the better part of her life in Paris and London. But there were mysterious blanks in Lisolette's background, and she not only fell silent but actually appeared frightened when pressed, so Eulalia stopped questioning her.

It was so easy to sympathize with the girl, who was attractive and sensitive, well-bred and highly intelligent. Eulalia couldn't help wondering what she was concealing and brought up the subject to Whip at supper one night.

As always, he was eminently practical. "It may be your imagination and nothing else," he said.

"I think not," she replied, wondering why he went out of his way to belittle her.

"I reckon most of the Russians have problems of one kind or another," he said, shrugging. "If the girl wants to talk, she'll open up to you. If she doesn't, there isn't much you can do about it."

That ended Eulalia's open speculation on the subject.

The following morning Whip accompanied Eulalia into the village to buy some nails from Ted Woods and to bid farewell to Captain Ingalls. The *Washing-*

ton was sailing shortly before noon, and the settlers would be on their own again.

Eulalia went directly to the barracks. This was an important day for the Russians. At noon Ernie von Thalman would administer the oath of allegiance to them. Immediately thereafter, the Americans who were offering the Russians refuge would come to Fort Oregon, make their individual arrangements with the newcomers, and take them off to their temporary homes.

The troops paraded to the waterfront for the farewell to the frigate, and the crack of their rifles was answered by the roar of the *Washington's* guns as she sailed toward the mouth of the Columbia and the open waters of the Pacific. The ceremonies completed, Major Moser marched the troops back to the fort.

Whip, who had little else to occupy him for the moment, decided to accompany Lee Blake to the barracks to watch the ceremonies that would incorporate the Russians into the community. Ernie had been waiting for Lee, the symbol of American authority, to appear, and as soon as he came into the large dormitory, the ceremony began.

One by one the Russians came forward, formally relinquished their status as subjects of the Czar, and agreed to obey the United States Constitution, the laws of the nation, and those of the Oregon country. Parents carefully repeated the formula on behalf of their minor children.

Their health restored, the Russians were in high spirits. Their bleak existence had changed, and their future was far brighter than ever before in their lives. They knew, too, as Ernie had taken care to explain to them, that he would seek a ruling from the State Department as to whether they would now acquire full American citizenship. Inasmuch as virtually all immigrants to the United States became citizens without delay and were entitled to the privileges of that standing, he felt reasonably certain no hitches would develop. The peasants and kulaks who, like their ancestors before them, had known stern repression and had been subject to the unpredictable whims of czars and the nobility, were overjoyed by the prospect.

Only Igor Doznevkov and two insignificant, ordinary-looking men were less than wholehearted in their renunciations of Imperial Russia. The two men mumbled their responses of acceptance of responsibility to the United States. Doznevkov, however, who came forward partway through the ceremony, was arrogant, reading the oath in a voice dripping with sarcasm. Even the least knowing of the spectators realized that he was being anything but sincere.

Lisolette Arbo did not volunteer to come forward and, Eulalia thought, seemed to be trying to make herself invisible in the background. Not until all the other Russians had participated and Ernie asked if any remained did she come forward slowly. Eulalia saw that she was deathly pale and that her hands were trembling.

Lee and Whip, standing at one side of the dormitory, were also watching, and the former, his experience making him alert to every nuance in such a situation, noticed that Lisolette glanced very quickly in the direction of Doznevkov, her body rigid.

The man inclined his head only a tiny fraction of an inch. Only then did she take the oath.

"Come with me to my office," Lee said to Whip. "There's something I want to show you."

They walked in silence across the parade ground, and when they reached the office, even though only an orderly was on duty in the outer room, Lee closed his door before speaking. "I'm sure you remember the problems that plagued Tonie Martin, long before she married Bob, during the early stages of your journey across the country," he said.

Whip nodded. "Sure. Because she had been born in

Russia and her parents were still there, the Russian legation in Washington City tried to nail her to a wall and force her to work for them. They even sent agents of their secret police who did their damnedest to make her commit sabotage against the wagon train, but she wouldn't do it." Whip was slightly puzzled, unable to imagine why that subject should arise now and why the commandant of the American garrison was being so secretive.

"I believe we face a similar problem right now," Lee said. "I've suspected Igor Doznevkov from the first time I saw him. I spent years in military intelligence work, you'll remember, and I'm ready to swear that he fits the pattern of a secret police agent. His manner, his bearing, his attitudes all suggest it."

Whip nodded.

"Well, I believe he has a hold over that young woman, Lisolette Arbo. I'm also willing to wager that the two Russian men who muttered the oath may be under his influence. So far I'm just going on a hunch, perhaps a little more."

"What makes you think Doznevkov is forcing the Arbo girl to work for him?" Whip asked.

Lee related in detail what he had seen before she had taken the oath of allegiance. Rarely did Whip Holt demonstrate a sense of excitement, but now his eyes lighted. "At supper, just last night," he said, "Eulalia was talking about some secret or other that she thinks the Arbo girl is harboring. To be honest with you, Lee, I thought it was just one of those whims women get, and I didn't pay much attention."

"What else did Eulalia say about her?"

"Well, the girl is half-French and half-Russian. She was brought up in France and England, and she didn't go to Russia until her folks died and she wanted to claim her father's estate. The court ruled against her, and then they wouldn't allow her to leave the country."

"That fits!" Lee exclaimed.

"I don't remember if there was anything else, but we can ask Eulalia."

"If you don't mind, I'd like to keep her completely out of this. I'm mentioning this whole subject only to you, Whip, and I'd very much like your help."

"You bet," was the immediate response. "I'll do anything I can."

"I know, and that's why I'm turning to you. Also because I know I can trust you implicitly."

Whip nodded his thanks.

"So far," Lee said, "I'm just thrashing around in a sea of uncertainties and conjectures. All I have are some half leads based on my background as an intelligence officer. I have no concrete information that would convict Doznevkov in a court of law. And far more important, in the view of our isolated position here, thousands of miles from American civilization, I have no idea what plans Doznevkov may be hatching to cause irreparable harm to the American cause in Oregon."

"Maybe we ought to throw him out of the settlement," Whip declared.

Lee shook his head. "That's the last thing I want to do. I prefer to let him begin to develop his plans—even to performing some overt act—and then catch him before he goes too far."

"I see."

"That's where the Arbo girl comes in. If, as I believe, he has a hold over her, he may include her in his sabotage plans in some way. He may make her a party to his scheme and try to compel her to work for him."

Again Whip nodded.

"That's where you come in. My rank and my job as commandant here make it impossible for me to do anything myself, but you're less visible. You're a member of the council, but to an outsider like Doznevkov, you're just another ordinary settler. So I want you to keep a close watch over the Arbo girl, Whip, to be sure that Doznevkov doesn't try to use her to hatch some scheme of his own against the settlement. If he communicates with her and she becomes upset, we'll know that something is afoot. Precisely how we'll react will depend on the situation that arises. In the meantime, we can at least be reasonably sure that the girl comes to no harm."

"The way I see it," Whip said, "there's one big obstacle in my way. How in thunderation can I keep an eye on the girl?"

"Insist that she stay at your house," Lee said. "I don't know who may be scheduled to take her in, but you'll have to ride roughshod over them. Make an issue out of it, if you must."

Whip nodded, then sighed. "That's all well and good. But you don't want me to mention any of this to Eulalia?"

"Not yet. She might say something to the Arbo girl or confide in one of her friends. And this situation demands secrecy."

"Well," Whip said, "I hope she understands."

"Of course she will! You have a solid marriage." Lee spoke with assurance, but privately he hoped that Whip didn't return the continuing interest that Cathy inadvertently showed in him.

Hitching up his belt, Whip spoke grimly. "I'll do it!" he said.

VII

The presidential aspirations of United States Senator Henry Clay of Kentucky were recognized throughout Washington City, and that fact, combined with his leadership of the Whig minority in the Senate, made him a formidable opponent of an administration still struggling to overcome the effects of the Panic of 1837. So Martin Van Buren, who was certain to be the Democrats' candidate in a bid for reelection, responded with immediate courtesy when Clay sought a private meeting with him on "a matter of the most crucial national interest."

Taller than the President but equally balding and overweight, the Kentuckian could be benign and charming when he chose. In the presence of the man he hoped to oppose at the polls, however, his manner was grim, almost forbidding. He bowed stiffly, his handshake was formal as he entered Van Buren's office, and he perched uncomfortably on the edge of the chair he was offered, making it plain that in no way did he regard this visit as social.

Ordinarily the President would have offered him a drink of the whiskey that both occasionally enjoyed, but under the circumstances he was wary, and his own manner was restrained. "I gather you have a problem, Henry," he said, trying in vain to sound amiable.

"No, Mr. President, the United States faces a very serious problem." Clay tugged at his cravat of black silk, which made his high collar stand still higher. "A friend in the State Department has informed me confidentially that Russia is intending to announce her claim to the entire Oregon country in the immediate future."

"Your informant is correct." Van Buren silently damned the unnamed official who had talked out of turn. "I've been planning to notify the Senate at an appropriate time."

"I would have thought, sir, that you'd have felt obligated to tell us the news as soon as you yourself learned it!"

"That's a matter of opinion," the President replied coldly. "I don't want the information leaked prematurely to the press. I see no need to alarm the general public."

"The American people have the right to be told about this ridiculous claim!" The Senator's tone was sharp.

Van Buren replied in kind. "I require no instructions from anyone—not even you, Henry—regarding my obligation to the people of this country."

"Before I make an address on the subject in the Senate," Clay said, "I wanted to do you the courtesy of inquiring what steps you may be taking to counter the position taken by the Russians."

"Their legation has already been notified that the United States has established a prior claim. We have also made it clear to the Czar's Minister here that our first settlers have already established their homes in Oregon and that additional wagon trains are even now traveling to Oregon."

"Mere words, sir. My State Department friend says the Russians also have sent an expedition to Oregon, sponsored by Prince Orlev, who recently was appointed First Minister. In other words, the Russian government assumes responsibility for their settlers."

"Your information is quite accurate." Van Buren allowed himself the luxury of a tight smile.

"Exchanges of communications with the Russian legation are nothing but lawyers' letters, Mr. President. We need to show our teeth to the Czar."

The President assumed control of the conversation. "You're thinking in my terms, Henry. I wanted to take strong, affirmative action before I notified the Senate, much less the public at large. And that's precisely what I've been doing in the past ten days."

The Kentuckian's expression indicated that he had hoped the President had been negligent. "Are you prepared to tell me any of those actions, sir?"

"Of course—in confidence, pending my receipt of confirmation of various steps. A navy frigate was scheduled to sail from Charleston this very morning with two hundred and fifty soldiers on board to augment our new garrison at Fort Oregon."

Clay couldn't help but feel relieved. "I'm pleased to hear that!"

"General Scott is to keep close watch on the situation, and he plans to send still more men if Colonel Blake believes he needs them."

"Ah!" The Senator didn't quite know what to say.

"It will also interest you to know that earlier this week I held a private, unpublicized meeting with John Jacob Astor, who came here from New York at my request. He and his associates are meeting the Russian challenge and the continuing opposition of the British to our settlement of Oregon. They're currently organizing an expedition consisting of four merchant ships that will sail to Oregon as soon as possible. Those ships will carry supplies of all kinds that our settlers will need, including one shipload of live cattle."

The Senator was impressed. "It appears that I owe you an apology, Mr. President."

"In addition," Van Buren said, sitting back in his chair and folding his hands over his paunch, "just yesterday I had a visit from Paul Thoman, the Boston shipbuilder. His son is a member of our settlement in Oregon and apparently he intends to build a shipyard there. So the father is sending a merchantman carrying tools and other equipment the young man will need."

Clay realized he could no longer accuse the Administration of indifference or laxity. "I must commend you, sir."

"There's one thing more." Van Buren was smiling broadly now. "I've authorized the expenditure of a large sum of federal funds—one hundred thousand dollars, to be exact—to be spent on various items such as plows for our settlers in Oregon. These supplies will be forwarded overland by way of Sam Brentwood's depot in Independence. Each settler will be given whatever he needs and will be granted a very generous, long-term loan to repay the government."

Clay tried to make the best of a political situation that, rather than help his own cause, would bring great credit to the present occupant of the White House. "I must congratulate you for being so farsighted and thorough, Mr. President," he said lamely.

Only now did Martin Van Buren finally offer his visitor a drink of whiskey.

The vigorous opposition to Great Britain's Whig government led by Sir Robert Peel was so vigorous and insistent that members of the Cabinet were kept busy daily in the debates that raged without end in both Houses of Parliament. So the Prime Minister, Lord Melbourne, always was relieved when he could slip away to his country estate outside London for the weekend. Only here, as he frequently remarked, could he and the members of his cabinet find the peace and quiet that would enable them to discuss their long-range problems and establish policies.

The Prime Minister's guest on this particular weekend was his Foreign Secretary, Lord Palmerston, and they worked well together because they were cut from the same mold. Both were born aristocrats, yet both had strong liberal leanings in spite of their callousness to the lot of the common working man. Here their similarities ended.

Melbourne, handsome and dashing, had lived a bachelor's existence since his separation, a decade and a half earlier, from his wife, Lady Caroline Lamb, whose affair with the poet Lord Byron had created a scandal. He was the political tutor of young Queen Victoria, who was only one of many women who admired him greatly. Noted for his caution, he was slow to make up his mind on a question of state and slower to act.

The far more gregarious and socially inclined Palmerston was so ordinary in appearance and dress that he frequently passed unnoticed in a crowd. He was unaware of the phenomenon, however, because his mind churned so furiously that he was invariably preoccupied. Far more brilliant and daring than his superior, he was accused by Peel and the Tories of being too impulsive for his own or Britain's good, and there was a measure of justice to the charge.

Nothing had been said about affairs of state when the pair had arrived in time for dinner the previous evening, and instead, somewhat to Palmerston's dismay, Melbourne had gossiped idly about their many mutual friends. This morning they had gone for a brisk canter, and only now, at the breakfast table, did the Prime Minister appear ready to settle down to business.

He ate sparingly, as was his custom, while Palmerston loaded his plate at the sideboard and ate with great relish. "This joint of beef tastes better cold this morning than it did hot last night," he said. "And these kippers are delicious. I must find out where your housekeeper buys them."

Melbourne did not reply and instead asked abruptly, "What's your reaction to the announcement in St. Petersburg, Henry?"

Palmerston instantly put frivolity aside. "I assume, William, you refer to the Russian claim to the Oregon country."

"I find it ridiculous," the Prime Minister declared.

"Quite so. They had Oregon but never attempted to settle it and then formally abandoned it. No claim they might make now should be regarded as valid."

"Then," Melbourne said, "we tell them—in polite terms, naturally—to go to the devil."

"I disagree, William," the Foreign Secretary said, returning to the sideboard. "I recommend that we remind them rather forcibly of our claim but that we refrain from discouraging their ambitions."

Melbourne looked startled.

"Their navy is weak, their merchant marine is puny, and even if the expedition they sent to Oregon has managed through some miracle to get there, they lack the means to support a colony. They're finding it almost beyond their capacity to maintain themselves in Alaska."

"All the more reason—"

"Hear me out, William. Which claim threatens us more, that of the United States or that of Russia?"

"The Americans can cause us great harm, that's obvious. Their first settlers are digging in, they're sending many more, and I was surprised to read in a War Office report that they've built a fort and staffed it with experienced soldiers."

"Now you begin to understand my point," Palmerston said, smiling slightly.

"I do not. And I don't enjoy riddles at this time of day," Melbourne said peevishly.

"The Americans may steal Oregon from under our noses, that much is plain," the Foreign Secretary said, his manner patient. "But we have literally nothing to fear from the Russians. So I advocate a policy of limited and private cooperation with the Russians in Oregon."

"You're joking, Henry."

"Indeed I'm not, William. To whatever degree the Russians may be able to create mischief, I prefer to see it directed against the Americans than against us. Anything they might do to loosen the American hold on Oregon would be welcome. We'll have ample time later to squeeze out the Russians."

"A Machiavellian maneuver," the Prime Minister said, smiling.

"I think of it as Palmerstonian," the Foreign Secretary replied. "Keep in mind that our position there is becoming precarious. The Hudson's Bay factor is cooperating far too freely with the Americans."

"Can't he be restrained?"

"It isn't that easy," Palmerston said, frowning. "I've lunched with several of the Hudson's Bay directors—strictly on an informal basis, you know. It wouldn't do at all if the Tories thought we were trying to influence what a privately owned company does. Be that as it may, the directors haven't been encouraging. Some of them are in sympathy with the position their factor has taken."

"Then there's nothing more we can do."

"There might be one thing. Members of the Royal Family are major stockholders in Hudson's Bay, and you have great influence over Queen Victoria—"

"No, Henry." Lord Melbourne spoke with quiet emphasis. "I've been Her Majesty's adviser in matters relating to government and administration. But I'm quite certain I'd be given a very chilly reception at Windsor Castle if I presumed to interfere in anything relating to her private investments."

"The empire stands to lose a large portion of Oregon, William!" Palmerston exclaimed.

The Prime Minister shrugged. "The empire is expanding rapidly all over the world, Henry. I'll grant you that Oregon is a rich and fertile country, but I simply cannot take advantage of my friendship with Her Majesty by approaching her on this matter."

"Then we must make every effort ourselves to insure that the territory will be British."

"Every effort short of an act of war," Melbourne said. "The establishment of an American garrison there speaks for itself, and the Yankees are a belligerent lot."

"Perhaps we can turn their belligerence to our own advantage in some way, William. I intend to keep a close watch on the situation there. Oregon is a great prize, and I don't intend to lose a single acre of it!"

Eulalia Holt was troubled. Perhaps she had been wrong when she thought Whip was still interested in Cathy Blake. She had been stunned when he had first suggested, then insisted, that they give Lisolette Arbo refuge. She herself liked and felt sorry for the girl, but it seemed strange that her husband, so fully occupied breaking in his new horses and working with Stalking Horse to put a fence around the property, should concern himself with the plight of the young Russian woman.

She had to admit that since Lisolette had been living with them, Whip had paid relatively little attention to the Russian woman when she was in his presence. He was polite enough, but he remained slightly removed, which was his way in his relations with most women. All the same, he was curious about her, frequently asking whether she had received any visitors at the ranch and, on her rare trips into the village, wondering whom she had seen there.

Unable to discover any impropriety in Whip's relations with Lisolette, Eulalia gradually relaxed somewhat, the process hastened by her own sympathy for the girl. Lisolette eagerly offered her help around the house and worked as hard as Eulalia to put the place in shape. But she seemed to shun social life, often finding excuses to refuse to visit the village and accepting no invitations from the Russians she had known on her long journey. Her only real friends appeared to be the busy Dr. Wizneuski and Olga Runkova. She appeared pleased whenever she learned that one or the other had inquired after her, but she made no attempt to see them.

Lisolette's seemingly deliberate self-isolation was a matter of growing concern to Eulalia, and one day she insisted that the girl accompany her into the village. They went first to the blacksmith shop. When Paul Thoman came in to pick up some special tools that had been made for his new shipyard, Eulalia introduced Lisolette to him. To her surprise they were soon chatting, and while she attended to her other errands, they remained outside the shop, discussing literature.

Of course! All at once Eulalia realized that what Lisolette needed was the company of young men with whom she had interests in common. Acting on sudden impulse, Eulalia invited Paul to the ranch for Sunday dinner after church, and he quickly accepted.

Whip approved heartily when his wife told him what she had done. "Good!" he said. "The more she sees of Americans, the better it will be for her." He offered no explanation of his cryptic remark.

On Sunday Paul was in high spirits, and while the venison that would provide the main course was roasting, he said that he was making better progress than he had anticipated in building his small shipyard. "Two of your Russians are helping me," he told Lisolette. "Dmitri Haznyev and Boris Sakolov."

"I know them only slightly," Lisolette said. "They and their wives are good people, but I find their peasant Russian difficult to understand and even more difficult to speak."

"We're just beginning to talk a little," Paul said. "They work hard, I can tell you, and they have spirit!

As that great English poet of the last century, Oliver Goldsmith wrote, 'Forc'd from their homes, a melancholy train, To traverse climes beyond the western seas—' "

"I beg your pardon," Lisolette interrupted, "but you have made an error. 'Beyond the western main' is what Goldsmith wrote."

Paul reddened. "You're right," he muttered in embarrassment.

Whip choked down a laugh, and Eulalia averted her face to hide her smile.

Paul hastily changed the subject. "I suppose you've heard the latest news. Your friend, Olga Runkova, is going to open a small tavern in the village. She's going into partnership with Dolores."

"Dolores!" Eulalia was surprised.

"It seems she's always wanted to own a place that sells food. Hosea is building the tavern, and Ted Woods has been dragooned into helping him. I look forward to taking my ease there. I believe it was Voltaire who said, 'There is nothing which has yet been contrived by man, by which so much happiness is produced as by a good tavern or inn.' " He looked pleased with himself.

"Forgive me for correcting you," Lisolette said, "but it was Samuel Johnson who made that observation. In the past fifty years it has been attributed to many people, including Napoleon Bonaparte, who lacked the good sense and the wit."

"It was Johnson, of course," a chastened Paul said. "I always push him to the back of my mind because I don't consider him one of the great philosophers."

Eulalia jumped to her feet, announcing that she had some final preparations to make in the kitchen. As soon as she closed the door behind her, she began to laugh aloud while she washed the salad greens.

A few moments later Lisolette followed her into the

kitchen. Eulalia bit the insides of her cheeks so she could stop smiling, then said, "Stir the soup, if you like. Add a little flour if you think it needs thickening."

Lisolette was silent as she attended to the chore. Then she asked, "Were you and Whip laughing at Paul Thoman or at me just now?"

"Both of you," Eulalia confessed. "But more Paul than you. We've learned to take his quotations in our stride and ignore them. You're the first person who has ever put him in his place."

"Oh, dear. It was unintentional."

Eulalia wasn't certain Lisolette was as innocent as she sounded. In any event, she had stopped brooding, at least for the moment.

When dinner was served, it soon became apparent that Paul had been thinking hard, trying to find some way to strike back. A remark Whip made about horses inspired him to say something at length in Greek.

Lisolette immediately responded in the same tongue. "We were quoting Euripides, the Greek playwright," she explained to her host and hostess.

Paul tried again over the roast venison, launching into Latin. Concluding with a flourish, he looked at Lisolette, his expression challenging her.

She glanced down at the table, her manner demure, and then, very quietly, spoke even longer in Latin. "Those quotations were from Ovid," she said to Whip and Eulalia.

The confusion in Paul's eyes indicated that he didn't quite know whether to admire her or become annoyed. Now it was the girl's turn, and she said something to him in a strange tongue. He looked blank.

"I couldn't resist teasing you," she told him. "I was quoting an obscure Russian poet of the last century who was one of my father's favorites."

Unable to control themselves any longer, Eulalia and Whip roared.

To their surprise Paul joined in the laughter. "You're extraordinary," he told Lisolette, and it was evident the compliment was sincere.

She made no reply and looked shy and vulnerable.

Paul indulged in no more quotations, and Eulalia wondered if his feelings were seriously hurt. He made his attitude clear when the meal had ended. "I don't believe you've seen my shipyard, what there is of it so far," he said to Lisolette. "If you'd like to ride down to the cove with me, I'll have you back here before sundown."

"I'd enjoy that very much," she replied promptly and went off with him.

After Eulalia washed the dishes and cleaned the kitchen, she joined Whip in the yard outside the front door, where he was transplanting two wild cherry trees he had found in the forest. He stopped digging in the ground, wiped the back of a hand across his forehead, and said, "If the ranch fails, you could set yourself up in business as a matchmaker."

She was sure now that his interest in Lisolette had not been personal; he was too pleased with what they had witnessed. "It was a stroke of good luck, that's all. Paul is never at a loss for words, so I thought he might be able to draw her out of her shell. I had no idea she's as much of a walking encyclopedia as he is."

"Well, they hit it off together like nothing I've ever seen. And to think it was all accidental."

"Accidental?" Eulalia smiled. "You may know all there is to know about wilderness trails and Indians and horses, Michael Holt, but you know nothing about women."

He slid his broad-brimmed hat to the back of his head and looked hard at her.

"Lisolette," she explained, "decided for reasons of her own that she liked Paul. So she deliberately waited until he made a mistake—and then pounced on him. No matter what he said, she beat him at his own game. She gained his complete attention in the only way a man like that can be captured. Any woman would have recognized what she was doing."

"But she seems so young and inexperienced."

"She is. Her reaction was instinctive." It wasn't often that Eulalia gained an advantage over Whip, and she was enjoying the experience.

"Well, the way those two spout off like geysers, I can't help wondering what their children are going to be like." He resumed his digging.

The mention of children sent a chill traveling up Eulalia's spine. Whip still made love to her only infrequently, but whenever he did she prayed she would not have a baby. It was of paramount importance to her that they have no children until they solved the problems that kept them apart—if they ever solved them.

"The kitchen needs to be about four or five feet longer," Olga Runkova declared. "The dimensions of the front room are just fine now, but we'll need more room for our stove and for the shelves to hold the dishes and glasses we'll buy, little by little."

Ted Woods, his hammer in one hand, sighed quietly. "I wish you two would make up your minds. A tavern ain't like an accordian that can be stretched and shrunk. It's a building, and the way we're putting it up, it will be here for a long time to come."

"Olga is right, as usual," Dolores said. "The kitchen must be longer."

Hosea made no comment and grinned amiably at the two women as he continued to pound nails into a section of wall.

"This is the last change I'm going to make," Ted

said. Walking to the lumber pile, he selected a long board. "You realize we'll need to extend the kitchen roof, too."

"We appreciate all the help you give us," Olga said, smiling at him.

Mollified for the moment, he went to work on the extension, first digging several holes, then driving uprights of oak into them. His strength was so great that each support required only a few blows with his sledgehammer to make it secure. Trouble developed when he wanted to nail his first crossbeam in place almost seven feet off the ground. He was able to reach the place easily, but it was too high for the diminutive Hosea to hold the other end of the board for him.

"I reckon we've got to make ourselves a ladder," Ted said.

Olga intervened. "I will hold the board for you," she said.

He was outraged. "That's too much! I'll be hanged if I'll let any woman do a man's work."

"If it needs to be done," she replied sensibly, "I do not see what difference it makes if it is done by a man or a woman." She picked up the heavy piece of lumber. "Just show me where you want me to hold it, please."

His unhappy grunt signified his surrender. He took hold of one end of the beam, then held it in place against an upright. "Make it parallel," he said.

Olga had to reach high over her head, but her hands were steady, even when he drove the other end into the upright with several savage blows of his hammer. Grumpily he came to her end, caught hold of the crossbeam with one hand, and glared at her. "All right, if you can hold a nail in place, I'll make it secure."

She did as he directed and had to curb a desire to laugh. "You see how much I trust you?" she asked, holding the nail for him. "If you wished, you could smash my hand with that hammer."

"I've got to admit I'm tempted." Once the nail was in place, it held the crossbeam, and Ted waved Olga away with an impatient gesture. Taking the nails she was holding, he drove them into the wood.

Meanwhile, at Dolores's request, Hosea had lighted a fire at the rear of the yard behind the uncompleted building, and Olga calmly went off to join the other woman there.

Hosea could reach high enough for the additional crossbars that were needed for the frame, and for the next half hour he and Ted worked steadily. They were quick and efficient, each anticipating the needs of the other. Concentrating on their labors, they paid no attention to the two women.

"It is time to stop now," Olga called.

The exasperated Ted wiped perspiration from his forehead with the back of his sleeve. "We're just starting to sweat," he said. "Why in the devil should we stop?"

"Because dinner is ready," she told him. "You have been working since early in the morning, and you need food."

Now that she mentioned it, he realized he was hungry. He washed his hands in water he poured from a bucket, then went to the fire, where unfamiliar but appetizing odors assailed him. "What are those?" he demanded suspiciously, pointing to some irregular-shaped objects in golden crusts that were still sizzling in a pan.

"Try one," Olga suggested.

The food was very hot, but he held it without discomfort and bit into it. Inside the pastry shell was a mixture of chopped meat, wild onions, and peppers, along with several herbs he could not identify.

"Well?" Olga demanded.

Ted hated to admit the dish was delicious, even though it was totally unfamiliar. "Not bad," he admitted grudgingly.

Olga began to eat, too, and watched him as he

devoured his food. "They are Russian meat pies," she told him. "Help yourself to more. There are many."

Ted reached for another pie. "Why did you go to all this bother? Some cold venison or elk meat would have been plenty good enough."

"You are spending your whole day off from your own work to help us," Olga said. "Early every morning and late every day, when you are done in the blacksmith shop, you do more and more for us. The least we can do is to prepare a nourishing meal for you. How else can I thank you for being so kind?"

"I don't want thanks," he muttered.

Dolores exchanged a knowing glance with Hosea, then looked away quickly so Ted wouldn't see her smile.

Olga remained unflustered. "Tomorrow night," she said firmly, "you will come to our house for supper. I am roasting the wild goose that one of your customers gave to Hosea yesterday in payment for work he did."

Ted hated to be indebted to her, but it had been a long time since he had eaten roast goose, one of his favorite dishes. Helping himself to yet another meat pie, he succumbed with an ungracious shrug of his massive shoulders.

Olga was satisfied. Never had she seen a man more in need of a woman's ministrations, and although he didn't yet even suspect what she had in mind, she had already decided that Ted Woods would marry her. Perhaps, Olga thought, the idea of making her his wife would dawn on him by the time he and Hosea finished building the new tavern. If not, he would think of it eventually, and she was content to wait. She had been a widow for so long that, having found the new husband she wanted, a delay of a few weeks or months didn't matter to her in the least.

Harry Canning stood on his quarterdeck and sighed with relief when he dropped anchor near the junction of the Columbia and Willamette rivers. His voyage to Oregon had been delayed interminably because the Mexican authorities in Yerba Buena, wanting to gain a share of the American trade for their own merchantmen, had found one excuse after another to prevent him from leaving port. Only when he had threatened to shoot his way out had he been permitted to leave.

His arrival created a profound stir. The *Wendy Anne* was the first merchant ship flying the American flag to reach the settlement, and the members of the community were quick to recognize the significance of the event.

Harry soon became popular with the settlers. Not only was he carrying all kinds of merchandise that the pioneers wanted and needed, but his prices were reasonable. Soon realizing that little cash was available, he proved himself amenable to barter deals, accepting smoked meat, furs, and lumber in return for the goods he was offering. He did a lively business and quickly became friendly with several members of the community.

Paul Thoman came on board the *Wendy Anne*, admired the soundness of the schooner in spite of her age, and in return invited Harry to visit his as yet uncompleted shipyard. Impressed by the younger man's industry, Harry made several suggestions that proved valuable.

"It strikes me," he said, "that you're being too ambitious. You say you plan to make only fishing boats at first."

"Sure," Paul replied. "I'd need a whole team of carpenters to make anything bigger."

"Then cut the size of your dry dock in half. You'll finish it faster and get into production that much sooner. From what little I've seen here, there's a real need for fishing boats, and you ought to be able to sell them as fast as you can make them."

Tilman Wade, who made a barter deal for a number of tin milking pails he would need on his dairy farm, established such a solid relationship with Harry that he invited the ship's master to his house for supper one evening. Tilman asked Sally MacNeill if as a special favor, she would prepare the meal. She agreed to do it, but Olga and Dolores, who were sharing her house until their own dwelling behind their new tavern was built, intervened and took charge. Ted Woods and Hosea also were invited, and the group spent a convivial evening.

Ted, who made friends slowly, expressed the thoughts of the others the next day. "That Canning puts on no airs," he said. "It's like he's one of us."

The cordiality that marked Harry Canning's relations with the community did not extend to his raffish crew. The sailors soon discovered that they could buy a raw, barely potable whiskey from a Canadian trader who frequently did business at Fort Vancouver. Paying scant attention to the American settlers, the seamen concentrated on their drinking.

Even Murillo and Billy Sullivan, on whom Harry was relying, caroused with the others. He spoke separately to the two men, but he had no duties for them to perform on board the *Wendy Anne* during the weeks the ship was in port, and he had no control over them ashore. He had hoped both would develop into reliable subordinates, but their conduct did not particularly surprise him. Only those who could earn a living in no other way signed on as members of a tramp schooner's crew.

A few days after the *Wendy Anne* dropped anchor, Olga and Dolores opened their tavern, for the present serving meals only at noon, when a number of settlers might be in the village making purchases. They were pleased when they aroused the immediate interest of the British in Fort Vancouver. So many customers crossed the Columbia for dinner that the establishment was crowded every day.

At the insistence of Olga and Dolores, Ted and

Hosea dropped in daily for their own dinner after other customers had left. As Olga said pointedly, it was the least they could do for the pair who were now engaged in building a house behind the tavern. Ted balked, but he found Olga's cooking more than he could resist, and after his first meal he stopped protesting.

One day, about a week after the tavern opened, the place was jammed. The settlers who came into the village on business were finding it increasingly convenient to eat there, bartering fresh, raw food for their meals, and the customers from the far side of the Columbia paid in cash, so the success of the tavern was assured. On this particular day the crowd was so large that a line formed outside, and the frantically busy proprietors had to ask help from Sally MacNeill, who had come into town on an errand of her own. She gladly went to work for them as a waitress.

The last customers left, and Olga came out of the kitchen to slump wearily into a chair for a few moments, while an equally exhausted Sally leaned against a wall. Only Dolores, who didn't know the meaning of fatigue, continued to work in the kitchen, preparing dinner for Ted and Hosea, who would be arriving soon. Even though Olga was tired, she looked around the main room with pleasure. The floor was bare, there were no decorations on the walls, and the eight tables, each with four chairs, were made of raw, unpainted pine, but the atmosphere was cozy. She had come a long way for a penniless immigrant from Russia who had arrived in Oregon only a short time earlier.

Now she was half-owner of a place of her own, soon she and Dolores would move into their house at the rear, and one of these months Ted would recognize the inevitable, that he was falling in love with her.

Olga forgot her aching feet and stood.

At that moment the front door opened, and three

men in rough sailors' attire walked in. Sally instinctively disliked the way they looked at her and became tense.

"I am sorry," Olga told the trio, "but we are serving no more meals today."

"It's not food we're after," Billy Sullivan replied. "We have a terrible thirst." Murillo and the third sailor nodded and grinned.

"We sell no liquor here, and it will be months, I am afraid, before we can offer locally brewed beer," Olga said. "Until then, we must wait until a ship comes in that will sell us a supply."

Sullivan's smile faded. "Not in all me born days did I hear of a tavern that sells no spirits!"

Murillo's eyes narrowed. "I wonder if these good ladies do not want honest seamen as patrons."

Sullivan bristled. "Ye mean they lie?" The Mexican shrugged.

That was all Billy Sullivan had to hear. "We'll make our own search for a bottle!" he declared.

It occurred to Olga that the trio was dangerous. All of them had already been drinking, and they all carried knives in their belts. Nevertheless, she had no intention of allowing them to rummage as they pleased in the new establishment that meant so much to her. "I have told you the truth," she said quietly but firmly. "We have no beverages for sale here, and we are no longer serving dinner. Be good enough to leave."

"Seems to me she needs a lesson in manners," Sullivan said. "Maybe we should smash up the place a bit." He picked up a chair and lifted it over his head, intending to send it flying against the wall opposite him.

The kitchen door opened, and a silent Ted Woods filled it, a sledgehammer in one hand. He had been alone in the blacksmith shop when an alarmed Dolores had summoned him, and he had come at once.

Ordinarily Billy Sullivan feared no man, and he

believed he and his companions could hold their own in a brawl. But the menace in the eyes of this brooding giant who faced him was so intense that he slowly lowered the chair to the floor.

"Get out!" Ted commanded, his knuckles whitening as he took a tighter grip on the handle of the sledgehammer.

The third seaman needed no convincing and began to back toward the front door.

"I'd as soon squash in your head like an eggshell as I'd kill a fly," Ted said in a low tone.

Sullivan was ready to accept the challenge, but Murillo, even though intoxicated, knew this tall, heavyset man was dangerous. Perhaps they could subdue him, but he would do great damage, and one of them might be killed before they could overcome him. "Billy," he said nervously, "we'll find more to drink at some other place."

"Get out of here and don't come back," Ted said. "If you do, I give you my word that you'll die."

No one moved.

Ted raised his sledgehammer and started to move forward very slowly. Murillo's experience had taught him to recognize murderous intent when he saw it, and he fled. Billy Sullivan tried to hold his ground, but when Ted came within arm's length he, too, lost his courage and took to his heels. A shaken Sally MacNeill closed the front door behind the trio.

Olga Runkova thought she had come to know Ted, but this mood of black rage was new to her. A demon had taken possession of him, and he was indeed ready to kill. But the rage in him subsided swiftly, and he placed the sledgehammer on a table and sighed almost plaintively. "Too bad," he said. "I would have enjoyed giving them sailors a lesson in manners. Anyway, they won't bother you again."

"They must be members of Captain Canning's crew," Sally said.

Ted nodded. "No doubt of that. I'll have me a word

with Harry and tell him to keep his men on a tight leash."

"Sally," Olga said, "you have given us more than enough of your time today, and I know there are chores that wait for you at home. I'll see that Ted is served his dinner." Happy to be on her way, Sally left quickly.

Olga turned to Ted. "I am very grateful to you."

He was embarrassed. "Hosea and I worked too hard building this place to let some drunken sailors wreck it," he said. "Besides, nobody is going to threaten you when I can help it."

As Olga went to the kitchen to bring him his meal, she realized he was moving even more rapidly than she had hoped to a recognition of his affection for her.

Meanwhile, Sally started off at a brisk pace on the trail that led to her new farmhouse. That morning she had walked to the village rather than ride one of her workhorses, and she was so enamored of the Oregon countryside that she always enjoyed the half-hour walk. She was making slow progress on clearing her land, but didn't really mind. Tilman Wade and other friends helped when they could, and in the meantime there was plenty to eat. She was sinking her roots here, and now that she was succeeding in forgetting her dream of marrying Paul Thoman, she was better able to face reality.

After walking for a quarter of an hour, Sally paused at the crest of a hill. To the west, at the shores of the Pacific, lay the Coast Range, to the east were the Cascades. She never failed to stop here to admire the view. Nowhere else in the world, she felt sure, could anyone find its equal.

Sitting quietly, enjoying the view, she heard the sound of heavy footsteps. Turning to look, she was numbed by the discovery that the three drunken seamen were following her. Her first instinct was to run, but she knew that would impel them to pursue her with even greater determination, so she curbed the desire and instead got up and walked at a steady, even pace.

She could hear the boots of the sailors crashing through the underbrush behind her. Curbing her panic, Sally hoped she could reach her house in time to slam and bolt the door behind her, then reach the loaded rifle she kept in her bedroom. She had never used firearms, but the sailors didn't know that, and the sight of the weapon might give them pause and help to change their minds.

No! She simply wasn't thinking. Instead of going home she would go a little farther, to Tilman's house, and seek his aid. He would know how to deal with the problem.

One of the men called out to her, and a cold chill moved up Sally's spine. She could well imagine what might happen to her if they caught her. Almost imperceptibly she increased her pace, and her heart hammered in her ears.

At last she reached Tilman's property. She caught a glimpse of him in a field behind his house, working with two of his horses pulling up tree stumps. Concentrating on his efforts, Tilman did not become aware of her proximity until she called out to him. As he straightened, Sally could control her fear no longer and broke into a run. Breathlessly she explained the situation.

The trio emerged from the woods, saw the girl talking to a slender man in his thirties, and then resolutely pressed forward again. This was no burly giant like the man they had encountered at the tavern, and they were confident that any one of them could break this man in half.

"Are they armed?" Tilman asked.

"They have knives," Sally replied.

He turned his back to the approaching trio for a moment, took a pistol from his belt, and handed it to the girl. "Keep this hidden until I tell you otherwise," he said. Then he walked a few feet to the place where he had thrown his coat to the ground, and there he halted, folding his arms.

The sailors exchanged grins and continued to advance. "We will throw a coin," Murillo said, "to see which of us gets the girl first."

"You're trespassing on private property," Tilman Wade called. "What do you want here?"

The trio did not reply, but continued to march forward, shoulder to shoulder.

Tilman bent down, reached under his coat, and stood erect again, cocking his rifle. The sight of the weapon caused the men to halt.

"I'm told you followed this young lady from the village," Tilman said. "I'm afraid you picked the wrong person for whatever you have in mind. We're peaceable folks hereabouts, so I urge you to avoid trouble and clear out."

"We want the girl," Billy Sullivan shouted.

Tilman beckoned Sally closer, and she moved to a place beside him. "I've given you fair warning," he said and raised his rifle. Their intoxicated grins indicated their belief that he was bluffing.

Tilman took careful aim, then squeezed the trigger and put a bullet through Murillo's hat. Calmly handing the rifle to Sally and taking his pistol from her, he said, "Reload, please, and quickly. Ammunition and powder are in my coat pockets."

Sally moved quickly. Here, at least, she knew what she was doing, thanks to the practice in reloading weapons she had had during Indian attacks on the wagon train.

A pale Murillo stood with his hat in his hands, staring at the hole. Only a disbelieving Billy Sullivan was still smiling.

Tilman pointed a finger at him. "Sailor," he said, "if you aren't off my land by the time I count to five, I'm putting a bullet between your teeth. That smile will be frozen on your face for all eternity."

The third member of the trio had heard enough and began to edge away.

"One!" Tilman called.

The third sailor lost his nerve and moved off in the direction of the woods.

"The rifle is loaded," Sally said.

"Good," Tilman told her, speaking in a low voice. "Now I'm ready for both of these fellows." Then much more forcefully, "Two!"

Murillo lost his desire for the girl and decided to take himself elsewhere. These American settlers in no way resembled the lackadaisical Spanish ranchers who lived near Yerba Buena.

"Three!" Tilman called.

Billy Sullivan hated to be bluffed or bullied. Maybe he could draw his knife and throw it at the American.

"Keep your hands away from your belt!" Tilman called. "Or I won't go on with the counting. Four!" He raised his pistol, sighted down the barrel, and held the weapon in a steady hand.

Sullivan knew when he was beaten. Blaming his two comrades for cowardice and telling himself they were responsible for this predicament, he began to move toward the woods, his walk a slow swagger.

"All of this cleared land is my property, so you're still trespassing, sailor," Tilman called.

Almost feeling the pistol aimed at the back of his head, Sullivan ran, gathering speed until he reached the woods. Tilman and Sally could hear the crashing of his footsteps through the underbrush as he continued to run.

Only now did Tilman lower his pistol. "I'm glad you came to me, Sally," he said. "Those three have just enough liquor in their bellies to be mean."

"I—I was desperate," she said, and now that the danger had been averted, she started to weep.

Still holding his pistol and watching the woods in case the seamen changed their minds and returned,

Tilman patted her shoulder. "Now, now," he said. "What's a neighbor for if it isn't to be helpful in a time of trouble?"

Sally controlled her tears, and her relief was so great that she started to giggle.

"What's so funny?" Tilman demanded.

"You're so calm. A body would think you help maidens in distress every day of the week."

"I don't reckon I'll get any more work done in the fields today," he said, ignoring her remark. "You keep a sharp watch for me while I unhitch my team and take them to the barn. Then you're coming to my house and making us a pot of herb tea. You aren't going home until I know that Dolores and Olga are there, too."

Sally nodded, thinking as she watched the woods, where there was no longer any sign of the three seamen, that not since her father had died, had she known any man as wonderful as Tilman Wade.

Whip Holt and Stalking Horse returned late at night from their second expedition into the Cascade Mountains, so Eulalia didn't know her husband had come home until the following morning.

"I didn't want to wake you up," Whip explained to Eulalia as she prepared breakfast the next morning, "so I slept in the main room."

"The parlor," she told him automatically, wondering how long it would take him to learn its name. What was really on her mind, however, was something far more significant. Perhaps he was finding an excuse not to sleep with her any more, and she felt a deep stirring of restlessness.

He grinned as he joined her at the kitchen table for a platter of fried fish and a loaf of her bread. "We had good luck again," he said. "We caught two more mares, both of them young and healthy. Now, what with a couple of stallions on the ranch, we have enough mares to start breeding. One of those mares is going to be something special, I can tell you. She's a real spitfire. I barely got started taming her before we got back here, and a half-dozen times she nearly got away."

"I'd like to see her," Eulalia said.

After breakfast they went together to the yard behind the stable where the new horses were tethered. Eulalia picked out the little mare instantly. Her coat was a deep, shiny reddish-brown. She lifted her ears as they approached, and her bushy tail stood out behind her. She tried her best to get rid of the rope that held her captive, kicking her hind feet and shaking her head.

"I want her," Eulalia said, "for my very own. We can return Tonie Martin's mare."

"Fair enough," Whip said. "I'll turn her over to you as soon as I've tamed her enough so you can ride her."

She shook her head. "No, I want to break her in myself. That way she'll really be mine."

When he started to protest, she said, "I ask for very little, Michael Holt."

"As long as you think you can do the job," he said.

"If I didn't think I could," she replied with asperity, "I wouldn't have asked." She headed back toward the house.

Whip was about to accompany Stalking Horse on a ride out to the range when Eulalia appeared, and her husband stared at her. Damned if she wasn't wearing men's pants!

"I made these for myself with that cured elk skin you gave me," she said. "If I'm going to be a rancher's wife, I can't ride in skirts. And there's no way I can break in that horse in a dress."

He promptly changed his plans for the day. "I'll hang around, then."

"I wish you wouldn't," she said. "Gwen and I will get to know each other better if we're by ourselves."

"Gwen?"

She shrugged. "The name just came to me."

Obviously Whip wasn't wanted. He gave the two-toned whistle he used to call his horse, and his stallion appeared at the entrance to the barn, then came to him at once.

Whip followed his custom of reaching into his pocket with great deliberation and giving the animal a carrot, which the stallion nibbled with care while his master continued to hold it in the palm of his hand.

Ordinarily the trick amused Eulalia, but today she was too much out of sorts. In fact, she couldn't help wondering whether Whip was daring her to teach the wild mare similar tricks. No, that was going too far. He and his stallion were close. In a way she would never be close to him. She realized it was as absurd to make the comparison as it was to read hidden meanings into the simple act of Whip's whistling for his horse, then feeding the animal a vegetable, but she couldn't help it.

Unaware of the thoughts seething in his wife's mind, Whip calmly mounted the stallion bareback, then rode off with Stalking Horse. His one desire at the moment was to put distance between himself and the woman with whom he wrangled so frequently, most of the time without good cause.

Eulalia waited until he disappeared from sight before she went to the stable for the saddle and other tack she had used on Tonie's mare. Returning to the field, she reached into the pocket of her doeskin jacket and produced an apple, which she extended on the palm of her hand. "Here's my introduction to you, Gwen," she said. The mare took the apple and ate it but watched the young woman warily.

Eulalia was uncertain of her reasons for wanting to break in the animal. She had been no more than fifteen years old the last time she had broken in a horse, after accepting a dare from her father, and to this day she had told no one that Claiborne had helped her.

All she knew now was that she had voluntarily accepted this challenge and could not fail. Perhaps she was restless because every other phase of her life was so unsatisfactory; she and her overly casual husband were almost strangers living under the same roof.

Reaching into her pocket again, she partly unwrapped a folded paper and shook a little precious sugar into the palm of her other hand. "Here's a special treat, Gwen," she said. "You'll get the rest when you're really broken in."

Then Eulalia placed the saddlecloth on the horse's back. She reacted violently, both of her rear hoofs flailing. The task of saddling and bridling her took half an hour and wasn't accomplished until the mare finally realized there was no escape. But even when she stood trembling, suffering the indignity, her nostrils flared.

Gathering herself for a spring, Eulalia leaped into the saddle, first getting a firm hold on the reins, then took a knife from her belt and cut the rope that held the horse captive.

Gwen made a determined, persistent effort to throw her rider, snorting in anger as she reared and plunged forward, halted abruptly and, lowering her head, kicked her hind legs high in the air. She ran in circles, alternating these movements with unpredictable, irregular patterns, bucking incessantly.

Somehow Eulalia managed to hang on. The task she had set for herself was far more difficult than she had anticipated, and the experience was unlike any she had ever known. She no longer had the resilient body of an adolescent in her mid-teens, she was a mature woman in her twenties. She felt as though her insides were being torn out of her, and she wondered how long she could tolerate the brutal punishment.

The contest was between her will and that of the horse, and she was determined not to give up. It would be shameful to be forced to admit to Whip that she had been unable to complete the chore she had given herself. In some strange way, by challenging the mare she was also challenging her husband.

The struggle went on and on, with neither of the participants yielding. Gwen resorted to guile now, occasionally halting and standing still for a few moments before renewing her violent, erratic tactics. The young woman was not fooled, however, and remained alert, always ready for a renewal of the deadly game. She lost all sense of the passage of time and told herself repeatedly that her stamina required her to do more than match that of her mount.

The mare made a supreme effort, rearing and flailing with her front hoofs, then bucking vehemently and kicking furiously with her rear hoofs. Eulalia flew through the air over the horse's lowered head and landed in a heap on the ground. She lay there for a few moments, too dazed and exhausted to move. Then, slowly, she pulled herself to her feet, not realizing or caring that her long hair had become snarled and matted with dust and perspiration, unaware of the fact that her clothes were as soaked as they would have been if she had poured several buckets of water over herself.

Gasping as she tried to regain her breath, she looked at the horse, who was standing immobile a few paces away, watching her. "Girl," Eulalia said grimly, "you won that round. Now it's my turn." She reached for the reins.

The mare shied and tried to sidestep, but Eulalia caught and managed to keep a tight grip on the reins. Moving very slowly until she reached Gwen's left side, she suddenly vaulted into the saddle. The duel was resumed.

Once again the horse began to buck, but she was as

weary as her mistress, and this time her efforts were halfhearted. She fought for another half hour and then quietly surrendered, her reddish-brown coat drenched.

Eulalia patted her, took the rest of the sugar from her pocket, leaned forward, and held it out on the palm of her hand. The mare twisted her head in order to obtain the treat and licked it carefully.

Eulalia had won, but she was too tired to exult. Her task was just beginning, as she well knew. Now, while the horse was docile, was the best time to teach her to respond to gentle pressures on the reins and orders given through pressures of the rider's knees. The lesson began.

The mare was still spirited, but having lost, she entered into the pleasures of this new game without hard feelings. Her intelligence was extraordinary, and she picked up the meanings of instructions with surprising rapidity.

Eulalia walked the mare slowly, then rapidly, turning her right and left, halting her and starting forward again. Never had she known any horse to respond with such sensitivity. The time came to canter, then to go all out in a full gallop, and both rider and mount enjoyed themselves thoroughly.

The last lesson was the most difficult, that of teaching the animal to trot. As one who had learned to ride in the South, Eulalia posted, rising in her saddle and returning to her seat almost effortlessly, matching the horse's own rhythms. Whip, like most mountain men, regarded posting as an effete affectation, but that was just too bad. Gwen was Eulalia's very own horse and would be taught her mistress's ways from the outset.

They spent a long time on the trotting lesson, and the mare finally caught on, doing what was required of her. Eulalia rode in triumph now.

She was astonished when she looked up and saw

Whip and Stalking Horse approaching. Then she glanced at the sun and realized it was already mid-afternoon. The better part of the day had passed.

Whip rode up beside her, grinned, and said casually, "I see you made out all right."

"We've become very good friends." Eulalia kept her tone equally casual.

All three riders went to the stable. After dismounting, Eulalia spent some time walking Gwen about, to give the animal a chance to cool down after the hard ride. Then she sponged Gwen with water and began to brush the mare carefully.

Stalking Horse offered to help Eulalia with these tasks, but she shook her head. "Thank you all the same," she said, "but I'm going to allow no one else to groom her. Ever." She picked up one of the nosebags she had made from the canvas of her wagon cover, filled it with oats they had purchased at the Hudson's Bay store, and looped it over the animal's head. "I intend to feed her myself, too, and no one else will ride her."

"That's smart," Whip said, falling in beside her as she started toward the house, while Stalking Horse remained behind to take care of the other horses. "You did better than I expected."

He rarely offered praise, and even a few grudging words were better than none. "Thank you," she replied simply.

Suddenly he halted, a new excitement in his voice. "Your limp is completely gone!" he exclaimed.

Eulalia knew he was right. The long hours of violent exertions in which she had engaged while breaking in the mare had paid handsome, unexpected dividends. She was whole again, totally recovered from the debilitating effects of the fever she had suffered.

A feeling of such relief swept over her that she wanted to weep, but she had learned that displays of emotion made Whip uncomfortable. So she spoke with as much calm as she could muster and had no idea she sounded coolly remote. "I'll always be grateful for the help you gave me," she said. "If it hadn't been for your insistence, I couldn't have accomplished what I did today." She paused, then added, "I'm afraid I lost count of time today, so dinner will be delayed. I hope you aren't too hungry."

"I can wait," Whip said and stood still, watching her as she continued on her way to the house, her walk that of a normal, healthy woman.

Had he been more demonstrative, he would have hugged and kissed her to show her his pleasure over her recovery. But her remoteness, combined with his own natural shyness, caused him to freeze, and he made no attempt to join her in the kitchen. Instead, he wandered aimlessly, circling the house and wondering why the problems that were making their marriage less and less tolerable seemed to be growing worse. Would he have achieved greater contentment had he married Cathy? He had no idea. In fact, much as the thought shocked him, he couldn't help speculating on the possibility that he had actually still been in love with Cathy when, drawn to Eulalia as much by his sympathy for her as by her beauty, he had impulsively proposed to her.

All he knew for certain was that whatever the obstacles were that prevented Eulalia and him from enjoying a happy marriage, they were growing bigger and were becoming increasingly difficult to penetrate.

During the best of weather, rain fell at least twice each week in Oregon, but in the winter it was a rare day when there was no chilly rain. The settlers went to church one Sunday in a downpour. Most, regardless of their denominational beliefs, were so grateful to God for bringing them safely to this land of plenty that no bad weather could deter them from attending services. So the church was crowded, as it always was.

The rain stopped as the congregation sang its last

hymn, but there was still a chill in the damp air as
people emerged from church. People who had spent
so many months together on the long journey across
the continent refused to be denied the pleasure of
visiting, however, and groups formed everywhere on
the broad yard as the settlers brought each other up
to date on the progress they were making in establishing their new homes. Only a few, Dave Evans among
them, kept to themselves and soon went off.

Lisolette Arbo, who had attended the services with
Eulalia and Whip, greeted Paul Thoman with a bright
smile that belied her shyness. Harry Canning had
come to church with Paul, and Lisolette was reserved
in his company, but she glowed whenever Paul addressed her.

Cathy and Lee, the latter in uniform, had been
required to sit in a front pew, and because of the
Colonel's presence, his officers, virtually without exception, had made it their business to be present, too.
After the service, when Lee drew Whip aside for a
few private words, Major Eli Moser promptly materialized at Eulalia's side. His presence relieved her because, in spite of her long and close friendship with
Cathy, both felt a sense of strain when they were
alone with each other these days, and both were finding it difficult to keep up more than a surface conversation.

In order to ease her almost inexplicable embarrassment, Eulalia flirted with Eli even more strongly than
she had intended. He responded but remained cautious, unable to decide whether she was inviting him
to have an affair with her or whether she was inno-
cently outgoing in all of her relationships.

Everyone, the officers in particular, couldn't help
smiling at the sight of Ginny Dobbs being escorted by
Sergeant Major Hector Mullins, who wore his full-
dress uniform. As Lee had remarked only recently,
"The Sergeant hadn't seen the inside of a church for

twenty years. I honestly didn't think any woman was capable of taming him."

Those who didn't know of Ted Woods's work in building the new tavern and the house behind it were surprised to see him in the company of Olga Runkova. Claiborne and Cindy Woodling came face to face with the blacksmith and the Russian woman, and Cindy knew at a glance that Ted had recovered from his infatuation with her. She squeezed her husband's arm as they made small talk with the couple, but he failed to grasp the significance of the gesture, and she reflected that only a woman would realize that Olga's attitude toward Ted had become proprietary.

Danny, the former bound boy, who was living with the von Thalmans, was the first to realize that trouble was brewing. Grasping the arm of Chet Harris, his best friend, he muttered, "Watch out."

A half-dozen members of the crew of the *Wendy Anne* had arrived at church, and all of them were intoxicated. Before anyone quite knew what was happening, Billy Sullivan caught hold of Lisolette and tried to kiss her. Paul intervened instantly and landed a hard punch on the sailor's cheek. Sullivan retaliated, and Harry Canning, outraged by the conduct of members of his crew, roared a command to stop.

Ted Woods took no chances, however. Wading into the melee, he caught hold of Sullivan's shoulder, spun him around, and then felled him with a single blow that sent him sprawling.

Murillo and another of the seamen drew their knives. This was too much for Hector Mullins, and he entered the fray, his fists flailing. Although none of the spectators quite knew how it happened, Murillo dropped to the ground, and blood spurted from the other sailor's nose.

Within a few moments, thanks to the aid rendered by a number of the settlers, order was restored, and the sailors were restrained.

While scores of the settlers milled around, many of them talking simultaneously, Tilman Wade drew his fellow members of the council aside, and they learned, for the first time, how he had prevented three of the seamen from assaulting Sally MacNeill. At Olga's insistence, Ted—still ready to take on the entire crew single-handed—came forward and briefly told how he had cut short what might have developed into an unpleasant incident at the tavern.

Ernie von Thalman took a grave view of the situation. "We are a law-abiding community," he said, "and we tolerate no brawls here. Colonel Blake," he asked formally, "do you have room in your detention barracks for these seamen?"

"Ample room," Lee replied succinctly. "Sergeant Mullins!"

Hector came forward at once from his place beside Ginny. "Sir?"

"Fetch a squad from the garrison. Lock up these sailors in the detention barracks. Make sure they're separated, with only one in each chamber, and then post a guard detail. We'll hold them until further notice, so they'll have plenty of time to sober up."

Murillo, in the grip of two settlers, cursed loudly. Ted took a step toward him, then smashed him across the mouth with the back of a huge hand. "Keep a civil tongue in your head when there are ladies present!" he said.

Within a short time the seamen were marched off to Fort Oregon.

A mortified Harry Canning approached Ernie and Lee, who were conferring in low tones. "Gentlemen," he said, "I can't tell you how sorry I am that all this happened. I'm afraid I have no control over these scum when they come ashore. The worst of my problem is that I can't hire reliable sailors of a higher caliber in Mexican ports like Yerba Buena and San Diego. Murillo and Sullivan, who appear to be two of the worst offenders, made a good impression on me when I first hired them, but I'm afraid they don't wear well."

"We're not holding you to blame in any way, Captain Canning," Lee said. "But they've seriously disturbed the peace more than once, and we can't take the risk of allowing it to happen again."

"The next time," Ernie said, "someone might be shot."

Harry sighed. "I was hoping to stay on here for another week, but it's plain I'll have to sail as soon as possible. I'll dismiss the offenders as soon as I drop anchor at Yerba Buena, and I'll do everything I can to sign on men of a different class. If and when I succeed and buy more merchandise, I hope I'll be allowed to return here."

"You're always welcome in Oregon," Ernie told him. "You've already been a big help to us."

"Thank you," Harry said. "I believe in this settlement, and I hope with all my heart that the American occupation of Oregon succeeds. What you're trying to accomplish here will influence the future of the United States permanently."

"That's the way we look at it," Ernie said and shook his hand warmly.

Harry spent the rest of the day rounding up the members of his crew who weren't in the detention barracks. He took on water and fuel, then confined his men to the ship.

At dawn the following morning the incarcerated sailors were marched to the shore, and the soldiers who escorted them remained in place, each holding a loaded rifle.

"If you come ashore again," Sergeant Major Mullins said in a harsh rasp that Ginny Dobbs would not have recognized, "you'll be treated in a way you won't forget, but won't want to remember. What's more, I promise you that before we lock you up again and throw away the key, I'll take you on one by one in a free-for-all. There's little I'd like better than beating the tar out of all of you."

The merchant sailors looked at him sullenly, but none replied.

Harry Canning stood on his quarterdeck, knowing it would serve no useful purpose to lecture his crew. They were competent enough when they had the willpower to stay sober. but drunk, they were men of the lowest order, and their type usually drifted from one berth to another.

Waiting until all were on board, he gave the command, "All hands to sailing stations!"

The crew members scattered.

"Hoist the jib and the lower mains'l," he commanded. The Columbia River current was so strong he would need no additional sail until he reached the open waters of the Pacific. "Weigh anchor!"

The old schooner creaked as she bobbed, then slowly made her way to mid-stream and began her voyage.

Harry couldn't resist looking back for a final glimpse of the village before it disappeared behind a bend in the river. What his fellow Americans were doing in Oregon inspired his awe and envy, and he hoped that, in some way, he could hire new men and return with enough of the goods the settlers needed to solidify their position, create a permanent colony, and win their dispute with the British.

He had lived a hard life for so many years that he entertained few illusions any more, but the Oregon settlers were turning an idea into a reality, and he wanted to play an active role in their enterprise. Then some day, perhaps, when he could no longer earn his living at sea, he would settle there himself. New York, Boston, Baltimore, Philadelphia, and Charleston no longer challenged him, and even old, bustling New Orleans was jaded. Oregon represented the America of the future.

The forest of cedar, oak, and pine closed in on both sides of the great river, and signs of civilization soon vanished. Harry breathed the sweet, pure air. It was absurd to admit, but he was already homesick for the raw, new community that he had first seen only two weeks earlier.

The *Wendy Anne* sailed serenely under reduced sail for the better part of an hour without incident. Then several members of the crew came to the quarterdeck. Harry wondered if they intended to apologize for their conduct. Well, no matter what they said, he didn't intend to become involved in a prolonged discussion with them. As soon as they reached Yerba Buena, he would pay them off and be rid of them.

Suddenly Billy Sullivan came up behind Harry and put his arms around him, holding him in a viselike grip. The astonished Harry struggled to break free, but others came to Sullivan's assistance. Harry was borne to the deck and disarmed, and then his hands were tied securely behind his back.

"I am taking command now," Murillo announced as he moved to a place beside the helmsman, whose lack of surprise indicated that he was a party to the conspiracy.

"This is mutiny!" the incensed Harry declared. "You'll be hanged for this."

"First they'll have to catch us," Sullivan replied, "and who will do the catching? There's nary a British or American ship within many days' voyage of us. We made sure at both Fort Vancouver and the American village that none are expected."

"You talk too much," Murillo said sourly.

But the exuberant Irishman could not be silenced. "By the time we reach Yerba Buena, this tub will have a new name, and her appearance will be changed so much the Mexicans won't recognize her."

"Shut up," Murillo said.

Other seamen were congregating, and Harry realized that the entire crew had participated in the plot.

"It matters not what I say," Sullivan declared. "Canning will soon be dead." He drew his knife.

"No!" Murillo turned, a pistol in each hand. "We voted, remember. It was agreed not only that I would take command until we reach port and get our price for this ship, but we also agreed that we would put Canning ashore without harming him. I want no charge of murder over my head, and neither do you, if you are sensible."

Sullivan looked into the muzzles of the pistols and shrugged. "Do with him what you please," he said, and stalked off.

Harry's faint hope that a fight might develop between the ruffians who had seized his ship quickly dissipated.

Murillo edged the schooner toward the south bank, then ordered the anchor dropped when they reached the shelter of a tiny peninsula that offered shelter from the Columbia's current.

The gig was lowered, and Harry's hands were untied so he could climb down the ladder to it behind three crewmen, one of them armed with pistols. Others, lining the deck, kept their own pistols pointed at the Captain.

It would do no good to protest, Harry knew. All of his savings were in this schooner, and the scum would laugh if he asked for his strongbox or any of his personal property. He supposed he was fortunate that they were not murdering him.

He crouched in the prow of the gig as it was rowed toward the shore and weighed his chances of turning the tide on the desperate band, but they were slim. Not only was the armed man who sat in the stern keeping a sharp watch on him, but those on board who were observing the scene from the deck carried firearms, too, and he presented a target easily within their range. He knew he would have to submit to the theft of all he owned in the world.

OREGON!

As the gig drew close to the mossy bank, the man in the stern gestured with one of his pistols. Harry stood, balanced himself for a moment, then leaped ashore. The gig immediately headed back toward the schooner.

Harry, aware that the sailors might change their minds and fire at him, plunged into the deep woods and started back up the river. By the time he returned to the bank of the Columbia, the schooner had vanished.

His rage turned cold but remained just as strong as he trudged toward the Oregon village. It was ironic, he told himself, that he was returning to the settlement far sooner than he had expected.

The ship had traveled a considerable distance by the time he had been put ashore, and he estimated that the village was as much as ten miles away. The watery sun, when it broke through the clouds briefly, stood directly overhead.

Harry's progress was slow, his anger still so great that he felt neither hungry nor thirsty. He just hoped he would encounter no wild animals with a taste for human blood, for he carried no weapon of any kind. His pockets were empty, and his only possessions were the clothes he was wearing. He was being forced to start life again from the beginning, as he had first done when he had gone to sea as a cabin boy.

It was mid-afternoon when the heartsick, footsore Harry heard the sound of sawing and hammering ahead. Soon, after he turned a bend, he saw a little cove directly ahead and immediately recognized it as the site of Paul Thoman's shipyard.

Paul stood on his uncompleted dry dock, where he was adding a new section. He stopped work and stared at the bedraggled figure who approached him.

"If you'd like to hire a new hand who'll work for his keep," Harry called, "I'm your man."

Paul climbed to the ground, still staring, and Harry told him what had happened, restricting his narrative to a few biting words.

Paul Thoman was so shocked he could think of no adequate literary quotation to summarize the situation.

"There you have it," Harry said. "There are no ships in port at Fort Vancouver, and by the time one shows up, it will be far too late to catch those scoundrels. So here I am, without a penny or even a penknife to my name. I have nothing but the clothes in which you see me—and the knowledge of ships that's stored in my head."

"But what knowledge that is!" Paul exclaimed. "We've talked about nothing but ships and more ships many times these past weeks, and you know them all—schooners, brigs, and warships. You've even advised me on the fishing boats I plan to build when my yard is done. I believe you know as much about ships as my father, and that's the highest compliment I can pay you."

"In that case," Harry said, laughing grimly, "maybe you'll give me the job I seek. I wasn't joking just now. Whether I like it or not, I'm stranded in Oregon."

Paul took a long nail from his hip pocket and absently used it as he would a pen, scribbling meaningless circles on a plank of wood that stood on the top of a pile beside him. "No," he said finally, "I can't let you come to work for me." Harry was startled. "What I can and will do," the younger man continued, "is to offer you a full partnership here. I'll never know as much about ships as you do. I spent a few summers working in my father's Boston yard, but you have years and years of experience at sea in all kinds of ships. From now on this is the yard of Thoman and Canning, Oregon's first shipbuilders!"

VIII

The winter rain tapered off at sundown, and after supper one night the air was bright and clear, giving the snow-covered mountains that lay to the east a bluish tinge. Clouds forming in the distance indicated that the respite was only temporary, but the settlers had learned to take advantage of breaks in the weather. So Ginny Dobbs accepted Hector Mullins's offer to go walking with him, even though she knew they might become soaked before the evening ended.

Hector wore his full-dress uniform and took the precaution of carrying a loaded pistol because they were venturing beyond the limits of the village. They wandered along the river bank, and although they had come to know each other well enough to talk animatedly, Hector was unusually quiet, and Ginny respected his silence.

He led her to the top of a wooded hill that looked down on the fast-flowing waters, and there he carefully spread a large bandanna on the ground. Unaccustomed to such gallantry, she lowered herself onto it, even though she didn't particularly feel like sitting and knew the bandanna certainly would not keep her dry for long.

Surprised to find Hector playing the role of a gentleman, she looked up at him as he leaned against the trunk of a cedar tree, but she said nothing.

Rarely at a loss for words, Hector drew in a deep breath. "What do you think of Oregon?" he asked abruptly.

"Well," she said, "the scenery is pretty. But I lost my taste for scenery when I crossed the Sierra Nevada."

"If you had your choice, would you go back to New Jersey?"

She found his questioning odd, but nevertheless she replied honestly. "The years I spent in the orphanage spoiled my taste for the East. I prefer living here. Not that I'm all that crazy about my work, but just about anything is better than becoming a seamstress again." Ginny saw no reason to tell him that she had developed a strong dislike for Dave Evans, resenting him because she had thought he was paying court to her when he merely had wanted her to work for him.

Hector was more shrewd than she had realized. "I've seen you bristle when Evans comes into the office from the sawmill." A sudden thought occurred to him, and his voice hardened. "He don't try to get fresh with you?"

"He'd better not!" she replied, bristling. "I wasn't born a lady, but I demand respect from a man!"

Her attitude delighted him, and he grinned at her. "If anybody steps out of line, you just let me know."

"Thank you, but that won't be necessary. I can look after myself."

"A little bit of a thing like you, Ginny?" he scoffed. "Suppose I was to grab you all of a sudden—"

"I wouldn't advise you to try it!"

"I ain't done it yet, and I ain't likely to," he said, his tone indicating he was offended. "I was just giving you an example."

"I'm not complaining about the way you've behaved. I just didn't want you to get the wrong notions in your head."

"Don't worry about what goes on inside my head. I got my own future all planned, and that's more than you can say for yourself."

"I know that I don't have any plans," she said, becoming rueful. "I've had to live one day at a time for so long that I can't afford to think ahead. I hardly know what I'll be doing tomorrow or the next day, much less what will become of me in a year."

Hector's manner became solemn. "In three more years I'll have earned the army's maximum retirement pay. And when I take off this uniform for the last time, I'm going to settle right here in Oregon. I don't rightly know what I'll do to keep busy and earn extra money, but I sort of figure by that time enough people will have come here to create a need for an inn. A little place of about fifteen rooms, with a livery stable."

"When I was little, I always thought that owning a hotel would be wonderful. I still think so, but I know now that there's a lot of hard work in running a hotel."

"I've never been afraid of hard work," Hector declared.

"Neither have I!" she retorted.

"You don't have to tell me that. I see you down at the sawmill, where you can't call a minute of the day your own. Whatever Evans is paying you, it ain't enough."

She nodded, and all at once a horrid thought came into her mind. Was it possible that Hector, like Dave, was going through the motions of paying court to her because he wanted her to work for him? She decided to test him. "You'll need competent people on your staff when you open your inn."

Hector waved deprecatingly. "It ain't even built yet, and maybe it never will be. All I know for sure is that Colonel Blake has promised me I can stay on at Fort Oregon until my retirement. So I have three years to look around and make up my mind."

Ginny was sorry she had doubted him.

"I was just wondering about you, that's all. I've heard tell that you was heading East when you came across the wagon train and joined up because there was no way you could travel all the way to New Jersey by yourself. But with more and more trains coming, pretty soon there will be armed escorts traveling across the continent both ways."

"I made a mistake when I went to California," Ginny said slowly. "I haven't told this to anybody else, but I'd like you to know it. I went there to marry a rich Spanish rancher who advertised for a wife. Not long after I got there he died, and his children wanted nothing to do with me. The only reason I was going East is because I couldn't stay in a Mexican colony. There was no work there for a single woman who wanted to stay decent. I have no reason to go back to New Jersey. I have a job here, and that's cause enough to stay in Oregon."

"That ain't much of a reason."

"It's better than none."

"Most women," he said clumsily, "think about marrying and settling down."

"What I think on that subject is my business, sir!"

"I'm making it mine," Hector roared in a tone that had often caused recruits to shudder. "If you could plan to marry some Spanish rancher you never even met—"

"He proposed to me," she said calmly.

Hector's voice became even louder. "What in the name of all that's holy do you think I'm doing right now, woman?"

"I don't know," Ginny said, seemingly becoming very meek, even as she rejoiced inwardly.

Hooking his thumbs in his broad leather belt, he said, "Well?"

"I am not a private soldier in your regiment." She tried to stand, but the feat was difficult to accomplish with dignity on the side of the slope.

Hector took her hand and hauled her to her feet. "You're the most exasperating female I ever knew. You can't even answer a simple question."

"I didn't hear you ask any simple question." She brushed pine needles from her skirt.

He picked up the bandanna, stuffed it into a hip pocket, and then turned to face her. "Will you or will you not marry me, woman?" he demanded through gritted teeth.

Never had Ginny known a moment of such great triumph, and she savored it. "Now I understand your question."

"Well?"

"In spite of your lack of romance, I'm considering it."

"I ought to spank you," he said.

"Try it and you'll regret it!" She faced him defiantly.

Hector glared at her, then began to laugh. "I've got to hand it to you, woman. You ain't afraid of anybody or anything."

"That's better. If you'll stop shouting at me and threatening me, I'll be happy and proud to become Mrs. Hector Mullins. But I will not be bullied!"

Hector could scarcely believe his good fortune. "You'll really marry me?"

"I always mean what I say." She expected him to kiss her, but she waited in vain and finally had to take the first step toward him.

Only then did he reach out, his touch very gentle. When he kissed her, he betrayed an awkward self-consciousness.

When he released her, Ginny knew beyond doubt that here was the man she had always wanted. He would try to dominate her, as he dominated his subordinates, and most of the time she would give in to his wishes. But she had already discovered the tenderness behind his gruff front, and she knew that when an issue really mattered to her, she would win.

"Colonel Blake will give his permission for me to build us a house off the post," he said. "I'm sure of it."

"That sounds fine to me, Hector," Ginny said, taking his hand and holding it. "But I wonder if we could discuss all this on our way back to the village. The rain has started again."

He grinned sheepishly as they descended the hill and began to climb another that stood even higher. "My ma always said I didn't have the sense to come in out of the rain. You're just like her. If she was still alive, she'd ask you why a girl like you—who could have any man she wants—would marry a tough old soldier like me."

"I refuse to give you an even better opinion of yourself than you already hold, so I refuse to tell you my reasons." The climb was too steep now for conversation.

Suddenly, as they neared the crest, Hector halted and stared down at something. Then, gesturing for silence, he roughly thrust Ginny behind the trunk of a tree and drew his pistol. The clicking sound it made as he cocked it seemed very loud.

Rain was falling steadily now, and Ginny peered in the direction of the river, but she could see nothing at first. Then, slowly, as her eyes became accustomed to the darkness, she made out the shape of a large ship, its sails ghostlike as it hovered a short distance off shore. The light of a lantern blinked three times from the deck of the ship, penetrating the gloom. Someone standing at the base of the hill removed the hood from a lamp he was carrying and blinked the light three times in response.

For a long time nothing more happened, and then the couple at the crest of the hill heard the sound of oars. A boat was being rowed toward the bank of the river.

"Stay right where you are," Hector whispered. "No matter what happens, don't let on you're here. I give you my word you'll be safe, but right now I got to find out what's going on." He slipped away and began to ease his way down the hill toward the water.

He was remarkably quiet for someone of his size, Ginny reflected. For a moment, prompted by curiosity, she was tempted to disobey and follow him. But common sense told her Hector was right, and she realized he could protect her only if she followed his orders.

Three men, each carrying a bulky sea bag, stepped ashore, and the boat returned to the waiting ship.

The man who awaited the trio greeted them in a deep, guttural voice, but Ginny couldn't make out what he was saying. She guessed that Hector was close enough to hear the brief conversation that ensued, but he made no attempt to intervene.

The sound of the voices began to fade as the four began to walk up the river bank, then cut inland. A moment later Hector reappeared silently at the crest. "Hurry!" he said. "We've got to get to the fort as fast as we can."

Ginny followed him as he walked rapidly down the slope, her mind filled with questions. But she had no opportunity to ask them; Hector set a rapid pace and appeared to be on the verge of breaking into a run.

He turned and called over his shoulder, "Can't you walk any faster?"

"No," Ginny gasped. "Go ahead without me."

"I'll do no such thing," he declared. He continued to push her to the limit.

This was a Hector Mullins she had never before seen. He was cold, ruthlessly determined, and it was clear that her comfort was not important to him in this situation, whatever it might be. He glared at her, spurring her, forcing her to walk even more rapidly, and he showed no sympathy when she stumbled or when she had to pause for a moment to ease the pain in her side or catch her breath.

OREGON!

By the time they reached Fort Oregon, Ginny's legs felt like jelly, and she was ready to collapse.

To her dismay Hector went straight to the commandant's house, where an oil lamp and several candles were burning in the parlor. Giving the girl no chance to compose herself, he pounded hard on the door. Lee Blake answered the summons in his shirtsleeves.

"Sir," Hector said as he saluted, "I apologize for coming here at this time of night, but this is urgent!"

"Come in," Lee replied mildly.

Cathy, who was sewing a quilt, immediately stopped her work and, aware that Ginny was on the verge of collapse, quickly offered her a chair.

"Colonel," Hector said, "me and Miss Dobbs was taking a walk down the river, and she did me the honor of accepting my proposal of marriage."

Lee thought Hector had come to obtain formal permission to marry, and he smiled.

"Then we ran across something that smells to me like a serious threat to the settlement of Oregon!"

Lee's smile faded.

Hector repeated what they had seen, then added the details that Ginny had been so eager to hear. "That troublemaker, Igor Doznevkov, was the man waiting on shore. Him and the ones that came off the ship talked in a language I couldn't understand, but I guess it was Russian. One was very much in charge, and damned if—excuse me, ladies—blamed if he wasn't wearing some kind of uniform with gold braid all over it. I never saw that kind of uniform before."

"Where did they go?" Lee wanted to know.

"They headed into the forest. If it wasn't for Ginny here, I would have followed them, but I didn't want her involved. They started in the direction of Doznevkov's cabin deep in the woods, so it's my guess they went there."

"Can you find your way to that cabin?"

"Yes, sir."

"Very well. Take a detail with you, with spare mounts for Doznevkov and his friends. Bring them back here. Major Moser and I will be in my office when you arrive. Use force only if it should be necessary to apprehend them, and don't be any rougher with them than you must. Disarm them as a precaution, but don't use firearms yourselves. They've broken no laws, as far as we know, so I don't want anyone shot."

"I understand, sir." Hector stood at rigid attention.

Ginny watched him with admiration. He was so sure of himself, so ready to cope with the emergency that had developed, and she readily forgave him for the indifferent way he had treated her.

"Assign ten men to the squad, Mullins, any ten you wish. We'll see to it that Ginny is escorted home."

"Thank you, sir." Hector cast a quick glance in the direction of the young woman who had accepted his proposal of marriage, his expression asking her to understand there were times when he had to place his duty ahead of her welfare.

She smiled at him fleetingly as he saluted again and raced out into the night.

Cathy had never liked Ginny, regarding her as too belligerent and abrasive, but their relationship was changed now. As the wife of the garrison commander, it was her responsibility to show hospitality to the future wife of her husband's sergeant major. "Let me give you a cup of tea before you're taken home," she said. "You've had an unpleasant experience."

Ordinarily Ginny would have rejected the invitation, but she, too, was aware of the change in their relationship. This woman whose beauty and poise she resented was the wife of Hector's commanding officer, and she couldn't allow herself to forget it. Colonel Blake could make life miserable for a subordinate if he felt vindictive.

"Is it—real tea?" she asked, thinking she could no longer refer to Cathy by her first name but unwilling to address her as "ma'am."

Cathy shook her head. "The same herb tea that everyone else here is drinking. You'll soon discover that we enjoy no special privileges in this house."

"I—I'd like a cup of herb tea very much, thank you," Ginny said, then accompanied her into the kitchen.

Cathy filled a kettle with water and placed it on her stove, Oregon's first, which was made with sheets of metal that had been a gift from the officers of the U.S.S. *Washington*.

Lee came in, wearing his tunic and hat and buckling on his sword. "I may be very late, depending on how long it takes Mullins to round up Doznevkov and his crew," he said, "so don't wait up for me, Cathy. Ginny, I'll send a corporal to take you home, but you needn't rush."

Cathy waited until he had gone before she smiled and said, "You'll soon find that Hector's sergeants and corporals will treat you like royalty." The water began to boil, and she spooned dried herbs into the kettle to steep.

"Why should they?" Ginny debated whether to take a chair, but the Colonel's wife was putting on no airs, so she sat.

"Army life is different for those of us who never knew it before. Soldiers are conscious of rank at all times, but their rules don't apply to you and me. We're still civilians. So feel free to come to me for any advice or help I can give you. I believe that some of the officers and sergeants who are coming here as reinforcements are bringing their families with them, so it will be up to you and me to make them feel at home." She poured steaming, aromatic tea into two mugs, then seated herself at the table.

Ginny realized she had to revise her estimate of this beauty she had regarded as haughty and self-centered. "It will take me a little time to become accustomed to army life," she confessed, giving a nervous laugh. "It can't be much more than an hour ago that Hector proposed to me."

"I know how you feel. The day Lee's troops arrived here I wanted to run off into the forest and hide. But soldiers are people, just like everyone else, so just be yourself."

"I'll try." Ginny sipped her herb tea, then paused for a moment. "Why are you being so nice to me?"

"Why shouldn't I be? We had our differences after you came into our Wyoming camp last winter, but all that is past. My husband and the man who will become your husband spend their working lives together. And they need to depend on each other. So it's up to you and me to relieve them of additional burdens by becoming friends."

A slow smile appeared on Ginny's face. "I have to admit I hated you when I first met you, Cathy. You and Cindy and Eulalia were the kind of people I'd always wanted to be, and I envied you. But now, all of a sudden, everything is changed."

"I'm discovering that only our attitudes change. We're as happy or as upset as we want to be and allow ourselves to be." Cathy privately hated herself for sounding so smug and wished she could take her own advice. She wouldn't be truly happy until she could put Whip Holt out of her mind for all time and reconcile herself to the fact that she would spend the rest of her days as Mrs. Leland Blake.

The worst of her predicament was that her marriage was anything but a failure. Lee loved her, and she knew she could love him, too, once she could force herself to forget what might have been with Whip. As she had just finished explaining, she had accepted serious responsibilities and was discharging them to the best of her ability. The time had come for her to stop behaving like an adolescent who craved the admiration of every boy she saw.

A tap sounded at the door, and Cathy was glad to put her own problems out of her mind as she admitted a young corporal of the watch.

"Evening, ma'am," he said, removing his hat. "The Colonel wants for me to take Miss Dobbs home."

Ginny was ready to depart, and, after thanking Cathy again for her kindness, she left.

The soldier fell in beside her, his rifle in his right hand. "Colonel Blake says you'll be a-marrying the Sergeant Major," he declared, his tone stilted.

"Yes, that's right," she said.

He chose his words with care. "I wish you every happiness, ma'am."

Only one other man had ever addressed Ginny Dobbs as "ma'am," and that was Hector. She realized that, at least, within the confines of the garrison, her status was being drastically altered.

In spite of the late hour, an entire company of infantry had been placed on an alert, augmenting the sentries on watch and taking up posts around the headquarters building. Two oil lamps were burning in the office of the commandant, where he and his deputy awaited the results of Hector Mullins's mission.

Eli Moser was eager to talk, but his superior made it plain he preferred to learn facts rather than speculate, so they spent the time setting up the orientation and training schedules for the reinforcements that Washington City was sending them by sea.

More than two hours passed, and then they heard the Corporal of the guard call, "Advance and be recognized!"

"Sergeant Major Mullins, with prisoners and an escort!" Hector responded in a voice that echoed across the parade ground.

Lee allowed himself the luxury of a tight smile of satisfaction. Hector Mullins was unfailingly reliable.

A few moments later a heavy knock sounded at the door, and Eli Moser opened it. Lee looked up from his desk without rising as Mullins shoved the four prisoners into the office. Two were very young, obviously bewildered and frightened, and their drab attire indicated they were menials. Igor Doznevkov was angry, his face red, but it was the fourth man who immediately caught the commandant's attention.

He was tall, fully bearded, and wore the full field uniform of a Colonel of the Imperial Russian Household Guards. His mere presence in such attire halfway around the world from Russia was startling.

The furious Doznevkov launched into a tirade, giving no one else a chance to speak. "Colonel Blake," he shouted, "you have no right to have us arrested as common criminals! I demand our immediate release."

The bearded Colonel silenced him with an imperious gesture. "I will take charge," he announced and turned to Lee. "By insulting me, sir, you have insulted Czar Nicholas. I must insist upon the return of my sword and an official apology from the government of the United States."

Lee looked him up and down coolly. "And who are you, sir?"

The officer clicked his heels. "I am the official and personal representative of His Majesty, Czar Nicholas. I carry his commission as the Military Governor of the Imperial Russian colony of Oregon!"

Eli Moser covered the lower part of his face with his hand in order to conceal his broad smile.

Lee remained sober faced. "And these two?"

"My servants."

"Your name and rank, sir?"

Again the officer clicked his heels. "I am Colonel Mikhail Menshikoff, on detached service from the Second Division of Imperial Household Guards."

Lee rose. "Colonel Leland Blake and Major Eli Moser, United States Army," he said, then resumed his seat. "Sergeant Major Mullins!"

"Sir?" Hector appeared in the door frame.

"It's a mite crowded in here," Lee said calmly, "so I

suggest you have someone take these two young fellows to the mess hall and rustle up something for them to eat. Have them kept under close watch, of course."

"Yes, sir." Hector motioned the two young Russians out of the office, then repeated the commandant's orders to a subordinate before returning to his place outside the door.

"Perhaps you'll be good enough to explain why you were landed here surreptitiously, Colonel Menshikoff."

"I am under no obligation to reply to your question, Colonel Blake." The Russian's dark eyes were stubborn, but he kept his temper.

"I'll answer for him," the seething Igor Doznevkov said. "We knew you would do everything in your power to interfere with His Excellency's landing!"

Lee ignored the interruption. "Am I correct in my understanding, Colonel Menshikoff, that you came here with only two personal servants? Apparently you have landed no troops, no supplies, and no civilian settlers."

"I have come to take charge of the Czar's subjects who arrived at an earlier date," Menshikoff replied firmly.

"Those people are no longer Russians," Lee said quietly. "All of them, including Doznevkov, have sworn an oath of allegiance to the United States."

"They were coerced!"

"I beg to differ with you. No force was used. Any who wish to leave are free to accompany you."

Eli Moser wondered why his superior was being so polite. He himself would have shown far less patience.

Lee Blake well knew that, on the surface, the situation was ludicrous. The uniformed Russian officer apparently was supported by no troops or warships, so his commission as Military Governor was meaningless. But, as one who had been trained in the complexities of international relations, Lee knew Menshikoff represented a threat to the American claim to the region. Even though he was virtually alone and powerless, he had nevertheless come to America as the viceroy of the absolute monarch who ruled Europe's largest nation.

"May I see your commission?"

Menshikoff reached into an inner pocket and removed a folded sheet of parchment, which he handed across the desk.

"Don't give it to him," Doznevkov said. "He'll destroy it!"

Lee glanced at the man in contempt, then unfolded the parchment. He knew enough Russian to make out the gist of the document, which seemed genuine.

"Allow me to make my own position clear," Lee said. "The United States claims the Oregon country, and that claim is supported by my troops and the members of our civilian community. We seek no trouble with anyone. So you and your servants may stay here as long as you please, either living with Doznevkov or building a dwelling of your own. I won't insult you by demanding that you swear allegiance to the United States, but as long as you are here, you will be required to obey our laws. If that doesn't suit you, go where you please. There are hundreds of thousands of square miles of unoccupied land in the mountain chains that lie to the east of us, in a region that no nation as yet has claimed. Set up your colony there, and, if you wish, invite those who came here earlier from Russia to join you. We'll keep no man here against his will."

Doznevkov was still badly upset. "You know you've subverted our people, Colonel Blake. You've taken them into your homes, granted them parcels of land, and even encouraged your settlers to help them build houses and clear forests for farming. They have become so comfortable here that you know they will not choose to leave, particularly when they are protected by your cannon and your soldiers!"

Lee paid no attention to him and carefully returned the parchment to Menshikoff. "You've heard my offer, Colonel. Take it or leave it, as you wish."

"There is an old saying in Russia," Menshikoff replied. "He who commands the most regiments gives the orders." He smiled ruefully, then shrugged.

The man was creating grave diplomatic problems, but Lee couldn't help admiring his realistic acceptance of the situation. Obviously, he was unlike Igor Doznevkov, who was perpetually hostile to his American hosts.

"For the present," Menshikoff continued, "you give me no choice, and I assume I shall receive similar treatment from the British at Fort Vancouver. But I must warn you, Colonel Blake—as I intend to warn the British—that I have made arrangements for a Russian trading ship to come to me at regular intervals. My report on the stand you have taken will be reported in full to St. Petersburg, and you will suffer the consequences."

Lee was relieved because the Russians were using a trading vessel rather than a warship to carry messages. "I'm sure you realize that I will send a report to Washington City at the first opportunity, too. I have already notified our government that the Russian settlers who came here previously have joined us, and I have no doubt that the State Department will communicate with the Foreign Ministry in St. Petersburg. For the present, welcome to Oregon." He stood and was ready to thrust out his hand, but the Russian officer clicked his heels, bowed, and started to leave.

Sergeant Major Hector Mullins blocked the door.

"Mullins," Lee said, "return the weapons you took from this gentleman and his companions. Fetch his men from the mess hall, escort the party to the fort entrance, and turn them loose."

The Sergeant Major stared incredulously at his superior for a moment, then recovered and saluted. As Lee closed the door behind the visitors, he could hear Mullins bawling commands.

"Colonel," Eli Moser said, "don't be offended by my criticism, but if I were in charge here, I'd have thrown those idiots into detention cells and kept them there until the next Russian trading ship came to Oregon. Then I'd send them on board in chains."

"I was tempted," Lee replied, "but we can't do it, Eli."

"Why the hell not, sir?"

"I don't want to give St. Petersburg any valid reason to break diplomatic relations with the United States or create any other embarrassment for our government. We know Doznevkov is a mischief-maker, but Colonel Menshikoff seems sensible, although only time will tell whether I'm right. Just keep in mind that he follows orders, as you and I do. So, if anyone creates a fuss, it will be the Russians who do it. We're fairly strong and growing stronger, so we're in a good position to sit tight and let them make the first overt move, if that's what they intend. Meanwhile, we're to keep an eye on these Russians and make sure they stay harmless."

Word of Colonel Menshikoff's arrival spread quickly through the community, and Olga Runkova expressed the sentiments of some of the other Russians when she said, "This Colonel may go to the devil, and I hope he takes the Czar with him! We are Americans now, and we take no orders from him!"

Dr. Anton Wizneuski, busily engaged in the medical practice he was sharing with Dr. Martin, merely smiled and made no comment. None was needed, in his opinion. The United States was an active force in Oregon, but St. Petersburg was continuing to bumble.

Lisolette Arbo was disturbed and frightened by the news, however, and Eulalia—thinking Lisolette's concern was due to the general fear Russians had for figures of authority—could not convince her that there was no way the newly arrived Russian official could exert authority over her. Whip was also concerned for Lisolette's welfare, but because of his promise to Lee Blake, he could not let her know that he knew just what was frightening her.

Paul Thoman did his best to soothe her, too, when he came to call at the Holt ranch the following Sunday. "You're too intelligent to be afraid of ghosts," he told the girl. "There are seven hundred and fifty Americans here now, including the troops at Fort Oregon. Just look at their cannon, and you'll feel better. I hear this Colonel is living with Doznevkov until his servants build a separate house for him nearby. When he moves into it, he can be governor of a colony of three people. So put him out of your mind!"

"You do not understand," Lisolette told him but refused to elaborate.

She remained so upset that Whip persuaded her to ride into the village with him one day so Dr. Wizneuski, who had long been her friend, could reason with her.

Anton was patient with her. "Colonel Menshikoff can cause you no harm," he said. "He has no army, no navy. He is like so many I have known in Russia. He takes postures and makes grand speeches, but he has no power to back up his words."

Lisolette had to struggle to prevent herself from trembling. "He may have no power over you or the others who made the long journey from Russia. But he still has power over me."

"How could that be?" Anton spoke very quietly. "All of us have become Americans now."

"Surely you don't think the ministers of the Czar and—and the secret police—will accept a change in nationality."

"The secret police?" He raised an eyebrow. "The

230

arm of the secret police is said to be long, but I don't think it reaches as far as Oregon."

Lisolette could not curb a shudder. "I am half-French, remember, so I am more vulnerable than you who had two Russian parents."

Her logic made no sense, but the young physician stopped trying to calm her. Speaking privately to Whip, he said, "Something is frightening her, and only the passage of time will convince her that her fears are groundless."

Whip well knew, thanks to his talk with Lee Blake, that Doznevkov was responsible in some way for the girl's upset state. But all he said was, "We'll look after her, never fear."

His feeling of calm would have lessened appreciably had he realized that, soon after he and Lisolette had ridden into town, Igor Doznevkov had appeared at the door of the ranch house.

In Igor's opinion his mission had become urgent. The arrival of Colonel Menshikoff made it essential that a strong, bold stand be taken in behalf of Russia. He could not believe that all of the Czar's subjects had accepted their change to an American status happily and without regret. But he had become so unpopular that there was no way he could test their loyalties himself. So he had decided to put Lisolette to work for him. He would order her to act in his stead, and after she found out which of the immigrants were still sympathetically inclined toward Russia, he would be in a far better position to intervene directly with them.

For two days he kept watch on the Holt ranch house from a distance, and this morning his patience had been rewarded. The Indian who worked for Holt had ridden out to the range early in the day, and a short time later Holt and his wife had gone off to the village.

What he failed to realize from his distant observation post, however, was that it was Lisolette who was riding with Whip. Doznevkov had seen her only from the rear, and she was wearing a doeskin shirt and skirt she had borrowed from Eulalia.

Eulalia was scrubbing a frying pan in the kitchen when she heard the tap at the door. At Whip's insistence she always kept firearms nearby when she was alone in the house, so she obediently picked up a loaded pistol before she went to the door.

The stridently unpleasant Russian was the last person she had expected to find at the threshold.

Doznevkov quickly realized he had erred, then just as quickly decided he might be able to utilize the situation to his advantage. Any woman as beautiful as Holt's wife had to be vain, and perhaps he could find some way to use her in behalf of his cause.

"I'm afraid my husband isn't at home," she said. "He's gone into the village."

"To be truthful," he said, smiling broadly, "I was hoping I might have a few words with you, Mrs. Holt. Provided," he added as he gestured toward her pistol, "that you won't shoot me."

Eulalia flushed. "Come in," she said, but she took care to jam the pistol into the broad belt that Whip had made for her. Experience had taught her to take no unnecessary risks in frontier living.

Doznevkov could be charming when he wanted to exert himself, and he continued to smile steadily as he walked beside her to the kitchen. "I hope I don't intrude."

"Not at all, if you don't mind my finishing what I was doing. I've got to leave soon to exercise my mare." Eulalia picked up her pan and brush and began to scrub again.

"May I sit?" Igor gestured toward a chair.

"Help yourself." She could imagine no reason this man would want to see her, but she had no intention of making the task any easier for him.

He watched her in silence for a moment. "It is astonishing," he said at last.

"What is?" She remained matter-of-fact.

"You Americans are remarkable. The most beautiful lady in Oregon, perhaps the loveliest I have ever seen anywhere, stands over a tub and scrubs a frying pan!"

"I prefer it clean to dirty. We have no more cash than most people here, and less than many. So I do my own housework, naturally." She was flattered by his reference to her beauty, but nevertheless remained wary.

"You are curious to know why I, a stranger, have sought you out, Madame Holt. It is because you are more sophisticated than the other Americans here, more worldly."

"I doubt that very much," she said. "I spent my whole life on a South Carolina plantation before my family and I joined the wagon train."

Here was the key he needed. "Exactly. When you lived on the plantation, there were many parties. You had many suitors. So you have learned much about the nature of people."

That much was true, she had to admit.

"It is my hope," he said, "that you will take pity on me." He felt his way cautiously. "Perhaps you, knowing human nature, can tell me why so many in Oregon dislike me. Is it because I am a foreigner to you?"

"Hardly that," Eulalia said, beginning to think that his request for her help might be sincere. "Ernie von Thalman, our appointed agent, who will be our delegate to Congress eventually, comes from Austria. And many of the Russians who have joined us are very popular. Everybody likes Dr. Wizneuski and Olga Runkova."

"And the Arbo girl who is living with you, they like her, too?"

"Well, not that many know her. She's a more private person."

"Perhaps some have told you why I am disliked."

"Not really," Eulalia said, drying the skillet and hanging it on a wall peg. "Perhaps it is because you were the leader of the party that came here from Russia, and sometimes people don't take kindly to those who have had authority over them. Of course, my husband was a leader of our wagon train, but he has a special way of handling people without their ever knowing it, so he's unusual."

Igor choked back his intense dislike of Holt. "Indeed he is," he agreed. "It may be there are some in the Russian party who do not hate me. Is that so?"

"I really haven't heard, one way or the other."

"Perhaps you could find out for me. A word here, a word there. Everyone likes and trusts you, not only because you are Holt's wife, but because no other woman here is as lovely. It is common knowledge that you stand apart."

Eulalia had not heard of such an appraisal and couldn't help glowing. She could begin to understand why this lonely, bitter man had come to her, and it would be wrong to refuse to offer him her assistance.

She was never free of the belief that Whip took her for granted, and her life was permanently soured by the realization. There was nothing she could do to ease that burden, to be sure. She had given herself to Whip without reservation and loved no other man. Certainly she was interested in no one else, and in spite of her natural flirtatiousness, a result of her South Carolina plantation upbringing, she knew that nothing could impel her, now or ever, to be unfaithful to her husband. Her degrading experience as an Indian captive had taught her that sex without love was cheap and disgusting, and she would spend the rest of her days living in the hope that, ultimately, Whip would feel toward her as she did toward him.

In the meantime it was pleasant, even exhilarating, to be appreciated. Something in the nature of this visitor continued to make her uneasy, but she couldn't define that characteristic, so she tried to put it out of her mind. He had come to her for help in solving his own problem, and it would require little effort on her part to learn which of his fellow Russians, if any, felt a measure of sympathy for him.

"I can't promise anything," she said, "but I'll be glad to do what I can."

Igor rose and bowed over her hand. "I shall not forget this kindness, Madame Holt," he murmured.

Eulalia was thrilled. It had been a very long time since her hand had been kissed, and, whatever this man's faults, she could not deny that he was a gentleman.

Doznevkov exulted as he took his leave. How much better it was to have the respected wife of the universally admired Whip Holt find out which of the Russians might be recruited for the establishment of a separate colony than it would be to rely on the half-hearted effort of a frightened Lisolette Arbo. His fortunes had changed, and this unexpected encounter promised to be productive.

He glanced at his pocket watch as he made his way into the woods, then walked slowly toward a pre-designated spot about a mile up the Columbia River from the American village. He would reach the place in about an hour, and then another, equally important test awaited him. He would prove to Colonel Menshikoff that he was the most competent of aides and deserved promotion in the ranks of the secret police. Mikhail Menshikoff, like most aristocrats, had a narrow field of vision and was slow-witted, so only a few successful ventures would be needed to persuade him to send a praise-filled report about Doznevkov to his own superiors. Then, Doznevkov thought, he would be able to leave this drab New World wilderness and return to St. Petersburg, where he would be appointed to the supervisory position he deserved.

The uniformed Menshikoff awaited him and was sitting on a rock overlooking the Columbia when his associate joined him. "I was afraid you would be late," he said.

Doznevkov greeted him deferentially. "I am never late, Your Excellency. Please observe that the long-boat is just now putting out from the opposite shore."

They watched together in silence as eight redcoats rowed the boat across the river. A junior officer, resplendent in scarlet and gold, leaped onto the bank, approached the pair, and saluted with a flourish. "I bring you Colonel Morrison's compliments, gentlemen," he said.

They accompanied him to the boat and were rowed across the river. There a British captain and a detachment of troops were waiting, and the two Russians were escorted to Fort Vancouver.

Someone had been watching for them, and Colonel Phillips Morrison came to the gate to greet them cordially. He then conducted them to the parade ground, where an honor guard stood in formation and was duly inspected. Only then did the British commandant conduct his guests to his house, where Major Roland Pitts and a skeptical Dr. John McLoughlin joined them for dinner.

Before the meal was served, they drank sack in the parlor, and Colonel Morrison offered a toast to Czar Nicholas. Colonel Menshikoff, not to be outdone, responded with a toast to the health of Queen Victoria.

The dinner was superb, far more elaborate than any offered to other visitors. Steamed mussels were followed by grilled salmon; the main course was venison steak; dessert was a deep-dish peach pie; and savories of wild mushrooms on toast rounded off the meal. Appropriate wines were served with every course, including a fine champagne the British commandant had been hoarding.

Throughout the meal Colonel Morrison was a genial and attentive host. Earlier in his career he had spent two years as assistant military attaché at the

British legation in St. Petersburg, so he was able to speak knowledgeably about the Russian army and life at the court. The far more parochial Colonel Menshikoff was unable to keep up with him, but Igor Doznevkov smoothly filled in the gaps, and the conversation flowed easily. Major Pitts spoke infrequently, which was fitting for the junior officer present, and Dr. McLoughlin was almost completely silent, his bushy eyebrows occasionally rising and falling as he listened to the talk.

When the decanter of port wine was passed to the left, according to the British custom, and new toasts had been consumed, the time for serious matters had come. "Gentlemen," Colonel Morrison said as he passed around a box of West Indian cigars he had had imported at great expense, "we face a dilemma. Great Britain and Russia were the principal allies in the titanic Napoleonic Wars that led to the defeat of Bonaparte. Since that time we have remained close friends. Queen Victoria's relations with Czar Nicholas are amicable. Nevertheless, we find ourselves rivals in Oregon."

Colonel Menshikoff was out of his depth, so Doznevkov replied for him. "I'm sure I know what you are thinking, Colonel Morrison. Neither of our governments would approve if hostilities broke out between us in a land as remote as Oregon."

"Precisely, sir." Morrison took his time lighting his cigar. "Both Britain and Russia have laid claim to Oregon, and the claims of both have a sound legal basis."

"That is one of our most vexing problems," Doznevkov replied, while Menshikoff nodded in vigorous agreement. "We came here before you and explored much of the area. On the other hand, you established Fort Vancouver and have achieved a notable success here. What shall be done?"

"The answer lies with none of us at this table," Phillips Morrison declared. "Higher authorities in

London and St. Petersburg will reach a solution, and I am confident that these two great powers will not resort to war."

"That would be catastrophic for all of us," Menshikoff managed to say.

"You take my point," Morrison said, then unconsciously used the language Lee Blake had used when speaking to him. "Gentlemen, I propose we allow those who control our nations to find the compromises that will result in a fair sharing of Oregon. In the meantime, let us be friends and help each other in every way we can."

"Admirable!" Doznevkov said enthusiastically. "We will only harm each other and ourselves if we fight. At present there are only a few Russians here, but if our dignity is harmed, you know and we know that the Czar and his ministers would not permit such a slight to go unanswered."

"We think alike," Morrison said. "And that brings me to the major point that none of us has mentioned. The upstart Americans. Not only have they sent a wagon train to Oregon—with more trains on the way here, as they tell us at every opportunity—but they have also sent troops and established a fort. This situation, as I see it, is intolerable!"

"You echo our sentiments, Colonel Morrison." There was a gleam in Doznevkov's eyes.

"They must be driven out," Colonel Menshikoff added firmly.

John McLoughlin cleared his throat loudly. The others had almost forgotten his presence, and they looked at him in surprise. "It strikes me you've neglected your history, all of you," he said. "Back in 1804, President Thomas Jefferson sent two young officers of the United States Army on a journey of exploration. Virtually nothing was known of the western portions of this continent at the time. Meriwether Lewis and William Clark are still regarded as heroes by the Americans. And rightly so."

Morrison became indignant and tried to interrupt, but Dr. McLoughlin silenced him with an icy glare. "Lewis and Clark spent their first winter in the Dakota country. The next year they reached the Columbia River basin and traced the river to its mouth—to the very place where we have been sitting and enjoying a splendid banquet. In case you've forgotten, they explored this entire area. I assure you that no American has forgotten these facts. The United States bases her claims to Oregon on the discoveries of Lewis and Clark. Combine that claim with the also undeniable fact that they're the first to settle here in large numbers, and the American position becomes formidable."

"The Russians were the first to come here," Doznevkov said emphatically.

"No nation denies that Russia sent expeditions of exploration to this region from Alaska," McLoughlin said sternly. "But at no time has St. Petersburg offered proof that your explorers preceded Lewis and Clark!"

"Czar Nicholas made the statement himself in a speech from the throne," Colonel Menshikoff said. "Who would dare to deny that the Czar speaks the truth?"

McLoughlin smiled. "Well, the Americans aren't impressed. For that matter, neither are the ministers of Queen Victoria's government. I'm not saying that London and Washington City are calling Nicholas a liar. That would be indelicate and undiplomatic. But a nation's claim to a rich country that is well able to support many hundreds of thousands of settlers—perhaps millions—needs to be substantiated with something more than a vague royal allegation."

"You insult my guests," Colonel Morrison declared.

"That isn't my intention," Dr. McLoughlin said. "I'm just trying to point out to all of you that the United States, which is far closer to Oregon than either Britain or Russia, can't be bluffed, talked, or frightened into leaving this territory."

"Ways must be found," Doznevkov said.

"We will find them together," Morrison replied.

The dinner ended on that optimistic note, and Major Pitts conducted the visitors to the longboat that would take them to the south bank of the Columbia.

John McLoughlin lingered behind. "Morrison," he said when he and the Fort Vancouver commandant were alone, "you're no fool. Surely you can't believe the Russians have a legally justifiable claim to Oregon."

Phillips Morrison laughed aloud. "The Russian position is preposterous."

"Then why did you go out of your way to encourage those two Russian representatives?"

"St. Petersburg would have sent troops and ships here from Alaska long before now if the Czar's claim was serious. What's more, the Russians are doing everything in the worst way possible. They're trying to win something at a very low cost. But they won't get it. Only the Americans are offering us genuine competition, and they've moved ahead of us."

"Then why—"

"For the very reason that the United States has taken the lead. I have no idea what the Russians may do to harm them, and I took care not to ask."

"That's unscrupulous," McLoughlin said.

"Call it what you will," Morrison said. "My principal aim is to get the Americans out of Oregon, and nothing would please me more than to see the Russians do the worst of the dirty work for me."

IX

Relations between Fort Oregon and Fort Vancouver remained correct, if not cordial, because of an unofficial policy established by the commanders of the two garrisons. British enlisted men were forbidden to cross to the American side of the Columbia River, and the north bank was declared out of bounds for American soldiers. Officers of both garrisons were allowed to cross at will, and no attempt was made to restrict the movements of civilians on either side. Peace was fragile, but no untoward incidents disturbed it.

In the main, the people of the two communities lived their lives separately, and only a few people regarded that separation as strange. The stakes for Oregon were enormous, so it was agreed that it was wise not to become too friendly with people who might become overnight enemies.

Then nature intervened, and in almost no time the relations between the Americans and the British in Oregon were changed.

Toward the end of the winter, there was an extraordinary shift in the weather. Ordinarily, rain fell heavily every day at this season, but now an unusual dry spell set in, and for three weeks not a drop of rain fell.

Hawkman, an unshaven, renegade trapper from St. Louis who preferred Olga and Dolores's tavern to the British establishments across the river, announced to anyone who would listen to him that in the ten years he had spent in Oregon he had never known such weather. Few people paid attention to Hawkman's pronouncements because he was rarely sober, but they had to agree with him that the drought was unlike any Oregon weather they had experienced.

One morning Paul Thoman and Harry Canning left the cabin they shared and walked to the Columbia in the hope of catching a salmon for their breakfast before going on to work at their boatyard. Both threw lines into the water, and Harry happened to glance upstream.

"My God!" he exclaimed. A forest fire was raging to the east, and the wind from the Cascade Range was blowing it in the direction of the village.

Fishing forgotten, the pair raced to Fort Oregon, and as they approached the sentry at the gate, they shouted, "Fire!"

The entire garrison was aroused. Bugles blared, drums rolled, and as the regiment assembled, Colonel Lee Blake sent two mounted messengers to alert as many residents of the village and outlying settlers as they could reach, particularly those who lived to the east.

Then the troops were marched in the direction of the conflagration, all of them carrying hatchets and axes. Along the way they were joined by settlers, similarly armed.

One of the first to arrive was Whip Holt, who had somehow guessed where he would find the regiment as he galloped at full tilt. Seeing the unit, he joined Lee at the head of the column.

"Thank God you're here," the latter said. "All I can think to do is to cut a broad path to stop the advance of the fire toward the settlement."

"It's the only thing," Whip agreed. "There's no way

in this world to stop a fire of that size except to give it nothing more to feed on."

They pressed on rapidly, and settlers continued to augment the line. The spirit that had animated these members of the first wagon train company was revived. As survivors of innumerable hardships and more Indian raids than they cared to remember, they were confident of their ability to win the battle against this new, unfamiliar enemy. A number of men began to sing and did not fall silent until Hector Mullins sensibly told them to save their breath for the struggle that awaited them.

Lee and Whip rode together near the bank of the Columbia, where open spaces made it possible for them to watch the fire. The speed of its advance was frightening. Here and there flames leaped high toward the sky, and a column of black smoke poured upward, fouling the clean air.

"The oaks and the other big trees may be scorched, but they won't burn too badly," Whip said. "The confounded evergreens are what cause the trouble. The pines are like sawdust."

Lee pointed several hundred yards upstream. "Look over there," he said.

A string of longboats stretched across the Columbia from the north bank, all of them filled with British troops.

Several had already landed on the south shore, and Major Roland Pitts hurried forward on foot. "Colonel Blake," he said, "I'm in acting command of Fort Vancouver because Colonel Morrison is away on a hunting trip. I saw the fire on my way to breakfast and thought you might be able to use our help. Every able-bodied man I could muster is on the way."

"I'm grateful to you, Major," Lee replied. "Obviously we can use all the help we can get."

Soon the blue-clad American troops and the British redcoats were enjoying the unique experience of marching side by side to fight a common foe.

After advancing for the better part of an hour, Whip called a halt. "This is far enough to the east," he said. "As it is we'll have to hurry."

Lee immediately assumed overall command. Civilians held the position nearest the river, with the redcoats deployed adjacent to them and the American troops taking their places farther inland. Within a short time there was no sound but that of axes and hatchets biting into wood.

Ernie von Thalman was one of the last to reach the scene and automatically took charge of the American civilians. Individual military units were under the orders of their company commanders. Lee, Whip, and Major Moser rode back and forth up and down the entire line, and Major Pitts joined them when a horse was found for him.

"It isn't enough to cut down trees," Whip said. "They've got to be hauled back out of harm's way, trunks and branches and all, or the fire will creep along the ground to this side and then start up again. As it is we've got to pray this wind will die down, or the flames may leap across the gap. If they do, they'll travel all the way to the Willamette."

"Then we've got to make the cleared area as wide as we possibly can," Lee said.

"Sure, but our first worry is length."

The fire line stretched toward the south for the better part of two miles, blocked only by a narrow lake that, providentially, offered protection for almost another mile to the south. The fire was not burning that far southward, so the men in charge reasoned that it could be contained if their cleared area was wide enough to prevent the flames from jumping across it.

The men labored unceasingly through the long hours of the morning, with almost eight hundred of them—the majority British—cutting and then hauling the felled trees out of the way. The sappers of both regiments speeded the process by exploding charges of gunpowder that caused other trees to topple.

By noon the cleared area was at least one hundred feet wide and in some places was even deeper. Lee was not satisfied and drove the men hard. "Make the path still deeper," he ordered repeatedly.

The men were weary but continued to chop. They needed no one to tell them that if the fire could not be contained, all their houses, built with such great effort and loving care, were in danger of being destroyed.

Little by little the fire crept closer, then closer still. The roar, faint at first, gradually became louder, and the hissing, crackling sounds, punctuated by the crash of burning trees as they toppled to the ground, became menacing. The wind subsided somewhat, but was still strong enough to carry the acrid odors toward the men who were making a supreme effort to save the American settlement from destruction. Men's eyes watered, and when the smoke became thick they choked, gasped for breath, and had to withdraw temporarily in order to breathe some clearer air.

In spite of these obstacles they persisted in their efforts. Major Pitts and Major Moser were stationed with their respective regiments now, each cajoling and threatening as they nudged and prodded the troops into continuing their efforts.

Only Lee Blake and Whip Holt continued to patrol the entire line, and Lee behaved like a man possessed by demons. "Harder," he shouted hoarsely. "Keep cutting! Haul that cedar out of the clearing! Faster, men! We can't let the fire gain on us!"

Soldiers and civilians alike were exhausted, but they chopped and hauled automatically, calling on their reserves of energy to see them through the crisis. In places they could feel the searing heat of the fire, and sometimes whole clouds of black smoke enveloped them, but they found the courage and stamina to go on and on.

245

By mid-afternoon Lee and Whip had tied wet handkerchiefs over their faces to enable them to breathe more easily, and as the fire moved on toward the expanding clearing, they found it increasingly difficult to control their panicky horses. They could see the fire now, and Whip had to blink away the tears in his eyes.

"Maybe we'd better pull back now," he suggested.

"Not yet," Lee said stubbornly. "There's still time to bring down more trees."

A quarter of an hour later, when they reached the shore of the lake, they were relieved that the fire had not yet progressed this far to the south. If the flames failed to leap across the cleared area, the American community would be saved.

"We've done all we can now," Lee finally said. "We'll have to leave the rest to the Almighty."

The pair spurred northward, shouting, "Pull back!"

The bone-weary fire fighters needed no other command and immediately retreated into the forest, dragging their heavy axes on the ground. Some threw themselves onto grass or moss to rest, but the majority just stood still, sweat pouring from their faces and bodies as they peered in fascination at the still-raging fire.

At last Lee and Whip reached the bank of the Columbia. But their own work was not yet done. The conscientious Lee insisted they double back to make certain that every man had heard and obeyed the order.

As they came to the junction of the British and American line, a thick cloud of oily, almost impenetrable smoke blew toward them, propelled by a gust of wind. Whip spurred forward, and his stallion, although terrified, nevertheless responded and galloped rapidly enough to escape the worst of the cloud.

Lee was less fortunate. His gelding's panic was so great that it could no longer function, and it halted abruptly, unable to move in any direction. The cloud rolled over rider and mount, obscuring them from the view of the horrified troops who watched, unable to help.

Man and horse were immersed for what seemed like an eternity. When the smoke finally dissipated, the gelding lay dead on the ground, and Lee was crumpled in a heap near the animal.

Whip was the first to reach his side, with Major Moser and Major Pitts close behind him. They discovered that Lee was still alive but unconscious, his face smoke-blackened, his breathing shallow and labored.

"He needs doctors, not us," Whip said. "I'll take him to the hospital."

He mounted his stallion, then reached out as the two officers lifted up the unconscious Lee. After positioning Lee in front of him, Whip galloped rapidly toward the village.

By now the fire was consuming the last trees that stood on the far side of the clearing, angrily eating into the wood, causing branches to disappear while the still-burning trees to the rear cast a deep red glow. The American and British majors stood side by side and stared at the conflagration. The supreme test was at hand. Now they would discover whether the hard day's work had been successful or in vain.

The fire advanced no farther. Sergeant Major Mullins roared, "By God! The wind has died away!" Exhausted men laughed and wept and somehow found the strength to pound each other on the back.

Eli Moser, previously ever-eager to pick a quarrel with the British, changed his mind and extended his hand to his redcoat counterpart. "We owe our salvation to your troops, Major Pitts."

"I think we can share the credit," the British officer replied, giving him a tired smile.

Eli grinned. "We'll need a little time to rest, all of us," he said, "but I hope that your regiment will accept an invitation to dine with mine at Fort George the day after tomorrow."

Roland Pitts calculated rapidly. Colonel Morrison would still be absent on his hunting trip and would be furious when he learned his deputy's decision, but that couldn't be helped. "Major Moser, Her Majesty's Fort Vancouver garrison accepts with the greatest of pleasure."

Cathy Blake's friends rallied to her side. Cindy Woodling was the first to join her in the empty hospital cubicle where she was waiting. Bob Martin and Anton Wizneuski, assisted by Tonie Martin, were working on Lee.

Eulalia Holt put aside her jealousy of Cathy and rode into the village, too, as soon as Whip came home with the news. She found her friend and her sister-in-law sitting side by side on a cot, their faces revealing nothing. "How is Lee?"

Cathy remained stone-faced. "We haven't heard yet. I'm sure they'll let me know as soon as there's something to report." She rallied and tried to smile. "Tell Whip I'm grateful to him. Bob Martin said that —if they can save Lee's life—it's because Whip brought him here so quickly."

"I'm sure he wants no thanks," Eulalia said, "but I'll be sure to tell him." She sat opposite the other women.

For a long time no one spoke, and there was no need for verbal communication. They had sustained and supported each other on countless occasions during their long trek to Oregon, and now they were reunited, standing together in this new crisis. Cindy and Eulalia well remembered the hardships Cathy had endured on the trail, and they shared her dread that Lee might not survive. She, in return, knew how they felt, and their overwhelming concern for her gave her the courage to believe that all would be well.

At last Cindy broke the silence. "When Claiborne came home, he told me the fire was petering out," she said. "It must have been a terrible battle. His eyebrows and hair were burned, and he was so tired he went straight to bed. I couldn't even persuade him to eat something first."

"If Whip was tired he didn't show it," Eulalia said. "But he rarely does."

"He's extraordinary," Cathy agreed.

A horrible thought passed through Eulalia's mind. If Cathy was widowed she would be free and would become an even greater threat. Whip might even throw off all restraints and go to her. "Lee is remarkable, too," she murmured.

"We've always expected so much from both of them," Cindy declared, "and they've never let us down. We wouldn't have reached Oregon without them, just as we wouldn't be secure here without them. That's one reason Lee simply must pull through, Cathy. We all need him—almost as much as you do."

Cathy nodded, but made no reply. Besieged by a feeling of guilt because she believed she didn't love her husband, she prayed with all her might and all her soul for his recovery. She didn't know how she could live with herself if he died.

Only Cindy stood outside the mainstream of conflicting emotions. Aware of the complications, she felt closer to Eulalia, her sister-in-law, but her affection for Cathy was not diminished. Somehow, perhaps through their loyalties to each other, they could adjust to the loyalties that marriage demanded of them.

Wise far beyond her years because of her past, Cindy knew there was no escape for either of her friends. American moral conventions were rigid, unyielding, and when a woman married she had to accept her lot. "For better or worse" was not a glib phrase but a fact of life. Society forbade divorce and would not condone a marital separation. People always blamed the wife when a marriage failed, and even those who were close to her felt compelled to reject her. Oregon might be thousands of miles from the heart of American civilization, but the values back home also prevailed here.

Certainly Cathy and Eulalia understood what was at stake, and both were sensible, forced by their experiences to abandon false romantic illusions. As one who felt very close to both of them, Cindy could only hope they possessed the determination to solve their problems without hurting each other or themselves.

After an eternity of waiting, a weary Tonie Martin appeared in the entrance to the room and addressed herself to Cathy. "Bob and Anton think Lee will be all right," she said quietly. "His breathing is gradually becoming closer to normal, and his pulse rate is improving. He's still unconscious, but they aren't too worried about that. They're going to take turns staying with him through the night, and unless new complications develop, which they don't anticipate, they believe he'll be fine."

The dam broke, and tears glistened in Cathy's eyes.

"Bob says Lee should be over the worst of it in a week or less," Tonie continued. "Once he recovers consciousness, he'll be permitted no visitors except you, Cathy. It will take much longer for him to return to normal if his strength is taxed."

Cathy could only nod.

"It's late," Tonie said, "and there's nothing you can do here tonight, so go home and rest. I'll come to fetch you if you should be needed."

Cathy was reluctant to leave, so Cindy took matters into her own hands. "Come along, Cathy," she said. "Sleep will do you good."

They left the little hospital together, with Eulalia and Cindy leading their horses as they walked the short distance to Fort Oregon. They were surprised to discover that the night was far advanced, but a heavy rain was falling, ending the drought, and, hopefully, putting out what was left of the forest fire.

Leaving Cathy at the entrance to the fort, the two

young women mounted their mares and started off on the trail toward their homes. The cold rain drenched and chilled them, but it was useless to complain. Besides, they had known far worse weather on their trek across the continent.

A horseman loomed up in front of them, and a hollow-eyed Whip addressed them in obvious irritation. "I had a hunch you'd do something stupid like this," he said. "When it got to be midnight, I hoped both of you would have the sense to stay at the hospital or the fort overnight. Instead you come traipsing through the forest as though this was Charleston. Or Louisville. The wilderness is no place for women riding without escorts late at night!"

Eulalia cut her husband's diatribe short. "Lee Blake is going to be all right," she said. "We just found out."

"Of course he is. It would take more than a forest fire to kill a man like Lee! Now, fall in behind me, ride close, and don't lag." Whip turned his stallion and started back up the trail.

Duly reprimanded, the young women followed him meekly. He was right, as they well knew; they hadn't thought about their own safety. His highhanded manner annoyed Eulalia, but she told herself she should be grateful that he thought enough of her to ride into the village in search of her this late at night.

Cindy was deposited at her own home, and then a silent Whip rode beside Eulalia to the ranch house. Lamps were burning in the kitchen, and Eulalia was touched when she discovered that Lisolette had prepared a pot of hot soup for her. What was more, the girl kept her company while she ate it. Whip, however, went off to bed without speaking another word.

Discovering she was ravenous, Eulalia ate two bowls of soup, and, after insisting that Lisolette go back to bed, she cleaned the pot and her bowl before retiring.

Whip was sound asleep when she climbed into bed,

and she felt miffed. Certainly he should have understood the concern she and Cindy had felt for Lee and Cathy. She realized he had to have been very tired after his own exhausting day, but in her opinion his weariness was no excuse for the way he had spoken to Cindy and her.

Lee Blake regained consciousness at noon, but he was so weak that Cathy was permitted to remain at his side only long enough to feed him some broth. Then the physicians sent her away, and that evening her stay again was restricted to a visit of a few minutes' duration.

The following day Lee showed improvement, but Dr. Wizneuski warned Cathy not to discuss anything of importance with him or to linger too long in his room. He spent most of his time sleeping and wouldn't begin to feel like himself again for another forty-eight hours.

That afternoon the Americans at Fort Oregon entertained the redcoats from Fort Vancouver, and the event was a great success. Sides of venison and elk were roasted in pit fires, and the cooks baked loaves of fresh bread. The guests, mindful of the fact that food supplies were limited and would not be replenished until ships arrived, contributed beans flavored with venison meat that had been simmering over low fires since the previous day.

Each soldier was served only one tot of rum, and the restriction on the consumption of alcoholic beverages contributed to the amity; quarrels were few, no fights erupted, and the members of both garrisons enlarged on what they had discovered while fighting the forest fire, that they really had a great deal in common.

Members of the American civilian community also were present, as were John McLoughlin and most of his employees. But this was a day primarily for the military, and those who watched the troops from both garrisons eating and chatting with each other thought it unlikely that they would go out of their way to create incidents that might spark a war.

The higher-ranking officers and civilian leaders speculated on the number of trees they had cleared to stop the fire, and Eli Moser, with the enthusiastic support of Ernie von Thalman, offered Dr. McLoughlin more than half the wood. "After all," he said, "British soldiers also cut it down. So it wouldn't be fair for us to keep all of it."

McLoughlin accepted graciously but attached a condition. He would accept the felled trees, he said, only if the Americans, civilians and the military alike, would avail themselves of an offer he was making them. The following day he would sell wheat and dried beans, bacon, marmalade, and other provisions imported from England by the Hudson's Bay Company at half the normal price. The new spirit of friendship across the Columbia, he declared, was far more important than profits.

All of the American women who had any cash to spare were excited by the offer. Most of them agreed with Eulalia's comment, "Bargains like that are irresistible! I'm going to spend every last penny I can find!"

Ernie and McLoughlin promptly arranged to send longboats back and forth across the river throughout the day. And Ernie expressed the sentiments of virtually everyone when he said, "It has been unnatural for the people of two small, English-speaking communities, living so near to each other, to be separated by enmity. I believe that period is ending, and our friendship will force our governments to solve the problems of territorial claims peacefully."

Eulalia asked Lisolette to accompany her to Fort Vancouver, but the girl refused, saying there was nothing she wanted or needed there. Her shyness,

obvious in all of her relations except her growing
intimacy with Paul Thoman, appeared to be responsible for her decision.

The following morning Eulalia retired to her bedroom immediately after breakfast and took a long
time preparing for the journey across the river. Whip
had given her twelve dollars, and for that large a sum
she would need to take a pack horse to the village
with her in order to bring all of her purchases home.
Certainly she would have enough flour and bacon for
many months to come, and with any luck she might
even be able to buy a few boxes of genuine tea from
India.

Tired of the doeskins she wore most of the time,
she selected one of her South Carolina dresses, which
was far too light for Oregon weather, and for one of
the few times since arriving in Oregon, she applied a
rim of kohl around her eyes, used rouge on her lips
and cheeks, and dipped into her precious supply of
rice powder to dust her nose. When she emerged from
the bedroom, feeling more attractive than she had in
many weeks, Lisolette had already gone out to the
range to help Stalking Horse. Whip, who planned to
escort her as far as the village, was waiting alone for
her.

He rose slowly to his feet, staring at his wife.

At last, Eulalia thought, he appreciated her appearance.

"What in the devil have you done to yourself?" he
demanded.

Eulalia felt as though he had slapped her across the
face. "What's wrong with the way I look?" she retorted.

Whip had to study her for a long time before he
could put his reactions into words. "Your dress is too
tight, and the neckline is cut too low. And how do you
expect it to keep you warm?"

"This gown happens to have been made for me by

one of the best seamstresses in Charleston. Everyone who has ever seen me in it has complimented me."

He grimaced. "For another thing, you've got all that paint on your face."

"We're not spending the winter in the Wyoming mountains, you know. Fort Vancouver is a real town, and I see no reason why I have to go over there looking like a frump!"

Whip failed to realize she was bored and restless. After spending all of her life in the company of many people on a busy plantation, she had been surrounded at all times on the wagon train journey. Now she lived an isolated existence on the ranch, with only Lisolette to keep her company most of the time, and she was so busy, as was Cindy, that she and her sister-in-law visited each other infrequently.

In his sudden spurt of anger, Whip went too far. "You look like a whore!"

She immediately thought he was referring to the weeks she had spent as an Indian captive, and color burned through the rouge on her cheeks. "How dare you? I'm a lady, and I look like a lady!"

He realized he had hurt her, but he didn't know how to compensate for his mistake. "I reckon I spent too long living in the Rockies by myself," he muttered in an attempted apology. "We'd best get started if you're going to meet Cindy in the village. I'll saddle your mare for you and round up one of the pack horses."

They rode into town in a stiff, uncomfortable silence. Eulalia blamed Whip for taking the edge off the pleasure her appearance had given her. He, on the other hand, guessed he should apologize more fully, but he was damned if he would. She was so pretty that the combination of her dress and the paint on her face made her much too flamboyant by wilderness standards.

Eulalia left her mare and the pack horses in the

new stable that Ted Woods and Hosea had built behind the tavern.

"Tell me when to meet you," Whip said, "and I'll be here."

"I should be back by midday," Eulalia replied coolly, then walked off to a longboat waiting at the river bank.

Rather than return home for such a short time, Whip decided to stay in the village. First he paid a brief visit to the hospital, where he was pleased to learn from Bob Martin that Lee Blake was finally making rapid progress. "If he continues to improve as he's been doing," Bob said, "he'll be ready to go home in a few days."

Wandering aimlessly and chatting with various people, Whip encountered Tilman Wade, who had escorted Sally MacNeill into the village so that she, like so many of the women, could take advantage of Dr. McLoughlin's generosity. The pair went down to the waterfront and, sitting on tree stumps, discussed a variety of matters that would require action by the council.

One new problem had arisen, that of the disposition of the American share of trees cut down to prevent the spread of the forest fire. "I've heard," Tilman said, "that Dave Evans is letting it be known he'd like as much of that wood as he can get."

"That doesn't surprise me," Whip replied, absently plucking a dead weed from the ground. "But I'm blamed if he's going to have it. Those trees are common property and belong to everybody. But if he gets his hands on them, he'll cut them into planks and sell them for a big personal profit. I'll vote against any such disposition at the next council meeting."

"So will I," Tilman said, "and I don't think we need be too concerned. Ernie and Emily had Sally and me over for supper last night, and Ernie will vote the same way."

"Good. That settles it." Whip was silent for a moment, then grinned. "You and Sally MacNeill?"

"She's my neighbor, that's all," Tilman replied almost too quickly. "I help her out when I can, and she's been lonely since Paul Thoman lost interest in her."

"Speaking of Paul, I wonder if his boatyard is finished yet."

"Let's go find out."

They walked along the river bank, and when they came to the cove, they found Paul and Harry Canning struggling to lay the keel of a seventeen-foot fishing boat, the first they would produce.

"Looks like you need help from a couple of lads with muscles," Whip said. A moment later he and Tilman were helping lay the keel in place. The physical exertion, he discovered, gave him the release he needed from the tension between Eulalia and himself.

Lee Blake was sitting up in bed when Cathy came into his room. A natural color had replaced the pallor in his face, and his eyes were clear.

"You've shaved," she said, bending down to kiss him lightly.

"That's because I knew you'd be here this morning," he told her.

"You're really looking much better today."

"That's how I feel. I can't bully Bob Martin, but I've squeezed a half promise from Anton Wizneuski that I can go home the day after tomorrow."

Cathy seated herself in the cubicle's only chair. "There's no rush."

"They won't allow anyone other than you to visit me here, and I want to hear directly from Moser about the visit of the British garrison."

"The information will keep. And so will whatever news there is in Dr. McLoughlin's sale today. But I can tell you this much right now," Cathy said. "Just about all the women here—and a surprising number of the men—have been going over to Fort Vancouver this morning. I've seen boatload after boatload leave. John McLoughlin is being wonderful to us."

"He's a farsighted man." Lee studied her. "I presume you'll be going sometime today?"

She shook her head. "The British would make a fuss over me because I'm your wife, and I wanted to avoid all that. So I gave Ginny Dobbs the money to make my purchases for me, and Sergeant Major Mullins went with her. I don't think he allows her out of his sight," she added, smiling.

"The outing would have done you good, Cathy."

"If you want the truth, I preferred to stay right here, near you. They restrict each of my visits, so the least I can do is to keep coming here several times a day."

"You're being very good to me," Lee said.

"How could I be otherwise?"

"Very easily." Again he looked hard at her. "I don't remember anything about the day they brought me here. And the next day, when I was fighting for my life, is still a blur. But since then, I've had a lot of time to do some hard thinking. Cathy, I don't want to upset you, but I wish you'd tell me something. Are you sorry you married me?"

Cathy caught her breath. "What an awful question!"

"That's no answer."

"The question doesn't even deserve an answer."

"I courted you," Lee said, "when you turned away from Whip after you discovered he'd lived with the Indian girl, La-ena. Until then you had eyes for no other man. So I haven't been able to help wondering —if I hadn't stepped in when I did—whether you would have patched up your differences with Whip and ultimately married him instead of me."

She was treading on treacherous ground, and she told herself not to forget the doctors had warned her that Lee should remain calm. "I am Mrs. Leland Blake," she said, "and that's quite good enough for me."

"You have no regrets?"

"I have no cause for regrets." She hoped she sounded firm and convincing.

Lee sighed. "Maybe it's my imagination. But when Whip and you are together, an electric current seems to pass back and forth between you."

"For an army officer of high rank who takes pride in being practical," Cathy said, "you have an overdeveloped romantic streak."

"I just wanted to be certain, that's all."

She rose and bent down to kiss him again. "Now you know," she said. "And Bob Martin will be badly upset if you don't take a nap before dinner. I'll be back this afternoon." She tucked the bedclothes around him and left quickly.

When Cathy emerged into the open, she halted and took a deep breath, aware that she felt badly shaken. Lee was too keen an observer to fool permanently, but in his present condition she had been forced to lie to him.

No, even when he was healthy again she would lie. One of these days she would recover from her infatuation with Whip, and she would no longer have to lie. Her marriage was solid, and she had to succeed in it. Paying scant attention to her surroundings, she started toward the fort.

"You'll bump into people, ma'am, if you don't watch where you walk."

"Whip," Cathy's hand flew to her throat.

His tight grin failed to hide his own discomfort. "You were a thousand miles away just now."

"Not really. I've come from the hospital, and—"

"How is Lee?"

259

"So much better that he's dreaming up schemes to persuade the doctors to let him come home. What brings you into the village?"

"Oh, I'm killing time waiting until Eulalia comes back from shopping at Fort Vancouver. I settled some council problems with Tilman, helped Paul Thoman and Harry Canning lay the keel of their first boat, and taught Olga a new recipe for elk liver."

Feeling very wicked, she said, "If you have nothing better to do while you wait, come home with me, and I'll give you a cup of my own horrid acorn coffee."

Whip's face lighted. "There's nothing I'd like better," he said.

It felt natural to be walking together as they made their way to the fort. The sentry on duty saluted Cathy, and Whip and Cathy went to the commandant's house, neither of them speaking. Cathy led the way to the kitchen.

The first time he had ever seen her, Whip thought, she had been working in her Long Island kitchen. Never had he encountered such an attractive girl, and he tried to shut the image out of his mind.

When the coffee was heated, Cathy poured two mugs, and they sat opposite each other at the little kitchen table.

"This—feels—right," Whip said, the words escaping before he could stop himself.

Cathy nodded. "I know just what you mean. I sometimes wonder how much coffee we drank together between New York and Wyoming."

"I could add up the number of cups, and I wouldn't be far off the mark."

"Please don't, Whip."

What Lee had said was true. There was an electric current that passed back and forth when she and Whip were together. "There was a time," she said, half hiding her face behind the large coffee mug, "when everyone on the wagon train would have bet that you and I would marry each other. I thought so myself until poor La-ena showed up. And I learned about the two of you."

"La-ena and I—"

"In those days," she interrupted, speaking very rapidly, "I was terribly straight-laced. It didn't occur to me that a man who hunted and trapped alone in the mountains had the right to whatever happiness he could find. I did you an injustice, Whip, and I offer you my belated apologies."

"Don't apologize. All that matters is whether you're happy now," he said.

Cathy stared down at the black acorn coffee, and its bitter aroma assailed her nostrils. "Lee is much more than an exceptionally competent officer. He's a wonderful man. And he's devoted to me. I don't think any woman has the right to ask for more than that in a marriage."

He was silent for a time, then couldn't resist saying, "You haven't told me whether you're happy."

She was reminded of her talk with Lee at the hospital a short time earlier. "I'm not actively unhappy," she said. "When I was married to Otto, I knew I was miserable. He treated me like a nasty stepdaughter, and he was such a miser. But I—I can't analyze the way I feel now. It may be that I'm deliriously happy and don't even know it."

"I hope you *are* happy," Whip said.

"I do my part. I'm loyal to Lee—because he deserves my loyalty. I do everything that's expected of a wife. I've learned a great deal about the army, and I'm trying to become the perfect colonel's lady. A colonel's wife is in the army, too, you know. I'll never let Lee down, just as I know he'll always stand behind me. Perhaps that's happiness. I honestly don't know."

"I'm no expert on that subject."

She stood, went to the stove for the coffee pot, and deliberately stood with her back to him.

"Seeing that we're being honest, Cathy, could I

speak to you in confidence? Eulalia's been your friend for a long time."

"Yes. My good friend."

"Well, my marriage is crumbling into dust. And there doesn't seem to be a thing I can do about it. When a mountain river rips down through its gulch in the spring thaws and tears out chunks of rock, nobody can stop the process of nature. Well, I don't seem to be able to stop my marriage from falling apart."

"Surely it isn't that bad, Whip." She forced herself to return to the table and refill their mugs.

"We bicker about nothing. No matter what I say, she takes it wrong. And whatever she says or does gets my dander up. Eulalia and I seem to live in different worlds. I never know what goes on in her mind, and she has no idea of what's happening in mine."

Only when he was deeply concerned, Cathy knew, did he become so talkative. "As long as you love each other—"

"That's part of the problem. For a long time I— well, I thought I was in love with you. Then you turned away from me when La-ena came down out of the Rockies, and I couldn't blame you. I felt like shooting myself when La-ena went off to the peaks to die—"

"You mustn't blame yourself for that."

"Let me finish while I'm still galloping. Pretty soon after all that, you married Lee. And I felt like a cyclone out of the Great Plains had twisted me into knots."

Of all the men Cathy had ever known, none was more sure of himself or better able to cope with an emergency than Whip Holt. Yet even he was vulnerable, prey to the same emotions that caused those less strong to be hurt, bewildered, and upset, and her heart went out to him.

"The next thing I knew, Eulalia came down with

the bad fever and was crippled. Lord, I felt so sorry for her! She's so beautiful and sweet, and it looked like her life was ruined. Well, I married her, as you well know."

Cathy tried to determine for herself whether he had married Eulalia out of love or pity, but there was no way she could judge, and she wondered if he himself knew.

"There was a fighting chance," Whip continued, "that physical exercise would cure her. I'd seen it happen before. So I hounded her. I admit I gave her no peace, and even though she's cured now, she still hates me for it."

"I can't believe she really hates you, Whip," Cathy said, partly out of loyalty to her friend and partly because she believed that what she said was true.

"Lisolette lives with us, and I'm sure she's noticed how wrong things are. Eulalia has big smiles for everybody but me. I support her, she's my housekeeper, and that's that. Sometimes I think it was bad for me to marry and settle on a ranch. I should have gone back to the mountains and stayed there. Hunting and trapping aren't what they were a few years ago, but it's the only life I really know."

"I wish I could help you," she said.

He gulped the last of his acorn coffee, stood, and faced her squarely.

This was the climactic moment, the culmination of all that had happened over the years, the time when the accumulated tensions that had grown until they had become unbearable had to be recognized or rejected.

Cathy realized that a tiny smile of encouragement, even a hint in her eyes, would bring him to her. One part of her being wanted him to take her in his arms. She knew, however, that if they kissed, they would discard all judgment, all sense of responsibility, all reason.

It would be so easy to flee from Oregon together and take up a new life elsewhere. But she didn't know whether either of them would be able to tolerate the guilt that would haunt them for the rest of their lives. Surely the ghosts of Lee and Eulalia would give neither of them a single day of peace.

Whip desperately wanted Cathy, but he was beset by doubts, too. He was a married man, and she was the wife of a comrade who trusted him.

So much more was at stake than their personal happiness, and both of them knew it. On the long journey across America, Whip Holt and Cathy van Ayl had been more than leaders of the expedition. They had become symbols to the entire company, and people who had looked up to them still regarded them as models of what they themselves should be. Those settlers were still leading a precarious existence, with their future far from assured, and their need for leadership and inspiration was as great now as it had been on the trek across the continent. By going off together, these two would destroy the illusions of those who still needed examples of courage and perseverance.

Not a word was spoken during this electric moment, yet Cathy and Whip reached the same conclusion simultaneously, and their tension subsided.

"If you'd like more coffee, I'll brew another pot," she said calmly.

"Thank you kindly, ma'am, but Eulalia will be coming back from Fort Vancouver any time now." He was equally in control of himself.

As the door closed behind him, a chapter in both of their lives came to an end. They would remain friends, but they would go their separate ways, abandoning their daydreams and working out their problems to the best of their abilities. Their obligations were far more important than desires that might prove fleeting.

Eulalia reluctantly admitted to herself that Whip had been right: her dress was too revealing and her makeup too exotic for a shopping trip to Fort Vancouver.

Cindy, who was equally attractive and who accompanied her for a time, was sensibly attired in a dark gray dress of linsey-woolsey, with her face scrubbed clean. Consequently, the men paid virtually no attention to her. She made only a few purchases, and as she had many chores awaiting her at home, she soon returned to the American side of the river.

Eulalia was alone now, and her torment became worse. The clerks who waited on her in the three shops where she bought various items of food merely ogled her and made no comment, and while in the stores she enjoyed a measure of protection because she knew the other American women who were also shopping. But walking from one store to another was torture. Two redcoats followed her, discussing her physical attributes in loud voices, and only her dislike of making a scene prevented her from giving them a tongue-lashing.

Eulalia endured the most humiliating of her experiences when she emerged from the second of the shops. A bearded French-Canadian trapper in faded buckskins who had been loitering nearby approached her, his manner making it plain that he had seen her earlier and had been waiting for her.

"You come with me," he said, "and I pay you plenty much Yankee dollars."

She pretended she hadn't heard him and brushed past him without glancing in his direction, but her face burned. Good Lord! Whip hadn't exaggerated when he had said she looked like a whore.

After Eulalia completed her purchases, a clerk on the Hudson's Bay staff piled them into a wheelbarrow, which he pushed toward the longboat that would be next to cross the river. She walked beside him and was unprepared for his sudden comment. "I'll gladly give a fortnight's pay for an evening with you, m'girl," he said in a clipped English accent. "Where will I find you?"

"You won't," she replied icily. "I'm afraid you've come to the wrong woman."

The clerk fell silent but looked puzzled.

There were only a few other passengers in the longboat, and Eulalia's ordeal was not yet ended. The bo's'n in charge of the oarsmen stared at her steadily as the craft crossed the Columbia, and after they reached the south bank, he unloaded her parcels for her. It could have been no accident that, although she tried to avoid him, he brushed against her repeatedly.

She breathed a sigh of relief when the longboat pulled away. Leaving her purchases until she could fetch her pack horse, she hurried to Dolores and Olga's tavern to meet Whip. She owed him an apology but would have to word it carefully because she didn't want him to know the extent of the stir she had created. He was already annoyed, and she didn't want him to become even angrier.

Hawkman, the renegade trapper, was sitting in the road opposite the tavern, his back propped against the wall of an as yet uncompleted building. Beside him lay a partly consumed flask of cheap whiskey. He looked Eulalia up and down slowly, insolently, but she paid no attention to him and went into the tavern. Only Dolores was there.

"Whip was here about fifteen or twenty minutes ago and said he'd come back," Dolores told Eulalia. "The last I saw of him he was talking to Cathy Blake, walking with her toward Fort Oregon. He should be back soon."

A stab of jealousy shot through Eulalia. "I don't think I'll wait for him. Tell him I've started for home, if you will, please." Her excuse to herself for leaving without delay was her desire to change into more suitable clothes and remove the cosmetics from her face.

"Wait for him," Dolores said, gesturing in the direction of the renegade trapper. "That man is very bad, and when he drinks he becomes nasty."

However, Eulalia wanted to change her appearance before Whip saw her again, particularly on the heels of his chat with the ladylike Cathy. "I'm really in a hurry to get home," she said and left.

Quickly she went to the stable behind the tavern for her mare and pack horse. She led the animals to the waterfront, and as she loaded her packages on the broad back of the pack horse, she felt rather than saw someone observing her. Cautiously glancing back, she saw that Hawkman had followed her.

Refusing to give him the satisfaction of even recognizing his proximity, she completed her task, mounted her mare and, picking up the pack horse's tether, started off toward the ranch house. The work animal was so heavily laden that she had to walk her mare.

Not until she had left the village did it dawn on Eulalia that Hawkman was still following her. She was angry rather than frightened. Then, about halfway home, she remembered Lisolette had gone off for the day at Paul Thoman's invitation to watch him and Harry Canning build their first boat. Since Stalking Horse was somewhere on the range, the ranch house would be empty. She began to feel uneasy, but it was impossible to increase her pace.

As she drew nearer to the ranch house, however, she could no longer hear the man's footsteps behind her. Apparently the combination of the liquor he had consumed and the long walk were too much for him, and he had gone back to the village.

Arriving at the ranch at last, Eulalia paused and listened intently, but could hear no sound in the woods through which she had just ridden. So she went straight to the stable, where she removed the mare's saddle and relieved the pack horse of its burden. Laden with bundles, she walked to the kitchen, then returned for more.

After making several trips, her arms were tired, and she decided to change her clothes before moving her purchases from the kitchen to the larder. As she started to close the kitchen door behind her, Hawkman suddenly loomed in front of her, a knife with a long blade in one hand.

Eulalia involuntarily took a step backward but quickly realized it would be a mistake to let him see she was afraid of him. "Get out!" she ordered.

He leered at her, but made no move.

"What do you want here?" she demanded brusquely.

His leer broadened, revealing stumps of blackened teeth. "You know damn well what I want," he said in a rasping voice. "You!"

Her pistol and rifle were in the bedroom, and he blocked her path to the corridor. "My husband will be here soon," she said, "and I expect our foreman to come in from the range at any moment."

"Don't you worry, there's plenty of time for you and me to get together," Hawkman said.

Eulalia tried to curb her panic and made an attempt to think clearly. She could reach her kitchen knives before the man could stop her, but such a move would be certain to make him even more antagonistic. She had seen enough of frontier dwellers by now to realize that someone of his type would not hesitate to stab her, perhaps kill her, if he felt threatened. Her only hope was to stall, persuade him to relax his guard and then reach her firearms. She had no way of guessing when Whip might return home, so she could not rely on his assistance.

"No woman is going to be friendly when a man threatens her with a knife," she said, trying hard to speak calmly.

Hawkman grinned at her, thought for a moment, and then jammed his knife into his belt. "Does that suit you better?" he demanded.

"Much better."

"Then prove it. Show me how friendly you're going to be." He took another step toward her.

Eulalia tried to sidle past him, but he had anticipated just such a move, and he caught hold of her arm and spun her around, then jerked her toward him. Losing her balance, she was afraid she would fall against him and raised both hands to ward him off.

"I'll teach you how to be friendly," he said, then slapped her hard across the face.

The sharp blow stung her, prodding her into action. She lashed out at him, clawing his face with her nails. In return, the infuriated Hawkman struck her with his fist, then systematically began to beat her, his powerful blows repeatedly battering her face. Eulalia opened her mouth to scream but was so terrified and in such pain that she could not make a sound. Then a particularly vicious blow sent her crashing to the floor, and she moaned involuntarily as she landed on her back.

Hawkman loomed above her, an expression of grim satisfaction on his face as he reached for his belt buckle. He would rape her now, and she knew there was no way she could escape.

The kitchen door opened, and Whip Holt took in the scene at a glance.

Hawkman, hearing the sound of the door creaking, turned instantly and reached for his knife, almost simultaneously leaping at the man who had interrupted him.

Whip had no opportunity to draw one of his own weapons, but he had survived in the Rocky Mountains for years and was capable of coping with the unexpected crisis. Sidestepping just enough to avoid being bowled over, he concentrated his full attention on the hand that held the knife. As his assailant brought his arm down, trying to stab him, Whip caught hold of his wrist.

No mountain man was more expert in hand-to-hand combat than Whip Holt, no man was a deadlier foe when his ire was aroused. And at this moment he was coldly furious. His home had been invaded, his wife had been beaten, and had he arrived a few minutes later, she would have been violated.

Hawkman was no match for him. A sharp twist of the man's wrist sent the knife clattering to the floor. Eulalia, finding it hard to see clearly because one of her eyes was already so badly swollen that it was almost shut, nevertheless had the presence of mind to pick up the blade. She pulled herself painfully to her feet and leaned against the kitchen wall for support.

Whip had no need for his pistol, knife, or rawhide. His fists were his only weapons, and every blow he delivered was an expression of his fury and frustration. He had returned home upset by his talk with Cathy Blake and their unspoken farewell. He had vowed to make an effort to improve his relations with Eulalia, but he knew the way she looked today was at least partly to blame for her predicament.

The scum who had beaten her became the sole object of Whip's outrage. His fists hammered Hawkman unmercifully, smashing into his face, catching him in the pit of the stomach, then sending him reeling with a drive to the cheekbone. The trapper did his best to protect himself and retaliate, but Whip shrugged off his punches. Then Hawkman tried to kick him and was sent sprawling for his pains.

Whip pulled Hawkman to his feet again, propped him against a wall, and continued to pummel him, each blow delivered with the icy fury of one who had been forced to endure more than he could tolerate. No man could take such harsh punishment, and Hawkman sagged, then slowly collapsed onto the floor.

Leaving the man where he had fallen, Whip at last was able to turn his attention to Eulalia. "Are you all right?"

Her lower lip was split and swollen, and she could only mumble before lowering herself onto a kitchen chair.

Hawkman somehow pulled himself to his feet, and staggered out of the ranch house, painfully making his way toward the sanctuary of the nearby woods.

Whip slammed and bolted the kitchen door. Gently removing the attacker's knife from Eulalia's still-clenched hand, he picked her up as though she were weightless and carried her to their bedroom, where he lowered her to the bed.

She thought, as she moaned, that he intended to say something to her, but instead he vanished. Her heart sank, and she was convinced he was rejecting her.

A few moments later he returned with a cloth he had dipped in a bucket of cold water. "Put this on your face, and I'll fetch another for you," he said.

Her bruised face ached when she applied the cold, wet compress, but she stifled another moan.

Again Whip returned, and in addition to another cloth he carried a glass. "First drink this," he said and helped her to a sitting position.

"What happened—was—my fault," she was able to say. "You were right—this morning. This dress—and all those cosmetics—got me—into trouble."

"What's done is done," he said. "You'll be all right in a couple of days. Now drink this."

The raw whiskey burned her throat, and she coughed. He gently lowered her to the bed again, and when she tried to speak, he silenced her. Taking the original compress from her, he placed the fresh one over her eyes. "Go to sleep," he said.

She hoped he would kiss her, at the very least as a way of indicating that he forgave her folly. Instead, he quietly left the room.

Aching and ashamed, Eulalia could remain awake

no longer, and she was glad the cold compress hid her tears as she cried herself to sleep.

Whip returned to the kitchen, aware that he should have made some gesture to his wife but uncertain as to what he should have said or done. Cathy Blake was no longer in his mind as he stared reflectively at his scraped knuckles. A feeling of pity for Eulalia engulfed him, as it had when she had been crippled by fever.

One thing was certain. His wife needed him to protect her. Perhaps no deep love, such as he might have known with Cathy, bound them together, but he was obliged to remain faithful to his marriage vows. Half a loaf, he guessed, was better than none.

X

A fire blazed in the cabin hearth, and the badly battered Hawkman slept near it, comforted by its healing warmth.

Igor Doznevkov sat nearby, ignoring the obvious irritation of Colonel Mikhail Menshikoff, and stared absently at the man to whom he reluctantly had given refuge. He felt deep contempt for this creature and suffered no false illusions about his worth. There were many like him in Russia, lazy, shiftless opportunists, unreliable and certainly untrustworthy.

But years of service in the secret police had taught Igor that such men could be used. An idea had already formed in his mind, and he weighed it, examined it for flaws, and then made up his mind. Rising abruptly, he beckoned to Menshikoff, then walked out into the open.

The Colonel followed him into the damp, chilly air but was indignant. "At least it was warm inside, even with that loud snoring."

Igor waved him to a tree stump. "Never mind, Mikhail, we have matters more important than the weather to discuss."

"Couldn't we have talked indoors? That American idiot surely doesn't understand Russian!"

"In some matters it is best to take no chances, ever."

Igor lowered himself to another tree stump. "Mikhail, our situation is not good, and St. Petersburg will not be pleased with our efforts."

Menshikoff's shrug was fatalistic. "I fail to see what we can do that we have not done."

His defeatist attitude brought a slight smile of contempt to his colleague's lips. "Our settlers are sheep who have taken the easy path and joined the Americans. There are some, like Dr. Wizneuski and the Runkova woman, who are already more American than the Americans themselves. I wish I had destroyed those two while I still had the opportunity! I have applied the maximum pressure to the Arbo girl, but we learn nothing of value from her, and now I am forced to rely on what I can glean from Madame Holt about which of our own people may be reliable and useful to us. The only bright spot in our picture is that the British commandant, Morrison, is a fool who thinks we are harmless."

"I'm afraid he is right," the Colonel replied. "Our teeth have been pulled, and we bite only with our gums."

"We must try another approach," Igor Doznevkov said. "You brought a small fortune with you in gold rubles. Now we shall spend some of them."

"On what?"

"Hawkman."

"He would spend it on drink."

Igor shrugged. "Cattle respond to a prod. A few very small payments—with a promise of much larger sums to follow—will make Hawkman our serf. And there are others like him. Three or four of these strange creatures who live alone in the mountains come to Fort Vancouver every week. They have no nationalities, no loyalty to anyone or anything but themselves. I am annoyed because I did not think of using them long before now. All will jump to do our bidding in return for a little of the Czar's gold."

Colonel Menshikoff pondered. "Do you truly think we can rely on them?"

"Certainly not! We make tiny payments to show them they can trust us. But they receive no substantial amounts of gold until they produce results for us."

"It may be that you have found a way for us to win this struggle, Igor."

"I'm sure of it, Mikhail. For the present we do nothing to disturb the British. No matter what harm comes to the Americans, Morrison will not interfere. His turn will come later."

Menshikoff showed a growing enthusiasm for the scheme. "How many of these riffraff do you think we can enlist?"

"From what I have seen at Fort Vancouver, at least six or eight, perhaps as many as ten or twelve. The numbers are not that important. There will be enough to set fire to the houses and barns of the Americans, to destroy their village, to cause many kinds of catastrophes." Doznevkov spoke incisively. "What I like best about the idea is that we ourselves are not directly involved. The Americans will believe these renegades are their enemies."

"True. Once we actually pay a man in gold rubles, he will go elsewhere to spend the money. At Fort Vancouver he cannot buy a girl, good liquor, or a new gun. It will be difficult for the Americans to trace their troubles to us."

"Then you approve, Mikhail?"

"Of course!"

Igor Doznevkov rubbed his hands together. "By the time we are done with the Americans, they will wish they had never come to Oregon!"

The spring air was balmy, giving promise of the long growing season ahead, and the farmers in the American community devoted virtually all of their time to preparing the ground for planting. Even though they were busy, however, practically everyone in the settlement came to church in the village on Sunday morning. This was a special Sunday.

Immediately prior to the regular service, the Reverend Cavendish performed a double wedding ceremony, uniting Dolores with Hosea and Olga Runkova with Ted Woods in marriage. Dolores and Hosea were at ease, as always, and chatted amiably with Whip and Eulalia, whom they had asked to stand up for them. But Olga, wearing an old-fashioned gown of silk taffeta, seemed tense, and Ted appeared to be his customary somber, brooding self. As soon as the ceremony ended, however, and he had kissed his bride shyly, his face was creased by a radiant smile that none of the people who had crossed the continent with him had ever before seen.

No one was more pleased than Cindy Woodling. She had been relieved to see Ted outgrow his infatuation with her. And Olga would be a good, steadying influence on him.

The newly wedded couples took seats in the front pew, and the regular church service was held. Reverend Cavendish took full advantage of the larger than usual congregation by preaching a long, impassioned sermon on the subject of universal love. Some of the children grew restless, but no one left prematurely.

The service was interrupted near its end by the totally unexpected booming of the Fort Oregon cannon. So the closing hymn was eliminated, and Reverend Cavendish hastily bestowed a blessing on all those present.

People lost no time going out into the open and were startled by the familiar sight and sounds of an approaching caravan. Chet Harris broke the news to those still inside the church when he shouted, "The second wagon train is here!"

The wagons were drawn into a circle, and scores

moved forward to welcome the newcomers. The group consisted of one hundred and seventy-five men, women, and children, who revealed that more than thirty persons had died on the long journey.

The presence of the entire community was fortuitous, and the members of the council took full advantage of the situation. Ernie von Thalman hurried to his village office for the land claim forms he would make out for each family, and volunteers clamored for the right to offer temporary housing to the newcomers. The veterans offered advice, introductions were made, and countless eager questions about the availability of fertile land were answered. It appeared that everyone was talking at once, and the babble of voices was deafening.

Then an exceptionally pretty girl with flowing hair emerged from one of the wagons wearing her only silk dress, into which she had just changed, and her full-throated Indian war whoop momentarily halted all conversation. "There's my cousin!" she shouted. She threw herself at Tilman, almost knocking him to the ground in her exuberance.

Nancy Wade had made her fitting entry into the American settlement.

The members of the new train were formed into a line to receive their land claims. Under arrangements previously decided by the council, each family also received an appointment at the hospital, where every individual would receive a physical examination by Bob Martin or Anton Wizneuski.

The members of the council stood near Ernie observing the proceedings and were pleased when they learned there were several masons and bricklayers in the ranks of the newcomers. Nancy Wade, clinging to her cousin's arm, chatted with Cathy and Eulalia as though she had known them for years, and they found it almost impossible to interrupt her breathless monologue.

Whip, Tilman, and Lee Blake exchanged an occasional comment, and soon were joined by Jeremiah Olberg, a former New York shopkeeper who was president of the second train. He was promptly invited to join the council, and Lee asked, "Where's your guide?"

"He'll be along," Olberg said. "He's probably making sure our work animals have been unhitched. That's a job he never left to anyone else."

Some minutes later a short, wiry man, whose face resembled the faded, stained leather of his buckskins, sauntered toward the church lawn. His walk was self-confident, and he carried a rifle in the crook of an arm with the assurance of one who knew how to use it.

Whip stiffened but made no comment.

The new arrival came closer, then waved casually. "Hello, Holt," he said. "I heard tell you were here."

Whip's lack of cordiality matched that of the other man. "I didn't know you were the train's guide, Ramsey," he said.

"Well, you know it now." The wiry mountain man's tone was flat, indicating neither hostility nor amicability.

As Olberg introduced Richard Ramsey to the other members of the council, Lee noted that Whip had refrained from shaking hands with the man and that his face had become as blank as that of an Indian.

Ernie von Thalman looked up from the claims he was signing. "Are you planning to settle with us, Mr. Ramsey?"

The mountain man shrugged. "Not if I can help it. I'll stay around these parts for a spell because I have a hankering for salmon, but before summer comes I'll probably head back to the Rockies."

Whip remained tight-lipped.

Lee waited for an opportune moment, then drew him aside. "I gather you don't care much for Ramsey."

Whip nodded, but did not reply.

"Why not?"

"I don't hold with turning folks against a man. I'd rather let Ramsey do it himself."

"I've never known you to condemn anyone unfairly," Lee replied, "and the council should be warned if you know of anything against him. You know we'll keep confidential any information you give us."

"Oh, he's competent enough," Whip said. "He brought a wagon train all the way from New York, and most of them seem healthy. So that's an accomplishment that speaks for itself."

"Now you're being evasive, and that isn't like you."

Whip sighed. "If you must know, I caught him cheating a poor, drunken old trapper in a card game about five or six years ago. Later that same night I heard something in the trapper's tent and looked in. There was Ramsey, emptying the man's purse of the money he'd been paid for his furs that day. I beat the daylights out of Ramsey."

"I see."

"Maybe he's changed, Lee."

"And maybe he hasn't."

"Well, seeing he's going to be around for a time, I'll keep an eye on him," Whip said. "He knows what I think of him, and I don't believe he'll try any of his tricks with me watching him."

Lee let the matter drop, but a short time later he approached Jeremiah Olberg. "What's your opinion of your guide?" he asked.

The elected leader of the second expedition spoke with great care. "A man is innocent until he's been proven guilty, Colonel. Ramsey wasn't very popular, especially during the final stages of our journey. I don't play cards myself, so I don't like to make accusations."

Jeremiah had confirmed Whip's view, and Lee needed to hear nothing more. Oregon wouldn't suffer if Richard Ramsey confined his visit to a short stay.

Paul Thoman thought of the idea, Harry Canning approved, and when Lisolette Arbo endorsed it, the matter was settled. All single members of both the old and new wagon trains were invited to a salmon feast, and Paul promised that he and Harry would catch the fish, going out in their newly completed boat for the purpose.

The Holts were asked to act as chaperones, and Eulalia insisted that the party be held at their ranch. She had been so depressed since her unfortunate encounter with Hawkman that Whip, hoping her spirits would improve, readily agreed.

A pit was dug behind the kitchen, and Whip built a fire of hickory wood early in the day. At noon Paul and Harry appeared on horseback, having gone fishing at dawn. The pack horse they led was laden with more salmon than the guests could eat. Harry wanted them baked in clay, in the Indian fashion, so Whip showed them how to prepare the fish by painting them with bear grease before wrapping them in the clay.

Established settlers contributed food for the party. Tilman Wade, who would be bringing his cousin and Sally MacNeill, provided onions from his vegetable garden. Others brought squash, cornmeal, spring berries, and early melons. Dave Evans, whom it had been impossible to exclude, not only appeared with a keg of fermented apple cider, but was accompanied by Richard Ramsey, with whom he had become friendly.

Sally, Nancy, and Ginny Dobbs, who was escorted to the affair by a civilian-clad Hector Mullins, banished Eulalia from her own kitchen and took charge of preparing the vegetables and fruits. Nancy, whose enthusiasm for the task was greater than her talents as a cook, was given the task of baking cornbread, which she claimed she could do expertly.

Eulalia was subdued and, more sensitive than ever before to her husband's likes and dislikes, noticed that his greeting to Ramsey was distant. She was somewhat surprised, thinking it odd that he failed to show friendliness toward a fellow mountain man. Nevertheless, she followed his example, and she, too, was cool to the second expedition's guide.

Her manner was so restrained that Eli Moser and several other officers from the garrison chatted with her only briefly before turning to others for more animated conversation. In fact, she rarely smiled and bore little resemblance to the vivacious, flirtatious young woman she had been.

Whip stayed in the background with her. They had loaned the house to friends, but this was not their party, and he was content to observe the guests, approving of some of the bachelors and young women from the second train. If they followed the example of their predecessors, as he felt sure they would, many of them soon would be married. It was difficult, in a land cut off from the rest of the United States, for anyone who found a suitable mate to stay single indefinitely.

Sack races and blindfolded games of tag quickly broke down the barriers that separated the established settlers from the newcomers, and within a short time virtually everyone was at ease.

Only Dave Evans and Richard Ramsey, Whip saw, consumed more than small quantities of the fermented apple cider. Tilman also realized the pair were drinking rather heavily and was prepared to intervene at his host's side if the need arose.

Paul hovered constantly beside Lisolette, and she, in turn, smiled whenever he spoke to her. Their interest in each other was so plain that even the newly arrived settlers were conscious of it, and bachelors from the second train wasted no efforts on a woman whose future obviously had been determined. Sally MacNeill saw that Paul and Lisolette had drawn close to each other, but she no longer cared. In fact, she couldn't help wondering, as she looked at Paul, how she had ever imagined herself in love with him. Oh, he was bright and good-looking, but he simply didn't interest her. If and when she married, she wanted someone solid, a quiet, predictable farmer like her father.

One of the more complicated races involved passing a raw duck's egg back and forth between a man and a woman with a spoon every ten paces as they ran, and when an egg fell and broke, those contestants were eliminated.

Harry Canning regarded himself as too mature to participate in the game, so he did not step forward. His reticence challenged Nancy Wade, who immediately approached him. "What's the matter?" she demanded. "Don't tell me you're afraid to race."

Harry, who feared only a raging gale at sea, looked at the girl coldly. She was pretty enough, but she was too damned forward. "Let's just say I'm too old for games," he replied.

"You're no such thing!" she retorted. Giving him no chance to protest further, she caught hold of his hand and dragged him forward. "Here's my partner," she called.

It was small consolation to Harry that Hector Mullins and Tilman Wade, who had also been dragooned into taking part, looked as sheepishly uncomfortable as he felt.

Eulalia placed a raw duck's egg in the spoon held by each of the women contestants. Whip stood one hundred paces away, at the finish line, where he would act as judge. "Ready!" Eulalia called. "Steady! Go!"

The teams started forward, and Eulalia, lifting her skirt so she could move more easily, walked rapidly beside them, ready to disqualify those who dropped their eggs or who failed to pass them back and forth at the appropriate intervals. Shouts and gales of laughter erupted each time an egg was dropped and splattered on the ground.

Tilman and Sally were among the first to be eliminated, and he shook his head. "I think I need eyeglasses," he said. "I'm really too old."

"You are not!" Sally replied indignantly.

Hector and Ginny advanced cautiously but steadily and made such good progress that they took the lead before the halfway point was reached. Conscious of each other at all times, they accomplished each transfer of the raw egg with great care, slowing their pace for a moment or two, then gradually increasing it again. Their marriage, Whip decided as he watched their approach, would be the best thing that could ever happen to the once impulsive Ginny.

Somewhat to Harry Canning's surprise, he and Nancy Wade challenged the other couple for the lead, then moved ahead. They ran somewhat erratically, even sprinting when necessary, and Harry, who was aggressive in all things, realized he had a compulsion to win. Evidently the girl felt the same way, and so far they made a well-matched if unpredictable team. In spite of his initial reluctance to participate, he found himself grinning, enjoying the contest.

"Steady now," he called as Nancy passed him the egg.

"I'm plenty steady," she said. "Just look out for yourself, and we'll do fine."

They took a fairly commanding lead by the time they reached a point only ten to fifteen paces from the finish line, and then disaster overtook them. Perhaps overconfidence made them careless. Whatever the reason, the duck's egg fell to the ground and broke as Nancy tried to pass it back to Harry.

The still-careful Ginny and Hector continued to forge ahead and were the first to cross the line to the cheers of everyone present.

Nancy and Harry glared at each other. "You oaf!" she said.

"You clumsy woman!" he replied.

"All you had to do was hold out your spoon, but you jiggled it," she declared.

"You threw the egg instead of dropping it into my spoon," he insisted. All at once he began to laugh. "Not that it really matters. We had a good time."

Nancy softened, too. "For two people who don't even know each other, we worked pretty well together."

Harry became gracious. "If you're willing, we'll work together again the next time there's a game that requires a team."

She extended her hand. "Good! And we'll win!"

They offered their congratulations to Hector and Ginny, then strolled together toward the fire.

"What's so special about baked salmon?" Nancy asked.

"Once you've tasted it, you'll know."

"Back in Pennsylvania we never ate fish, but I'm willing to try anything." She paused, and her next remark indicated that either Sally or Tilman had briefed her on Harry's background. "I hear you not only caught the salmon, but you built the fishing boat."

He nodded. "That was her trial run. We're selling her to a settler from Delaware who wants to fish instead of farm for a living. And that's just the beginning. My partner and I hope to turn out a boat every month."

Nancy was curious about everything she encountered. "When you're building a boat," she wanted to know, "how can you make sure it won't sink after you put in into the water?"

Harry laughed. "When you're cooking a meal," he countered, "how do you know it will be edible?"

"I don't," she replied cheerfully. "I'm a terrible cook. Cousin Tilman ate two of my meals, and now he keeps finding reasons to invite Sally to supper, so she does most of the cooking."

"Come out to the boatyard any day you're free," he said, "and I'll show you how we work. And why."

"I'll be there," Nancy said, meaning it.

Whip and Eulalia showed the newcomers how to crack the clay containers, and the salmon was so delicious that there were many who followed Paul Thoman's example and ate third and fourth helpings. The vegetables were tender, and the inner birch bark with which they had been cooked gave them a flavor that was unique.

Only the cornbread was less than perfect. It was dry, virtually tasteless, and crumbled as soon as it was touched. "I've done it again," Nancy said to Harry as she sat beside him on the ground. "Another miserable failure to add to my list."

He saw that her distress was genuine, even though she was trying to make light of the situation. "Don't you believe it, not for a minute," he said, stuffing a wad of the cornbread into his mouth. "This is so good I'm going to have more of it."

The girl looked at him, a gleam of admiration in her eyes. Sally had told her that Harry Canning was a rough sailor, but he was far more: he was the first true gentleman she had encountered since she had left home. Suddenly the ten-year difference in their ages seemed unimportant. Harry's days as a bachelor were numbered.

As Harry forced himself to eat the cornbread, he saw the changed expression in her eyes, and he couldn't help responding to her warmth. Now that he was spending his life ashore, he reflected, there was no reason to remain a bachelor. He was still cautious, to be sure, and had no intention of flinging himself headlong into a romance, but it could do no harm to cultivate a friendship with this girl. In time she might even learn to cook.

After the meal was finished, Hector Mullins surprised everyone by proposing that some of the men wash the dishes and scrub the pots and pans. He was joined by several volunteers, who went off to the kitchen with him, and the women had nothing to do except collect the dirty dishes and carry them away.

Ginny laughed when she walked into the kitchen and saw Hector, his sleeves rolled up and his arms plunged into soapsuds up to his elbows. "Don't get any wrong ideas," he told her. "After we're married I might help you out on Sunday nights, but the rest of the week I won't come near your kitchen."

She was still smiling broadly as she started back toward the fire to collect another load of dishes. Someone loomed up in front of her in the dark, and she halted abruptly.

"How about sharing your joke with me?" Richard Ramsey asked.

Ginny saw at a glance that he was somewhat unsteady on his feet, and she tried to move around him. But Ramsey moved, too, and continued to block her path. "Don't be in such an almighty hurry," he said. "It's been a long time since I've had anything to do with a pretty girl."

A shout would bring Hector to her side immediately, Ginny knew, but a fight would be certain to ensue, and she wanted to avoid an ugly scene. Perhaps she could handle this mountain man without summoning help.

"All I want is a few kisses," he said, watching her with care.

"Are you quite sure that's all?" she asked sweetly.

"Maybe something more. I sort of figured you and I would hit it off good together."

Ginny moved a step closer to him. "Let me show you what I'll give you," she said, then kicked him as hard as she could in the shin.

Ramsey hopped backward, holding his injured leg in the air and cursing the young woman under his breath. Without a backward glance, she moved on toward the fire. His temper rising, Ramsey started to follow her, but a lean, tall figure intervened, halting him.

"I wouldn't go after her if I were you," Whip said quietly.

Ramsey glowered at him. "Mind your own goddamn business, Holt!"

"That's exactly what I'm doing. If Sergeant Mullins finds out you've made advances to the woman he's going to marry, he'll take off your head."

"Maybe I'll take off his!" Ramsey was drunk enough to be reckless.

"Well, it won't happen either way on my property. You're abusing my hospitality, Ramsey, so I advise you to clear out. For that matter, if you're smart you'll get out of the territory. Folks who have come to Oregon are peaceable, and they don't need your kind to rile them up."

"Are you threatening to throw me off this property, Holt?" the smaller mountain man demanded.

"I never threaten," Whip said, "but I'll do what I must."

Dave Evans approached, and even though he, too, had consumed more of the fermented apple cider than was good for him, he was still in control of himself. "What's wrong?"

"Your friend here has insulted a lady," Whip said. "And all hell will break loose if the man who's going to marry her finds out about it. Get him out of here, Evans, and save me the trouble of running him off my land."

Dave took offense. "That's downright unfriendly of you," he said.

"Very unfriendly," Whip said, "and the same goes for you. For your sakes I hope you don't doubt that I can do it."

For a moment it appeared that Evans would stand up to him, but suddenly he wilted. "Come on, Rich," he muttered. "There's more cider back at the sawmill."

Whip stood unmoving as he watched them go to their horses, mount, and ride off into the night. They were two of a kind, and good riddance to them. Not until they were out of sight did he return to the fire, where only Ginny realized that an unpleasant incident had been averted.

The men who had washed the dishes rejoined the company, and someone produced a fiddle. Paul Thoman demonstrated his versatility by playing it expertly, and the entire group sat around the fire and listened to him. Night had fallen, the sky was filled with stars, and the mountains off to the east were plainly visible, as were the limitless forests, their color a deep green-black.

Few people were familiar with the music that Paul was playing, but no one really cared. Men and women who had come from every part of the United States were united in this distant wilderness so far from their original homes, drawing comfort and solace from each other's presence. They were foreigners in a benign but alien land, and behind their sense of fellowship lay the determination to make the Oregon experience succeed.

When Paul paused in his playing, Lisolette, who sat beside him, asked softly, "Do you know the tune of 'La Jeune Fille?' It was very popular in France a few years ago."

"I'm not sure," Paul said. "Hum a few bars."

She did, and his face cleared. "Of course! Will you sing it, Lisolette?"

The girl hesitated but was encouraged by his positive attitude and finally nodded her assent. She began to sing, with Paul accompanying her, and her voice, although small, was sweet and true.

The song told the story of a girl, Marie, whose lover had been lost at sea. Marie haunted the docks of Brest, wandering from boat to boat, living in the hope that her lover would return to her, and even as she grew older, she never lost the conviction that he would come back to her.

Lisolette sang in French, and only Paul understood the words. They inspired each other, and Lisolette's voice gained strength as she repeated the plaintive melody of the refrain.

Some of the others managed to piece together the meaning of the song, but even those who didn't were stirred by it. Ginny Dobbs rested her head against Hector Mullins's broad, muscular shoulder. In him she had found the security she had never before known. And he, knowing he was loved, gave unstintingly in return.

Nancy Wade lost her sense of exuberance and huddled near Harry Canning in the dark. For some reason the tune struck a responsive chord within her, and tears streamed unheeded down her face. Harry silently handed her a clean handkerchief, and Nancy dabbed at her face, feeling no sense of shame. When she returned the handkerchief to him, she smiled. A feeling of warmth suffused him.

Sally MacNeill knew now what she had long suspected, that Paul and Lisolette belonged together. She herself had been wrong to pursue Paul. She had succumbed to an adolescent's dream, but she was a grown woman now.

Inadvertently her glance strayed to Tilman Wade, who sat beside her, the firelight playing on his face. He was so mature, so self-possessed that she was afraid he thought of her only as a child who happened to be his immediate neighbor and Nancy's contemporary.

Tilman became aware of the girl's gaze and grinned at her. Suddenly he looked vibrant and alive, much younger than his years, and Sally's heart inexplicably beat more rapidly.

Whip and Eulalia sat outside the circle around the fire, part of the group yet separated from it. The haunting refrain and Lisolette's sweet voice filled Eulalia until she thought it would consume her. She wanted to clap her hands over her ears to shut out the sound, yet at the same time she drank it in avidly, as though her soul thirsted for it.

If Whip was moved by the song, he did not show it. He stared off into space, his face seemingly carved out of granite, his eyes hooded and his mouth set. Never had Eulalia felt so alien to him. Their relationship had grown worse—no, more remote—since the day he had saved her from Hawkman's attack. She had recovered from that harrowing experience, at least physically, and her bruise marks had disappeared. She still suffered inner torments, however, and was convinced she alone was to blame for what had happened.

If Whip had been kinder, if he had forgiven her frivolity or had shown her sympathy, perhaps she might have put the incident out of her mind. Instead, his only reference to it had been oblique. "From now on," he had remarked several days later, "don't go anywhere alone unless you're armed."

She had no idea if he was angry, perhaps even disgusted with her. All she knew for certain was that the chasm that separated them had become wider and deeper. They had so little in common that their conversations were exclusively perfunctory, concerning only the essentials of daily living.

She prayed he would take her hand or slip an arm around her shoulders. Instead he sat immobile, as distant and cold as the snow-capped peaks of the Cascades he seemed to be staring at as he listened to the music. Tears came to Eulalia's eyes, but she brushed them away impatiently. It did no good to weep for a marital relationship that might have been. Somehow, she had to find the strength and courage to accept a reality that she found unbearable.

"A trapper named Hawkman told me it would be worth my while to see you," Richard Ramsey said.

Igor Doznevkov motioned his visitor into the cabin, then closed the door behind him. He knew Ramsey by sight and, aware that he had guided the second American wagon train across the continent, realized that here was someone of higher caliber than the shiftless trappers he had been recruiting. This man required special treatment.

Opening a sea chest, Igor removed a jug of French brandy. Pouring a liberal measure into his guest's cup and a smaller amount into his own, the agent settled back in his chair.

Ramsey enjoyed the liquor. "This is good brandy."

"I'll order a jug for you."

The mountain man smiled. "Thank you. But you're wasting your time if you think I'll accept spirits as pay."

Igor reached into the leather purse at his waist, fished out a gold ruble worth at least twenty dollars in American money, and handed it to his visitor.

Ramsey weighed it in his hand, bit it to test it, and was impressed. "Now you're talking my language," he said.

It was Doznevkov's turn to smile. "Accept this piece as a sign of my good will and my desire to do business with you," he said. "Help me and you will receive many more coins."

"What do you want done?"

"Not so fast, my friend. Do you know who I am?"

"Hawkman doesn't know for certain, and neither do several other trappers who are accepting favors from you."

"It is no secret that my colleague, Colonel Menshikoff, who has gone salmon fishing, carries the appointment of Czar Nicholas as the Imperial Russian Governor of Oregon. I stand at Menshikoff's right hand."

"You're going to have hell's own time taking this territory away from the Americans and the British," Ramsey said bluntly.

"It can and will be done," Doznevkov said. "That is

why I am willing to be generous—in return for the right help and cooperation. If you intend to betray me to the Americans, however—"

"I don't," Ramsey interrupted. "They paid me as a guide, but I've fulfilled my contract with them. I live under no nation's flag. I'm my own man, and I look out only for Richard Ramsey's good."

"Very well." The agent sipped his drink. "I wish to be rid of the Americans here before I dispose of the British. What contributions can you make to that cause?"

Ramsey thought for a time. "Well, quite a few hunters and trappers came out here when game became scarce in the Rockies. I'm acquainted with most of them, and I can bring you some recruits."

"Men like Hawkman?" Igor raised an eyebrow.

"Most are of his quality, but I can do better than that. Dave Evans, who operates the American sawmill, is becoming discouraged. Not only are the British across the Columbia giving him stiff competition, but most of the Americans pay him in bartered goods, and Dave is partial to cash. He loves the sight and feel of gold."

"I'll speak to him; he could prove valuable. But I am disappointed, Ramsey. I was hoping you could make a truly major effort on our behalf."

"So I can, but it will be expensive."

"The expense is of no consequence!" Igor exclaimed.

Ramsey drained his cup but wanted to demonstrate his sense of responsibility, so he refrained from asking for more. "Are you familiar with the Rogue Indians?"

"I have never heard of them."

"They're a tribe who live in southern Oregon, near the border of Mexican California. Most of the Indian nations hereabouts are lazy because living is so easy for them. They hunt, fish, and even farm. Their lodges and lifestyle are solid, permanent—they aren't warring nations. But the Rogue are different. They're greedy devils who have learned that gold will buy them liquor, guns, and blankets. The Mexicans have been paying them a subsidy to keep them quiet, but I don't think the authorities in Yerba Buena would become too upset if the Rogue launched a campaign against the American intruders."

At last! Here were the potential allies Doznevkov had been seeking! "How many men can they send into a campaign?"

The mountain man grinned. "That would depend on how much you're willing to pay them. In all, they have five hundred to a thousand warriors."

Igor felt like celebrating. "I will secure payment for all of them, ample payment," he said. "You understand, of course, that it will take time to arrange the transfer of gold with the Imperial Viceroy in Alaska."

"Take all the time you need to make sure your campaign succeeds. But don't wait to establish your alliance with the Rogue. Give me five hundred dollars in gold—four hundred for the Rogue and one hundred for myself—and I guarantee they'll become your allies."

The terms were outrageous, but Doznevkov was backed into a corner. He knew nothing about the native Indians of the New World and had to depend on this mountain man to make his arrangements for him. "I will give you four hundred to bind the Rogue to the cause of the Czar," he said. "Bring me positive proof that you have arranged a treaty with them, and you'll be paid one hundred."

"I'll take fifty now and fifty when the treaty is secure," Ramsey replied, gloating inwardly because the Russian would be paying him an exorbitant fee— as much as he had earned guiding the wagon train all the way from New York to Oregon. "Those are the best terms I can offer you."

Igor well realized he was taking a grave risk by accepting the mountain man's word. Ramsey well might take all of the money and disappear permanently from Oregon. The secret police believed in keeping controls over those with whom it dealt, and Ramsey was no exception. "How much time will you need?"

"I'll go to see the Rogue at once, and I'll return in no more than a month."

Igor knew now how to handle the situation. He went to a strongbox, removed a heavy pouch, and, one by one, removed an appropriate number of gold rubles. "Here is the equivalent of four hundred dollars for the Indians and fifty for you," he said.

Ramsey's deep-set eyes gleamed.

"I place a condition upon this transaction," Igor said, his voice becoming harsh. "If you have not returned in six weeks from today with proof you have paid the Rogue and that they have accepted an alliance, Colonel Blake and the territorial agent von Thalman will be notified that you are a traitor to the United States."

Ramsey reacted as though he had been struck in the face.

"These are the best terms *I* can offer *you*," Igor added, smiling coldly. "Accept or reject them, as you wish."

For a moment Richard Ramsey made no move. Then, very slowly, he reached for the piles of gold coins. "I accept," he said hoarsely.

Members of the second wagon train found the land they wanted, built their homes, and began to move into them before clearing away the forest. Meanwhile, as the spring advanced, the original settlers discovered that the climate of Oregon was perfect for the growing of wheat and other grains. Soon the first of the year's crops would be harvested.

A British sloop of war and two merchant ships flying the Union Jack put into Fort Vancouver, bringing dispatches and mail as well as supplies for the Hudson's Bay Company outpost. The warship left a few days later, but the merchantships remained to take on a cargo of furs and lumber.

Less than a week later the settlers rejoiced when an American flotilla sailed up the Columbia. Leading the procession was a newly commissioned United States Navy frigate, the *Philadelphia*, her decks lined with the two hundred and twenty-three officers and men who would bring the regiment up to full strength. Also on board were five officers' wives.

The three merchant ships included two brigs sent by John Jacob Astor and his associates, and the third flew the ensign of the Thoman shipyard of Boston. Sheep and cattle filled the decks, and the holds were crammed with provisions and hardware, seed and farm implements. A holiday atmosphere prevailed in the village as the cattle and sheep from the Astor Company were distributed to those who wanted them and the supplies from Paul Thoman's father were stored in the new warehouses that had been built during the winter months.

"Soon we will become self-sufficient," Ernie von Thalman said as he watched stores being unloaded. "Neither the British nor anyone else can force us to leave Oregon now."

The regiment was kept busy assimilating the new troops, settling them in their barracks, and assigning them to infantry, artillery, cavalry, and sapper units. Cathy and Lee Blake gave an official dinner welcoming the new officers and their wives, and thereafter they were kept busy entertaining the commander of the *Philadelphia*, his officers, and the masters of the merchant ships.

Paul Thoman was overjoyed when he saw the adzes and other shipbuilding tools his father had graciously sent. Even the pragmatic Harry Canning was moved to observe, "With all this new equipment, we can build coastal traders that can sail as far south as San Diego and as far north as Alaska."

Huge quantities of cedar, oak, and spruce had been accumulated by various members of the settlement from land cleared for homes and farming, and when the holds of the merchants' ships had been emptied, the wood, which was traded as payment for the supplies, was carried on board. John McLoughlin held a near-monopoly on what was left of the fur trade, and out of deference to him the Americans did not try to compete with him. Besides, John Jacob Astor had determined that the market for furs from the Pacific Northwest was dying. Instead, there was a growing demand for lumber superior to that found anywhere else in the United States.

The captain of the *Philadelphia* and the masters of the merchant ships gave dinners in return for the hospitality they had received, inviting the senior officers of the garrison, members of the council, and their wives. Eulalia Holt had a temper tantrum when Whip told her he planned to go off in search of more wild horses instead of attending the dinners, and she made such a fuss that he postponed his trip until the vessels were scheduled to depart.

Immediately prior to the frigate's departure, three more cannon, each of them twelve-pounders, were added to the Fort Oregon armaments. Again Lee Blake was aware of British sensitivities across the Columbia and took care not to point any of these new guns in the direction of Fort Vancouver. Major Pitts, who had attended some of the festivities, had indicated that Colonel Morrison was already apoplectic over the reinforcement of the American garrison.

Igor Doznevkov and Colonel Mikhail Menshikoff quietly bided their time. Several more renegade trappers joined them in their cause. A far more important recruit was Dave Evans, who became furiously angry when he learned that the new equipment received by

Thoman and Canning included saws that would enable the partners in the embryo shipyard to cut their own lumber. The return of Richard Ramsey was eagerly awaited.

On the day of the flotilla's departure, Colonel Blake paraded his entire regiment, almost five hundred strong, in honor of the ships' officers and crews. Everyone came to the village for the ceremony, which included a fife and drum corps of twelve men playing martial music.

Approximately seven hundred civilians lined both sides of the dirt road to watch the spectacle, and their cheers could be heard in Fort Vancouver across the river. Perhaps Tilman Wade best expressed the spirit of the day when he said to Sally and Nancy, "You know, we're growing so fast I hardly recognize the place. Why, there are more people in American Oregon right this minute than there were in the Pennsylvania towns nearest to the farm I left behind."

Ernie and Whip took a more somber view. Standing behind their wives at the waterfront, the latter remarked, "With two more wagon trains already on their way out here, folks will soon be spreading all over the place."

"Including the north bank of the Columbia," Ernie observed.

"Exactly what I meant," Whip replied. "I sure hope that Martin Van Buren—or whoever is elected President this year—will make a deal with the British and divide the Oregon country fairly. There are nearly two thousand men, all of them armed, sitting in the two forts. So far we've been lucky, but I'm afraid that one of these days there will be a misunderstanding, and then all hell will break loose."

After the ships sailed away, life gradually returned to normal. Crops were planted and tended, orchards were nurtured, cattle and sheep were turned loose to graze. The members of the second wagon train, aided greatly by the tools that John Astor had sent them, continued to clear their land so they could start to grow crops of their own in the immediate future.

Whip, accompanied by Stalking Horse, went off to the mountains again on his belated trip and returned with a stallion and three more mares. "I have enough horses now for the next year," he told Eulalia. "Two of the older mares will be having their colts soon, so the ranch is starting to produce. By this time next year, after the next couple of wagon trains arrive, we'll start to get cash for our animals."

For his sake she was pleased that the ranch promised to be successful, but her own future remained too clouded for her to rejoice. Perhaps the strain in their marital relations was having an effect on her, but she felt a sense of foreboding that would not dissipate.

The council asked for volunteers to take part in a major building project, and the regiment was the first to respond. Goaded by Sergeant Major Mullins, the troops offered as much of their time as was needed. Colonel Blake obligingly gave them extra leave for the purpose. Civilians were quick to answer the call, too, and so many men showed up for work that it was possible to start several portions of the program simultaneously.

A new wing was added to the hospital and included three new wards and several smaller rooms. Bob Martin and Anton Wizneuski would be stretched to their limit, and Bob had already sent several letters to colleagues in the East, asking them to think about migrating to Oregon. The church was enlarged to accommodate a larger congregation, and a permanent schoolhouse was also built. Arrangements were made with a woman member of the second train, who had taught in Cincinnati, to take charge of the school. Paul Thoman was increasingly occupied at his boatyard and no longer had the time to teach.

Then all of the men went to work together, a short

distance inland, to construct a meetinghouse that could be used for gatherings of many kinds. Whip suggested it be called Andrew Jackson Hall, and his idea was endorsed so heartily that it proved unnecessary to take a vote on the matter.

The exterior of the meetinghouse, like the hospital and school, was made of logs, but planking was needed for the floor. When Dave Evans was reluctant to provide the wood free of charge, Thoman and Canning donated their own services and the use of their saws for the purpose.

The settlers were delighted by the growth and solidity of their community, and almost everyone attended a dedication ceremony at Andrew Jackson Hall one Sunday, immediately following church services.

That same day, Richard Ramsey returned from his mission to the Rogue Indians.

XI

Igor Doznevkov examined the strange object he held in his hand, turning it again and again. Made from the trunk of a small tree, it was cylindrical, about six inches high, with three columns of carved human heads covering its surface from top to bottom. Although crudely done, it was possible to distinguish Indian features on some of the grotesque faces, while others seemed to represent white men. All were gaudily painted in bright blues, greens, yellows, and reds.

"I don't understand," he said.

Richard Ramsey was patient. "All across North America except in these parts," he said, "the Indians use wampum—beads made from shells—as money and as symbols. Here they carve what they call totems. After they accepted my terms for an alliance, their artisans took three days and nights, working in shifts, to make this miniature totem pole. Look at the small fish and the owl at the very bottom. They're the signature of the Rogue. This is their equivalent of signing a treaty."

"Barbaric," Igor said.

"Call it anything you please," the mountain man said in irritation, "But I've done what you asked, and they've agreed to fight the Americans with you."

"I must take your word for it, apparently." Igor

301

took some gold coins from his strongbox and handed them to Ramsey.

"The Rogue have a condition of their own. Their weapons are primitive, and they know they'll be fighting men armed with guns. So they insist you supply them with rifles or muskets, along with plenty of ammunition and powder, before they'll make war."

Igor was sorry he had paid the man the rest of his fee. "Where will I obtain hundreds of rifles?"

Ramsey shrugged. "That isn't my problem. I suppose you can send to Alaska for them."

"Impossible. There are no weapons to spare in the arsenals there."

The former guide became defensive. "Well, I sure can't blame the Rogue for wanting something more than spears, bows, and arrows if they're going into battle against Americans who carry firearms. These Indians may be barbaric, but they aren't stupid. No more than one hundred of their warriors already carry rifles, although they've taken turns at target practice, and most of them seem to be able to handle our kind of weapons."

"I will find a way to obtain what they need," Igor said firmly. "It won't be easy, and it may take a little time, but it will be done. And if you and the trappers want to earn more money from me, you won't stray too far from the area. When the appropriate time comes, I'll need all of you."

Later in the day the Russian agent went to the bank of the Columbia River and draped a large square of bright yellow cloth across the branches of two trees. That evening at sundown he returned to the spot and waited.

After dark, when traffic across the river could not be seen by the Americans at Fort Oregon, a longboat crossed the Columbia and transported Doznevkov to the north bank. A short time later he was closeted with Colonel Phillips Morrison in the British commandant's office.

The surprised Morrison listened with growing interest as the Russian outlined what he had done. The idea of using Rogue Indians, supported by renegade whites, to drive out the American settlers was a masterful stroke, and he wished he had thought of it himself.

Doznevkov handed him the miniature totem pole. "I've been told this signifies the acceptance of the scheme by the Rogue."

Familiar with the symbols used by the Indians of the Pacific Northwest, the British commander studied the cylinder, then nodded. "This is legitimate," he said. "You've made an agreement they'll honor."

"Only if I procure firearms for them," Igor said. "That is why I've come to you for help, Colonel."

Phillips Morrison frowned. "Two years ago we issued a new type of rifle to our infantry, so we've stored one hundred to one hundred and fifty of the older, less accurate rifles in our arsenal. How many will the Rogue need?"

"Far more than one hundred and fifty. Enough to provide every warrior with firearms. Hundreds more will be needed."

"I don't have them here."

"Then the entire plan will have to be dropped." The Russian scowled. "I find it a great pity. By this autumn, perhaps, yet another American wagon train will arrive here. More will come next year, and by then no one will be able to dislodge them, not even your troops, should you risk a major war with the United States by launching an attack on their people."

"I recognize the beauty of this situation," Phillips Morrison replied. "I'll grant that Colonel Blake and the settlers might learn you inspired the Rogue and the trappers, and they might well find out that Britain supplied them with arms. But it would be difficult to prove, and our governments could deny any participation in a conspiracy."

"I think it unlikely we will be given another such

opportunity," Doznevkov declared. "Either we strike this year, or we abandon the Oregon country to the United States."

The British commandant opened a desk drawer, removed a sheaf of papers, and studied them. "There is a way," he said. "We have set up a string of small forts across central and western Canada, most of them near Hudson's Bay Company trading posts. They've been issued new rifles, too, so most of them should have their old arms stored somewhere. I can send a cavalry company to visit those garrisons and collect whatever they may have in the way of old rifles and muskets."

The agent brightened.

"It's a task that can't be performed overnight," Morrison continued. "And even after the arms are brought back here, I'll have to wait for a Royal Navy warship to put in here and then persuade her captain to drop off the weapons in the Rogue country. I estimate we may need at least six months to provide these Indians with the arms they'll need to wage an effective war."

"As long as we know they will go into battle, Colonel, I am willing to wait."

"Don't forget that the Americans will continue to grow stronger during those months," Morrison said.

Doznevkov nodded. "All too true, I am afraid. But there is no need to wait. There are men eager to earn the Czar's gold right now, so it should not be too difficult to arrange blows that will weaken the Americans, cause them serious problems, and make it difficult for them to consolidate their position."

Doznevkov timed his second visit to the Holt ranch with precision, waiting until Whip and Stalking Horse rode out to the range and Lisolette Arbo saddled a mare and then rode out for an hour's exercise. So Eulalia was alone when the Russian came to the door. As she always did now, she carried a rifle.

The sight of the weapon made Igor uneasy, but his smile was ingratiating. "I hope I do not intrude, Madame Holt."

Eulalia was eager to ride her mare after performing her morning's chores, but she was polite. "Come in."

Doznevkov wanted to waste no time. "I am wondering," he said, "whether you have learned if any of my fellow Russians are inclined to be friendly toward me."

Eulalia hesitated to tell him the truth. Lisolette became upset at the mere mention of his name, refusing to discuss him, and Olga Woods and Anton Wizneuski spoke of him with such scorn that she had refrained from asking the other Russian settlers their opinions of him. "I'm afraid I have nothing of value to tell you," she said.

He seethed inwardly, but his seeming composure was unaltered. Not even this vain, empty-minded woman would cooperate with him, but she—and every other American in Oregon—would pay dearly for their attitude toward him. He murmured his apologies for disturbing her, then quickly took his leave.

Not until he returned to his own cabin did he allow his rage to erupt. "Mikhail," he said to his companion, "I am tired of doing nothing. In the very near future we shall strike a terrible blow against these Yankees."

Colonel Menshikoff was cautious. "Plan well," he said, "and make certain there are no mistakes in the execution. No matter what happens, you and I will be suspected, and the Americans are such barbarians they would not hesitate to execute us if they learned we were responsible for some catastrophe."

Igor smiled. "According to their legalities," he said, "I am one of them. I was required to swear an oath to obey their Constitution and their laws, remember. So you and I will be present in their midst when the catastrophe, as you call it, strikes them. We will choose some festive occasion, when all of them are gathered together, and we will join in their celebration."

"I hope you are right," Menshikoff said, still dubious.

"You must trust me, Mikhail. I have spent a long time building a cobweb. Now the spiders who have taken our gold will begin to destroy the American flies."

The year's first harvest exceeded all expectations. Oats and rye, flax that would be made into linen, and a variety of vegetables were plentiful. Apples, pears, and other fruit were still growing and were not yet ready to be picked, and the wheat crop was so large that members of the council believed it soon would become unnecessary to bring flour to the territory from other parts of the United States. One of the new settlers who had arrived with the second wagon train was a miller by trade, and he was already in the process of building a gristmill.

Fish ran in such numbers that tons were smoked over hickory fires for preservation. The hunting, according to Whip, was better than it had been in years, and after immediate needs had been met, large amounts of meat were smoked or pickled in vinegar for future consumption. Supplies of wildfowl proved more than sufficient, too, as hunters shot down geese and ducks flying north. Oregon truly was a land of plenty.

A communal spirit still prevailed. Each family kept what it required of its produce, game, and fish, and the rest was stored in the warehouses that had been constructed at the edge of the village. As people needed more they were free to draw what they wished from the common stores. No permission was required, and heads of families were asked only to notify the council what they had taken.

Spirits were high, and when Ernie von Thalman suggested that the community hold a festival for the early summer harvest, the idea was received with almost universal enthusiasm. A date was set in late June, and it was agreed that the party would be held at Andrew Jackson Hall. If the weather permitted, the meal would be served on the spacious lawn of the meeting house.

Volunteers by the score offered to bake breads and cakes, and a week before the event, teams of hunters and fishermen became active, with two of the boats built at the yard of Thoman and Canning being utilized. Every family contributed a dish, but for old times' sake Cathy Blake and Emily von Thalman reactivated the group of women who had done the cooking for the first wagon train. All happily agreed to serve, and it was arranged that they would prepare the fish and meat.

Cooking pits were dug behind the meetinghouse by the men, who built fires the day before the party, so beds of hot coals were ready in advance. Whip and Tilman butchered the game, and sides of deer, elk, moose, and antelope were placed on spits. The cooks, wearing aprons over their party dresses, reported early in the morning, and a short time later many of the teen-age girls showed up to help them. Chet Harris and Danny offered to fetch the fish, which had been kept alive in watering troughs set aside for that purpose. In addition to the incomparable salmon, there were crabs, Pacific herring, and a number of large fish with white flesh that had no name but nevertheless were delicious when fried in deer fat.

In mid-morning families began to appear in the village. Games of skill were organized for the children of all ages under Paul's supervision, assisted by Lisolette and the new schoolteacher. Late in the morning the sun, which had been playing hide-and-seek for hours, came out to stay, and the clouds cleared away. Men who were pitching horseshoes soon removed their coats and rolled up their shirt-sleeves.

The entire regiment, with the exception of the unfortunate who had drawn sentry duty, marched from Fort Oregon behind the fife and drum corps. Lee promptly instructed Sergeant Major Mullins to dismiss the formation, which he did, and the troops joined in the festivities.

There was a minor stir at noon when Igor Doznevkov and Mikhail Menshikoff unexpectedly appeared, followed by the latter's two servants. The Russian officer looked uncomfortable in civilian attire. Many of the Russians snubbed the pair, but members of the council made it their business to greet the Russians with as much cordiality as they could muster. This was the first time the Czarist officers had shown up at a public function, and Ernie took the position that it would be inhospitable to ignore them.

At the sight of Doznevkov, Lisolette seemed to withdraw inside herself. Thereafter, Paul saw to it that he remained close beside her at all times.

Someone began to sing one of the songs that had been popular on the long march across the continent, and soon hundreds of voices were raised in unison. One trail song followed another, and people applauded themselves vigorously. "We have a right to be proud of what we've done," Tilman remarked. "We've come three thousand miles for this jubilee."

Shortly after noon a contingent from Fort Vancouver appeared, led by Dr. McLoughlin and Major Pitts. More than a score of British officers were in the party, but Colonel Morrison, as always, was conspicuous by his absence. At no time had he deigned to formally recognize the existence of the American settlement.

Around one o'clock in the afternoon the meal was ready, and a number of the men carved the meat on makeshift tables. Members of the cooking detail, aided by other volunteers—about forty women, in all—waited to serve the food, and the hungry celebrants formed in long lines.

A bugle sounded, everyone fell silent, and the Reverend Cavendish offered a brief prayer. "Lord," he said, "we thank you for your manifold blessings and your loving kindness to us. Your Divine guidance and your help have enabled us to conquer the wilderness. Help us now, as we enjoy this feast of plenty, to remember the comrades who sacrificed their lives for all of our sakes on the trail. May the memory of our martyred friends enable all of us to lead better, fuller, and more productive lives. Amen."

Plates were heaped high with steaming food, and so much had been prepared that even such enormous eaters as Paul could return repeatedly for more. "This is like Thanksgiving," Nancy Wade told Harry Canning.

After the meal Paul and several other volunteer fiddlers joined the fife and drum corps. As the musicians struck up a lively air, hundreds of the settlers formed a ring to play the game, Circle Prisoners. It was inevitable that Cathy and Lee Blake should be the first couple to be thrust inside the circle. According to the rules, they would be required to dance continuously until the crowd approved, at which time they would be released.

They accepted their "capture" in good spirit and danced together until they were applauded. Then they joined the circle. Emily and Ernie von Thalman were next and surprised the spectators by demonstrating the vitality of people half their age. After the von Thalmans had been applauded, someone called, "Get the Holts!"

Eulalia needed no urging to move into the circle.

But Whip, standing on the outskirts of the throng, smiled and shook his head. "My wife is the dancer in our family, so I'm sure she'll oblige you. Me, I've never danced a step in my life and wouldn't know what to do."

There was no man present who was foolhardy enough to try to drag him into the circle against his will. Eulalia stood alone inside the ring, flushing in deep embarrassment.

Tonie Martin felt sorry for her and called, "Eulalia needs a partner." Major Eli Moser worked his way through the crowd and entered the ring.

Mortified by her husband's refusal to dance with her, Eulalia swayed in time to the music, then began to dance rapidly, forcing her partner to keep up with her as best he could. The musicians increased their tempo, but she challenged them again, twirling and bending, her body in constant, fluid motion.

The spectators watched in fascinated silence. Even those who had participated in the game many times had never seen a woman dance with such reckless abandon.

Cindy and Claiborne Woodling exchanged uneasy, silent glances. They were aware of Eulalia's chronic unhappiness, and both correctly interpreted her present mood. But they were afraid she was going too far in her attempt to thumb her nose at her husband. Not even the girls who danced in the waterfront taverns of New York and Philadelphia were so shameless.

Whip's eyes narrowed, and he seemed to hold his breath as Eulalia danced. He could blame no one but himself for her exhibition, to be sure, but she was going out of her way to spite him, and he found it difficult to curb his anger.

Claiborne started to cheer and applaud before Whip's temper exploded. Others followed his example, and a laughing, gasping Eulalia and her partner were permitted to leave the circle. Whip's face was wooden, and he did not look again at his wife.

Claiborne realized it was imperative that the tensions be alleviated swiftly, so he called, "Ted and Olga Woods go next!"

The heavyset man and his sturdy bride protested in vain as they were propelled into the circle. Paul Thoman winked at his fellow musicians, then led them in playing a stately fifteenth-century air.

The crowd watched in astonishment as Ted and Olga, never touching, moved around the circle with delicacy and charm, their feet moving in unison. No one would have believed that two people of their size could be so graceful, and a storm of applause interrupted them.

The blacksmith and his wife smiled at each other, but did not halt. They finished their dance before they glided, still at arm's length, toward the throng.

The applause became louder, and Ted responded by enveloping his bride in a bear hug. He and Olga made a perfect couple, and he was delighted the whole community was aware of their relationship. Olga beamed, too, as Ted took her hand and they walked together to the outside of the crowd.

A mischievous glint appeared in Sally MacNeill's eyes as she shouted, "Nancy Wade and Harry Canning!"

The pair were standing together and tried to escape, but the throng closed in on them, and they were half carried, half pushed into the open space. Nancy tossed her head and tried to make the best of the situation, but Harry groaned aloud.

Paul looked at his partner, chuckled, and said something in a low tone to the other musicians. Then he raised his bow, and they began to play far too rapidly for dancing.

Nancy did her best to keep time to the beat, while Harry deliberately moved at half time. Their efforts were totally uncoordinated, and people began to jeer.

Then Paul purposely played a more sedate tune. Nancy tried to be helpful by setting the tempo, but Harry stubbornly refused to let a woman take the lead, and he did what he pleased. Nancy became annoyed and persisted, and although both were graceful, they appeared to be doing two different dances.

"Keep them prisoner until they do it right!" Sally called. Others echoed the cry, and the musicians played for a third time.

Aware that they would be held in the circle until

they cooperated with each other, Harry and Nancy finally settled down. He deliberately moved in a simple step, which she quickly picked up, and at last they were dancing in unison. Several people cheered halfheartedly.

Then Harry's dancing became more complicated. Again Nancy matched him step for step, somehow anticipating what he would do next. By now the cheers were becoming genuine and enthusiastic.

But Harry was not yet satisfied, and Nancy was a kindred spirit. They realized that a misstep or stumble would undo all they had accomplished, but they insisted on dancing in increasingly intricate patterns, both of them utterly determined to persevere to the end. They were remarkably nimble now, communicating without words, their efforts superbly coordinated.

Paul brought the song to an end, and Nancy curtsied and Harry bowed low as the crowd responded with good humor. The exhausted but triumphant couple had more than redeemed themselves.

While the settlers, members of the garrison, and the guests from Fort Vancouver were enjoying their sport, an activity of a far different kind was taking place at the opposite end of the village.

A nervous, apprehensive Dave Evans stood at one side of the road, peering in the direction of Andrew Jackson Hall. He could not see the meetinghouse or its grounds because his view was cut off by the church, schoolhouse, and hospital, but he could hear the music and laughter, and he was afraid someone would come wandering down the dirt path at any moment.

"Hurry up," he called softly over his shoulder. "We don't have all day."

A grim-faced Richard Ramsey emerged from one of the larger warehouses, an almost empty bucket of pine tar in one hand. From it he took a length of rope

312

impregnated with the tar, then lightly but carefully stretched it down the road.

"Where the hell is Hawkman?" Dave demanded.

The renegade trapper, also carrying a bucket of pine tar, came into the open from another warehouse. "No names, you idiot," he hissed, and not waiting for a reply, he followed Ramsey's example and laid out a length of rope soaked in pine tar.

"Take your bucket with you," Ramsey reminded him. "Remember that we won't be paid if we leave any evidence behind."

Hawkman nodded, then turned to Dave. "You take over now," he said. He headed toward the woods that lined the river bank, and Ramsey quickly followed him.

Dave knew they would run separately for about two miles, meeting at a predesignated spot up the Columbia, where they had hidden a boat that would take them safely to the opposite bank.

His own position was far more dangerous, and at the moment he found little consolation in the thought that he was being paid more of the Russians' gold than his comrades would receive. His hands trembling, he struck sparks using steel and flint, and set fire to the outer, frayed ends of the ropes.

Shoving the flint and steel into a pocket, Dave curbed a panicky desire to break into a run and forced himself to walk sedately toward the meeting-house, which he knew he could reach at that pace in no more than three minutes. Doznevkov had assured him the wicks would burn for at least ten minutes, and he hoped the Russian could be trusted.

In any event, he had now done his part, and if his companions had been equally reliable, the warehouses soon would be on fire. Pine tar, like the sawdust he had also supplied, burned furiously.

Regardless of the outcome, he would demand full payment from Doznevkov, the equivalent of what he could earn in two months of hard work at the sawmill. But he couldn't think of that now. He had to remain alert, proceed one step at a time, and improvise as he had never before done.

The music became louder as Dave approached Andrew Jackson Hall, and he saw hundreds of people gathered in a circle on the lawn. Food scents assailed him, and he realized he was ravenous, but he couldn't afford to think about his personal comfort, either.

Luck was with him. He saw Whip Holt standing alone outside the circle. Deliberately moving into his line of vision, Dave drew a cigar from his breast pocket, then took his time lighting it. So far so good.

He sauntered on, behaving as though he didn't have a care in the world, and puffed on his cigar with relish. Ah! Off to his left he saw Ginny Dobbs and Hector Mullins. Moving toward them until he made certain they noticed him, he waved casually, but did not halt.

He was relieved when they returned his wave. Their lack of enthusiasm left him unperturbed; all that mattered was that they had seen him, which helped him establish his presence here.

Dave's luck remained good. Several American and British officers stood together nearby, among them Majors Moser and Pitts, and he heard the American say, "We'll have to get a splinter from the cooking fire for your pipe, Roland."

Without hesitation Dave intervened. "Permit me to help, gentlemen," he said, lighting Major Pitts's pipe. The boldness of his act, he told himself, was a brilliant maneuver.

Next he joined the crowd watching the dancing and made it his business to laugh and cheer loudly. If necessary, he was prepared to swear he had been standing in one place for a long time. Others were so engrossed in what was happening inside the circle that they had lost all sense of time's passage.

Dave smelled smoke, and only the exercise of great

self-discipline enabled him to refrain from craning his neck and looking in the direction of the warehouses. If they were burning it would be a grave tactical error for him to make the discovery.

Nancy Wade and Harry Canning, tired but grinning, moved past Dave after they were allowed to leave the circle. He made a point of congratulating them.

The thought entered his mind that perhaps he should maneuver so that he and some woman were called into the circle to dance together. No, it would be wrong to call too much attention to himself. What he had done so far was just right.

In the distance he caught a glimpse of Igor Doznevkov, but he totally ignored the Russian. Never would he acknowledge that they were even remotely acquainted.

Bored by the dancing, Dave glanced surreptitiously at his watch, which he removed from his waistcoat pocket. Thirteen minutes had passed since he had walked away from the burning fuses. Surely the fire would be well started in the two warehouses now and would spread to the smaller storage building that stood between them.

If something untoward had happened and the fuses had failed to burn or had been extinguished, eventually the settlers would know that a deliberate sabotage attempt had been made. Pine tar and piles of sawdust would be found in the warehouses, and the fuses themselves would be evidence. But none of it could be traced to him, not even the sawdust. Regardless of the outcome, he was safe.

Sixteen minutes. Assuming the fires had caught, the warehouses would be infernos by now.

Dave joined in the laughter and applause as another pair of dancers won their reprieve.

Twenty minutes. His nerve was breaking, and he did not know how much longer he could stand the suspense. He tried to concentrate on the dancing of

Tilman Wade and Sally MacNeill, who were now inside the circle, but he couldn't help thinking they were making fools of themselves. Certainly Wade was old enough to know better.

Twenty-seven minutes. Dave mopped heavy perspiration from his face with a bandanna. His eyes were glazed, and he neither knew nor cared about the identity of the dancers who had just been forced into the ring.

Suddenly aware of the enormity of what he had done, Dave gave in to a total sense of panic. Breaking away from the crowd watching the dancers, he left the hall and fled in the direction of the forest.

No one in the settlement ever saw him again.

The high-pitched sound of a woman's scream cut like a razor blade through the music. Then a man shouted, "Fire!" Columns of dense smoke were billowing skyward at the far side of the village.

Dozens of people started to run in the direction of the blaze. Both of the large warehouses were burning fiercely, and the smaller storage building that stood between them was in flames, too. The fuses had burned, leaving no trace, and the fire was so intense that no one would be able to find evidence of pine tar or sawdust. Ironically, Dave Evans would never see that the act of arson had succeeded and that its perpetrators were safe from detection.

The military reacted to the emergency promptly and vigorously, with the soldiers forming double bucket brigade lines that stretched to the river. Meanwhile, residents of the village and scores of volunteers rounded up all the buckets they could find.

But they were too late, and their efforts were in vain. The fire was so far advanced that the water thrown on it failed to halt the all-consuming flames, and within an hour all three of the log warehouses were reduced to piles of glowing rubble.

Only now did people begin to comprehend the significance of the catastrophe. Individual families had kept enough food supplies in their homes to last two or three weeks, but the bulk of the provisions that were to have sustained them until the next harvest— including grains and vegetables, smoked fish and preserved meats—had been destroyed.

The members of the council convened informally, standing together and watching curls of smoke still rising from the ruins. "This is bad," Ernie von Thalman said as he shook his head. "We're going to be on short rations for the next few months."

"We'll have to do without beans and corn and most vegetables, that's sure," Tilman said.

Whip took a more positive attitude. "Nobody will starve," he declared. "Starting tomorrow morning we'll send out teams of volunteer hunters and fishermen. The salmon are still running, and the forests are filled with game."

"Oh, we'll make out all right," Lee Blake said. "But there are more than a thousand of us here now, so it won't be easy. The garrison has a month's supply of flour and bacon in its own warehouses, and we'll share that with the civilian population, but I'm afraid that it won't go very far."

"We'll have to tighten our belts for the next few months, that's all there is to it," Ernie said. "It won't be pleasant, and people will be as hungry as they were when we spent a winter in the Wyoming wilderness. But we'll survive somehow."

One thought was uppermost in the minds of the council members, but no one voiced it. No merchant ships carrying provisions were expected to arrive over the summer, and the situation would become even more ticklish if the third wagon train reached the settlement before the next harvest. If that should happen, the shortages would become critical.

John McLoughlin, who had also watched the fire in horror, approached the group. "Forgive this intrusion, gentlemen," he said, "but perhaps I can help you."

They looked at him.

"My warehouses across the river are filled," he said. "I have more kegs of corn and beans than I can count, and I must have several tons of pickled and smoked meats on hand. Most of it came to Hudson's Bay in barter with the Indians, and I'm not sure—in fact, I never have been—that it is worth our while to send food on to London. So your people are welcome to all I have."

The members of the council were stunned by the generous offer. "We're overwhelmed, Dr. McLoughlin," Ernie said. "But there's one very serious problem. Our people haven't yet accumulated much cash, and they won't for at least another year, until we establish regular trade with the cities in the East. So we have no way to pay Hudson's Bay for the supplies."

John McLoughlin smiled. "I'm well aware of your situation," he said, "so I'm perfectly willing to extend credit to the Americans. Individuals can sign for what they need, and they can repay us whenever they get their hands on cash. In a year, two years—or however long it may take."

Ernie silently shook the Scottish factor's hand, his eyes suspiciously moist.

"Why are you doing this for us?" Whip asked.

McLoughlin shrugged. "I am no philanthropist. I have spent my entire life making money for Hudson's Bay and myself. But there comes a time in every man's life when he discovers there are things more important than money. I have loved Oregon ever since I came here. I'm thinking of retiring here rather than going home. This country is unique in all the world. This is the land of the future."

As his listeners watched him, they were impressed by his fervor. His eyes sparkled, and his lined face looked more youthful.

"I don't care and have never cared who settled

here," he said. "Americans are as welcome as the British. So are the Russians—and anyone else who wants to come. You Yankees have earned the right to possess the territory. I've begged London to send settlers, but no one has listened to me. You've suffered trials and hardships, and you've earned the right to call Oregon your own. I hate politics, and I don't think very highly of politicians. What's important to me is this land. I've been watching your men plant crops and nurture them. I've seen you live by fishing and hunting. I've watched you tame the forest. So how could I refuse to offer you my hand in help when you're in need?"

That same afternoon four boats that had been built by workers under the direction of Thoman and Canning began to ply back and forth between the south and north banks of the Columbia, all of them laden on each return trip with barrels of corn, beans, and preserved meats from the Hudson's Bay Company storehouses. John McLoughlin kept his word and was generous to a fault. Those who wanted the provisions he offered, and most of the settlers eagerly accepted his generosity, were required only to indicate to the chief clerk how much they had taken, then sign their names or make their marks.

John McLoughlin stood at the oversized window in his office near the waterfront, a faint smile on his face as he watched the boats taking on supplies, then carrying them to the Americans on the far side of the river.

The door opened behind him, and he turned. It was Colonel Morrison, who was obviously furious. McLoughlin braced himself, his smile fading.

"You've gone too far this time, McLoughlin," the commander at Fort Vancouver declared. "I'm sorry the Americans suffered a serious accident, but if you hadn't meddled, their hold on this country would have been severely weakened. As it is, you've strengthened them and made it possible for them to stay on here."

"I have no wish to drive them out," Dr. McLoughlin said quietly.

"You've given me no choice. You act contrary to government policy. So I intend to write to the War Office and the Foreign Office recommending that you be placed on trial for high treason!"

"Write as many letters as you please, Morrison, and be damned to you," the Scotsman declared. "I can't believe honorable Englishmen have sunk so low in their own esteem that they'd hang me for making a gesture to hungry people in the name of humanity!"

Morrison was so upset that he had to compose himself before he could speak again. "I appeal to you, close the doors of your warehouse immediately! Send no more provisions to the Yankees."

"You already know my answer. I refuse."

"Then I shall order my troops to close the doors, stand guard over your storehouses, and permit nothing more to be removed from them!"

A hint of amusement appeared in the factor's eyes. "You exceed your authority, but my clerks and I won't take up arms to prevent you from sealing our doors. However, you'll pay a heavy price for your actions, Morrison. Hudson's Bay is a privately owned company, and you have no jurisdiction over us. We and the British government have worked hand in hand without major disputes for nearly two hundred years. But if there's a parting of the ways now, my directors won't take the insult meekly, I can assure you. The man responsible for using force against us will be cashiered and drummed out of the Royal Army. You have my word that your career will end very abruptly, and when you're dismissed, you'll also be denied a pension."

Morrison reddened, then turned white. "How can you justify giving food to the enemy?"

"I know of no enemy," McLoughlin declared. "Apparently you refer to the Americans, but Great Britain is at peace with the United States. The settlers across the river happen to be my best customers, and if I choose to help them in their time of trouble, I do it strictly for business reasons. In the long run their gratitude will bring in a substantial income—in return for provisions that cost me little or nothing. The Hudson's Bay directors will see the situation precisely as I do. So send your troops to shut my doors—but pay the consequences."

Colonel Morrison's bluff had been called, and he hesitated.

"And be prepared, too, for a riot. The Americans know what I've promised them, and if you deny them the food they need, they'll storm across the river by the hundreds. Think of how it will look on your record when you're forced to report that American civilians were wounded, perhaps killed, by troops under your command. Right here in Fort Vancouver! Even if you escape court-martial in some miraculous way, you'll be laughed out of the Royal Army!"

The commandant turned on his heel, walked rapidly through the town. Upon reaching his own office in Fort Vancouver, he slammed the door behind him. He remained in isolation for a time and then summoned his principal military intelligence officer.

"Lieutenant," he said, "I want you to cross the river as soon as it grows dark and you can't be seen from the American fort. You know where to find the Russian, Doznevkov?"

"Yes, sir. I've twice visited his cabin."

"Good. I want you to fetch him immediately. Tell him I must see him without delay—and don't return without him."

Time dragged, and Morrison, normally a hearty eater, had no appetite for supper. He stayed closeted in his office, pacing impatiently until, in mid-evening, Igor Doznevkov finally appeared.

The Russian was in an expansive mood. "The sabotage today was very effective," he said. "I'm even thinking of giving my agents a bonus. The Americans have been badly crippled."

Colonel Morrison had no intention of explaining that, thanks to John McLoughlin's generosity, the settlers across the river would not suffer. Instead, he said harshly, "I sent for you because the schedule for your Indian attack must be advanced. The Yankees are already so well entrenched that our cause will be hopeless if we wait until late in the autumn."

Igor was startled. "The only reason we're waiting," he said cautiously, "is to give you time to accumulate the firearms that the Rogue demand before they'll go to war. Can you procure them sooner?"

"A number of old muskets will be arriving from some of the nearer outposts in the immediate future."

"But you know the Indians won't move until they receive enough arms to satisfy them."

Desperate measures were required to overcome a desperate crisis. "I have decided," Morrison said, "to supply the Rogue with arms from my own arsenal!"

The Russian was astonished. "You'll give them your new rifles, Colonel?"

"Yes. As many as they need." The odds in favor of the Americans had become so great that Phillips Morrison was gambling by playing his last trump.

The American settlers could not lavish enough praise on John McLoughlin, and they agreed that he well deserved to be called "the father of Oregon." He was inundated with more dinner invitations in the settlement than he could possibly accept.

But relations with the British garrison deteriorated rapidly. A decree issued by Colonel Morrison prevented the officers from visiting the south bank of the Columbia, and not even Major Pitts was immune. The redcoats not only doubled their sentry details, but, egged on by Morrison, were so surly to Americans who visited the Hudson's Bay stores at Fort Vancouver that several fights were narrowly averted.

Lee Blake weighed the situation carefully, then called in Whip Holt for a private talk. "It appears to me," he said, "that Colonel Morrison is spoiling for a battle. He seems to be looking for an excuse to start trouble, even though we and the British are still at peace."

"It could be," Whip said. "I hear tell he's been giving food and lodging to no-good trappers like Hawkman."

"I doubt that he'll make a direct attack on Fort Oregon," Lee said. "That would be an act of war without an actual declaration of war by London. But I'm not losing sight of the fact that his garrison outnumbers us by three to one, so there are a great many things he could do to harass us. And I have the feeling in my bones that Doznevkov and that joke of a Russian colonel are cooperating with him."

"Slap the Russians into jail, Lee."

"We have no evidence that would condemn them in any court, and we're still bound by the rules of American law, Whip. All the same we've got to take precautions. For one thing, I'm asking Ernie to request that our women carry firearms with them at all times, as they did on the wagon trains. And even more important, I want to form a militia battalion to augment my regiment."

"I think you'll find that every able-bodied man here will want to join."

"So much the better! I'm offering you a brevet, Whip—a temporary commission as a lieutenant colonel to command the battalion."

"Many thanks," Whip said. "But shouldn't the post go to Ernie?"

"He holds the seal of the President and the Congress as a government-appointed agent, so he isn't eligible. Besides, he's growing too old for an active military command."

"All right, then, I'll accept."

"Your most important task is to establish a network so the word can be passed quickly if there's a need for the civilians to mobilize. How we'll utilize the militia will depend on developments. The principal object is to get everybody together quickly in an emergency. How many men would you guess you can muster?"

"Maybe two hundred and fifty. Give me some officers and I'll start recruiting right off."

"Appoint your own officers."

"I'll ask Tilman to be my second-in-command, and I'll make Claiborne my adjutant. Three of us should be enough to get the recruiting organized. Then the companies can elect their own officers."

"I hate to alarm people, but we can't take chances. The formation of the militia will cut down the British odds against us."

They parted solemnly, and Lee's mood was somber for the rest of the day. Hereafter, he knew, the farmers and ranchers would carry weapons with them whenever they went into the fields. Children from outlying properties would be escorted to school. In effect, the American community would live under siege conditions. But Colonel Morrison's attitude made it impossible for Lee to react in any other way.

At the end of his work day, as he walked the short distance from his office to the commandant's house, Lee had to steel himself before telling Cathy of the preparations for trouble that he was making. She and all of the other women who had made the long trek across the continent had endured so much on their travels, and since their arrival in Oregon, they had worked incessantly, enjoying few luxuries in a frontier society that would take years to develop. It would be a long time before they knew real comforts, and at the very least they deserved peace of mind, but now even that would be denied them.

Festive candles were lighted in the parlor, and Cathy greeted her husband in her ivory satin gown.

Lee tried to remember their social calendar. "Is someone coming to supper tonight?"

She shook her head. "Nobody, but we're having a special supper. Harry Canning brought us a gift of shrimp, and then we're having baked venison."

"A real feast."

She poured him a small glass of sack.

"Join me in a drink?"

Cathy shook her head again and smiled as she sat opposite him. Lee was puzzled. "Why the party atmosphere?"

"Well, this is a special occasion."

"Is it?" He searched his mind and knew it wasn't their anniversary or either of their birthdays. In any event the news he dreaded telling her would have to wait.

"Very special." Cathy was cheerful but spoke quietly. "I stopped in at the hospital today, and Anton confirmed what I've guessed for several weeks. We're going to have a baby, Lee."

He caught his breath.

She looked at him and laughed. "Say something!"

"I—I'm speechless!" He stared hard at her for a moment. "Are you happy or sad, Cathy?"

"I'm just delighted, and I hope you are, too."

"If you really want to bring my child into the world," he said, speaking slowly, "then I'm elated, too. This may not be the time to bring certain things into the open, and I know we should have talked long ago. But it's better to be frank now than keep silent forever. I know I took you away from Whip when you were disillusioned with him. And for a long time after we were married, I had the feeling you were still in love with him. More recently, well—we've both been busy, and daily routines can paper over cracks in a building's structure."

"Once upon a time," Cathy replied, speaking with equal care, "I was a little girl, married in name only to an old miser. As I was still an adolescent, I became infatuated with Whip Holt. He was my escape from reality. After Otto died I couldn't hide any more, and I had to live in the real world. I married again, and this time it was a real marriage. Now I—I hope we have a son. He'll be named Leland Blake, Junior, and by the time he becomes a cadet at West Point, his father will be one of the most distinguished generals in the army. Do I make myself clear?"

"I'm beginning to get the point," he said.

Cathy looked at him, her smile warm, her eyes tender. "I'm a fortunate woman because I've learned to face reality without flinching or hiding my head any longer. I'm married to a wonderful man, whom I happen to love with all my heart."

Lee went to her, lifted her gently to her feet, and kissed her. "If we have a daughter," he said huskily, "we'll name her for you."

Cathy laughed, but there were tears in her eyes. "We'll do no such thing, Colonel Blake. One of me in the family is quite enough!"

Tilman awoke at dawn, went out to the barn to milk the cows, and after feeding them, turned them out to pasture. Then he returned to the house, where Nancy, showing no improvement as a cook, prepared a breakfast of tasteless pancakes.

Tilman went off to weed in his wheat fields, a task made necessary by a recent, heavy rain. Nancy promised to join him later, and after hurriedly washing the dishes she walked the short distance to Sally MacNeill's house. Every morning since Nancy's arrival, they had got together for a cup of herb tea before settling down to the day's chores.

Sally, who had been living alone since Dolores's marriage, kept a well-ordered house, and the tea was ready when her friend arrived.

"I thought I'd see you last night," Nancy said, bubbling as usual, "but Tilman went out recruiting for the new militia, and before he left he made me promise not to leave the house. Imagine! As though I were a child."

Sally felt certain she would be treated to a new development in her friend's budding romance with Harry Canning, and Nancy did not disappoint her. "I've been invited to a very special party," she said. "A barbecue at the boatyard."

"What's the occasion?" Sally no longer objected to mentions of Paul Thoman.

"Harry and Paul want to celebrate the keel-laying of their first coastal sloop. It will be huge, a real ship —sixty feet long. They're asking quite a few people, so I'm sure I can get an invitation for you, too, if you'd like."

"Don't bother," Sally said, smiling at the change in her own attitude. She glanced idly out of the window in the direction of the new barn at the rear of the house, then stiffened and grasped the other girl's arm.

"What's wrong?"

"Ssh. There he is again!"

"Who?"

"An Indian!"

Nancy laughed. "I've been in Oregon long enough to know that the only Indians around here are the braves who take their furs to Fort Vancouver."

Sally gripped her arm harder. "There are two of them," she said and reached for her rifle.

Nancy looked out of the window and saw she was right. Two Indians, both short, stocky, and very dark, wearing buckskin trousers and shirts decorated with seashells, were cautiously making their way to the front of the barn.

Having forgotten to bring a weapon of her own, Nancy had to borrow a pistol. Sally handed it to her, then started toward the kitchen door.

"What are you doing, Sally?"

"It looks to me like they want to steal my horses. Maybe I can scare them off. Anyway, the sound of my gun will bring Tilman here in a hurry." Sally flung open the door, raised her rifle to her shoulder, and fired blindly.

It was impossible to determine where the shot went, but the Indians scurried to safety behind the barn.

"Keep watch," Sally ordered as she reloaded her rifle.

The Indians did not reappear, but as Sally had predicted, Tilman arrived on the run, his own rifle under his arm. "What's the matter?" he called as he approached.

Both girls spoke simultaneously, and as he tried to make what he could of their babble, a second shot rang out, coming from the direction of the barn. The bullet buried itself in the log wall only inches from Tilman's head.

He went into action immediately, raising his own rifle to his shoulder as he peered toward the barn. The instant he saw the two intruders he fired, and one of the savages threw his hands high in the air, then sprawled lifeless on the ground. The other Indian fled into the woods behind the barn.

Tilman took Sally's rifle and handed her his. "Reload this," he said curtly and continued to look out toward the barn.

The girls were so frightened they remained silent for a long time. Then Sally asked in a small voice, "Is he dead?"

"I can't be sure, but it looks that way." He walked cautiously out to the barn, prodded the dead man with his foot, then bent down to pick up the rifle the Indian had dropped.

Still scanning everything in his line of vision, he returned to the kitchen. "Where there are two, there may be more, so I'll take no chances. Nancy, saddle my gelding and ride as fast as you can to the Holt ranch. I've never seen an Indian quite like this one, and I want Whip to identify his tribe. Don't tarry, now, because I'll be keeping watch right here."

For once Nancy wasted no words, and, still clutching her friend's pistol, she hurried off to the Holt property.

Tilman sensed that Sally was badly upset and wanted to console her. "It could be they were just a couple of renegades looking for something to steal."

Sally began to tremble violently. "Everything is going to be just fine now," Tilman assured her.

She could not control her trembling body. "I—I'm sorry I'm such a coward," she murmured.

"You had a right to be scared." Still scanning the area behind the house, never allowing his gaze to wander elsewhere, Tilman placed an arm around Sally's shoulders.

She moved closer to him. Reacting instinctively, he tightened his grip, and gradually she became calmer, her trembling stopped, and she sighed.

Still holding her, Tilman was thunderstruck when the realization dawned on him that the girl who nestled close to him was no longer an adolescent. She had become a woman, mature beyond her years because of the tragedies and hardships she had suffered. Inadvertently he glanced down at her for a moment. Sally was looking up at him with an expression that needed no interpretation.

"Well," he said aloud.

"Well, yourself," she replied, a hint of a giggle in her voice.

He took in a deep breath and asked, "How long have you known?"

"I haven't kept count," Sally replied happily. "Quite a few months." She leaned her head on his shoulder, and when she sighed again, it was plain that she was contented.

"You knew the way I felt about you, too?"

"Of course. Nancy and I have discussed it many times, and we agreed that sooner or later you'd wake up."

Tilman wanted to kiss her but would have to wait.

It was imperative that he continue to keep watch for the Indian who had raced off into the woods. Perhaps it was just as well, he thought, because he found it almost impossible to believe that he and Sally could have fallen in love. "I still think I'm much too old for you," he said.

"Oh, no, you're not," she said. "You know that age doesn't matter in the least."

"It doesn't?"

"Why should it?" she countered. "You're a man, and I'm your woman. Nothing else is important."

Tilman was silent for a time, absorbing her statement, and finally murmured, "You're right." His grip became still tighter.

"There's only one problem I can't solve," she said. "After we're married, I don't know whether we just add my land to yours or sell this place to somebody who'll be coming here on the next wagon train."

She would always be a step ahead of him, and he couldn't help laughing. "That's a detail," he said, "that doesn't need to be settled right now."

Before she could speak again, Whip and Stalking Horse arrived at a gallop. Nancy, who had been unable to maintain their blistering pace, followed them, but did not arrive for several minutes.

Taking in the scene quickly, Whip dismounted and, keeping his rifle ready, went to the side of the barn and studied the dead Indian. "Rogue," he said with finality. Stalking Horse came up behind him and nodded in agreement.

"This is strange," Whip told Tilman. "The Rogue are a coastal tribe who live near the southern border of Oregon, near California. They're mean, and so greedy that not many people—other Indians or trappers—deal with them much. But they'd have no reason to go on the warpath this far from their homeland. Unless—" He broke off, leaving the thought unfinished.

"Unless they were put up to it," Tilman said. "That means the British or the Russians—or both."

Whip looked at the warrior's rifle that Tilman had picked up and examined it briefly. "This was made in Sheffield, England," he said. "It is exactly like the new-style British rifles we picked up after the last big Indian attack we fought off on the trail."

Tilman whistled under his breath. "We're in for trouble," he said.

Whip nodded gravely. "Lots of it. We'll have to let Lee Blake know right away so the regiment can take steps, and we'll have to put the militia battalion on the alert, too. Unless this is an isolated incident, which I find hard to accept, all hell is going to bust loose around here!"

XII

Lee responded quickly to the threat, sending platoons of infantry and cavalry to patrol the perimeters of the farms, ranches, and groves of fruit trees that comprised the American settlement in Oregon. The newly formed militia were placed on alert, too, but Whip instructed its members to continue doing their normal work until further notice. As yet there was no concrete evidence to suggest that the Rogue intended to attack in force, and until they did, there was no visible enemy to fight.

The army's infantry and cavalry gave the settlers valuable protection, but the defenses were not foolproof. The homes of the settlers were scattered over such a wide area that even the most efficient troops could not be everywhere simultaneously.

This unfortunate fact became all too evident when small bands of Rogue warriors began to conduct lightning raids on isolated homes, then vanished again into the deep forest. One house was burned to the ground, and an entire American family, the parents and three children, were killed. The next night one of the Russians died while trying to defend his property, but his wife and son managed to escape and gave the alarm. By the time troops and militia reached the place, however, the braves had vanished. As earlier generations of American settlers had learned in the Colonial era, it was almost impossible to establish airtight defenses against a foe who utilized hit-and-run tactics.

Lee sent a stiff note of protest to Fort Vancouver, his officer courier presenting the rifle picked up at Sally MacNeill's farm as evidence that the Rogue were using the newest of British weapons. Colonel Morrison made no attempt to deny the charge that he was supplying the Indians with arms. Instead, he placed his garrison on a full war alert.

His belligerence forced Lee to reply in kind, and the cannon at Fort Oregon were moved into new positions so that virtually all cannon faced the potential enemy across the Columbia. The wall built earlier to conceal the armament from British view was knocked down. It appeared almost certain that an outbreak of major hostilities between the forces of the United States and Great Britain could no longer be averted.

This situation made it necessary to keep the bulk of the regiment on duty at the fort at all times. Therefore, the burden of patrolling the outer limits of the settlement had to be assumed by the militia. Whip's ranch became the battalion's headquarters, and small groups of men came and went constantly, particularly at night. Eulalia soon learned to keep pots of herb tea and acorn coffee on the stove, no matter what the hour.

The raids conducted by the Rogue were still sporadic, however, and fit no discernible pattern. The community continued to depend on the crops and fruit that individuals grew, and the cattle and sheep required care, too. So more than a semblance of normal living had to be maintained.

There were almost two hundred men in the militia, and Whip solved the problem by assigning forty at a time to active duty on a rotating schedule, with each group conducting patrols and scouring the countryside for periods of twenty-four hours. This allowed each militiaman time to earn his living.

The raids continued on an irregular pattern. The elder of two brothers on a remote farm was killed and the younger wounded, but this time the militia found the intruders, and four Rogue warriors were shot. Everyone knew this punishment would not deter or discourage the Indians, and the settlers braced for still more assaults.

Some were in favor of leading an expedition to the land of the Rogue and attacking the Indians there. But Whip pointed out that this would leave the settlement relatively unprotected. And the greater threat of war with Great Britain had to take precedence, so the battalion had to be kept at home, ready to join forces with Lee's regiment of regular army troops if the need should arise.

Members of the council agreed with Lee's growing belief that Russia had a hand in the troubles, so Ernie von Thalman signed a warrant for the arrest of Igor Doznevkov, Colonel Mikhail Menshikoff, and the latter's two servants. A squad of troops was sent to Doznevkov's cabin to apprehend the four men and bring them to the village, but by the time the soldiers arrived there, the quartet had fled, taking all of their possessions with them.

Certainly their involvement with the Rogue was established, making it possible for Lee and Ernie to write strong reports to the War and State Departments in Washington City, but the knowledge offered the settlers small consolation. The Russian troublemakers were still at large, presumably having joined the Rogue somewhere in the forests, and consequently they were free to continue harassing the settlers.

Like the pioneers in other parts of America during earlier times, people acclimated as best they could to a new way of living. Fear was ever-present now, but the settlers refused to succumb to it. Sally MacNeill and Tilman Wade were married in a simple ceremony by the Reverend Cavendish, with Nancy Wade acting as her friend's maid of honor. A small party was held for the bride and groom at the Holt ranch, and Tilman was granted a forty-eight-hour leave of absence from the militia and then returned to duty as the deputy commander.

Paul Thoman and Harry Canning were lieutenants in the militia, arranging to serve together so they could devote the rest of their time to their work at the boatyard. The keel-laying of their first coastal sloop was necessarily delayed, but the feat was accomplished at last, in spite of obstacles. They were still determined to celebrate the event, but the times did not permit extravagance, so they pared their guest list to a dozen people.

Harry caught several salmon, Paul brought down a deer, and they built their cooking fire several hundred yards from the boatyard, on the cove, in order to prevent damage to their property in the event that the wind carried the flames in the wrong direction. They began their preparations for the event early in the day. Lisolette Arbo and Nancy Wade offered to bake the bread and cook the vegetables, and they arrived together late in the morning.

Nancy and Harry began to bicker, as usual, and the shy Lisolette exchanged amused glances with Paul, but made no comment. She shucked a few dozen ears of corn and peeled half that number of potatoes, disposing of the husks and peels in the fire, over which Paul was slowly turning a side of venison on a spit. They were happy to be engaging in these homely activities together, neither felt talkative, and they tried to shut out the sound of the latest argument.

"This isn't the first time I've baked bread, you know!" Nancy declared.

"Well, it looks to me like you don't know what you're about," Harry replied. "Add more yeast, or that dough will never rise!"

Lisolette waited until they paused for breath before

asking Paul, "Where is your iron kettle, the big one? I'll put the potatoes on to boil now, but I won't put the corn in until the rest of the company gets here and dinner is almost ready."

"I left it in the boatyard office," Paul said. "The frying pan is there, too. If you'll turn the spit for me, I'll fetch them for you."

"No," she said. "I might be too slow or too fast, but you know how to turn the spit at the right speed. I'll get the kettle and pan."

"You're sure they won't be too heavy for you?"

"Hardly," Lisolette replied, laughing as she started to walk around the edge of the cove to the boatyard. Granted that she lacked the brawn of such women as Olga Woods, but she wasn't as frail as Paul appeared to believe.

Leaving the water when she reached the scaffolding of the dry dock, Lisolette headed inland toward the small office-storeroom, an ungainly log cabin located at the far end of the boatyard. The door was open, and the thought flickered through her mind that the partners usually kept it closed, but she assumed they had been careless because the site of the party was so near.

She paused at the threshold, then recoiled in horror, gasping involuntarily. Two men in greasy, faded buckskin shirts and trousers, both with stubble on their faces, were ladling pine tar from buckets as they moved from one end of the cabin to the other. They heard the girl's gasp, and Hawkman sprang toward her.

"I'll take care of the woman," Hawkman called to his companion in a low voice. "Keep on with what you're doing, Smitty, and don't waste any time"

Lisolette started to scream, but the renegade trapper clapped a hand over her mouth, then bore her to the ground. She struggled furiously, kicking and scratching, but she was no match for him.

"Shut up, damn you!" he ordered, and his strong

fingers closed around her throat as he choked her.

At the end of the cove, Paul thought he heard Lisolette scream, but Harry and Nancy were arguing even more loudly, and he couldn't be certain. Feeling uneasy, he left the spit, picked up his rifle, and started to walk toward the office. Perhaps he had been imagining things, but if he had been right, he had no business loitering. His sense of disquiet propelled him to move more rapidly, and he began to run.

The sight that greeted Paul stunned him. Lisolette was sprawled on the ground, her eyes closed, and it was impossible to tell whether she was dead or alive. Squatting above her, his fingers closed around her neck, was the itinerant trapper Hawkman.

Paul's temper soared, but the year he had spent in the Rockies as a mountain man stood him in good stead, and he knew the situation called for a cool mind. Afraid to shoot at Hawkman, who was only inches from the prone Lisolette, Paul grasped his rifle by the muzzle and, swinging it like a club, caught Hawkman with the butt. It crashed against the side of his head, forcing him to release his grip on the girl's throat and knocking him unconscious.

Paul started forward to examine Lisolette, but at that instant Smitty, whom Paul had not seen, lunged, his knife in one hand. Instinct prompted Paul to duck, and the blade grazed his shoulder, cutting through the fabric of his shirt and inflicting a hairline cut that drew blood. Barely aware of the cut, Paul caught hold of his assailant's wrist.

Trying to disengage himself, Smitty used his free hand to punch the young mountain man in the stomach, then in the face. But Paul hung on grimly, his long fingers wrapped around Smitty's thick wrist. He knew he had to act quickly, before a lucky punch disabled him, so he deliberately tripped the man, using his free hand to shove him violently.

They fell to the ground together, with Paul still clamping his hand on the other's wrist, and they began a wrestling match in which the loser was sure to die. Smitty tried to drive his knee into his foe's groin, but Paul had anticipated the move and managed to jerk his body out of the way in time.

In better physical condition than his shorter, heavier foe, Paul gradually assumed the offensive. They rolled over and over, and when Paul landed on top, he stayed there, his knees pinning Smitty to the ground, his hand still clutching the knife-wielding arm.

Only now could Paul give in to his rage, and his free fist drove methodically, repeatedly into his opponent's face. Giving no quarter, just as he had been given none, he struck again and again. Bone smashed against bone with sickening thuds, and Smitty's face was reduced to a bleeding, bloated pulp.

The man seemed to lose consciousness, but his body was still tense, so Paul knew he was resorting to a trick, hoping his assailant would release his wrist. Smiling through clenched teeth, Paul continued to batter him without mercy.

Lisolette regained consciousness gradually and needed a few moments to remember what had happened to her. In spite of her grogginess she knew, when she saw Paul, that he had somehow managed to save her. But at almost the same instant she saw a sight that made her blood run cold.

Hawkman had regained consciousness, too, and managed to pull his own knife from his belt, then crawl toward the entrance to the office, where the fighting men were still locked in a death struggle.

Lisolette had just enough strength to suck in her breath and scream at the top of her voice. The sound paralyzed all three of the combatants. Paul looked over his shoulder and not only was relieved to see that the girl was alive, but also became aware of Hawkman moving slowly toward him. He had no time to lose now.

Wrenching Smitty's wrist with his remaining strength, he forced the man to drop his knife. Then, seizing the blade, Paul drove it into the burly man's body again and again, and with each blow life drained more rapidly from the trapper's body.

Now it was Hawkman's turn, and Paul had no respite as he turned to confront the renegade, who had hauled himself to his feet. They circled each other warily, each clutching a knife, each awaiting the right moment to leap forward and strike a death blow.

Then a pistol shot rang out, and Hawkman crumpled to the ground as Harry Canning raced forward, his still-smoking weapon in his hand.

Only a moment was needed to make certain that both of the trappers were dead. Then Paul turned and hastened to Lisolette's side. She had struggled to a sitting position and managed to smile at him.

"Are you all right?" he demanded.

She felt her throat, wincing slightly. "My neck is sore," she said, "but otherwise I—I think I am fine." The scene she had interrupted came back to her, and she related it in detail.

Harry ran into the cabin, and when he emerged into the open again his face was pale. "It's true," he said. "Those bastards smeared pine tar all over. They were intending to burn down the boatyard."

Paul made no reply, but began to search through the pockets of the dead men. At last he found what he was seeking, a gold coin in the purse of each. "Here's the proof Colonel Blake will want to see," he said. "These are gold rubles. These men were paid by Russians to commit sabotage against us!"

By now Nancy had come to the office, and soon the other guests arrived. The women were taken to the cooking fire, and while Paul and Harry told the story of what had happened, a shallow grave was dug in the nearby woods for the bodies of the trappers.

Tilman, the only official of American Oregon present, shook his head as he looked at the gold coins. "These confirm the worst fears of the council and the military," he said. "Only God and Igor Doznevkov know how many good-for-nothing trappers, hunters, and guides are on the payroll of Russia, doing their dirty work for them!"

The grisly fight that had just taken place put a damper on the festivities. But Lisolette, who swore she had recovered, insisted that everyone remain for dinner. "With so much happening," she said, "there is no way of knowing when all of us will have a chance to get together again. Besides, a wonderful meal will go to waste."

Her arguments made sense, so the women took charge of the final food preparations, while the men helped Harry and Paul clean pine tar from the office, scaffolding, and even the keel of the new sloop.

For the first time it dawned on those present that the destruction of the community's food warehouses by fire had been no accident.

"My hunch is that Dave Evans may have had something to do with that fire," Tilman said. "No one has seen him since the night the warehouses burned. From now on we'll arrest every vagabond trapper and hunter we see. A man is innocent until he's proven guilty under our system, but we seem to be at war with Russia now, so we've got to act accordingly."

The party was subdued, but the meal was delicious. A roving platoon of militiamen appeared, and Tilman instructed the lieutenant in command to keep a sharp day and night watch on the boatyard. Then, long before dusk, the cooking fire was extinguished, uneaten food was shared to be taken home, and the party came to an end, with the whole group going together as far as the village. There was no need for anyone to mention that the deep woods might not be safe for lone travelers.

Tilman and Sally offered to drop Lisolette off at the Holt ranch on their way home, and the arrangement would have been sensible because Nancy was going back to the Wade house and Harry was accompanying her, intending to stay for supper. But Paul insisted he would escort Lisolette.

They followed the others, riding sufficiently far behind them to be out of earshot, and when they had left the village behind, he edged his gelding closer to her mare. He was tense but tried hard to sound casual. "It was Rabelais, you know, who wrote that necessity has no law."

"It was also Rabelais who first said that one must make a virtue of necessity," Lisolette replied almost automatically.

She had fallen into the trap he had set for her, and Paul smiled. "That's precisely the point I wanted to make. Under ordinary circumstances I would have waited until the boatyard was somewhat better established before proposing to you. But these are such dangerous times, as today's events proved, that procrastination for any reason is foolish. Do I make my point?"

"Not quite." She spoke with difficulty now. "You are asking me to marry you?"

"Yes. Because I love you. Because I almost lost you today, and I don't care to run that risk again. You need someone to protect you. And I nominate Paul Thoman."

Lisolette averted her face so he wouldn't see her tears. "I can't marry you," she murmured.

"That's absurd. You've given every indication that you love me, too."

"What if I have?" she demanded fiercely. "I cannot marry you—or anyone. And that's the end of the matter."

"The devil you say," he replied firmly. "If I must, I'll throw you over my shoulder and carry you off to the Reverend Cavendish's parsonage."

All at once the anger drained out of the girl, and she looked desolate. "You don't understand."

"Correct. But I don't enjoy guessing games, and

since I believe I'm capable of comprehending almost anything that might be said to me in any of the languages you speak, excluding Russian, I demand an explanation."

"I'll tell you in plain English," Lisolette said in a broken voice, "because I'm tired of keeping the secret locked up inside me. I am responsible for what happened today, just as I am responsible for the burning of the warehouses in the village."

"You?" He stared at her. "Impossible!"

Lisolette's story suddenly spilled out of her, and she told Paul how Igor Doznevkov had recruited her in Alaska, threatening to send her back to Russia if she failed to cooperate with him.

"Nothing you've said so far surprises me," he said. "Just how much did you do for him?"

"Very little. I gave him a few minor reports before we sailed here from Alaska. But ever since we have been in Oregon, I have done nothing for him. I—I guess he thinks I am not reliable, because he did not insist too hard after I failed him several times."

"Then how could you be responsible for arson and attempted arson?" Paul wanted to know.

"I was so frightened I kept quiet," Lisolette said, "when I should have gone to Colonel Blake—and Whip and Mr. von Thalman—and told them that Doznevkov is a secret agent dedicated to the destruction of the American settlement in Oregon."

"You wouldn't have told them anything they didn't already know," Paul said. "And I refuse to accept such an excuse as a valid reason for refusing to marry me."

"You would have me as your wife even though I was an informer?"

"Doznevkov enrolled you by scaring you out of your wits. Was anyone ever arrested or actively hurt by something you told Doznevkov?"

"No, because we found the Americans already settled here when we arrived, and all of our people were so happy to join you. Doznevkov had no more power over them."

"He had no more over you, either, just as he has none today. Now you'll marry me—immediately, because two days from now I go on active militia duty again—and I give you my word he'll never come near you again. 'Cudgel thy brains no more about it,' as Shakespeare said in *King Lear*."

"That happens to be a line from *Hamlet*," Lisolette replied, her voice restored to normal.

The others, riding far ahead of them, wondered what caused Lisolette and Paul to indulge in peal after peal of laughter.

A Royal Navy sloop of war sailed up the Columbia and dropped anchor at Fort Vancouver, her arrival unexpected.

A deeply disturbed Lee Blake summoned his deputy. "Eli," he said, "the British have an added advantage now, if they want to utilize it. The combination of a warship and their larger garrison would be hard for us to beat."

"What can we do, sir?" Major Moser asked.

"Very little, other than take preventive steps. You spent ten years as an artilleryman, so I want you to take personal charge of our batteries. Tonight, after sundown, train three of our best guns on the warship. Set them as accurately as you can for both range and trajectory. If it appears that she's going to open fire on us, we might be able to blow her out of the water first."

Eli's eyes gleamed. "Nothing would give me greater pleasure, Colonel!"

"I wouldn't doubt it," Lee said dryly. "But you'll open fire only when you're given the order by me, personally."

"Yes, sir." Moser seemed afraid the war might not start.

"Send Mullins to me, please."

A few moments later the Sergeant Major stood at attention in front of the commandant's desk.

"Mullins, all leaves are cancelled, effective as of now and until further notice."

"Yes, sir. Expecting trouble from that limey warship?"

"I hope not, but we've got to be ready in case it develops. Send a messenger to Whip Holt with this letter, too. I'm requesting him to put the entire militia battalion on active duty until the crisis is resolved one way or the other."

So the American preparations for war increased, and tension rose accordingly on the south bank of the Columbia. Uniformed army troops and militiamen, whose only badges of military identification were white armbands, leaned on their rifles and stared across the river. Never had silent Fort Vancouver seemed so menacing.

So many women and older men came to the church that Reverend Cavendish held an impromptu service. Every seat was occupied, and the congregation joined in the fervent prayers for peace. But every member of the community was prepared for the worst, and almost without exception the churchgoers carried loaded firearms as they returned to their homes.

For their mutual protection they rode in groups, but the Holt ranch stood alone at the far edge of the settlement, so Eulalia made the last portion of the journey alone. She was so weary and dispirited that she felt no fear. Locking herself into the house, she kept her rifle nearby, and she reflected that it would be a relief from the monotony of her existence if she had to use it. She almost hoped that a band of Rogue warriors, Doznevkov, or such traitors as Richard Ramsey launched an attack.

The immediate cause of her depression, she knew, had been the sudden wedding of Lisolette and Paul. She had attended the ceremony alone because Whip had been called away at the last moment by one of the countless militia crises that erupted these days. Lisolette and Paul were so much in love with each other that just looking at them had pained Eulalia. She had been aware, too, of the strong attraction drawing Nancy Wade and Harry Canning together, and she felt certain they, too, would marry in the near future.

There was love everywhere—except in the Holt household. Whip was in his element, guarding the community from marauding braves, and he spent the better part of his days and nights roaming through the nearby wilderness. Not only was Eulalia charged with the full operation of the ranch during his absence, but when he did come home for brief periods, he was always accompanied by various members of the militia, and he seemed to take it for granted that she would provide food and a hot drink for him and his companions. He slept only in snatches and even then was interrupted by couriers.

Eulalia knew better than to expect normal relations with her husband during this critical time. But she would have appreciated some sign of an awareness on his part that she, too, was carrying a far heavier burden and was discharging her obligations faultlessly. Instead, he seemed to be taking her efforts for granted, and at no time did he offer her a private word or a tender gesture. The crisis, she thought, shouldn't mean she had to abandon all rights as a wife, partner, and companion. Other men who were equally involved didn't forget they were married.

Perhaps, if Whip had shown some sign that he cared for her prior to the emergency, she would have been better able to tolerate his present indifference to her. Well, if and when the problem was resolved and normal living conditions were restored, she would be compelled to leave him. The prospect filled her with dread, and she hated the prospect of being forced to seek sanctuary with Claiborne and Cindy.

But anything was better than the mockery of her

present existence. She was rapidly reaching the breaking point, and almost any life was better than one in which love was one-sided. It seemed irrelevant that she knew, deep inside herself, that she would continue to love him, even if they separated. There was no real escape from her dilemma, so she would have to face the future with all the strength, resolution, and courage she could muster.

Colonel Phillips Morrison sat at his desk in a daze. The communication from the War Office in London that had just been delivered by the captain of H.M.S. *Dauntless* was so totally unexpected, so shocking that he could scarcely believe its content. He read it again, his stomach churning, his mind in a whirl:

> Her Majesty's Government have determined that the United States is in earnest when she informs us that, if necesary, she is willing to go to war for possession of what she believes is her due share of the Oregon Territory.
>
> Inasmuch as a presidential election will take place later this year, the Prime Minister, with the unanimous concurrence of the Cabinet, has decided it would be unwise to make the Oregon issue a matter of debate in that campaign. Both President Van Buren, the Democratic candidate, and General William H. Harrison, the Whig candidate, would outdo each other in their promises to the American electorate that they would preserve the American presence in Oregon at all costs.
>
> Consequently Her Majesty's Government have embarked on a new policy. Henceforth, friendly relations will be established with the Americans in Oregon, and the dispute between Great Britain and the United States will be settled by diplomatic means.

All that Phillips Morrison had tried to accomplish, all that he had worked so hard to achieve had been negated. And knowing the way that higher echelons delighted in shifting the blame when a policy collapsed and was reversed, he would be made the scapegoat. At best he would be transferred to an insignificant post as an archivist, at worst he would be retired without further ado. There was no doubt that his career had come to an abrupt end. The curt order that had accompanied the letter was explicit:

Effective immediately upon receipt of this order, you will relinquish command of Fort Vancouver to your designated successor and will return to London on board H.M.S. *Dauntless* for consultations and possible reassignment.

That was it. A lifetime of loyal service had been rewarded with a kick in the groin. There was no alternative: Morrison had to accept defeat. His shoulders sagged, and all at once he looked far older than his years as he summoned his orderly. "Ask Major Pitts to join me, please," he said. "And ask Dr. McLoughlin if he'll be good enough to pay me a brief visit."

Apparently the factor and Roland Pitts had already been conferring in the latter's office because they came to the commandant's room together. Phillips Morrison was so filled with his own misery that he failed to notice the younger officer was wearing the insignia of a lieutenant colonel. There was pity in Pitts's eyes, and he took care to salute with precision.

Colonel Morrison slid the copies of both of the War Office communications across his desk. "Look at these, gentlemen," he said. "They tell their own story."

"Colonel Pitts received copies, which he's already shown me," John McLoughlin said.

"*Colonel* Pitts?" Morrison noticed his deputy's new insignia and forced a weary smile. "Congratulations," he said. "I assume you've been appointed to succeed me."

"I have, sir." A lesser man might have been tempted to gloat, but Pitts was still sympathetic. Regardless of the stubborn attitude shown by the older officer, regardless of the acts that had caused so much harm in the American community across the Columbia, he had been consistent in doing his duty according to his principles.

Morrison could not curb a deep sigh. "We'll hold the transfer-of-command ceremony at once," he said. "As soon as I can gather the strength to control myself."

There was a long, uncomfortable silence. John McLoughlin was the first to speak. "I've spent a lifetime watching London officialdom change policies as rapidly as a weathervane spins. No government anywhere can maneuver more adroitly. For a long time I've felt certain the Oregon policy would change. The Americans—here and in Washington City—took too firm and uncompromising a stand. Trust our officials to find the perfect excuse to meet the demands of necessity. The Americans refuse to be driven out, so London has seized on the coming presidential election as the reason for changing its own stand. Ingenious—and marvelously clever. Why, even the Americans might accept their so-called reason as genuine."

The American Lieutenant in charge of the sentry detail stood on the ramparts of Fort Oregon and watched the longboat putting out from the north bank of the river. The craft was filled with redcoats, but before giving an alarm, the Lieutenant studied them through his glass. Then, wasting no time, he bolted for the headquarters building and ran to the office of the commandant.

"Sir," he said, "a British boat is crossing the river. There are two officers on board. Major Pitts, who seems to be wearing the insignia of a lieutenant colonel, and a junior aide."

Even if Pitts was delivering an ultimatum, protocol

had to be observed. "Mullins!" Lee Blake shouted. The Sergeant Major appeared on the threshold. "Send an honor guard to the waterfront to conduct two British officers here. And ask Major Moser if he'll be good enough to welcome them as my representative and bring them to me."

The old man was unflappable, Hector Mullins thought as he hastened to obey the order. A full-scale war might break out at any moment between the United States and her primary adversary, but no one would know it from Colonel Blake's attitude.

A short time later Roland Pitts was escorted into Lee's office, and the door closed behind them. Lee offered his congratulations on the other's promotion, and Pitts inclined his head in thanks, then reached into his tunic. "I believe you'll find this memorandum just received from the War Office of interest to you, Colonel," he said.

Lee felt a stab of foreboding as he reached for the paper, but he was smiling broadly by the time he finished reading it, his relief mingled with incredulity.

"I've assumed command of Fort Vancouver within the past two hours," Colonel Pitts told him. "My first act was to order our cannon aimed elsewhere than at the south bank. My second is this visit."

They grinned at each other, and Lee extended his hand. "You and I, working together," he said, "won't find it difficult to establish and maintain harmony."

"I'm sure of it," the new British commandant replied. "At Dr. McLoughlin's suggestion I intend to lift all restrictions on American visits to our side of the river."

"I'll be delighted to do the same in return," Lee said without hesitation.

"There's one thing more I can and will do," Colonel Pitts said. "As you know all too well, my predecessor was responsible for supplying arms to the Rogue.

That won't happen again. And I shall forbid all mercenaries who have been employed to fight you the right to take sanctuary on British soil. If I could, I would also place Igor Doznevkov and his cardboard Colonel under arrest, but I'm afraid my orders won't give me that freedom. However, I feel certain Doznevkov is too shrewd to come to Fort Vancouver again."

"These circumstances require a whole new approach," Lee said. "Once Doznevkov's scheme against us collapses, as it is sure to do without British support, I feel confident that St. Petersburg will deny that he was authorized to conduct an unofficial war against us. The Czar's advisers will recognize the inevitability of the American presence in Oregon, and Russia will abandon her claims to the territory because she will have no choice."

Before Colonel Pitts left, he extended a dinner invitation to all officers of the American garrison. No single gesture could have been better calculated to signal the start of a new relationship.

As soon as his visitor departed, Lee sent couriers to summon the members of the American council, and then he broke the news to his own officers. "Turn the cannon away from Fort Vancouver," he said, "and hereafter allow all British subjects to come to our side of the Columbia whenever they please."

The council members began to arrive at Fort Oregon, one by one, and each registered joy and disbelief when he learned of the new truce with the British.

The last to arrive was Whip, who had been leading a patrol in the wilderness beyond the settlement. As always, he was quick to grasp the strategic and tactical implications of the new agreement with the British. "This means," he said, speaking in his customary slow drawl, "that we'll be able to devote all of our efforts to getting rid of the Rogue and the trappers hired by the Russians."

Jeremiah Olberg, the president of the second wagon train company, immediately saw what he thought was a great opportunity. "Now we can send a real expedition to the land of the Rogue and teach them the lesson they deserve."

Whip shook his head firmly. "That's the last thing we want to do," he said. "The Indian tribes hereabouts, every last one of them, have been peaceful and friendly. We've left them alone, so they haven't bothered us. But if we invade the Rogue country and destroy their towns, every tribe between the Cascades and the Pacific will take up arms against us. We'll be at war with them for years to come, and hundreds of people will die needlessly."

Lee deferred to him as the expert on all matters concerning Indians. "What do you suggest?"

"I recommend that the militia wage an all-out campaign to drive the Rogue out of our area," he said. "I'd like to keep the whole battalion on active duty until we've done the job. The Rogue aren't stupid. Once they realize we're hurting them bad—and that they're getting no support from the British—all the Russian gold in the world won't tempt them. They'll go home. It'll be a spell before they realize we're not following them, and then they'll understand: if they stay out of our terrain, we won't bother them."

Lee nodded in approval.

"As for the mountain scum, they'll scatter like rats, taking their Russian money with them. They're the type who always look out for themselves, first and last, and if I know them the way I think I do, you won't see Ramsey or any of the others in Oregon again. As for Doznevkov," Whip added grimly, "I just hope I'm on the patrol that finds him. I'd like to settle with him personally."

"How long do you estimate the campaign will last?" Ernie von Thalman asked.

Whip shrugged. "That depends on how fast we can flush out the Rogue warriors. Their tactics aren't like those of the big Indian nations, and there are only a few warriors in every party. I'd guess it'll take us anywhere from two weeks to a month. I know that's a long time for men to be away from their farms and ranches, but it can't be helped, not if we want lasting peace."

"I'll gladly place my three cavalry troops under your direct command," Lee told him. "And you can take as many of my infantry companies as you want, too."

A tight smile appeared on Whip's face. "In that case," he said, "we should be finished in two weeks at the most."

The vote in favor of the campaign was unanimous, and two hundred and sixty soldiers were assigned to special duty with the militia. The leaders moved swiftly, and a short time before sundown that same day the officers of all units involved gathered in the yard behind Whip's ranch house.

The militia commander's address was brief. "Those of you who traveled with us on the first wagon train already know how we'll operate. For those who don't know my system, I'll explain. Over there are four men who have worked with me as scouts: Stalking Horse, Arnold Mell, Mack Dougall, and Pierre le Rouge. They can smell a hostile Indian a mile away and can pick up any trail. Each of them will be assigned to a sub-battalion. They'll find the Rogue bands for you. Then you'll take over. Stay on the prowl, never let up the pressure, and shoot to kill. But don't worry if an occasional brave escapes. Let them carry the word to their comrades that their cause is hopeless. Good luck and good hunting."

Tilman Wade stepped forward with a list in his hand and began to read individual unit assignments aloud. Two to three companies of foot soldiers and at least one troop of horsemen were being assigned to each of the scouts.

While the final orders were being given, Whip hurried to the ranch house for a quick word with Eulalia, whom he hadn't seen for two days. He found her in the kitchen, where she awaited an explanation of the officers' presence on the property.

"We're in the final stage of our drive," Whip told her, "and we won't stop until the Rogue and renegades are gone. Lee and the British have reached an agreement, so there won't be any big war. Now it's just a question of finding bands of Rogue and sending them packing."

Eulalia nodded, but made no comment, knowing he expected none.

"Our patrols will stop off here several times a day, and they'll be in the neighborhood at night, too. So you should be safe, but take no needless risks. I'm afraid you'll have to look after the horses while I'm gone. Feed and water them, of course, and keep them in the stables. And make sure the stallions are locked into their pens." He went to a barrel and, removing the lid, filled a leather pouch with smoked meat.

"How long will you be gone?" Eulalia felt desolate.

"No more than a couple of weeks. If we're lucky I should be home much sooner. If I have the chance, I'll stop by here now and then."

Apparently he had said something wrong. He saw a fleeting expression of hurt in her eyes, but it was replaced immediately by haughty disdain. He had wanted to kiss her goodbye, but that look in her eyes held him at arm's length.

At that moment Tilman rapped at the kitchen door. "The unit commanders have gone, Whip," he called. "The battalion staff is ready to go whenever you're ready."

"Coming," Whip called. He looked again at his wife. "I'll be back whenever I can," he said lamely, then went out of the door.

A long time passed before Eulalia moved. Then she

sank slowly onto a kitchen chair and covered her face with her hands. She wanted to weep, but no tears would come.

Each of the scouts was assigned to a specific sector, and the units accompanying them spread out over a wide wilderness area, thereby serving a double purpose. While hunting for the elusive Rogue warriors, they were also forming a protective shield for the American community that the Indians would find difficult to penetrate.

Stalking Horse and the elderly Arnold Mell soon demonstrated that they had few equals anywhere. Both practiced the same technique, constantly studying the ground as they moved slowly, then halting, dismounting, and making careful examinations of twigs, bushes, and bent grass. Again and again they signaled silently to the unit commanders behind them, and the troops raced forward to discover they had cornered small bands of braves. Occasionally the warriors tried to hold their ground before being crushed, but in most instances they fled and were cut down from behind.

Mack Dougall and Pierre le Rouge were less skilled than the other scouts, but they carried their fair share of the burden, and the troops they led racked up impressive scores, too. The hunt began every morning at daybreak and sometimes continued long after night fell. Whenever the moon shone sufficiently to light the way, the scouts remained active.

At best the augmented battalion snatched a few hours of sleep every night. They subsisted on rations of parched corn and smoked meat that were sent forward every night from the garrison at Fort Oregon. Men who felt the pace was too grueling grumbled to each other, but none protested aloud, principally because of the example set by Whip Holt.

The battalion leader was tireless, his energy seemingly inexhaustible. He and the few officers who comprised his staff spent at least eighteen hours out of every twenty-four in the saddle, riding from one sector to another. Whip was as adept as Arnold Mell and Stalking Horse at reading signs in the forest, and twice he and his staff encountered small groups of warriors whose ranks they decimated with their accurate rifle fire.

One night, after they had spent a full week in the forest, they did not halt until the small hours of the morning, and only then did they eat their final meal before resting. Tilman Wade stretched out beside Whip and, as he ate his meat and corn, became reflective. "The warriors are becoming harder to find," he said. "I think the Rogue are beginning to understand what we're trying to tell them."

"It could be." Whip shoved his hat onto the back of his head and slowly chewed a strip of smoked venison. "But we won't know for a couple of days whether they've really given up the campaign."

"According to my figures," Tilman told him, "we've killed eighty-four braves. We'll never know how many we've wounded because they take their injured with them. But we've already hurt them plenty, and only three of our lads have been wounded. That's a good record."

"Good, but not complete," Whip replied. "Are you suggesting we call it quits?"

"Oh, we'll keep going, if that's what you want, Whip. But the men are tired, and those with families are worried about them."

"Our patrols look in on every family several times every day, so the need for worry is reduced, although I'll grant you it isn't eliminated, even for you and me."

"I'll pass the word to the unit commanders in the morning," a resigned Tilman said. "The hunt will go on."

"I don't like all this any more than the rest of you,"

Whip said. "But I won't stop until we're done for all time. I want this to be the very last time the battalion is ever called up for duty. I want to establish a permanent peace in Oregon, and we won't have it until the Rogue know they're beaten and go home to stay."

Tilman knew he was right and realized, too, how much the Oregon settlers were in Whip's debt. He had contributed so much to the establishment of the territory, first, through his leadership on the initial wagon train and, more recently, through his continuing guidance of the community. When he set a goal, he allowed nothing to stand in the way of his achievement of it, and in situations like the present he was too stubborn ever to quit. Regardless of whether history gave him credit for his contribution to Oregon, every American and every former Russian in the community recognized it.

His light meal consumed, Whip wrapped himself in his blanket and instantly fell asleep. Years of self-disciplined training had taught him how to conserve his strength for the mission at hand.

So the campaign continued for another two days and nights, and only when he felt certain that the last of the Rogue had vanished was Whip ready to call a final halt. Two of the renegade trappers also had been killed by the militia, and although there was little chance that Igor Doznevkov or Richard Ramsey ever would be seen in the area again, it was unfair to hold the entire battalion on duty to search for the trouble-makers.

"We're disbanding this morning," Whip told his staff as they sat in a circle eating their meager breakfast. "Tilman, order the army troops to return to the garrison, with our thanks. You and I will visit Lee Blake later in the day and thank him in person. But before we go home ourselves, I want to ride from unit to unit and congratulate our lads on a job well done."

Rising to his feet, Whip placed his thumb and forefinger behind his teeth and whistled. His stallion came to him without delay. As always, Whip reached into his pocket and produced a carrot. "You're lucky we're going home, my friend," Whip said. "I'm out of carrots until I pick up some more for you from the kitchen larder."

Tilman finished repeating the orders to the other members of the staff, then laughed as he watched Whip. "That's a wonderful trick," he said, "but why did you waste your time teaching it to him?"

"It was no waste of time," Whip replied, his face serious. "When I lived alone in the Rockies, I never knew when I might be shot or injured. If I was on foot at the time, I wanted my horse to come to me, no matter what. Circumstances have changed now, of course, but my friend and I can't seem to break our old habits. So I still whistle, and he still comes to me for his carrot."

Tilman understood, nodding as they mounted and rode off together.

By mid-morning the militiamen were returning to their homes, bone-weary but proud of what they had done. "You've brought peace to Oregon," Whip told them, and they believed with all their hearts that he was right.

At the Holt ranch Eulalia had no idea that the end had come. This morning was as dreary as the countless days that stretched out behind her. She went to the stables, where she fed the horses, gave them water, and made certain the stallions were secure in their pens so they could not harm the other animals. Her own mare was restless after such a long incarceration, and Eulalia felt sorry for her. Perhaps, just this once, she could go for a canter and exercise her mount.

The idea took hold of her as she returned to the house. As usual when alone she had little appetite, so she drank some acorn coffee, then went into the bedroom to change into her trousers. She would carry a rifle and a pistol on her ride, so she would be able to protect herself. Besides, she could not remain cooped up here any longer.

A heavy tap sounded at the kitchen door. Eulalia looked out through the bedroom curtains and caught her breath. Two mounted men sat some distance from the house, and she recognized one of them as Colonel Mikhail Menshikoff. Two others had dismounted and stood at the door; one was Richard Ramsey and the other was Igor Doznevkov. Both carried rifles.

Making sure her rifle and pistol were cocked, Eulalia quietly opened the bedroom window a few inches and called, "Get off this property, or I'll shoot."

The pair at the door turned in the direction of her voice and saw the rifle barrel protruding from the open window. "We've come to see Whip Holt," Ramsey called. "Tell him we're here."

"He isn't home, as you well know," she replied. "I mean what I say. Leave—or I'll shoot."

"We will go," Doznevkov replied. "But we ask you to give Holt a message when he returns."

"Tell him he'll know where to find us," Ramsey added. "He's been looking for us, and now we're going to oblige him. Tell him we're no harder to find than wild horses."

"Tell him also," Doznevkov declared, "that after we finish with him, we will return here and take our pleasure with you. All four of us."

The evil in the man's face made Eulalia shudder. Never had she seen so much hate, and she knew these men had come looking for Whip because they wanted revenge against him.

As for the threat of violating her, the very idea turned her stomach, but she recognized it as a deliberate goad intended to impel Whip into accepting their challenge. He might be very tired when he came home, but surely he was far too intelligent and experienced to rise to such obvious bait.

Not waiting for her reply, Doznevkov and Ramsey returned to their horses, mounted, and rode off with the other pair, heading in the direction of the Cascade Range. She watched them, still gripping her rifle as they crossed a portion of the ranch and vanished into the forest beyond it.

The message Ramsey had left made no sense, but she felt certain these men intended to kill Whip. They had indicated, too, that he would return soon, so, if they were telling the truth, his campaign had been successful. It seemed obvious to her that his defeated foes were seeking the opportunity to strike at the man who was responsible for beating them.

Abandoning her idea of going for a ride, Eulalia returned to the kitchen. If Whip was really coming home, she should prepare a hot meal for him, so she rolled up her sleeves, threw another log on the kitchen fire, and began to scrub potatoes.

The sound of hoofbeats sent her to the door, and when she heard Whip's shout, she unbolted it and threw it open.

"I'm back!" he called. "Stalking Horse will be along soon, and now that the campaign is ended, I don't mind telling you we're ravenous." He dismounted.

Eulalia was so filled with the incident that had taken place earlier in the morning that she repeated the story as he approached her. Whip halted, his eyes narrowing, and became so absorbed in what she was telling him that he forgot to kiss her. "Tell me that message of Ramsey's again," he said.

She carefully repeated the renegade guide's words. Then, hesitating for a moment because she didn't want to infuriate Whip needlessly, she told him about Doznevkov's threat to violate her.

Whip's eyes burned like live coals. He stood motionless for a moment, and then he slowly tightened his belt.

Never had Eulalia seen him so enraged. "Pay no

attention to that kind of talk," she said. "I don't. It was said to bait you into following them into the mountains."

"Sure it was. That's as plain as the whiskers on my chin. But nobody on earth can threaten to take my wife without answering to me for it."

"Calm down," she said. "You're tired, and after you stop to think about it, you'll know they were trying to set a trap for you."

"I don't need to think about it. I know their reason. But what they don't know is that maybe I'm the one who will not only set a trap—but spring it, too. I didn't spend years earning my living by trapping beaver for nothing. I may have a few tricks of my own up my sleeve. Dinner will have to wait while I do one last job."

"Please, Michael," Eulalia begged, becoming frantic. "Get some help first. Maybe you didn't hear me when I said there are four of them!"

"Odds of four to one aren't so high, especially when a man knows the Cascades as well as I do." He patted her on the shoulder. "I've been dreaming of a big platter of bacon, eggs, and potatoes for days now. Maybe you could do something about that before I get back. There might be time to bake a loaf of fresh bread, too." He mounted his horse and rode off at a gallop.

Eulalia was so stunned, so furiously angry with him that she felt paralyzed for a moment. Then, returning to the house for her rifle and pistol, she hurried to the stable and began to saddle her mare. She had no clear idea of what she intended to do, but under no circumstances was she willing to remain idle while her husband faced a pack of cutthroat scoundrels alone.

She was just finishing her immediate task when Stalking Horse appeared. Eulalia told him what had happened, the words stale by now because of repetition.

Stalking Horse, who never became flustered, listened quietly. "First we get Tilman Wade," he said. "Then Stalking Horse go with him to help Whip."

Eulalia rode beside him as he raced toward the Wade property, her eager mare easily keeping pace with his stallion.

Tilman was sitting at the kitchen table, regaling Sally with the story of the past nine days as she prepared a homecoming dinner for him. He jumped to his feet as Eulalia and the Cherokee burst into the house. Giving the startled couple no chance to speak, Eulalia told the story again.

Tilman was equal to the emergency. "Stalking Horse," he said, "go next door and fetch Claiborne Woodling. I'm afraid his welcoming home party will be delayed, too. I'm sorry, honey," he added to Sally.

Eulalia followed him as he went to his stable to saddle a horse. "Why would Whip be so insane? Why wouldn't he wait and take others with him before trying to round up four killers?"

Tilman looked at her and shook his head. "You're his wife, but it seems you don't know him. He went alone because there was a job to be done, and he was convinced he could do it. He's Whip Holt, and he's won so many victories over so many years that he believes he's invincible."

She followed him out of the stable, acknowledging with a wave the arrival of her brother, accompanied by Stalking Horse. "I'm coming with you," she said.

Claiborne, already aware of the situation from Stalking Horse, addressed his sister lovingly but firmly. "You'll just be in the way, and it may be dangerous. Go home and wait for Whip there."

Eulalia ignored him. "Tilman," she said, "you just reminded me that I'm Whip's wife. But I need no reminder. I know who I am, and no power in this world can force me to stay behind."

Tilman sighed and looked at Claiborne. "Even when she was little," her brother said, "she was the most stubborn female the good Lord ever put on this earth."

"We're wasting time," Eulalia said impatiently.

They gave in because they had no choice, and she accompanied the men as they started in the direction of the snow-covered peaks to the east.

Eulalia thought the journey took forever, even though they rode the better part of the way at a gallop, and she was surprised, when she looked up at the sun, to see it was early afternoon. They had made far better time than she had realized.

Stalking Horse took the lead now, and they made their way through the foothills to higher and higher ground. At last he halted and pointed. "Bald Cliff is there," he said.

The young woman saw the place and knew it was aptly named. The crown of the cliff, like its side, seemed to have been carved out of rock, and there was no vegetation on it.

"At bottom is ravine," the Cherokee said, pointing again. "Whip and Stalking Horse find wild horses there."

"And that's the place where those scum challenged Whip to meet them," Tilman said.

Claiborne turned to his sister. "You've come far enough," he said. "There may be shooting, and you'd be a liability to us. Wait here, and we'll come back with Whip."

Eulalia definitely was being excluded now, and there was no way she could force the men to take her any farther. She sat still, holding her mare in rein as the men moved off, and soon they disappeared from sight in the brush.

She sat for a long time, looking up at the stern heights of Bald Cliff. The sun beat down on her, its glare intensified by the snowfields above her, and she absently brushed away an insect that buzzed near her ear. Something was very much off-key with the deductions her escorts had made, but she couldn't put the problem into its proper perspective.

Ramsey's hint that he and his companions would be waiting for Whip in the ravine where he had caught the wild horses was obvious. But if animals could be trapped there, so could a man. From the brief description Whip had given her, she knew that the rear of the ravine was sealed by the cliff, making escape impossible.

No one knew the ravine better than Whip. Had he blundered into the ravine, his enemies could have cut him off, and with the odds four to one against him, it would have been exceptionally difficult for him to fight his way out. No, it was inconceivable that he would have allowed himself to be tricked into going into the ravine. It wouldn't even have been necessary for his foes to enter the ravine itself. They could have stationed themselves on Bald Cliff and shot him with ease when he appeared below them.

The cliff! Eulalia had been staring at it all this time, and now she felt certain she knew what had happened. She had learned something of the way Whip's mind worked in a crisis, and her instinct told her he had gone to Bald Cliff, where he could look down on his enemies.

Eulalia spurred forward, her mare climbing steadily. There was no trail here, and the horse had to make her way through bramble and fields of rocks. Occasionally the cliff was hidden from Eulalia's view, but she continued to press forward and upward, and ultimately she came to a broad, flat table strewn with rocks, on which a few scrub trees defied the altitude by thriving.

The predicament in which Whip was caught was her own fault, Eulalia thought miserably. If she had refrained from repeating Doznevkov's provocative threat, Whip would have been more reasonable, used his common sense, and rounded up a number of competent helpers instead of trying to capture or kill the group single-handed. She should have kept her mouth shut.

Directly ahead now, on the near side of the jumbled pile of jagged rocks, she saw five horses tethered to trees. One was Whip's stallion. He had guessed correctly, then, where his enemies had headed and had come here to confront them.

Forced to dismount, Eulalia looped her reins over a tree branch, then started to climb across the rocks. Some were loose and moved beneath her feet, causing her to stumble. She regained her balance in time but almost lost her rifle. Gripping it hard, she continued to make her way across the hazardous rocks.

Even before she reached the flat top of Bald Cliff, the sight she saw ahead of her froze her blood. Two bodies were lying on the ground, those of Colonel Mikhail Menshikoff and the Russian who had been one of his servants. Rifles, pistols, and knives were scattered everywhere, and directly ahead she saw the leather whip that had given her husband his nickname. It was useless now, having been severed by a knife only a few feet from its handle.

But it was the living rather than the dead or the shambles of battle that fascinated and horrified her.

Igor Doznevkov and Richard Ramsey, each with a knife in one hand, were using their rifles, which they had obviously discharged and had not had time to reload, as prods to nudge Whip, who had lost his weapons, toward the lip of the cliff. Dodging, sometimes taking a half step forward, Whip was trying to counter the harsh thrusts of his remaining foes. But their knives as well as the barrels of their rifles held him at bay, and he would be stabbed if he tried to leap at either of his antagonists.

Perhaps Doznevkov and Ramsey could have ended

the unequal match quickly, but they were enjoying themselves too much, prolonging the agony of their archenemy.

Eulalia's heart stopped beating for a moment. Then, her whole body trembling, she raised her rifle to her shoulder. Neither Whip nor his foes had seen her, so there was a chance she might be able to help him.

No, the three men were bunched too closely together, and a woman who never in her life had fired at a human being couldn't take the risk of hitting her husband. Frustrated beyond measure, Eulalia didn't know what to do.

To her astonishment she saw Whip raise his thumb and forefinger to his mouth, place them behind his teeth, and whistle. The familiar two-toned, up-and-down sound brought tears to her eyes. Whip's great stallion heard the whistle, and straining with all his brute strength, the beast snapped the leather reins that held him tethered to the tree on the far side of the rocks.

Little by little Whip was being inched toward the edge of the precipice, where a drop of almost two thousand feet to his certain death awaited him.

Somehow, the stallion managed to make his way across the seemingly impossible obstacle of jumbled rocks without breaking a leg. He whinnied, then broke into a gallop as he raced forward to obtain the promised carrot that his master would offer him.

The thunder of hoofs sounding on the hard ground echoed across the wilderness of the mountains. Doznevkov and Ramsey heard the sound and turned. The renegade guide thought the beast was coming straight at him and instinctively moved away.

Ramsey was in the clear now, and Eulalia at last had her chance. Again she raised her rifle to shoulder, and this time her hands and arms were steady. She knew what had to be done and steeled herself, keeping her eyes open as she sighted her target down the length of her barrel. At the last moment Ramsey saw and recognized her, the expression in his eyes that of a cornered animal.

Miraculously calm, Eulalia squeezed the trigger, and Richard Ramsey dropped slowly, almost lazily, to the ground, the bullet in his chest instantly ending his life.

Igor Doznevkov heard the shot but paid scant attention to it. The huge stallion was bearing down on him, or so he thought, and he scrambled madly in an attempt to throw himself out of the beast's path. Then he stumbled on a rock and, falling to the ground, rolled close to the edge of the precipice.

He came too close to the lip, his momentum carrying him toward oblivion. The agent made a desperate attempt to check himself, but could not. Slowly he slipped off the edge of the cliff.

Somehow he managed to grip the lip with his hands as his body disappeared from view. Eulalia felt ill, watching in horror as the Russian's hands clawed at the rocky edge of the cliff. Little by little his grip lessened, little by little he lost his last hold on life itself.

Igor Doznevkov's scream, fading as he fell and echoing through the ravine below, was followed by a deep silence.

Afraid she might faint, Eulalia closed her eyes for a moment. When she opened them again, she saw Whip patting his stallion, offering his mount a mute apology as he stared at his wife. Eulalia returned his gaze, then began to run toward him. At the same instant he started to race toward her, too.

They came within arm's reach but stopped short. The expression in Whip's eyes was strange, unfathomable, unlike any she had ever seen.

"I lived alone for so many years," he said in a hoarse voice, "that I got to thinking I had to rely only on myself, that I could do anything alone. But I was wrong, dead wrong." He paused, moistening his dry lips.

He was alive and unharmed, and even as Eulalia listened to him, she rejoiced.

"I learned today what I should have known long ago," Whip said. "I need you. Now. Always, for as long as we live."

With one accord they embraced, their bodies pressed close together, kissing hungrily. Then, still holding her in his arms, he said, "I owe you my life. It's a debt I can never repay."

"It's a fair trade for restoring my health after I had the fever," she replied, trying in vain to speak lightly. "So we're even now."

"Never," he said, then kissed her again.

Continuing to nestle in his arms, she looked up at him and demanded, "Why have you always been so indifferent to me?"

He looked puzzled.

"You almost never tell me about your work, about anything you do."

Whip's face cleared. "I've always wanted to tell you things, but I figured you'd be bored."

She laughed quietly, contentedly. "Everything you do concerns me. Why, I've already decided we'll take the horses of those terrible men back to the ranch with us."

He chuckled. "It hadn't crossed my mind, but you're right. We can sure use them."

Still clinging to him, Eulalia summoned all of her courage. "There's one thing more I must know. Why have you made love to me so rarely?"

Color flooded Whip's face. "You're so pretty I've had to fight myself to keep my hands off you. I didn't want you to think I married you for that. You're a lady."

Eulalia replied slowly and distinctly. "In the parlor I'm a lady. In bed I'm your woman."

Their eyes met and held.

In the distance they heard the other members of the rescue party. Reluctant to move apart, however, they stood with their arms around each other's waists and together looked out across the plateau.

Ignoring the death and havoc around them, they looked at the peaks of the Coast Range, bathed in afternoon sunlight. Then, together, they gazed at the rolling, green hills, with the silver ribbon of the Columbia River cutting through them. This was Oregon, their home, and they would stay here for the rest of their lives. Together.

★ WAGONS WEST ★

A series of unforgettable books that trace the lives of a dauntless band of pioneering men, women, and children as they brave the hazards of an untamed land in their trek across America. This legendary caravan of people forge a new link in the wilderness. They are Americans from the North and the South, alongside immigrants, Blacks, and Indians, who wage fierce daily battles for survival on this uncompromising journey—each to their private destinies as they fulfill their greatest dreams.

☐ 26822	INDEPENDENCE! #1	$4.50
☐ 26162	NEBRASKA! #2	$4.50
☐ 26242	WYOMING! #3	$4.50
☐ 26072	OREGON! #4	$4.50
☐ 26070	TEXAS! #5	$4.50
☐ 26377	CALIFORNIA! #6	$4.50
☐ 26546	COLORADO! #7	$4.50
☐ 26069	NEVADA! #8	$4.50
☐ 26163	WASHINGTON! #9	$4.50
☐ 26073	MONTANA! #10	$4.50
☐ 26184	DAKOTA! #11	$4.50
☐ 26521	UTAH! #12	$4.50
☐ 26071	IDAHO! #13	$4.50
☐ 26367	MISSOURI! #14	$4.50
☐ 27141	MISSISSIPPI! #15	$4.50
☐ 25247	LOUISIANA! #16	$4.50
☐ 25622	TENNESSEE! #17	$4.50
☐ 26022	ILLINOIS! #18	$4.50
☐ 26533	WISCONSIN! #19	$4.50
☐ 26849	KENTUCKY! #20	$4.50

Prices and availability subject to change without notice.

FROM THE PRODUCER OF WAGONS WEST AND THE KENT FAMILY CHRONICLES— A SWEEPING SAGA OF WAR AND HEROISM AT THE BIRTH OF A NATION.

THE WHITE INDIAN SERIES

Filled with the glory and adventure of the colonization of America, here is the thrilling saga of the new frontier's boldest hero and his family. Renno, born to white parents but raised by Seneca Indians, becomes a leader in both worlds. THE WHITE INDIAN SERIES chronicles the adventures of Renno, his son Ja-gonh, and his grandson Ghonkaba, from the colonies to Canada, from the South to the turbulent West. Through their struggles to tame a savage continent and their encounters with the powerful men and passionate women in the early battles for America, we witness the events that shaped our future and forged our great heritage.

☐	24650	White Indian #1	$3.95
☐	25020	The Renegade #2	$3.95
☐	24751	War Chief #3	$3.95
☐	24476	The Sachem #4	$3.95
☐	25154	Renno #5	$3.95
☐	25039	Tomahawk #6	$3.95
☐	25589	War Cry #7	$3.95
☐	25202	Ambush #8	$3.95
☐	23986	Seneca #9	$3.95
☐	24492	Cherokee #10	$3.95
☐	24950	Choctaw #11	$3.95
☐	25353	Seminole #12	$3.95
☐	25868	War Drums #13	$3.95
☐	26206	Apache #14	$3.95
☐	27161	Spirit Knife #15	$3.95
☐	27264	Manitou #16	$3.95

<u>Prices and availability subject to change without notice.</u>

"FROM THE PRODUCER OF WAGONS WEST COMES YET ANOTHER EXPLOSIVE SAGA OF LEGENDARY COURAGE AND UNFORGETTABLE LOVE"

CHILDREN OF THE LION

☐	26912	Children of the Lion #1	$4.50
☐	26971	The Shepherd Kings #2	$4.50
☐	26769	Vengeance of the Lion #3	$4.50
☐	26594	The Lion In Egypt #4	$4.50
☐	26885	The Golden Pharaoh #5	$4.50
☐	25872	Lord of the Nile #6	$3.95
☐	26325	The Prophecy #7	$4.50
☐	26800	Sword of Glory #8	$4.50

Prices and availability subject to change without notice.

Special Offer
Buy a Bantam Book
for only 50¢.

Now you can have Bantam's catalog filled with hundreds of titles plus take advantage of our unique and exciting bonus book offer. A special offer which gives you the opportunity to purchase a Bantam book for only 50¢. Here's how!

By ordering any five books at the regular price per order, you can also choose any other single book listed (up to a $5.95 value) for just 50¢. Some restrictions do apply, but for further details why not send for Bantam's catalog of titles today!

Just send us your name and address and we will send you a catalog!

BANTAM BOOKS, INC.
P.O. Box 1006, South Holland, Ill. 60473

Mr./Mrs./Ms. _____
(please print)

Address _____

City _____ State _____ Zip _____
FC(A)—10/87

Please allow four to six weeks for delivery.